Little Feather's Woman

Little Feather's Woman

Maeve Sidhe Fitzgerald

To order additional copies of this book, contact:
Xlibris Corporation
1-888-795-4274
www.Xlibris.com
Orders@Xlibris.com
24394

I dedicate this novel
to my son Lliam
who is my computer repairman.
Every time the computer says 'error',
'cannot connect to . . . ', or just hasn't worked,
Lliam has responded,

and to my daughter Angel
who has read every version until this one.
She said she'd read this one when it was in book form!
Well, here it is!   msf

Prologue

Somewhere in Ireland 1649

"I can no' do it, Da! Do no' be askin' it o' me!" Hot, bitter tears, leaving tracks in the dust and dirt on her cheeks, streamed down Shannon's pale face. Distractedly, she swiped the salty droplets away, leaving streaks of mud across her high cheekbones. As a result of the frantic race through the preceding night, her flaming-red hair was in wild disarray about her heart-shaped face, like the unruly branches of a sweet briar rose about its central treasure.

"I can no' do it, Da," she again whispered desperately, glancing up at Shamus and pleading silently for his assistance.

Her brother, a big and burly man, shoving his fingers agitatedly through his dusty, red hair, paced about the confines of the small cave with jerky, unsteady movements reflecting the rage and frustration that drove him. Back and forth he stalked restlessly, like a lion caged, kicking up thick, choking clouds of ageless dust. Pausing, he shrugged his broad shoulders and gazed at her in baffled hopelessness and helpless rage.

She sneezed into her shoulder, attempting to muffle the noise. No help from that source. She dragged her tortured gaze back to the man lying on the cold, dank floor of the cave. The chill air clutched at her with icy fingers on unseen currents as icy tendrils of fear clutched her heart.

Blood trickled from the corners of her father's greying, cracked lips, and a rag, soaked in blood and grime, covered the gaping wound in his chest. Once her father had been a large, robust man with auburn hair like her brother's. But years of fighting the British in a futile attempt to keep their homeland had taken their toll, and now he lay dying on the hard, cold floor of a lonely cave far from his ancestral home, only a shadow of his former self.

The grip on her hand was a death grip . . . and they all knew it.

"Please . . . Hinny! . . . fer . . . me . . . year at most . . . Shamus ought . . . reach ye in tha' . . . time." he rasped out and started coughing, his emaciated form convulsing and bringing up more blood. His calloused, work-hardened hand tightened over hers.

Leaning her head on his shoulder, she placed her tear-streaked face next to his. "Oh, Da! When did ye' plan fer this? Why did ye' no' tell me?" her voice trembled with pain and frustration. A boy? She had to pretend to be a damned boy? She had to travel to the colonies as an indentured servant? To that wild unknown world? Why?

"Hinny . . . traitor among . . . us," he whispered in a thin, reedy voice, his body again racked with spasms.

Shamus, who had come to rest and was leaning his tall, muscular frame against the cave wall at the entrance, glanced back over his broad shoulder, helpless rage stamped on his handsome face. "Listen, Shanny," he waited a moment, letting her listen to the sounds of the soldiers as they slashed their way through the undergrowth. "'ow do ye' think they found us s' quick?"

A traitor? A traitor among them? Like a snake slithering through the grass waiting to strike their heels? Shannon shook her head in stunned denial. "No! None of our own would 'ave done such a ter'ible thing!"

Her father and brother remained silent, watching, letting Shannon work through her own disbelief.

Fatigue lay upon her like a suffocating weight; cold embraced her like an unwanted lover; and her father—her beloved father— lay dying in a pool of his own blood in front of her. And she could do nothing about any of these things . . . and now they were telling her it was all because of a traitor—a damn traitor! Not one of their own! They all loved her father, he had always been a good leader. They had all eaten, or they had all gone hungry together. Most of his followers were alive today because of him. Who could do such a horrible thing? Slowly, reason began to make its voice heard. How could the soldiers have known where the rebels would be today for the ambush? And. if not a traitor than how could the soldiers have discovered this place—as well concealed as it was? It would explain the ambush today . . . the ambush that killed her brother Paddy and struck the fatal blow to her father. A snake in the grass, but who . . . ?

"Da 'as s'pected a traitor for some time now," Shamus, hair aglow in the early morning light like an avenging angel, explained quietly, kneeling down in the dust beside the dying man. "There's no other way, lit'le girl, and ye' know it well."

Shannon reluctantly admitted the truth of his statement in light of this new information, but she didn't have to like it.

"I did no' . . . tell ye' sooner . . . knew this would . . . be yer reaction . . . hoped we'd catch the bastard . . . and it would no' come to this."

The shouts from outside grew louder. She could hear the swish of swords and the soft 'thunks' as the metal blades cleared a path through the undergrowth as the soldiers approached the cave. Time was running out.

Her sword drew a squiggle in the dust as she moved by her father's side. In its sheath over her hip hung her ivory-handled knife-a gift from Paddy—while her flintlock, a prize capture from the English, leaned against the cave wall. She was a crack shot—they all were, the best fighters in Ireland-but someone had betrayed them!

Hysterical laughter bubbled up and choked in her throat—brought down by a traitor! One of their own! She wondered for how much he had sold his soul. It wouldn't be enough! She and Shamus would pursue him to the ends of the earth and slit his throat with no more compassion than if he were a pig!

Now the tears flowed freely as she whispered, "I'll do it . . . fer ye', Da. But under protest!" Vainly did she attempt to bring forth a smile through the tears. She had done much over the years 'under protest'.

Her father tried to return her smile, but his energy failed him. "Thank ye'," he whispered. "Daghdha . . . be with . . . ye . . . both and . . . protect ye'." He grasped Shamus's hand.

"Be takin' care . . . of herself," he whispered with his last bit of strength.

"I will, Da," the young man solemnly pledged, but his father had already slipped beyond hearing.

Shannon pulled the beloved head and shoulders onto her lap, sliding her fingers through the thinning, white hair. She rocked and cried, her heart breaking. Finally, she smiled slightly through her tears and said—somewhat hysterically, "Oh, Shamus! All his life he tried to be a good Christian for Father Michael, but at the end he invoked the Lord of the Green Wood to protect us!"

Shamus only smiled grimly and waited a few moments for her to regain some modicum of control and to say goodbye to their beloved father—a few moments being all they had—before gently tugging the lifeless form from her clutching arms and pulling her to her feet. "We must be going, lit'le girl," he murmered urgently. "There be nothin' more we can do for himself . . . except to save ourselves."

Shannon nodded her head, acknowledging the truth of his words, and allowed herself to be led to the rear exit of the cave—hopefully, a secret no one else knew about—making one final promise to her father. The traitor was a dead man when they found him.

Chapter 1

Somewhere in Iroquoia

The fringed buckskin shirt and breeches covered the woman's slender figure while a broad strip of leather made a futile attempt to tame her sunset-red hair. A primed and loaded flintlock rested easy in her hand—dangerous, that, Little Feather observed as he watched the woman. From her trim waist, a long, deadly, skinning knife dangled, tapping lightly against her thigh as she moved.

Bent, she glided like a wood sprite, weaving in and out among the tangles of brush and saplings that grew in great profusion along the meandering stream, searching.

Abruptly, she settled to a squatting position. Her shapely hands skimmed the ground gracefully, lightly touching here and there as she studied some marks in the soft, moist earth, and then, rising to her feet in a single, fluid motion, she turned towards the forest and disappeared among the trees and undergrowth like so much early morning mist vanquished by the rising sun.

Little Feather, squinting against the glare of the bright sun bouncing off the stream, spied on the stranger from the thick brush on the opposite side of the broad stream from where the woman had disappeared. Silently rising from his place of concealment, Little Feather bared his broad shoulders to the caress of the warm sun and cautiously slid his moccasin-encased feet through the cool, silvery water. He didn't wish to reveal himself to the beautiful huntress . . . yet. A burning curiosity to discover what this strange woman was doing invading his forest filled him.

The musty smell of moist soil drifted up about him, and birds scolded him for his intrusion into their territory as he squatted over the spot recently vacated by the woman. How come they hadn't scolded her, Little Feather grouched idly as he searched the ground. What could she possibly be hunting so diligently?

Curiosity died on the spot as shock grabbed him at the stomach and roared out along his peripheral nerves like a hundred-forked streak of lightening. The tracks were clear, imbedded deeply in the soft ground—and gigantic! The red-haired huntress pursued a gigantic bear, possibly a grizzly from the size of the tracks. Fear raced in the wake of the shock along his nerves as he frantically fled after the woman into the forest.

The wind shifted, and the foul odor of the bear slapped him in the face. The sly beast was circling and would catch the woman, unaware, from behind! Panic dragged from him an extra burst of energy like the last bolt of lightening from a dying storm. He had to catch the red-haired huntress—warn her, protect her! Somehow, his life depended upon it! His heart thundered in his throat as he raced after her, but, in the manner of dreams, she remained stubbornly and persistently beyond his reach, beyond his voice.

Viciously swiping sweat from his forehead as it trickle into his eyes, Little Feather stared in horror as the gigantic beast intercepted the woman's trail. Rising up on its powerful hind legs, it swung its massive head from side to side, spraying saliva in all directions in its attempt to scent its query. Then, dropping to all fours, it charged with a howl of rage, tearing through the undergrowth—splintering young saplings and shredding the brush—in its mad dash after the woman.

The air about Little Feather thickened . . . clutching . . . . restraining—like a monstrous spider web—preventing him from following the woman and the bear. Fear twisted his heart, and he screamed until his throat ached. But all he heard was his own tortured voice thrown mockingly back at him . . .

He bolted upright in bed, heart thundering in his chest and perspiration beading his broad forehead. The dream again! Little Feather sat on his bed, trying to calm his wildly pounding heart, feeling as though he had raced from the Kanien'kehaka door of the Long House to the Seneca door. Slowly his heart, beneath his bear claw necklace, returned to a normal rhythm. He flopped back on his sleeping platform and tugged his bearskin blanket about him against the chill morning air.

Four days ago, he had returned to the village to the welcoming arms of family and friends, and each of the four nights he had experienced the same dream! Of course, he had been hunting a grizzly each day. But where did the woman—the huntress—come into the picture? And why was she hunting the bear? Woman didn't hunt bears! They might accompany their husbands on hunts, but the man did the hunting, and the woman assisted with the butchering and hauling the meat back to the village. What could be the meaning of such a strange dream? Perhaps the time had arrived to discuss it with someone. Maybe his uncle Iron Fist? He was a good dream interpreter. Maybe he'd discuss it with his friend Tall Tree. Even though Tall Tree hadn't been in the dream, he might be able to lend some insight concerning it.

That resolved, he lay in the all-embracing dark, peacefully absorbing the early morning scents and sounds of the sleeping long house—broken only by a few coals that sputtered in their fire pit. Iron Fist's gentle snoring from behind him on their broad sleeping platform impinged upon the periphery of his thoughts, while Bright Eyes, his sister's toddler, whimpered from somewhere deep within the long house—a bad dream maybe? Other people were heard rustling about under their blankets. Over it all was the faint smell of yesterday's smoke, the pervasive scent of all the different soups and stews made by the many families in the long house, the smell of fresh wood strips that would be made into new baskets—just the many familiar scents and sounds of home. It was good to be back after his long absence.

He had accompanied the negotiators to the stubborn Huron to persuade them to come under the Great Peace. The negotiations had been a disappointing failure. When the Council had decided a blockade of the Huron trade routes might persuade the unruly Huron to come under the Great Peace, he had felt it his duty to volunteer. Even that had been a dismal failure for the League, although individuals such as himself had returned with an almost obscene wealth in pelts.

But when the Seneca and his fellow Kanien'kehaka decided to take the process to its natural conclusion—invasion—he had felt no desire to participate. However, he had stayed and continued to blockade the trade lines during the interval between the two invasions. The stupid Huron . . . where were they now? Nothing more than smoke on the horizon, vanishing with each puff of fresh air. The survivors had straggled down into Iroquois territory, like so much flotsam in a river after a flood, and been absorbed by the different nations. Little Feather grinned ironically to himself as he lay on his bed and reminisced—just what the League had originally intended for the Huron, but as an independent nation!

Four days he had been home now, and four times he had been plagued by the same nightmare. A bear—there was usually a bear in his dreams before a hunt—and the huntress who hunted the bear while the animal hunted the huntress as he helplessly watched.

He had dispatched so many of the great beasts over the years that his friends teased him and said his name should be He-who-slays-the-great-bear! But Little Feather suited him fine.

He remembered his mother saying that he had been no larger than a little feather when he had been born. She was dead now. Had been since the raid on his village years ago—and he was no longer the size of a little feather.

Shoving the heavy blanket off, he slid to the edge of the bed, aroused and restless. The bear, he could understand. His sister Running Feet's husband, when returning to the village from the fishing grounds, had been attacked and mauled by the bear. A few men had returned from the spawning grounds to hunt the bear and each day they had accompanied Little Feather, tracking the elusive creature and setting deadfalls.

He arose from his platform, stretched his long, lean body, and strolled quietly from his fireside, brushing aside the skin that separated their compartment from the storeroom. Passing through the basket-filled room, he stopped at the door that exited the long house. For a few minutes, he stood leaning against the door jam, one foot crossed over the other, gazing towards the east. The sky, a sheet of pearly grey, glowed over the tips of trees blackened by the receding night and standing stark over the stockade walls as morning approached.

Pushing off the jam, he strolled in long confident strides towards the stockade entrance. The dream troubled and excited him as usual. The redheaded woman with grey eyes—dressed in her man's clothing—was like no woman he had ever encountered. The musket had resided easily in her hand—as though belonging there—and the knife had appeared equally at home on her hip. Her stride through the forest had been long and indecently like a warrior's. But her shape through the buckskin shirt and her delicate facial features . . . ah! They had declared her a woman! A warrior woman!

Turning onto the path leading to the river, he relieved himself in the bushes beneath the overhanging oaks. She had been hunting the grizzly! All alone. No one else, except himself, appeared in any of his dreams, and he, only as an observer.

He sliced the icy waters of the river in a smooth dive, hoping to extinguish the flame within that these dreams kindled. He'd enjoyed his share of women, but none had appealed to him as a mate, nor had any ever stimulated him or obsessed his mind like his dream woman did, and this is what troubled him so. A huntress with the face of a Christian angel? Dreams always meant something. What could this one mean?

Again he dove into the water, leaving scarcely a ripple. As he broke the surface, a twig snapping in the brush alerted him that he was no longer alone.

Shortly thereafter, an older man with long black hair sprinkled with silver strolled into sight.

"The bright sun shine pleasingly upon you, Uncle," Little Feather greeted his favorite uncle.

Long ago, Iron Fist had saved him from sure death—the same night his mother had died—and Iron Fist's sister, Bright Flower, had adopted him into the Turtle Clan of the Kanien'kehaka.

"I see the sun shines bright on you also, Nephew," the older man returned the greeting before entering the water for his morning ablutions. No more than a few seconds passed before he burst from the water in a shower of sparkling droplets and shook his long hair out of his strong, angular face.

"What are you going to do with all those furs?" Iron Fist inquired, plowing through the icy water and sitting on a rock where he proceeded to wring out his long, silver-dusted, black hair.

"Oh, I'm sure the traders will start flocking in when they realize the blockaders are home," responded Little Feather with a slight grimace as he floated on his back on the calm river. A short time later, settling his feet to the pebbly river bottom, he followed the older man out of the river where he flopped down on a small patch of last years dried grass to let the early-morning sun, shining from a cloudless, blue sky, dry and warm him. His roach didn't require wringing out.

"I'm going to try and get some flintlocks with them. The powder doesn't get wet, and I've never had mine misfire."

"There aren't too many of them around, and even the Dutch have trouble getting them. I think I'll stick with my bow and arrows. I trust them more than one of those flintlocks. I can get off more arrows than you can balls in the same time." He gazed across the river to where a buck stood on the edge of the dark forest, his neck gracefully bowed as he drank, apparently realizing he was safe for the moment. Iron Fist pantomimed nocking an arrow to an imaginary bow and pulling the string. "And it's every bit as accurate as your flintlock."

"True," Little Feather admitted reluctantly, but he still liked his flintlock.

Both men remained in companionable silence for a few moments, soaking up the sun.

"Uncle, I've had a troubling dream each night since I got home. Would you mind listening and give me your opinion of what it might mean?"

"I'll give you what insight I can," his uncle replied and listened intently to Little Feather's description of his dream.

The older man remained silent for so long after the young warrior ceased speaking that Little Feather glanced up at him questioningly.

Many thoughts and images flowed through Iron Fist's mind as he listened to his nephew speak.

"Well," the older man responded slowly. "I think the bear is you, Nephew. And there is something you want or desire, which may not be good for you, but you're not going to be able to stop yourself from pursuing it. I think the woman represents what you want, and it is something you want to protect from yourself. I'm not sure about the woman—representing your desire and at the same time hunting you. Perhaps your dream will help you understand the situation when it arises and guide you in dealing with it."

The sun rose higher in the sky, and brightly colored birds flitted among the bare branches, the tiny buds, tightly closed, giving a pale green haze to the trees. Little Feather pondered his uncle's words for a long moment before slowly responding, "Well, Uncle, you have given me much to think about." As an apparent afterthought, he added, "Oh . . . I made some new arrows recently . . . one never knows when they might be needed," he grinned at his uncle who snorted derisively in return, "but I made more than I'll ever have a need for—what with my flintlock"—Iron Fist snorted again—"I would like to give some to you, if you will accept them."

"They will make a welcome addition to my quiver," Iron Fist graciously accepted the gift.

Again a short time passed as they sat in friendly silence, each occupied with his own thoughts.

"Has Wild Rose been to visit her Aunts since you got back?" the older man asked, distracting Little Feather from melancholy thoughts of his dream, and peering at the younger man from the corner of his eye.

Little Feather's burst of hearty laughter rolled out over the water before them and was muffled by the forest behind them. "Uncle! I've been out hunting every day. How could I possibly know? And stop trying to match make!"

"She's a fine, young woman. Hard worker, respectful . . ."

"She giggles, uncle! She drives me crazy after being in her company for five minutes!"

"You've been gone the better part of two winters. She may not giggle as much as when she was younger."

"Gigglers never change!"

Iron Fist smiled to himself. He had wanted to determine his nephew's feelings for the beautiful, young maiden in the village north of them. Whenever she had come to visit relatives in their village she had always trailed after Little Feather, and the young brave had always been very tolerant of her. But she was not the woman for his nephew.

"There are some Frenchmen up at Long Bow's village. They'll probably stop here next. They're pretty honest, at least as far as Frenchmen go."

"What are Frenchmen doing this far south?"

"Well, they came across the big waters as Dutch servants, worked their length of time, and are now free to do what they want . . . which is get as many of our furs as they can while giving us as little as they can!"

Little Feather glanced at his uncle and chuckled.

"Have they ever had any flintlocks?"

"Not that I remember—it wouldn't be worth their lives to provide us with flintlocks!" Iron Fist stated ruefully, "but they usually have a few new items each time they come." He paused, deep in thought, and then continued thoughtfully, glancing surreptitiously at his nephew again. "They have a kid with them, rather slow, doesn't say much. Strange though, when he's through with his assigned tasks, he often wanders off by himself. The children are seldom far behind and seem to really love him. They certainly look forward to his coming." He was silent for a moment, thinking.

"I've talked with the kid on a number of occasions, well, actually I did most of the talking. Something strange there."

Little Feather looked at the older man questioningly.

"I don't think things are quite what they appear to be where the kid is concerned."

"Okay, so what do you think is amiss?" Little Feather's interest was hooked.

Iron Fist grinned to himself. His nephew liked a good mystery, and this one was just for him. "There's nothing I can point to; it's just a feeling." Definitely a feeling! It was time Little Feather had something in his life besides duty. "I think it has something to do with the way we met."

Little Feather waited.

"I was strolling down by the river when I happened upon the traders' canoe. There was this child, hardly bigger than a mouse, trying to pull this sack of trade goods out of the canoe. It was bigger than the child! It must have been stuck on something. Anyway, sh . . . he gave one mighty tug on it, and it came flying up, spun he . . . him around."—goodness but he'd have to be more careful—but Little Feather seemed to notice nothing amiss.

"Missed me by a breath of air, but the kid came slamming into me!"

Little Feather examined his uncle, concern in his dark eyes, "You weren't hurt, were you?"

The older man snorted. "The kid isn't as big as Red Fox!"

"You could have been hurt, depending on what was in that sack."

"Well, I wasn't. It was like being hit by a butterfly . . . okay so a big butterfly!"

The arrival of other men for their morning ablutions ended the private conversation. Iron Fist, well-satisfied with himself for having introduced the subject of the 'kid' to his nephew, ambled jauntily back to the village. Well, the Frenchmen and the 'kid' should be here by late afternoon. Now, how could he bring them together?

As it happened, his planning was academic, as Fate intervened.

"Worried about that bear?" Tall Tree asked as he stripped ready for his morning swim.

"Actually, I was thinking about a dream I've had every night since I returned home. I discussed it with Uncle, and he gave me a lot to think about. But I thought I'd get another opinion."

"I'm not much on dream interpretation, but if you want to tell it to me, I'll think about it while I'm in the water and tell you what I think when I come out."

So Little Feather recited his dream again, explaining that his uncle thought the bear represented Little Feather himself. Then he waited patiently, listening to the birds worshiping the morning and watching water spiders skimming the water near the shore while Tall Tree considered the dream and finished his morning activities in the water.

"Have you ever desired a white woman?" Tall Tree asked, sitting down beside his friend.

Little Feather gave him a look of disgust. "You've seen the same white women I've seen. What do you think?"

Tall Tree burst out laughing. "It was only a thought! I take it back! But I really can't think of any other reason there would be a white woman in your dream, unless there is something whites have that you want."

"Flintlocks!" Little Feather replied without hesitation.

"Well, I don't see you trying to stop yourself from getting those! Actually, I predict you doing everything in your power to get more! But at this time we have a bear to catch, so we can return to the fishing grounds."

Little Feather, agreeing, pushed thoughts of his dream woman and the kid of whom Iron Fist had spoken to the back of his mind. There was something that Iron Fist had said that sounded strange, but at the moment he couldn't isolate it.

"Yeah, got to stop that bear before he causes any more harm," Little Feather answered, "or takes much more of our time from the spawning grounds."

The few men, who had returned to the village to hunt the bear, had been out every day tracking the beast with him, even the dogs they took had been unable to pick up the rogue's spore. Today was going to be different, Little Feather thought, as the hunters straggled to the river for their morning rituals. Today . . . they were going to catch that beast.

Chapter 2

"Hey, kid, get that stuff packed up."

"Ian Mcphearson!" Shannon muttered beneath her breath, sure she'd forget her pseudopersona. "Hurry up, kid!" "Unfold the sleeping blankets, kid!" "Fold the sleeping blankets, kid!" "Get some firewood, kid!" "Put the fire out, kid!" "Put that stuff in the canoe, kid!" "Get that stuff out of the canoe, kid!" "Don't burn the fish, kid!" "Careful skinning that squirrel, kid. Don't cut yourself!" "Don't sleep too close to the fire, kid, you might get burned!" "Do this, kid!" "Do that, kid!" "Slow down, kid!" . . . Well, she admitted to herself as she bent her slim, wiry form to the task at hand, she'd never heard that one—thanks to her brilliant brother Shamus.

But she'd kill him . . . a long slow death when she saw him again. Maybe she'd stake him out and let the ants eat him! Maybe she'd feed him to the bears, she thought bitterly, as she proceeded slowly and methodically to reach out her long, slender hands to pick up the items one at a time and place them in a neat pile in the center of the deerskin mat. What a ridiculous exercise! Everything was going to fall into a jumble as soon as she gathered the corners and lifted the makeshift bag. No one ever noticed the incongruity of the ritual! Her performance must be very good.

In spite of it being early spring, the sun beat down mercilessly upon her, making her scalp itch under her floppy hat and sweat trickle down her spine under the rough cotton binder beneath her buckskin shirt.

As Shannon gathered the items—metal knives, hatchets, colorful blankets, pans, sewing needles and beads of all colors and shapes—which were spread in an orderly fashion over the deerskin mat, she absorbed into herself every bird twitter, dog bark, and child's cry that passed her way. She didn't miss a single breeze that rustled playfully through the branches of the giant trees. Every tangled thicket, every stream gurgling away to larger streams and ultimately to the ocean, the laughter and each nuance of the speech and laughter of the people with whom the Frenchman traded—everything she saw and heard of the people and the strange, green world filled with spectacular plants and animals into which she had been dropped like so much bat guano, she stored for future reference. She listened . . . and she learned.

Pierre and Jacque, like some beneficent but false gods, were passing out cups of alcohol amongst the natives who wanted it, bringing false cheer with a demon lurking within it—and there was a large group of warriors surrounding them. Her knowledge of Kanien'kehaka, the name these people called themselves, was excellent and increasing with each trip to one of their villages. She was skilled in languages and spoke Gaelic, English, Dutch—thanks to her time in Breuckelen—Kanien'kehaka, French, and a smattering of other Iroquois languages, but this was her secret.

Now, unnoticed—the kid was never noticed any more than a tree in the background was noticed—she listened to snatches of conversation that buzzed about her. Loud, boisterous and arrogant! Some, definitely under the influence of Demon Rum. "They fought like women!" One tall, broad-shouldered man was saying disdainfully, gesticulating wildly with his hands. Another arrogant voice—"Thirty of them—men, women and children, filthy and starving came into our camp last week begging for food!" Shannon understood them to be talking about disbanded Huron. She had been hearing about them for weeks now. Apparently, there had been a raid into the Huron territory to the north that destroyed the Hurons as a nation. A real mystery there . . .

Others were discussing the raids on the Neutrals and Eries. "Past the Thundering Water . . ." "Fought like women . . . no challenge at all!" "More furs than we know what to do with. Well, not really . . ." a boisterous voice bellowed to a rush of deep, male laughter. "Flintlocks, and more flintlocks!" "We crushed them under our feet . . . !"

Shannon hated arrogant men, but couldn't help herself from admiring their success. The Iroquois were raging over the land like a flooding river, conquering everything in their path and leaving a trail of death and disrupted nations. The men about her were drunk on the nectar of victory—along with a strong portion of whisky. It was probably the cause of their exuberant and festive mood which made this trip so profitable for the traders without a lot of dickering.

With all the unsold merchandise packed in the center of the mat, she slowly folded the corners to make a sack and smiled to herself remembering the time Pierre had offered her alcohol. She had vehemently shook her head, pushing the bottle away and repeating, "bad . . . bad stuff" consistent with her pseudopersonna The traders had laughed their silly heads off, but had not tried to force the poison on her again. Thank goodness . . . she might have had to kill them out of necessity, and they were really good company, and she was covering much more territory in her search for Shamus than she would have without them.

Pretending to be mentally slow had been Shamus' idea, and in retrospect had proven to be brilliant. She would have to thank him for that, just before she killed him for taking so long to rescue her. Slow moving, seldom talking, monosyllabic responses—it had proven most effective.

Slinging the pack over her shoulder, head hanging low, she shuffled with an unsteady gait—listing like a drunk sailor—slowly towards the tunnel-like opening formed by the stockade walls overlapping. The heavily-traveled dirt path, leading to the river that lay a mile or so away and was her destination, lay just beyond the stockade opening.

Her floppy hat shielded her eyes from the bright sun while the scents and sounds of a new-born spring tickled her senses.

As she struggled along the path, she admitted reluctantly to herself that she was coming to love this wild land burgeoning with life.

Coming around a curve in the path, Shannon found herself behind a gaggle of young women whose chatter competed with the blue jays that flitted among the newly greening branches far overhead. Inadvertently, she became an eavesdropper to their lively conversation.

"Have you heard? Little Feather's back."

"No, I hadn't . . . When?"

Shannon was all ears, unable to prevent herself from being caught up in the women's chatter.

"Several days, I think. My brother was talking to my cousin, and I overheard them."

"I wouldn't mind going into the woods with him!" They all giggled.

"I thought he had eyes only for Wild Rose?"

"That woman from the Wolf Clan?"

"I think so."

Another woman scoffed. "You mean she's got eyes for him! I've never noticed anything special in the way he looks at her. He looks at her polite, the way he looks at everyone."

"Did you hear that Wolf Running had been mauled by a bear?"

"No, is Little Feather leading in its hunt?"

"I think so. He's run down so many bears over the years . . . the bear hasn't a chance!" They burst out laughing.

The women turned off down a side trail, their chatter absorbed by the surrounding forest.

Continuing down the river path, Shannon had much to reflect upon. Little Feather? So the man was a bear hunter. Could this hunter be the same person about whom her friend Iron Fist raved?

Several times during the past six months, they had visited Iron Fist's village, typical of Iroquois villages—long central paths with shorter side paths and long houses lined up neatly side by side on either side of the main path. At one end of the village was a large area for their famous, or infamous, stick and ball games. There were always men and women everywhere coming and going from the village, tending to every day business: women hauling water, tanning hides, making clothes, tending children and a hundred other chores while men tended their weapons, talked of war and hunts, repaired long houses, carving their wooden masks, and coming and goingt in hunting parties. And everywhere there were children, laughing, screaming and playing, and then the ubiquitous village dogs—yapping, yapping—always yapping!

Her first encounter with Iron Fist had been memorable and almost disastrous. She had very nearly killed him!

Pierre and Jacques had had an unusually large number of trade goods, and she had been struggling, as usual, to get the sack out of the canoe. A corner of the make-shift bag had gotten jammed under the seat, and she had tugged and pulled at the recalcitrant sack for several minutes trying, unsuccessfully, to free it. Finally, in sheer frustration and with a few choice Gaelic curses, she had jerked with all her strength. Unfortunately, the bundle had chosen that moment to release itself from its entanglement under the seat and to swing upward with sufficient momentum to send her spinning in a full circle. To her misfortune, a tall, broad-shouldered man had been standing directly behind her. The sack must have missed him by a whisker, but she didn't! She slammed into him with the force of the sack and her weight. He managed to maintain his balance and keep her from falling flat on her face at the same time. Quite a feat! She thought she had seen a look of surprise and pleasure pass over his face, but it had been so fleeting, she attributed the impression to her vivid imagination. Good thing she hadn't accidentally killed him. These Iroquois were so touchy, it would probably have caused a war!

Placing the bundle in the canoe, she turned and headed back to the stockade for the furs that now belonged to Pierre and Jacques. The men in the village were noisier and becoming more belligerent by the moment as the alcohol flowed freely. Trouble was brewing.

As she wrestled the last of the furs into the canoe, she heard loud voices coming down the river path. They all sounded well on the way to being inebriated, Pierre and Jacques the loudest of all.

The group came into sight, laughing, shouting and joking. Pierre carried a bundle of furs—payment for the drinks after the first ones. She took the furs and placed them in the canoe and climbed in herself, settling in the center, kneeling on some furs, and rocking back on her heels. A paddle lay beside her, but she was seldom expected to use it. Something about the 'poor little scrap of a thing' not being strong enough. It was okay with her.

The two traders said their good-byes, shoved the canoe into the water, leaped in a bit unsteadily, and took up their paddles, having some difficulty coordinating their strokes. Shannon sighed, hoping the two men wouldn't get them all drowned.

After a few futile attempts, they developed a sort of rhythm and started on a sporadic course down the river. Good thing they were away from the village. The villagers were on the verge of being mean.

"Goosh haulsh, kish, huh?" and Pierre started howling at his own speech.

"Ian McPhearson," Shannon mumbled under her breath. She had mumbled so much during the past six months that the men thought it was part of her mental slowness and paid it no mind.

"Whersh to nexsht?" Pierre called from the back end of the canoe.

"Iron Fist's village," Jacques replied, not as skunked as his partner. "It's been a few weeks since we visited him. Thought we'd head there."

"Goosh idea," Pierre yelled.

"And don't you go to sleep!" Jacques hollered back. "I don't want to do all the paddlin' like last time!"

"I'sh not too far gone!"

"Yeah," Jacques muttered.

Both men leaned their backs into their work, and silence ensued.

The only sounds that broke the stillness were soothing ones: the shushing of the paddles dipping into the water, the occasional splash as a fish leaped into the air and fell back into the river, and birds—chirping, twittering, chattering.

And smells . . . the very water had its own unique scent, cool to the nostrils while the scent of green—an April green—filled the air.

Great trees, some gnarled and some ramrod straight, their early-budding branches intertwined far above, crowded the banks of the river. Young trees vied for space beneath their giant brothers. Brush, tiny flowers blooming amongst the late melting patches of snow—all the colors of the rainbow—and vines competed for their place in the sun. Maybe Da's final blessing was protecting her. They had been very lucky.

She had heard of conflicts occurring before they arrived at a destination or after they left. Maybe Daghdha, Lord of the Green Wood, did exist. Maybe not. She didn't know. She did know that the Christian God hadn't been of much help, not even to his priest, Father Michael.

Ah, Father Michael, the good priest. How she had loved him, her childhood mentor. The good Father Michael and her father had sat up many long nights talking, vigorous, lively conversations. In the western mountains of her homeland, there were small enclaves where the Old Religion still lived. Yes, their conversations had been lively. But none of that mattered now. They were both dead at the hands of the English. Hopefully, the good father was with his Christ, and her father was in the Good Land just beyond the horizon.

She let her hand trail through the water. Silence was conducive to thinking, and she thought a lot on these journeys. And she worried.

The last time they had stopped to resupply, she had seen a wanted poster on herself and Shamus. There was a reward for each of them—a hundred muskets! Who could possibly want them that badly. The traitor?

And, she worried about Shamus. Had he gotten out of Ireland safely—they had gone by different ships—had he made it to the colonies? Where was he now? Had anyone turned him in for the reward? How would he find her with her trail six months cold? No plans had been made for her indenture contract being sold. But there had been no help for it.

The van Hooven's had fallen on hard times. The crops had failed, and they had had to sell most of their cattle, the very ones it had been her job to tend, the children had gotten sick, and she had been one more mouth to feed.

Pierre and Jacques had watched her work and knew she was a hard worker—not very smart—but a hard worker. They hadn't been looking for 'smart', just a strong back. They had offered to buy her contract, and the van Hooven's had accepted. It had turned out to be a good deal with everyone satisfied, except Shamus would have to work harder to find her.

The quiet was lulling her to sleep, and her chin nearly rested on her chest.

A sudden burst of gunfire broke the stillness sending the three of them scrambling to the belly of the canoe, not knowing what was happening. So much for protection! A second barrage followed the first. Pierre was now fully awake with a clear head. Not hearing any bullets hitting the water, the three poked their heads over the side of the canoe. The yelling and screaming came from somewhere in the forest on the west bank.

Pierre and Jacques grabbed up their paddles and paddled furiously in that direction.

"It might be the bear we heard about back at old Long Bow's village, They may need help!" Jacques shouted from his place at the front of the canoe.

Pierre didn't say anything, just leaned harder into his paddling. Shannon grabbed her paddle, and the canoe flew over the water. Moments later the canoe hit the bank, and the men were scrambling out and rushing towards the noise.

After pulling the canoe up on the bank, Shannon followed the men but more slowly. She was dismayed at her companions mad dash into danger without giving it any thought. A little reconnoiter was in order—maybe a little idea of what was facing them. It might be one of those skirmishes between natives that the traders had been lucky enough to avoid. Alcohol! One day it was going to kill them!

And her only weapon was her skinning knife—Long, and deadly—but against a bear? Hardly! Pierre and Jacques had tried to teach her to use a musket, but she had pretended to be too slow to learn. She had nearly shot Pierre. That had ended the lessons. She hoped it wouldn't end her life.

Pulling the knife from its sheath, she started circling the sound of battle. There were still men fighting, and the growling told her it was a bear—a very angry bear. Shouts, yells, growling and inhuman screams filled the air. Then she heard Pierre and Jacques' voices added to the melee.

She came upon an Indian lying unconscious in her path. Blood flowed from the gashes on his head and side, and one arm lay in a peculiarly twisted position. Quickly pushing aside his heavy bear claw necklace and putting her ear to his chest, she breathed a sigh of relief. His heart beat was strong and regular. A cursory examination revealed a large bump on his head. Apparently, he had been knocked against something, probably a tree, and crawled this far before passing out. Good thing he had such a hard head. Good thing also that he still held his musket—a flintlock, no less. She pried it from his closed hand.

A rapid search of his pouches revealed the ball and powder. Never had she loaded a flintlock so rapidly. She hoped she hadn't over done the powder in the flash pan or down the barrel. There were fewer human sounds now but still lots of animal growls. Gun in hand, she raced towards the clamor, taking refuge at the last moment behind the bole of a forest giant and peering around it.

Grizzly! Damn! the biggest bear—bleeding from multiple wounds—she had ever seen! Snarling, growling, swinging his massivse arms about like clubs, aiming for anyone or anything he could smell or movement he could see! Several Natives and dogs lay on the ground while other dogs were leaping at the bear or nipping at its heals, and other natives were still firing at the beast or shaking their bows to confuse and distract its attention.

Pierre was shaking his gun at the beast, trying to get its attention. Jacques was trying to get a clear shot.

Shannon raised the musket to her shoulder, took a deep breath and held it, waiting for Jacques to take his shot. Both shots needed to sound as one. After a couple of moments, Jacques had his opportunity and took it. Shannon slowly squeezed the trigger at the same time, and the shots resounded as one. At the last moment the bear swung, hitting Jacques' gun, before falling dead at the Frenchman's feet.

Shoving away from the tree, Shannon turned quickly, intending to put the gun back in the Native's hand. Unfortunately, he was standing directly behind her, his dark eyes burning into her own grey ones, and she slammed into him before she could stop herself. She grabbed his good forearm intending to keep him from falling, only to realize his feet were firmly planted on the ground. Well, damn! Now what?

After the slightest hesitation, she slammed the gun into the hand of his good arm and patted him on his good shoulder, saying, "Good shot! Nice gun!" in Kanien'kehaka. He looked a little confused. Hopefully, he was in enough pain and experiencing enough confusion that he wouldn't even remember her. She gave him a gentle shove in the direction of his companions, saying, "Go on. It looks like you need each other," again in Kanien'kehaka. She disappeared into the trees in the direction of the river. She could only hope she hadn't made a mistake.

Chapter 3

Three deadfalls along the clear areas by the river had been checked so far, and still no sign of the wily grizzly. Tracking him was like tracking early morning mist; if you see it at all, it tends to vanish quickly. And the dogs were behaving in a similar fashion—here one moment and gone the next as they pursued one blind trail after another in an attempt to locate the beast's scent.

Coming to a steep bank with trees close to the edge, Little Feather and Tall Tree turned into the forest, planning to intersect the river beyond the bank.

After a few minutes of pushing their way through heavy brush, Tall Tree suddenly dropped to the the ground.

"Little Feather, over here!" Tall Tree called, feathering his hand lightly over some half-rotted leaves.

The two men squatted, studying the imprints in the soft earth—bear prints, *huge* bear prints!

"If that's our bear, he's one monstrous creature, the biggest I've ever seen," Little Feather shook his head, frowning thoughtfully. "And he didn't come from the river; he's moving through the thick forest," he added as he stood up.

The men, each with a quiver of arrows and a bow bouncing against his back and a flintlock ready in his hand, followed the tracks a short distance, their dogs, whining and squirming around their feet, waiting for the order to search.

"We'd better get the others and stay together on this one," Little Feather decided, pausing to study the tracks and their direction more intently. His strong, angular face showed his concern. "Too bad Wolf Running is still unconscious, or he might have been able to tell us something about the bear."

Shrugging his broad shoulders, Little Feather stood, put his hands to his mouth and emitted a long, shrill call that pierced the forest sounds like the scream of a cougar. Silence momentarily covered the forest. Three times he repeated the call to regroup and then waited. A few moments later an answering call resounded from the west and another from the north. Within a matter of minutes the five men were together following the bear's tracks through the semi-dark forest, the scraggly dogs running and yapping ahead of them.

Little Feather was worried. It was unusual for bears to be in the thick forests. This made the bear more unpredictable than most. They liked the partially forested areas around open fields and along streams and rivers. This one could be old, sick or injured, any situation of which made this animal more dangerous than usual.

The trail wound and circled back on itself, more tangled than a creeper vine, several times leading the men through brush and bramble, almost as if the bear were trying to lose them or was lost and confused itself.

The men, spread out on either side of the trail, were moving rapidly when a sudden howl of rage burst onto the air. Where were the dogs that they had given no warning? The creature crashed through the brush and saplings to the side and downwind of the party—explaining why the dogs had not detected the beast—not more than eight feet from where Little Feather stood. Grizzly! a monster of a bear . . . at least nine feet tall and as destructive as a summer hurricane!

There was no time for Little Feather to finish loading his gun, so he swung it up by the barrel, using it as a club. In the middle of the swing his moccasined foot slipped on some rotted leaves. As his vision flew from the bear to the trees above, he saw the dogs leap at the beast and be brushed aside like so many flies.

The bear charged!The other warriors, who had loaded their weapons while the bear's attention was on Little Feather, fired, and general mayhem followed.

Little Feather's fall was fortunate—although it didn't feel fortunate—as the bear, instead of being able to clutch him, was only able to graze his face and down his side with its wicked claws and slam him into a tree hard enough to knock him nearly senseless, wrench his shoulder, and break his arm. The other hunters did everything but stomp on the beast to draw its attention away from Little Feather. Two of the men were beating on the bear with their guns, dodging in and out of range of its deadly arms and jaws, while the other two were reloading. They fired into the bear while dancing out of its reach, then they started beating on him, while the others loaded their weapons. The grizzly got in a lucky swing, disabling another warrior. Little Feather struggled to crawl away, but instead of collecting his wits, he passed out.

As Little Feather was regaining consciousness, he felt something press against his chest. He had no idea what it was, but at least it didn't hurt. If it was someone who was going to scalp him, they could have it. His body wasn't responding to his brain. His face and side were on fire. As he thought about it, his shoulder and arm didn't feel much better. His brain cleared as he felt someone take his gun. A moment later and they wouldn't have been able to remove it so easily from his lax hand. Well, he still had his scalp as he felt someone going through his pouches until they found the spare ball and powder. So maybe they were going to shoot him . . . with his own gun! They'd be doing him a favor at the moment the way he felt. And he just knew he was going to feel worse before he began to feel better. That bear!

Whoever had lifted his weapon and ammunition was moving rapidly away from him. Soft, light steps. A kid?

He dared to open his eyes, but all he could see was the ground. He was actually going to have to move. He was lying on his left arm, which after trying to move, turned out to be his good arm. The one that was on top and free was broken. That figures!

Blood, flowing into his eyes, blinded him. No hope for it. He was going to have to move to wipe the blood out of his eyes. Gritting his teeth and listening to the bones crunch in his arm and shoulder, he swiped the blood from his eyes and pushed himself up to his hands and knees. The world swam around him, and he waited until it stopped, then pushed himself to his feet.

Looking towards where the noise was still coming from, although a lot less than when he passed out, he saw a small figure dressed in buckskins and some kind of funny hat that came down to his ears, leaning against a very big tree. It *was* a kid! He managed to approach the boy without being heard, probably because the kid was so intent on what he was doing. His gun was up and ready to shoot. Little Feather hoped it was loaded. What was the kid waiting for? The bear certainly sounded alive to him. Then he saw the kid pull the trigger.

Little Feather's ears were acute enough that he heard the two shots although they were only a split second apart. What was going on here? Obviously, two people had fired at the same time with the kid matching the other shot. The kid didn't want anyone to know there had been two shots. Why? Little Feather knew, without a doubt, that the kid hadn't missed. Strange.

Little Feather noticed a strangely familiar scent. Before he had time to wonder about it, the kid swung around so fast that Little Feather didn't have time to get out of the way. The kid slammed into him with a force he wouldn't have believed possible for one so small, then grabbed Little Feather's arm as though to keep him from falling. As if he were in danger of falling, even though he was. He almost snorted. The impact was also very revealing. Little Feather's eyes widened slightly, and he found himself staring deeply into the greyest, stormiest eyes he had ever seen—now where had he seen those eyes before—also among the most intelligent. But the gun was slammed into his hand, and the woman patted his shoulder, saying, "Good shot! Nice Gun!" in Little Feather's own language! He was confused, he admitted and hurt like crazy, but he wasn't that confused! What was going on?

To make matters worse, the woman gave a him a little shove towards his friends and said, "Go on. It looks like you all need each other!" again in his language, well spoken, too. Before he could say a word, she had disappeared . . . and into his forest! But she was right, whoever she was, he definitely needed his friends right now.

Chapter 4

Ruthlessly, Little Feather suppressed the raging pain that jangled along his nerves and staggered back to the battle site, his mind reliving the scene with the strange woman. The woman was forgotten instantly when he saw the devastation the bear had created. One dog limped about on three legs and dripped blood from a gash on its head. Another lay gasping, unable to get up. The others seemed to have fared better.

Among the men, Tall Tree seemed to be the only one to have escaped injury. Grey Turtle had a slash on his head from which the bleeding had already ceased and was now helping his twin to his feet. The other warrior, scarcely more than a boy, seemed to have only minor scratches and bruises. Little Feather, himself, had sustained the most serious injuries.

He raised an expressive brow at Tall Tree as he observed two strangers skinning the bear.

His friend immediately pointed to Jacques. "Jacques' shot brought the grizzly down We had run out of balls and were trying to beat the bear to death," Tall Tree grinned ruefully. "It was a toss up whether he would succumb first or we would. Anyway, the traders happened to be in the area when they heard the noise. Fortunate for us. That bear was one mean, stubborn cuss!

"Jacques and Pierre trade frequently with our village. More honest than most of the traders."

"Anyone else in their party that you know of?" Little Feather, sweat beading his forehead, asked as he staggered to a log under a big maple and collapsed onto it.

"The two of them," Tall Tree answered, and added as an afterthought, "and some kid. The kid doesn't say much, kind of slow. I've never seen them with anyone else. Why do you ask?"

Little Feather shook his head, apparently deep in thought. Iron Fist! Now Little Feather realized what was 'wrong' with his uncle's conversation. A couple of minor slips—he . . . for him a couple of times! How? How did Iron Fist know? Little Feather's lips curled up ever so slightly—the same way he had learned the woman's secret, colliding with the 'kid', of course! How much more did Iron Fist know about the woman? Little Feather intended to ask when he returned to the village.

Gazing around the area, Little Feather saw no one but his party and the two Frenchmen. So where was the third member of their party? Where was 'the kid'?

Jacques looked up from his work as the tall, muscular stranger approached. All of the other members of the hunting party were familiar to him, except this man. The way the others deferred to him, Jacques knew he must be important. The warrior was bleeding from multiple wounds—a series of claw gashes on his face and neck and deep lacerations on his side and hip. He appeared in danger of expiring right in his tracks.

So this was the man who thought he had killed the bear. Little Feather doubted that the Frenchman had accomplished the killing shot but said nothing. Could the huntress—a chill crept down his spine—be the same person every one referred to as 'the kid'? That would explain her presence here more sensibly than that she inhabited his forest without his or his people's knowledge. He remembered the woman's winter grey eyes under that ridiculous hat and knew instantly where he had seen them before. The flaming-haired warrior woman of his dreams! So where was she now, and why did she disguise herself? What had Iron Fist said? Oh, yes! These people were on their way to his village now. He decided to make a point of becoming acquainted with the 'kid.'

His thinking was growing fuzzy he began to feel the loss of blood. They were going to have to start back soon, or he would have to be hauled on a travois.

"Grey Turtle, White Feather, we need some moss, lots of it, and some bark from a birch, if you can find any," Tall Tree directed the twins who immediately disappeared among the trees. Then he turned to the last Native, the teenager, and said, "Red Fox, I need you to hurry to the river and fill one of your pouches with water. There isn't much we can do now, but we'll try and stop some of this bleeding, and that shoulder and arm need to be straightened. The women can take over when we get home."

Tall Tree looked at Little Feather and shrugged. They were both thinking about Wolf Running. But Wolf Runnimg had been alone, and it had taken him three days to crawl back to the village. Little Feather should be home within a few hours.

While the Frenchmen were skinning the bear, Little Feather could hear them talking in soft tones, too soft for him to hear what they were discussing. After a few minutes they came to a decision, and Pierre approached the log where Little Feather sat.

"If you would allow, sir, we have a friend who might be able to help. You must understand,"—here he gave an eloquent shrug of his slim shoulders—"he's not all,"—tapping his head,— "together. He was following us here, but I think he might have gotten lost," he said apologetically with another shrug of his shoulders. "But he has the healing touch and knowledge of herbs."

Little Feather's attention was caught immediately, although no trace of his avid curiousity showed on his face. Healing and herbs, huh? Another side to his warrior woman, and he wouldn't have to wait until he returned to the village to see her again. A thrill of anticipation filled him along with a wave of nausea and weakness that he firmly squelched.

Waiting a few moments before replying, he pretended to ponder their suggestion. At last he responded in a seemingly reluctant voice, "We are some hours away from our own healers; therefore, if you have a healer, I will at least see him before I decide to let him tend my injuries. Go and fetch him."

Pierre soon vanished into the murky dark of the forest to bring the lad back . . . if he could find him. Hopefully, the kid wasn't wandering around lost in this primeval forest, and Pierre hoped he hadn't made a mistake offering the kid's services. But if the kid could help this man, Pierre knew it would mean a lot of furs for them, possibly enough to make them wealthy, enough to buy the piece of land of which he dreamed. There was something in the manner in which the hunters deferred to the man.

Pierre breathed a sigh of relief as he caught the first glint of sunlight bouncing off the river through the trees. He could just make out the kid's floppy hat by the canoe.

Shannon was sitting on a large bolder, looking out over the river and totally absorbed in the song of the rushing water. How she missed the rushing streams and cool glens from back home! Would she ever be able to return home? Who could have possibly betrayed them? A year had passed. Where could Shamus be? She couldn't accept the possibility that he might be dead. She just couldn't. As she wiped a tear from off her cheek, she heard a loud crack emanating from the forest as a twig broke. She listened intently as the noise came closer. No attempt was made for silence, or it was futile. One of her partners without a doubt! She waited.

"Hey, kid," Pierre, kneeling in front of Shannon, spoke slowly, enunciating each word carefully. It never occurred to him that he was speaking to 'the kid' in French or that 'the kid' had learned the language in the past six months, and they considered her slow! "Someone is bad hurt, and needs your help."

Shannon glanced quickly at Pierre, a blank expression, on her face and then turned her gaze back to the river. "Ian McPhearson!"she muttered under her breath. Then, aloud added, "Lost! You lost!" she accused Pierre, never taking her eyes from the water as the urge to laugh bubbled up inside of her.

He interpreted that cryptic statement to mean the kid had gotten lost trying to follow them but had managed to find his way back to the canoe.

"I'm sorry about that, kid, truly I am, but it couldn't be helped. Some people were in terrible danger, a big bear was attacking them." He gently turned Shannon's face towards him. It was imperative that he make 'the kid' understand what was needed.

She stared at him blankly, proud that she did it so well. Maybe when life returned to normal, she'd go on the stage.

"Bad trouble," he tried again.

She'd say they'd been in bad trouble, but not any more. From what she'd seen after the bear had fallen, the only one seriously injured was the warrior she had encountered in the forest. Could he have been more seriously hurt than she realized? Could the head injury have been worse than she had thought? Maybe his head wasn't so hard after all. She waited.

"Hurt, bad hurt, kid. He needs your help. Do you understand? Medicine, he needs your medicine." The kid wasn't usually this dense, but then maybe the stress of being lost in the forest was still effecting him.

"Ian McPhearson," Shannon muttered, adding aloud, "Hurt? Someone hurt?"

Pierre grinned in relief, having gotten his message through to the kid finally, "C'mon, kid., I'll take you there."

After searching through her private bundle and locating the bag of medicine, she started the journey back to the injured man.

Now what, Shannon wondered as she trudged behind the Frenchman along the narrow footpath surrounded by trees, some tall and majestic, others old and gnarled showing the signs of much tough time. She just knew the man needing her help was the warrior she had discovered in the forest. Now she wished she had kept her big mouth shut—Shamus always said she talked too much! But, maybe the warrior wouldn't remember the encounter; she could hope.

Reaching her hand down, she grasped her bag of medicine. It was soft as duck down and shiny from age. The bag brought back bitter-sweet memories. She had been healer to her father's band of rebels. Father Michael had made her study medicine from books he possessed—much of which she hadn't agreed with—and her grandmother had made her study the use of herbs from the time Shannon had been knee-high to a grasshopper. The bag had been her grandmother's.

She hoped the man's injuries were not such that if he died, she'd be blamed for it. She sighed. It was such a nice day. How had she gotten herself into such a mess? What devil had prompted her to speak to him? They had their own healers, so why was Pierre taking her to the wounded Indian? She had to admit to herself that there probably wasn't a healer in the immediate vicinity except for herself, and he had been bleeding a lot when she had last seen him. God, she hoped she wasn't being given a second chance to kill him. She wasn't in a killing mood today. He was too good looking.

She stopped short. Now from where did that stray thought come? Resolutely shoving the unruly thought to the back of her mind, she continued thinking about his wounds as she trudged on. He wouldn't have to worry about those gashes leaving nasty-looking scars. Her stitching ability would leave only fine lines where wide lacerations now existed. Of course, he wouldn't know that—and if he didn't develop putrification and die from that.

Voices from ahead alerted her that they were approaching their destination. Her head went down, and her face went slack— her usual pose. But this time her heart beat faster and cold sweat trickled down her spine. What if the warrior challenged her? Activate plan B? Take off on her own to find Shamus? After all, her promise to her dying father had been fulfilled.

Nothing for it now but to brazen it out and see what the warrior would do. She assumed her slumped position and followed Pierre into camp.

The camp was much less chaotic than when she had last seen it. As a matter of fact, it was much subdued. Even the dogs did little but whine and lie around. Jacques had finished skinning the bear and was butchering the beast with the help of a young lad in his early teens.

"Little Feather, are you sure you want a white to touch your wounds? Especially one whose mind isn't all there?" One of the hunters was asking the man sitting on the log.

Little Feather? This was the infamous Little Feather? the one with whom the woman would like to go into the woods? She knew what men and women did together—her father had not neglected her education—but she had never understood why they would want to do such a thing.

From under the brim of her hat, she studied him intently. Well, he was certainly easy on the eyes—at least he would be if not for all that blood—tall and broad shouldered, muscular, a long, narrow head consistent with a long body, and piercing black eyes boring into her own grey ones. He was studying her as intently as she was studying him! Was that laughter she observed in his eyes, and maybe a challenge hidden deep behind the laughter? A strange tingling started somewhere deep in her gut and trickled out along her peripheral nerves. She dipped her head in confusion but couldn't stop the color that flooded her face like the rising of a pond behind a beaver dam. Good heavens! What was the matter with her? If this man opened his mouth and revealed what he knew about her, someone might figure out who she was, and she'd probably end up hanging on some English gallows!

Pierre led her to the man called Little Feather.

From the trees that surrounded the hunters, blue jays scolded the strangers who had invaded their territory. An old racoon, oblivious to the unusual activity, waddled towards the distant river. A squirrel scurried to and up an old oak; then he sat on a branch and chattered at the people below. Coward! Shannon thought. She wondered if a condemned man was so aware of his environment. She kept her head down as she shuffled closer.

"Kid, this is the man who needs your help." That's obvious, Shannon thought caustically. Then to Little Feather Pierre continued in broken Kanienke'haka, "This is the Kid. He doesn't say much, but he's a wizard at healing. Make those slashes heal with scarcely a scar!" At least that was his intent, but Little Feather understood the gist of the man's words, not that he believed it for a moment. She might be able to cleanse some of the wounds and stop some of the bleeding, but he would have to wait until he returned home to have the broken bone set and his shoulder joint put back into place.

As he watched her approach him in her slow, unsteady step, he knew he was observing a master showman under that disguise. That ridiculous hat was the mark of his warrior woman. But even he had had a serious moment of doubt when he had first seen her shuffling into the camp site, her arms hanging limply at her sides, and her face—what he could see of it beneath her floppy hat—had been slack and expressionless, definitely not the animated face of the woman who had slammed his musket into his hand earlier. Then he had caught her studying him even as he was studying her. No doubt about it! There was a mystery here, and he was already planning his strategy to unravel it. How he loved a good mystery!

"Are you sure about this, Little Feather? We'll be back in the village in a couple of hours," Tall Tree asked with a troubled expression on his broad face and hovering about his friend as a mother bear moves between her young and danger.

"And I could bleed to death in that time! Don't be such an old woman, friend," Little Feather responded. Then added, "And please move away and give the kid room to work!" Already Little Feather was feeling woozy from loss of blood, and the last thing he wanted to do was faint and fall at his warrior woman's feet.

Tilting his chin with one finger, she intently assessed the gashes on his face. She gazed into his eyes and seemed to be waiting for something.

Then it hit him like a stray bolt of lightning. The head wound must be effecting his thinking. She was waiting for him to comment about the earlier encounter. Whatever she was hiding was hers to hide . . . for the time being. He kept his mouth closed and watched her, waiting for her to catch on to the fact that he wasn't going to reveal her secret.

Giving a slight nod, she acknowledged his silence and continued examining the bump on his head.

"Anything in that bag of tricks of yours, kid, to help him?" Jacques asked slowly in French.

"Ian McPhearson," Shannon muttered automatically under her breath.

Little Feather, hearing her, wondered if that was her name. He intended to find out—to discover all of her secrets. to peel away the layers until he found the heart of her.

Shannon grumbled aloud, "Not bag of tricks." Then she added softly, "Just hard, hard head," not realizing that Little Feather's French was nearly as good as her Kanien'kehaka.

"Yes, isn't it?" he spoke in a voice so soft only she heard him.

Her eyes flew to his, and she blushed to the roots of her hair which Little Feather found amusing. She did appear to blush easily for a warrior woman, but then he *had* seen her kill a grizzly, at least assist in killing the grizzly. His men and the Frenchmen had put a lot of bullets into that beast.

Jacques, having heard Shannon's comment but not Little Feather's, didn't know whether to laugh or slap the kid, but he did feel the need to translate her words for the big warrior.

"He just said that it's good the injury wasn't worse."

Little Feather stared up at the woman, his dark eyes alight with laughter, any worse and he'd be dead! He might still die from putrification, and they both knew it.

Shannon blushed again and shoved his face away from her to assess the wounds on his neck and wished that was what she had said. He grunted from the unexpectedly brisk treatment. She looked at him with chagrin on her dirty face. "Sorry," she muttered. What was the matter with her? She couldn't remember ever having blushed before. Now her face seemed to be aflame all of the time.

"Think nothing of it. Your roughness took me by surprise, and a warrior should never be taken by surprise."

"Well, that makes twice today, warrior," Shannon replied softly in his language, emphasizing the word 'warrior' and grinning slightly at him.

"Huh?" Little Feather asked, the loss of blood beginning to take effect.

"The bear!" Shannon answered, reaching into her bag and pulling out a smaller bag containing a dried yellow herb.

The animated expression slid from Shannon's face as she looked around for a moment. The blank, expressionless look was back in place. "Water?" she asked of no one in particular.

Red Fox hurried to Shannon and handed her the pouch he had previously filled, glad of the chance to help his big brother and only regretting he couldn't do more. Shannon gave him a bright smile of thanks, startling the lad as he had never seen any animation on the kid's face whenever he came to the village with the traders.

Little Feather sucked in his breath, her smile literally taking it away. He knew with a certainty that this woman had in some mysterious way invaded his dreams. He swayed on the log and fought to remain conscious as he studied her.

Both his warrior woman and the kid were bold, quick-witted, intelligent—only their hair was different; his warrior woman had hair like the setting sun while this woman had hair like . . . like *mud?*

After adding some of the yellow herb to the water, she bent over him and started the painful process of cleansing the gashes on his face, giving him a close-up view of her hair. Yep . . . mud! Then he noticed little red sparkles from the scalp by the brim of her hat. He'd almost missed them—dye? She dyed her hair! An unbelievable sense of satisfaction flowed through him.

Shannon, feeling his intense scrutiny, glanced quickly at him. Sure enough, he was eyeing her as a cat eyes a mouse! He already knew that she wasn't slow-witted. Was there something wrong with her physical disguise? She hadn't had time to dye her hair in a couple of weeks. That task took longer than going into the woods to relieve herself. Pierre and Jacques considered her unusual need for privacy as part of her abnormality, but the hair dying always took place in the middle of the night while the men slept—usually dead drunk! Business had been good recently, and most nights had been spent in native villages.

The only thing this man really knew was that she wasn't as slow as she pretended, she had a working knowledge of a flintlock, she could shoot, she spoke their language—fluently—and she wasn't what she pretended to be. So. what was there really for him to divulge? Anyone who knew her wouldn't believe him. She felt a little more relaxed.

"Water . . . more water," she requested of Red Fox. The lad immediately rushed to the river for more water as Tall Tree paced the temporary campsite like a caged bear, stopping every moment or so to check over the foreigner's shoulder the progress being made to his friend's wounds.

"Tell him to perch some place and to stop gawking over my shoulder!" Shannon hissed to Little Feather and then added, "Have him build a small fire." Little Feather obligingly repeated the message as if it were his own. Tall Tree glared at his friend and scowled as the kid continued to cleanse the gashes on Little Feather's face.

About that time the twins returned to the campsite with the moss and bark previously requested.

When Red Fox returned, she took the pouch and gave the lad Tall Tree's water pouch and sent the boy for more water.

Adding some birch bark to the water she was holding, she placed the pouch on a stick over the low burning fire Tall Tree was tending. Impatiently, she waited for the solution to simmer, and then removed it from the fire to cool. She wished she had some whisky.

When Red Fox returned for the third time, Shannon took the pouch and put a large handful of leaves into the cool water. She hung it from a low-hanging branch so it wouldn't spill but would be ready when she needed it. God, she hoped she knew what she was doing. Her life might depend upon it!

Finally, when the solution was cool enough to use, she motioned for Tall Tree to follow her. While Little Feather drank from the liquid she offered him, he wondered what she planned to do next. There wasn't much more he thought she could do, but he was reluctant to have her leave. At the same time he realized that if he didn't leave for the village soon, his friends were going to have to carry him.

"The shoulder and arm . . ." she instructed, pointing to the dislocated shoulder and broken arm.

Little Feather's eyes widened in surprise. She couldn't . . . she wouldn't!

"Are you sure you want this . . . person to do this? He could do more harm than good!" Tall Tree grumbled grimly at Little Feather.

Some streak of stubbornness made Little Feather nod his head in the affirmative.

A squirrel scampered from behind a tree and cocked its head at the strange activities of the people.

Shannon and Tall Tree assisted Little Feather to lie on the ground. At least now he shouldn't faint, Little Feather mused to himself.

"You hold!" Shannon instructed Tall Tree, pointing to Little Feather's good shoulder and hoping Tall Tree would understand what needed to be done. She had a better chance of pulling the shoulder back into joint than keeping Little Feather from moving. Tall Tree did understand and held his friend to the ground, although doubtful that the 'kid' had the strength to pull the shoulder into place.

"Grey Turtle can do this if you want, brother," Tall Tree suggested before Shannon could grab Little Feather's upper arm above the fracture. "He's stronger than the 'kid'."

Little Feather shook his head in the negative. "Ian can take care of it." In response to Tall Tree's startled expression, he added, "The kid's name is Ian."

"Okay, if that's what you want, brother." Scarcely were the words out of Tall Tree's mouth when Shannon grabbed Little Feather's upper arm, bent the elbow and placed the broken lower arm across his chest. Holding his wrist and elbow, trying to stabilize the fracture, she moved the bent arm towards his head and gently moved the head of the upper arm until it slipped into the shoulder socket.

Sweat beaded Little Feather's forehead as he looked at her with new respect. His arm ached abominably, and there had been some discomfort in the shoulder, but not nearly as much as the last time he had dislocated it. The pain in the shoulder stopped almost immediately.

Shannon pointed to one of the twins—she thought he was Grey Turtle. "Water," she asked, pointing to the pouch. As Grey Turtle collected the pouch, Shannon turned her attention back to Little Feather.

"Stay!" Shannon instructed Little Feather, as if he were going anywhere!

She quickly pointed to the forearm above the break, and Tall Tree immediately clasped it tightly. Grabbing below the fracture, she carefully pulled, bringing the bones back into line. Holding the bones in place, she pulled the large mass of wet leaves from the pouch Grey Turtle was holding for her and quickly smoothed it over the fracture. She took two small branches and tied them on opposite sides of the mass of leaves.

Little Feather was breathing hard but didn't say anything. Tall Tree was staring at her with new respect in his eyes. Well, that was two jobs they had expected the healers would have to do.

Tipping his head to the side as he lay on the ground, she poured a little of the solution over the open wounds. She knew it was extremely painful, but he never twitched.

She had to warn him about the stitches. "What I'm going to do next is going to be very painful, but it'll reduce the scars and hopefully the chances of putrefication. It's something done long ago by my Norse ancestors." The words were for his ears only, softly spoken and in Kanien'kehaka. Where had she learned his language so well?

When she started stitching him up the way a woman stitched clothing, he didn't think of much of anything, and Tall Tree protested strenuously, starting to jerk her away from his friend. Little Feather grabbed Tall Tree's arm. "It's okay, friend. Let he . . . him be. He knows what he's doing." From that moment on he was too busy building mental blocks against the pain, thinking about his dream woman. Well, that didn't help!

Shannon started with surprise when she heard his slip. Good God! He knew her deepest secret! How? He knew everything! Well, almost everything. He didn't know about the reward. But he was holding her secret to himself. She relaxed—a little, sure that her secret was safe for now. She didn't understand why but appreciated it anyway.

"Well, that's it on the face," she murmured and poured some more of the solution over the stitches. Taking the moss that was offered to her, she placed it over the neat stitches. Immediately, she realized her problem. How to hold the moss on his face besides using her hand. Well, she'd thought of *almost* everything!

He realized her dilemma also and opened his eyes to gaze up into hers, a slight smirk on his sensuous mouth. He knew the instant she realized he was aware of her problem. He only teased her for a moment and then reached into one of his pouches and pulled out a length of deer hide, handing it to her.

"That should work," he murmured. He would have smiled, but his face hurt too much.

"You, jerk!" she muttered, only this time in Gaelic which he didn't understand, but the tone indicated it probably wasn't complimentary. He smiled broadly—inside.

"Your side is next!" she said. Then she promptly proceeded to repeat the whole procedure over again.

She was as drained by the end of the treatment as he was, but she was still conscious. She had lost count of stitches at one hundred and fifty, and he had passed out.

A few hours later, she lay with her head resting on her arm on the side of the canoe, listening to the gentle song of the river. Jacques and Pierre's voices droned in the background. Little Feather was on his way to his village on a travois, still unconscious from the potion she had given him. The bear's carcass had been hauled up into a tree to be retrieved later. There would be a great feast in the village that night. And that was just where they were headed as honored guests. Her head hurt.

Chapter 5

Sweat dripped down her face blinding her, and her heart pounded painfully in her throat. No matter which direction she fled, she could not escape the wily serpent that pursued her. Its scaly body was at least twenty feet long and as big around as a man's thigh, and its gaping maw threatened to consume her whole! The glimpse she had gotten of its terrifyingly-ugly visage revealed a hauntingly-familiar face, but fear and flight prevented her from thinking on it.

She dodged behind a giant, gnarled old oak, and the creature slithered its repulsive, serpentine head around the tree. Again she leaped into flight, her heart in her mouth and pure adrenaline pumping through her veins. At that moment a gigantic grizzly came crashing through the trees and attacked the serpent. Something bumped her on the shoulder . . . and she opened her eyes.

"C'mon, Kid. Wake up!" Jacques was tapping her on the shoulder.

"Ian McPhearson," she muttered irritably.

Her head throbbed abominably, more than when she had fallen asleep. She hadn't meant to fall asleep. She always had weird dreams and woke up with vicious headaches whenever she slept too short a time. Fortunately, the dream—which definitely fell into the category of weird—was rapidly fading from her thoughts; but the image of a serpent that looked familiar and a grizzly remained. Now why would a grizzly help her?

Lifting her head from her arm resting on the canoe railing, she gazed about her, trying to collect her wits. Natives, greatly excited, bustled about between the village and the river.

"Ohhhh . . ." she moaned, putting her head back down on her arm.

"C' mon, Kid. Wake up!" Jacques repeated, slapping her briskly on the shoulder. "We've arrived. From all the excitement, appears that Little Feather's back, too.

While men from the village pulled the canoe ashore, a hand grasped Shannon's arm, assisting her from the canoe. Now why would anyone do that?. Without thinking, she looked up, seeing Iron Fist's strong, angular face close to her own.

"I owe you for helping my nephew. I hope you will accept my thanks and continue to attend him while you are here."

What to say to the man next to her? She schooled her face, only to hear him speak near her ear, "It's too late for that, my little friend."

Well, damn! She left her face blank and expressionless.

"Whatever your concealing is yours to conceal, but my nephew and another man in our long house need your skills. Tall Tree was impressed with your care of Little Feather." Iron Fist guided her towards the stockade entrance. "How long have you been tending the injured?"

Caught off guard, Shannon answered without thinking, "Six years."

Iron Fist's brows rose. "You're scarcely more than a child yourself!"

Since Iron Fist knew as much as he did, she saw no reason not to answer and replied, "One grew up fast where I lived before coming to the Colonies."

Her face remained expressionless as she returned to the subject of the injured men. "Your medicine societies? I don't want to run afoul of them," she murmured softly

"They will deal with the spiritual side of healing, and you will tend the physical."

As they strolled into the village, the sights that beset Shannon were familiar: long houses in neat rows, young girls playing with corn husk dolls, young boys playing with their bows and arrows, women working on skins, baskets, pottery or visiting with one another, and babies in their cradleboards hanging from low tree branches.

"What about those responsible for the physical aspects of healing?"

Iron Fist was surprised at the young woman's perceptiveness of the situation. But maybe he shouldn't have been—having heard of her assistance in killing the grizzly from Little Feather and her healing skills from Tall Tree.

"Perhaps you could enlist their grandmothers' help," he suggested diplomatically.

"Probably a good idea," Shannon agreed and grinned beneath her silly hat, but the man next to her observed it and smiled to himself. A good challenge for Little Feather.

"You started Little Feather's treatment, and he would like you to continue it. And maybe you could help Wolf Running . . . he's the man who was attacked by that bear five days ago."

Five days? That was a long time, but she heard her grandmother's voice saying, 'Where there's life . . . there's hope.'

"As long as there won't be any trouble—but you must ask Jacques and Pierre first."

Iron Fist anticipated a lot of trouble . . . between this woman and his nephew, but Jacques and Pierre would be no problem— not with all the furs his nephew had!

And Iron Fist was right, the Frenchmen were delighted with the pelts received in exchange for the 'kid's' services.

Wild Rose was leaving the long house and several men, in single file, in strange masks were entering it as Iron Fist and Shannon approached the building.

"We'll have to wait outside until the False Faces are finished," Iron Fist informed Shannon.

"Are they here to tend Little Feather?"

"I don't think so. He wasn't planning on sending for them when I left just a few minutes ago. Wolf Running's clan probably sent them. He's in pretty bad shape. They're thinking of taking him home to die. You're his last chance."

"Well, I hope you're not expecting too much."

"Only a miracle!"

"Ah, our little miracle worker," Wild Rose said condescendingly as she came abreast of Iron Fist and Shannon.

Shannon couldn't help glancing up at Iron Fist who grinned back at her. "Grandmother sent over some herbs that might help. We didn't realize he had already been treated by a white . . ."

Shannon said helpfully from her expressionless mouth, eyes cast slightly downward, " . . . healer," wanting to punch the beautiful woman in her oh, so, sensuous mouth. She didn't like people who were condescending. It made her hackles rise. Shannon added, "Dog."

Wild Rose took offense and huffed off like a ruffled hen.

Iron Fist hid his smile and guided Shannon to a couple of gnarled old tree stumps to sit and wait for the False Faces to leave.

"Don't mind Wild Rose. She can be a bit . . ."

"Unpleasant . . . . overbearing . . . obnoxious?" all spoken in fluent Kanienke'haka.

"Well, those weren't exactly the words I had in mind, but they work as well. She was visiting her clan's long house in the village when Little Feather was brought in. She came immediately to see what was occurring. They've been friends for a long time, but she can be . . . inconvenient at times. Little Feather managed to get rid of her and related to me the things you had done for them this morning." He paused for a moment, watching her closely, and then added mildly, "Incidentally, you speak our language very well."

She shrugged her slim shoulders. "I'm just good with languages." She sat for a few minutes watching children playing around the long houses.

"I had really hoped he'd be too confused to remember me," she muttered so softly to herself that Iron Fist had to strain his ears to hear her.

"No such luck, huh?" he murmured sympathetically.

Again she shrugged her slim shoulders in a very fatalistic gesture.

Iron Fist smiled to himself as he watched the door to the long house. He didn't think the woman needed to be so . . . negatively resigned to her future. Of course, he couldn't tell her that. Events would just have to unfold as they would.

After what seemed like an hour or so, the False Faces filed out of the long house. Their shoulders were slumped, and a couple of the masks turned in Iron Fist's direction and shook their heads.

"They don't give Wolf Running much hope," Iron Fist said quietly as he stood and pulled Shannon to her feet. "He's a very close and dear friend."

"I'll do the best I can, but that is all I can promise."

"It'll do."

They passed through a small vestibule that was cluttered with baskets of all sizes and shapes—nearly empty now that winter was past. From the walls hung skin sacks and a variety of gardening tools.

Beyond the storeroom, they entered the smoky atmosphere of the central corridor that passed through the individual firesides. Her eyes immediately filled with tears from the pungent smoke and odors.

"Bend over a little, and it's not so bad," Iron Fist suggested.

The aroma of food cooking over the various fires down the center of the building blended with the smoke that spiraled towards the high roof, seeking the escape holes.

Along each wall running the length of the building were a series of cubicles consisting of space for sleeping at night, sitting space for the daytime, and storage cells separated from the opposite living area by a central fire and from the next fireside by a bark or skin wall. Above the benches were more shelves upon which a variety of items were scattered. Something hung from every pole and bare spot in the long house.

Shannon gave Little Feather, who was sleeping in the first cubicle, a cursory examination. At the moment he was doing well.

"Wolf Running?" she asked, turning to Iron Fist. "Wolf Running's grandmother?"

Looking about, Iron Fist spied Red Fox lingering about Little Feather's sleeping platform and sent him to fetch Wolf Running's grandmother.

Then Iron Fist lead Shannon to the storeroom at the back of the long house where a small cubicle had been closed off. Every laceration on the wounded man's body was inflamed, and the man was ranting in delirium. This was going to challenge every bit of knowledge and skill she possessed.

Those festered wounds needed to be opened and cleansed, and a healing brew needed to be forced down his throat. Shannon knew that she, and the aging grandmother even with Iron Fist's help would not be able to do everything needed. They were going to need help.

A little old lady shriveled with age, but dark eyes sharp with intelligence bustled into the room and promptly opened a large bag she had brought with her. She spread its contents on a ledge near her grandson.

"So you are the one who earned Tall Tree's praises with your skill?" The old lady turned her sharp eyes on Shannon and scrutinized her closely, and then shook her head as though satisfied. "I stopped for a moment to observe the work you did on Little Feather. Not bad!"

Shannon had to be honest with Wolf Running's grandmother. "You know . . . we clean . . ." she pointed to the infected lacerations, "could kill."

The old woman stared at her sharply. "And he'll die if we don't."

Shannon pulled a piece of deerskin out of her bag of herbs, placed it on a ledge at the head of the sleeping platform and dumped her herbs on it next to the old healer's pile. There was very little after treating Little Feather. She removed some knitbone and held it out to the old lady, "More?"

The old lady stared at Shannon intently, nodded her head as though satisfied about something, and then pulled some knitbone from her herbs. It was a pitifully small amount.

"More?" Shannon asked, hopefully. Wolf Running's grandmother thought for a moment and then started out of the room. Shannon called to her, "Whisky? . . . lots of whisky!"

The old healer glanced at Shannon for a moment, grinned and left.

"And Tall Tree!" Shannon yelled after her.

Shannon was treating Wolf Running when his grandmother returned with the needed items and Tall Tree trailing behind her.

It was a long afternoon. They soaked some of Shannon's orange flower petals in some of the whiskey and forced it down their patient's throat. There weren't enough flower petals, but they were all they possessed as a painkiller—that and the whisky.

Although Shannon knew these people were known for their ability to withstand or create pain to the death, she couldn't deliberately cause pain; so they forced the whiskey—herb solution down Wolf Running's throat.

All afternoon, the two women cut open infected lacerations, cleaned them and packed them with knitbone. Her grandmother's voice rang in her head, 'Clean it well, Shanny. Knitbone heals so fast, any fester in it will grow and kill your patient'. So they cleaned, drained, poured a cleansing solution into the wounds and drained them again.

When they were satisfied that the wounds were thoroughly clean, they packed them with the knitbone. Several times the men had to hold Wolf Running down while the women worked on him, and they all took turns pouring whiskey into the man. A couple of times Shannon caught Wolf Running's grandmother looking at her strangely, but the old woman said nothing.

After packing the last laceration, Shannon forced more healing brew and whiskey into Wolf Running. If he survived the night, he was going to have a headache to remember! And tomorrow they would have to repeat the whole process again!

Finished! Finally finished! Her head throbbed, and she felt like she was going to vomit. Sliding to the floor in complete exhaustion, she leaned her head wearily against a post, closing her eyes.

Iron Fist took her gently by the arm and started to assist her to stand.

"Just leave me here to die!" she muttered, pulling her arm from his grasp.

Tall Tree and the old grandmother smiled at that.

"Come, little one," Wolf Running's grandmother said. "You'll feel better after you eat and get some rest."

Shannon opened one grey eye and looked skeptically up at the old lady.

"If Wolf Running lives, it will be because of what you did today!" the old woman asserted with tears in her tired, old eyes, while Tall Tree and Iron Fist nodded their heads gravely in agreement.

Shannon's eye drifted shut again. "What we all did!" she corrected tiredly.

This time when Iron Fist lifted, she rose to her feet without a struggle and let him support her weight as he lead her out of the injured man's room. Tall Tree followed while. Wolf Running's grandmother remained with the unconscious man.

Little Feather was awake as the trio entered the cubicle. Shannon staggered towards him to evaluate his condition. He couldn't refrain from saying, "You look more in need of help than I do . . . Ian."

A weary smile formed on her face by itself. "Why am I not surprised? But I do need some food and sleep," she murmured softly for his ears only and wandered over to where a pot was boiling over the median fire. Something smelled delicious. Iron Fist was there with a bowl and spoon in his hand which he handed to her. Squatting down on the floor, she started to spoon meat and vegetables out of the stew. In a few minutes, the bowl was on the floor scarcely touched, and her head nodded on her chest. Iron Fist picked up the slight form and put her on the bed next to Little Feather who covered her over with his bearskin blanket.

Iron Fist strolled outside and gazed up at the night sky. A few people still moved about the village, but most were settling down in their long houses for the night. He wondered for the umpteenth time where his wife, Shining Star and their son, Little Squirrel were. Were they well? What kind of man had his son grown into? Had they been enslaved, or were they free? His heart was heavy with grief and anger at the same time. He had been hunting when, while out berry picking, they had been kidnapped by a renegade band of Cherokees. It was during pursuit of their abductors that he had come across Little Feather and brought him home. The image of that blazing village would remain with him forever.

There had been nothing he, a lone warrior, could do to help the women and children who burned to death within the village. As he stood watching, a youth of about twelve or thirteen summers burst from the forest at the edge of the village. The youth stood, hidden by a forest giant from the raiders, and promptly shot seven arrows killing seven of the attackers—Iron Fist never had been able to understand Little Feather's obsession with the flintlock. At that point Iron Fist had intervened before the lad could get himself killed. Iron Fist smiled in remembrance. That had been one of the worst fights in which he had ever participated. He thought on the vagaries of life, he had lost a wife and child and gained a nephew. Some day he hoped to have his wife and son back.

His thoughts went back to the 'kid'. What could she be hiding? She obviously was a healer of great skill. What else was there at which she might be skilled? Well, that was a mystery for Little Feather to solve.

Iron Fist cast a last, lingering glance at the starlit sky and the full moon shining down upon the village and reentered the long house. Climbing on the platform behind Little Feather, he curled up in his own bearskin blanket—a gift from Little Feather—and fell asleep.

Chapter 6

In the distance, Shannon could see Little Feather holding his arms out to her. Brush and briars filled the area between them and constantly tangled in her hair and scratched every bit of bare skin. As rapidly as she slashed her way through the briars and brush with her hunting knife, they grew back bigger, thicker and more tangled. In spite of the tears and sweat streaming down her face, and blood flowing from a multitude of cuts and scratches, she continued to hack her way through the brambles to reach Little Feather. Reaching him was essential! She knew instinctively that with him lay safety. Every time she appeared to be making progress, his figure receded into the distance. Struggling to lift her arms, heavy with fatigue, she was hacking through the next briar bush when something massive fell on top of her. As she fell, her last thoughts were . . . safety lies with Little Feather!

What the . . . ? Something rested heavily across her chest making breathing difficult. The headache was gone. Slowly memory returned. Wolf Running. Had to see to Wolf Running . . . and then Little Feather. The last thing she remembered was eating. So how did she get here . . . wherever here was? And the dream . . . what was there about the dream? Her last thought as the dream had faded, or her first thought upon awakening was that safety lay with Little Feather. Now what would make her think that?

Something tickled the side of her cheek. Opening her eyes slightly, she rolled them in the direction from which the light touch came. She was on a bed. Bed? Two big, bright eyes stared back at her. Bright Eyes, Shannon's favorite little urchin when she visited this village, stood brushing the side of Shannon's face with a feather.

"Wha' you doin' on Uncl' bed, Ian?" the precocious little urchin demanded.

Uncle? Little Feather's bed? Well, damn!

Little Feather lay, not twitching a muscle, leaving his arm stretched over the woman's breasts. He had known the instant she had come awake. Her thrashing about had awakened him. A nightmare! He wondered if she had them frequently.

So his niece was familiar with his warrior woman's name! Although at the moment, she didn't seem much like a warrior woman, just a very soft feminine form next to him. What else might his niece know?

"Shhhh, Little Feather is sleeping. I saved his life yesterday,"—a slight exaggeration, but it might impress the child to silence—"and he needs to rest today. I tried to help your daddy to, and I need to go and see how he is."

Shannon's little white lie didn't work. Bright Eyes snorted. "No body save Uncl', he save others! and daddy real g'umpy this mornin'. He tell Mommy his head feel like it been on the 'ceivin' end a Huron war cub." She continued tickling the side of Shannon's face with the feather. "Wha' does 'at mean?"

Shannon could feel Little Feather shaking with silent laughter. So he was awake, was he? Pushing his arm off her, she rolled to the side of the bed. She couldn't deny the feeling of comfort and safety she felt in his arms or the tingling sensation that started to flower deep in her abdomen. She ruthlessly suppressed the latter.

Grabbing the child and the feather, she proceeded to tickle Bright Eyes. "It means your daddy has a really, *REALLY* bad headache, but he'll probably feel better later in the day."

Shannon continued tickling the child mercilessly for a few moments while the youngster wiggled and giggled. Then she spoke quietly but seriously to the child, "You remember our secret?"

"Course!" the offended child asserted. "Neve' tell 'bout your stories or you won' tell 'bout the 'ar' or Cu'lan!" The dark-eyed, precocious child stared from Shannon to Little Feather. "Why you in Uncl's bed?" she repeated.

"I really don't know, Sweetie. The last thing I remember was sitting over there," she nodded towards the fire pit, "and then I woke up here."

The child nodded wisely. "'at 'appens me lot!"

A deep voice whispered from next to Shannon's ear, "May the bright sun shine on you this morning, my beautiful, wise, little niece. Close friends and . . . brothers often share a bed when they visit. And I have a secret for you, too. Ian did save my life—and probably everyone else who was there," he added for her ears only, "yesterday and I won't tell anyone either that sh . . . he talks our language so well".

Shannon scooted from under the bearskin blanket . . . bearskin? Hesitating a moment, she recalled her dream of the serpent and the giant grizzly. Unconsciously, she rubbed the soft bearskin. Little Feather . . . the bear. No, it couldn't be.

As she sat on the edge of the sleeping platform, a young woman brought her a bowl of stew and a wooden spoon with which to eat it. "Thank you for what you did for my husband," she murmured with tears in her eyes.

" . . . welcome," Shannon responded from her slack expressionless mouth, keeping her eyes down—but not as low as previously—taking the bowl and starting to eat. By the time she had finished, Iron Fist, returning from his morning ablutions, and Wolf Running's grandmother had entered the long house. The three of them went to check on Wolf Running.

Bright Eyes had been correct—her father was in a foul mood. "What did you do to me yesterday?" he demanded of his grandmother. Then, before his grandmother could say a word, "And what is that idiot doing here?" referring to Shannon. "And what are you doing here? I'm not of your clan!" to Iron Fist. He ignored his wife who hovered in the background.

"Tall Tree was here, also. To help hold your worthless hide while your grandmother and Ian worked trying to save your life.

For some reason your grandmother thought it was worth saving. I can't figure out why!" Iron Fist said mildly.

"Grateful to be alive, isn't he?" Shannon muttered.

Iron Fist and the elderly woman refrained from laughing.

Wolf Running's grandmother had, in the course of the long preceding afternoon, learned that appearances were deceiving. The kid, whom she had accepted as slow and different, was truly different! The kid was a gifted healer, with skills that seldom developed until one was much older.

Something else had happened in the course of the long afternoon. As the kid got more and more tired, his head rose from his usual subservient position. Several times he had gazed into the old woman's eyes as they worked on her grandson, and his eyes were intelligent—tired but extremely intelligent. Now what had ever led her to believe the kid was slow? Because he seldom said anything more than monosyllables? Seldom interacted with others? Moved slowly? Strange how the idea had developed.

Wolf Running's grandmother stepped forward. "These people and I worked all yesterday afternoon on you that you might see the light of this day. We had given up on you, but this young person brought fresh hope and skills to your treatment. Stop acting like a child and be the man we all know you are!"

"You are the mate of my niece and my friend," Iron Fist added, undisturbed by the younger man's outburst. "What else could I do but try and save your worthless hide, and Little Feather was mauled by the same grizzly yesterday . . ."

"No!" Wolf Running interrupted, forgetting his own distress. "Is he all right?"

"Better shape than you!" his grandmother answered briskly.

"The Frenchmen were in the area, and it turns out this kid has great healing skills. He treated Little Feather, and Little Feather is doing fine today. Now he and your grandmother need to examine your wounds and redress them." Iron Fist explained the situation.

"Ian!" Shannon said vehemently. "No kid . . . Ian!"The two men and old woman stared at her with varying expressions.

"Okay . . . Ian and your grandmother need to examine you," Iron Fist repeated, using Shannon's assumed name. At least it was better than 'kid', Shannon thought.

"Whisky," Shannon requested, looking to the older woman.

"Grandmother," the sprightly lady said with a smile as she left the room

"No whisky!" Wolf Running shouted. "I don't drink that rotten stuff!" Then light dawned on him. "You gave me that stuff yesterday! How could you, Uncle? You know I never touch it!" He stared at Iron Fist with accusing eyes. "That's why my head feels like all the dancers in the tribe are dancing in it! You think I'm such a child I can't stand the pain!"

"You were in no shape yesterday to stand anything!" Iron Fist responded in a slightly raised voice.

"Enough!," Shannon interrupted, shaking her hands to get their attention. "Me . . . give. No give whisky today. Need whisky" she pantomimed pouring over his wounds.

"Okay," Wolf Running grumbled.

"Men!" Shannon grouched in Gaelic.

The lacerations were clean, no sign of infection, healing well started. The women worked together, pouring whisky into each wound and repacking with fresh knitbone the older woman had provided. The amount of healing present made stitches undesirable.

By the time they were finished, Wolf Running's skin was pasty under his usual brown color. Some imp of mischief made Shannon say, "Whisky?" offering him the bottle. His grandmother slapped her on the back and shoved her towards the door, but Shannon had seen the grin on the older woman's face and the twinkle in her eye.

"Sorry, Grandmother," Shannon muttered, not sorry at all, "couldn' . . . resist!"

A chuckle was heard from behind Shannon.

Wolf Running turned his head in the opposite direction, and Shannon shuffled—her step a little lighter—from the room, head down, a grin on her face. Wolf Running was going to be fine! Her grandmother would have been proud of her.

The first person she met was the child, Bright Eyes. She squatted down to the child's level. "Your daddy is going to be fine, little friend."

The child wrapped her chubby arms around Shannon's neck and hugged her. Then turning to the corn husk doll in her hand, she chanted, "Daddy's gonna be fine, baby. Daddy's gonna be fine."

As Shannon shuffled, eyes down, towards Little Feather at the far end of the long house, several people intercepted her, thanking her for what she had done for Little Feather and Wolf Running. Shannon muttered repeatedly, "Okay . . . happy," and a few other comments in Gaelic. Being slow did have its draw backs. She muttered a lot in Gaelic which was gibberish to everyone she met, and the People had come to accept that on the Frenchmen's trips to the village.

As she made her way down the central corridor between the firesides, she came to Little Feather's grandmother working by one of the fires. "Little Feather," Shannon muttered. "Little Feather . . . wounds." At some point she was going to have to get out of this trap she and Shamus had created for her. It was fine as long as she wasn't doing any major healing!

The older woman scurried quickly to her fireside and collected her bag of herbs and followed Shannon.

By the time they made their way to Little Feather's sleeping platform, he had company—Tall Tree, who had assisted her in treating Little Feather in the field and then Wolf Running, and the same young woman, Wild Rose, who was leaving the long house as Shannon was arriving. Irritation crawled up Shannon's spine like unwelcome spiders. She really tried to suppress it as it was illogical to feel this way. It crawled up her spine anyway!

As Shannon approached the trio, she overheard the woman say in a peevish tone,

"I don't know why you want this . . . this . . . this person to help your grandmother tend your wounds. You should at least have the False Faces bring the spirits to help you! And I could clean your wounds at least as well as . . ." She glanced scornfully at Shannon.

Shannon wanted to kick the woman in the back of her buckskin skirt, but all she said was, "Ian."

"Ian?" the woman questioned, startled that the idiot had spoken to her.

"His name is 'Ian'," Little Feather explained patiently. "And there's a good possibility that I don't need the False Faces today because of the treatment I got yesterday from Ian and Tall Tree."

"Not me!" his friend protested. He waved his hand in Shannon's general direction, adding, "It was definitely Ian!"

"Ian? What a silly name!" and the woman started giggling.

Little Feather rolled his eyes towards the ceiling. Wild Rose hadn't changed in two years!

Tall Tree smiled behind Wild Rose's back and shrugged his shoulders. The girl's giggling had driven the two men crazy for years, but neither of them had the heart to hurt her feelings. But the matter looked to be more serious now, as the girl had chosen Little Feather for her own. Everyone in the village knew of her intentions, although she had not yet presented the traditional basket of cornbread. It would be interesting to see how his friend avoided this net.

"Wild Rose," Little Feather addressed the woman. "Last night you brought a white flower for a tea. I really enjoyed it, helped me sleep,"—what a bold-faced lie that was! Nothing could have induced him to sleep with Ian's soft, feminine body curled up next to his own hard, masculine one. Too bad there hadn't been enough light to see what color her hair was under that ridiculous cap! "Do you think you could bring me some more of those flowers?"

Wild Rose blushed with pleasure at the opportunity to do something for her chosen mate. "Of course!" and she hurried towards the door.

"Don't hurry! It'll be hours before I'm ready for it!" Little Feather yelled after her.

"What are you going to do about her?" his friend asked, grinning broadly.

"I haven't the foggiest notion! At least Mother hasn't suggested the possibility of marrying Wild Rose. Not be here if she takes it upon her self to bring me her corn bread!" and both men burst into hearty laughter.

"She *is* planning to marry you, you know?"

"I hadn't heard that rumor since I got back." Little Feather lay back on the platform carefully, placing his good arm behind his head, so that his grandmother and Ian could tend his wounds.

Shannon offered him some whisky to kill pain before she and his grandmother started working on him.

He shook his head, adding, "I don't drink the stuff."

Shannon was inordinately pleased at his response, although she had no idea why.

"You men!" his grandmother interrupted their conversation, returning the topic to Wild Rose, "Wild Rose is a fine young woman, hard worker, good with children, make a good wife!"

"Grandmother, she giggles!" laughed Little Feather, suddenly aware that Ian was listening intently to their conversation as she helped his grandmother remove the moss and clean his wounds. Tall Tree was unaware that she spoke their language fluently.

"You know," Little Feather said slowly to his friend, "Wild Rose really is an attractive woman and a hard worker. She does beautiful work with skins and basketry. Great with children." Little Feather appeared to be giving consideration to Wild Rose's virtues.

"Do you want me to let her mother know that you would consider her for a wife?" his grandmother asked.

"Ah . . ." Little Feather muttered, immediately realizing the trap he had unwittingly put himself into. "Ah . . . not yet, Grandmother. I'm still considering!"

Tall Tree grinned from ear to ear while Little Feather frowned at his friend.

As Shannon assisted his grandmother in attending the warrior's wounds, his praises of Wild Rose irked her . . . recently she seemed to get irked easily. Must be her irritation with Shamus for not getting her out of this mess! Her mind told her that what Little Feather thought of the other woman was none of her concern, and she certainly had no right to be annoyed by them. Unfortunately, something was overriding her good sense, because she was annoyed at Little Feather's words . . . very annoyed!

During the whole exchange between the men, she had worked rapidly on his lacerations, eyes cast down and face slack

"Here now, boy! Attend to what you're doing!" the older woman said sharply.

Shannon had covered a wound with moss without first washing it with the whisky and herb cleansing solution.

Tall Tree, having no idea that she wasn't what she appeared to be, glanced at her sharply. At no time during the preceding day, during all the hours he had worked with her had she made any such mistakes. He had learned that she was a skilled healer, so now he wandered at her lack of concentration A brilliant healer one day—a dullard the next? Not likely, but the matter passed from his mind as he admired the healing that had already occurred. "I have never seen such rapid, clean healing, my friend."

Little Feather twisted to the side to admire the neat stitches. They were clean with no sign of redness or swelling. "Such skill is truly a gift from the Gods!" Little Feather murmured., adding, "Especially when one is . . ." and tapped his finger to his head.

Shannon, intent on her work, heard his words but didn't see the hand gesture. She still understood the implication and felt irritation—again. Logically, she realized that he was protecting her. The fewer people who suspected her deception, the safer she would be. But right now she had an almost irresistible urge to break Little Feather's other arm. First praising Wild Rose and then emphasizing her short-comings!

These urges bothered her. The feelings were irrational and uncontrollable, and she had always prided herself on being rational and self-controlled—unlike other women. And she *hated* feeling out-of-control!

She lifted her head sufficiently to show Little Feather that his words meant nothing to her—as they shouldn't—but all Little Feather saw were her stormy grey eyes.

The warrior almost shouted for joy! His ruse was definitely distracting his little wildcat from her duty!

She pulled the moss off with little concern for pain until his grandmother looked at her sharply, and Shannon pulled her mind back to the task at hand. Little Feather had scarcely noticed. He was too busy studying her small, heart-shaped face which was anything but slack at the moment, since he was the only one who could see it.

Together the two women cleaned all the stitches with the whiskey—herb solution and covered them with fresh moss. Little Feather was healing nicely, and in a couple of days would be up and about, and not needing her anymore. Sadness washed over her with the thought, which again she didn't understand. It was time to go looking for the Frenchmen.

After wandering about the village and not finding Jacques and Pierre, she shuffled purposefully down to the river. Their canoe was no where in sight. What was going on?

Hurrying, as fast as she dared without drawing attention to herself, she returned to Little Feather's long house.

"Pierre and Jacques are gone!" she confronted Little Feather.

"I . . . we need you more than they do. I had Iron Fist buy your contract. What you did for Wolf Running alone was worth the price I paid for it," he said smugly, thinking she'd be pleased. At least she would be able to be herself around him and Iron Fist.

He should have known better. His warrior woman wasn't pleased at all. The fury remained in her eyes as her head tipped down, and she sort of slumped right before him and shuffled out of the long house. And, of course, he had no idea what the problem was.

He fell back on his platform, hurting all over from the whisky they had poured on all—at least two hundred the way he felt—of his stitches. Women! Well, she would have to get over her anger. The deed was done, and she would just have to learn to accept it. After all he was doing her a favor, Little Feather rationalized.

Chapter 7

"Damn!" Shannon muttered. Now what was she going to do? Playing dumb for two dumb Frenchmen had been easy! But to carry it off for everyone in the long house? To carry it off for everyone in the village? And how would Shamus ever find her now? Or how would she get out and about to find her brother? What had ever inspired Little Feather to buy her contract? They had their False Faces, and wonderful old women every bit as knowledgable as her grandmother had been . . . well, almost as knowledgable as her grandmother had been—Wolf Running had been in bad shape. But at least with Pierre and Jacques she was constantly traveling and searching for her brother. Now she would be stuck . . . stuck in this place! "Oh, damn!" she muttered again.

Lying on the bank by the river, she mulled over her problem. Her hat covered her face, and she tried to blank out the sounds around her: the soft gurgling of the river, the lively chirping of birds—what did they have to be so cheerful about, Shannon thought grumpily—the breeze playing through the branches above her.

"Ian," a soft voice murmured next to her ear, and the hat was shoved off her face. Bright Eyes squatted next to her, eyeing her from bright, intelligent eyes as chipper as any of the noisy birds overhead. Now what on earth was the child doing down here by the river ? It was too dangerous.

"You shouldn't be here by yourself, little one," Shannon rebuked the child. "You might fall into the river, and we would never see you again!"

Bright Eyes gazed back at her from black, piercing eyes. "Bu', Ian, me no' 'lone. You wif me!" the child responded logically.

Laughter burst from Shannon. "Yep, you're right, sweetie," Shannon responded, wishing her life were as logical and as simple as the child's. She stood up, retrieved her hat and took the child's hand, and together they strolled back to the village.

As the two were crossing the broad field surrounding the stockade, two hunters strolled from the forest carrying a deer slung on a pole between them. They both carried quivers of arrows and a bow slung across their backs . . . no muskets. These people always needed muskets—like people in the desert always needed water, and she was the source of a hundred of them! Something was going to have to be done about that, but she hadn't the slightest notion what.

Bright Eyes chatted cheerfully at her side as they crossed the extensive garden area, now dormant, that filled most of the area surrounding the village. She clutched Shannon's hand tightly in one of hers, as though she was afraid that Shannon might disappear, and her corn husk doll in the other. Shortly after they entered the village, the child ran off to play with some other little girls. The high-pitched squeal of children's joyous laughter and chatter momentarily distracted Shannon from her problems. It was so pleasant, truly relaxing.

Then she continued her slow shuffle through the noisy village, eyes cast down and hidden by her floppy hat, no closer to any solutions than when she had visited the river. She was still furiously angry with Little Feather for his presumption and interference with her plans! In spite of the anger that burned within her at thoughts of Little Feather, those same thoughts stimulated a tingling along her nerves and that flowering sensation deep in her abdomen. How she wished her grandmother were here for her to discuss these strange feelings that were confusing her so. Even her father might have been able to explain what was happening to her.

"Ian!"

Shannon shuffled to a stop, and the lad Red Fox approached her. Once he was abreast of her, he scuffed his feet, at a loss for words. Then, "Little Feather is my brother!" burst out of him.

So, the lad from the hunt was Little Feather's brother. Shannon said, "Little Feather," then, touching Red Fox's chest, added, "brother."

Red Fox grinned, as though a great hurdle had been leaped successfully.

At the same time, an idea was blossoming in Shannon's head like the petals of the moonflower at night. How long would it take for someone who was slow to understand, someone who had never had understanding teachers, learn with some good teachers? And how much could such a person acquire? Could such a person learn enough to be taken on hunting, trading or raiding trips? If so, she would still be able to search for Shamus.

Tapping Red Fox on the chest, she said,"Brother!" She tapped herself, saying, "Ian!"

Red Fox burst out laughing. He touched his chest and said, "Red Fox," and pointed to her and repeated, "Ian."

Shannon continued shuffling slowly towards their long house with Red Fox accompanying her. She repeated several times, "Red Fox" and "brother" and gave Red Fox a timid smile.

They approached a group of young men and boys playing the stick and ball game—there seemed to be a game going on somewhere all of the time—that the Frenchman had referred to as 'lacrosse'. For a few minutes they watched the fast-paced game.

The young men's strong, agile bodies glistened with sweat as they dodged in and out among one another, trying to gain control of a ball that flew rapidly between the rackets. Sometimes it was above the heads of the players only to disappear and reappear elsewhere with all the men scrambling after it.

Racket slashed viciously against racket as everyone struggled desperately to gain control of the ball. Within seconds, several players had received slashing blows from the flying rackets. Each time, Shannon winced involuntarily. A stocky youth, Running

Weasel, chased after the man who had gained the ball and walloped him across the back with his racket.

Within a fraction of a second a knock-down, drag-out, free-for-all was in progress on the playing ground in which everyone seemed to be taking an active part with dust and dirt, arms and legs, and rackets flying in every direction.

"And here I thought he had me picked out as a target for his meanness," Shannon muttered in Gaelic. "Apparently, he hates everyone equally!"

"C'mon, Ian, we'll teach you to play," Red Fox offered, ignoring Shannon's mutterings which he had noticed had a very musical, pleasant sound.

"Little Feather . . . Wolf Running . . . need look," Shannon mumbled.

Red Fox shrugged his shoulders, replying, "Another time." and jogged off to join his friends in the lively game.

"Without a doubt!" Shannon answered in Gaelic, watching the game for a few more minutes. Running Weasel had caused her distress on more than one visit to the village. He obtained great pleasure from ridiculing the 'dummy'.

She turned towards the long house, her step a little less shuffling, a little more firm, and the birds' cheerfulness matched her own light-heartedness as a plan crystalized in her mind, but she was still furiously angry with Little Feather for his interference that made alternative plans and a delay in her search for Shamus necessary in the first place.

Little Feather was sitting up leaning against the end of his platform when Shannon entered the long house. He noticed the difference immediately and studied her intently to try and determine what had changed. At that moment she glanced up catching his stare, and his heart sank within him—she was still angry with him . . . *very angry!*

"Grandmother?" she asked, glancing about the long house.

"She's visiting Aunt and trying to locate more of this," he answered, pointing to the leaves that had dried in a solid mass over his fracture.

"Hmmm . . . knitbone, there's never enough of it." Shannon sat on the platform by his feet and stared around the long house. They seemed to be its only occupants at the moment.

"Why were you so angry about the contract? It wasn't meant to hurt you. It was only meant as a gift to you for what you have done for us."

Anger boiled up in Shannon all over again. "You have your False Faces, and your grandmother and Wolf Running's grandmother are excellent healers. You don't need me You don't need to own me!"

"Neither of them was there when you helped me, and everyone, including Wolf Running's grandmother had given up on him! You saved his life! And what do you mean, 'own you?'" Little Feather yelled at her, angry himself. "Why can't you accept it as the gift it is?" Little Feather never lost his temper, and suddenly he realized he was shouting at Ian—if that was even the woman's name, Little Feather thought cynically caught up in the heat of the moment. Whites had different names for men and women, and since she was pretending to be a boy, Ian was probably not her given name.

"What's your name?"

Her head jerked up. "Ian is good enough," she paused. "I owe six years on the contract," she said more calmly now. "Sha . . . I could buy myself out of the contract. I didn't plan on serving Jacques and Peirre for six years. Also being dumb around two dumb Frenchmen isn't the same as trying to be dumb around some not so dumb people!"

Little Feather burst into laughter and then groaned from the pain it caused in his face and side.

"Why the disguise?"

She had thought long and hard on this question just for this eventuality. So she lied smoothly. "Most companies and people in the colonies want married couples or single men. Well, I don't fit either category, and I wanted a chance at a better life than I had back home, so I pretended to be a boy and indentured myself."

"I can't imagine leaving my family for a better life."

"Life is different where I come from than it is in your village."
Shannon was silent for a long time. "If you really think I saved
your life and Wolf Running's, could I ask a favor of you."

Not only did he think she had saved his and Wolf Running's
lives but probably one or more of his party when she shot the
bear. He didn't accept her explanation about the disguise either.
It did not account for her expert use of a flintlock or why the
need to dye her hair. He had seen red-headed boys before. But
her request could work in his favor also, if she didn't ask to be
released from the contract.

"Ask away, and we'll see."

"The dumb act is really getting to me. and I know I won't be
able to maintain the ruse here in the long house and around the
village on a daily basis—too many astute people. But I think I've
figured a way out of it. But I'm going to need a lot of help. I'm
going to need good teachers . . . some really good teachers!"

Little Feather was intrigued and relieved that his fiesty little
warrior woman hadn't asked to be freed from the contract, the
only means available to him to keep her here until they became
better acquainted. He could keep her as a prisoner or slave but
that didn't seem appropriate to do to someone who had saved so
many of their lives. And he didn't think it would serve his purpose
anyway.

"I'm listening."

"Well, what if you, Red Fox and your friends teach me
everything I need to know to be a hunter and warrior. You know,
pretend that I'm a baby and you teach me everything from
scratch."

The warrior's first impulse was to laugh . . . and laugh . . . and
laugh some more. His second impulse was the same. He refrained.
Some deep seated instinct for self-preservation warned him that his
prickly little warrior woman wouldn't take that well. Once he had
suppressed his impulses and given her idea some thought, he
was intrigued. Who could he get to help? Tall Tree, of course,
and Little Feather's younger brothers, Red Fox and Little Wolf,

the twins—Grey Turtle and White Feather—if White Feather had recovered enough from the bear attack, and *if* they stayed in the village long enough. The stick-and-ball game developed skills used by every warrior and hunter, the bow and arrow . . . . what could she pull off with that, he mused ? He'd seen what she could do with a flintlock.

"It might work," he responded slowly, thoughtfully with a wicked gleam in his dark eyes. "You will provide healing services whenever necessary?"

"Of course!" she appeared offended that he had felt the need to ask.

He shrugged, "I needed to know."

"There's one more thing," she seemed hesitant to ask.

"Yes?" He had a sinking feeling that he wasn't going to like this request.

"I need to sleep some place else!" burst from her in a rush of words.

"Why? You heard me tell Bright Eyes that brothers and friends often share a bed when we visit."

"I don't see men and women sleep together except married couples."

"Yes, but no one knows you're a woman except Iron Fist and myself. How would you explain that you don't want to share my sleeping platform for now?" he asked reasonably.

"'Iron Fist?''Shannon groaned. "How did the two of you see through my disguise?"

"When you ran into us," he answered and grinned. "Sleeping arrangements?" he inquired mildly.

She groaned again, seeing no way out of the situation. "Okay," she acquiesced ungraciously.

"And why haven't you learned the things you needed to know in the past?"

After a moment's reflection, she replied, "No one had time to work with me because I *was* slow. It's going to take you a lot of time to teach me what I need to know!"

That fitted well with Little Feather's plans.

Little Feather looked past her and watched as his grandmother walked to his fireside.

Shannon glanced over her shoulder and seeing the elderly woman approach, slumped into her Ian disguise and slid off the platform.

"Grandmother, what do you think of teaching Ian some of the things our boys need to know: lacrosse, bow and arrow, some of our games and stories?"

The two woman were removing the moss from his face and side. His grandmother stared at Little Feather and then at Ian intently. "Might be a good idea. Might even bring him out of himself," she replied enigmatically.

Shannon glanced at the older woman and asked, "Wolf Running?"

"His grandmother is with him now. He's doing fine, cranky as a bear! Basket Maker says that if you're too tired or busy, she can manage tonight."

Shannon looked at Little Feather.

"You . . . not needed," he interpretted for Shannon's benefit to assist in maintaining her disguise.

The older woman glanced up from her work. "Perhaps, grandson, our Ian understands a little more than he can express," and returned her attention to her work.

Well, it appeared that she was going to be sharing Little Feather's sleeping platform for a time at least—like it or not! She had definite ambiguous feelings about that! If it had been her idea, it would have been fine. But it wasn't her idea, and she hated being forced to do anything. But she had to admit that there was a tiny thrill scurrying around inside of her at the thought. She ruthlessly squelched the thrill and focused on being forced to sleep with Little Feather—it didn't even matter that it was for her own protection. She hated being forced to do anything.

Chapter 8

The weight was across her side . . . again! On a bed almost as wide as Little Feather was tall, why was she clinging to the edge with him crushed up behind her? She gently lifted his arm and placed it in the tight place between them. His breathing remained deep and slow.

Shannon lay gazing at the few coals that glowed dimly in the fire pit that smoldered between their cubicle and the cubicle on the opposite side of the fire. She had awakened breathless and with all her nerves sensitized. She had struggled to remember the dream, but her subconscious mind swallowed it as rapidly as her conscious mind became dominant, and she had been unable grasp and hold on to the images. But it had something to do with Little Feather. Maybe the pictures would come later in the manner of dreams when she wasn't trying so hard to remember.

She did remember Wild Rose coming to the long house the day before and clinging to Little Feather like moss clinging to the branch of a tree. It had been disgusting, and really irritated her. And Little Feather made the situation worse by enjoying the creature's presence which annoyed Shannon even more! She still didn't understand her reaction to Wild Rose. It just happened, and she had gone in a huff to spend a couple of hours by herself down by the river.

For a few minutes, Shannon lay listening to other sounds in the long house. Someone was snoring, a baby whimpered, a platform creaked as its occupant changed his position. And then all was silent.

Slowly, she slid off the sleeping platform, and turning, gazed at Little Feather. There was insufficient light to see more than a dark shape under the bearskin blanket. Collecting her bag from the ledge above and setting her hat more firmly on her head, she crept from their fireside, through the storage vestibule and into the cold night air.

The sky over the stockade wall to the east glowed a pearly grey against the starlit sky far above her. A shadow separated itself from between the long houses and slunk to where Shannon stood. It licked her hand and whined softly, looking for something to eat. Finding nothing, it disappeared silently back into the dark shadows. The rest of the village slept on bathed in the silver light of the nearly full moon.

Shannon jogged through the quiet village and out the entrance. It felt so good to be herself if only for a few minutes. That was all she had, as soon it would be morning, and the village would be awake. She had to return to the long house before then.

Taking her hat off and clutching it in her hand Shannon alternately jogged and walked down the well-traveled path to the river, luxuriating in the feel of the breeze against her face. She had always loved to run, but a year had past since last she ran free.

Upon reaching the river, she traveled far enough upstream that, hopefully, no earlier riser would stumble across her.

Within moments, she had divested herself of her buckskin breeches and shirt. The binder followed, adding to the pile. Stretching her lithe, young body, free of all restraints, she breathed deeply of the invigorating air.

Reaching out her foot, she touched the icy water. She shivered. This was going to be one fast bath! Never had the water in Ireland ever been so cold!

The breeze caressed her most sensuously, and the image of Little Feather rose in her mind. She paused by the edge of the water, thinking. Fragments of the dream rose before her eyes. She and Little Feather were in a field of flowers . . . naked! And he had been running his hand over her breasts and . . . Well, a very erotic dream it had been—filled with Little Feather! She blushed from her toes to the top of her head! From where had such images come?

As she stood there with her foot poised above the water, her father's voice rang in her mind, and she saw again that peaceful day. "It's wild, Shanny, and wonderful," he said, skipping a stone across the stream they were sitting by. "Sometimes, you won't know if you're coming or going! That's the way it was with your mother and me. She was the sun in my days and the moon in my nights! That's what love is all about, Hinny! And some day, my darling daughter, it'll strike you down and then lift you higher than you've ever been! I hope I'm there to see it!"

Why would she remember that conversation now? It had happened years ago, when she was only ten. They had been sitting by a stream not far from the camp, during a lull in confrontations with the English, when her father had started talking about her mother. What could her subconscious mind possibly be trying to tell her? What had come into her life that could bear on this memory? Wild and wonderful? The only thing wild in her life at this time was the up and down feelings she had about Little Feather. Little Feather? No it couldn't be Little Feather . . . could she be falling in love with Little Feather? No, she couldn't be . . .

Now as she stood about to dip her foot into the icy water of a wild land far from home, sadness settled about her like a cloak. She had no memories of her mother except through her father's eyes. Eyes which themselves had been closed in death this past year. Paddy was dead, Shamus was missing, and somewhere, someone was responsible. Shannon renewed her promise to her dying father. Somehow she would find the traitor and bring him to justice.

Without further thought, she dashed into the icy river. A few seconds later, she dove into the water only to reappear in a burst of sparkling droplets, gasping from the extreme cold and laughing from the sheer exhilaration of being alive. Again and again she sank beneath the water to reemerge. Each time dark water swirled away from her on the current, and her hair became brighter and brighter until it was a flaming red in the rising sun.

Shivering, she rushed from the water, grabbed her shirt, and rubbed it briskly against her cold skin. While her skin was still damp, she picked up her breeches and tried, unsuccessfully, to pull them up over her moist legs. The fabric stuck, pulled and pinched against her skin as she hopped about on one leg.

An unusual sound was heard on the breeze, almost like a chuckle. She stopped and listened, but heard nothing more. Resuming her struggles with the offending breeches, she finally tugged them up her wet skin. After strapping her hunting knife about her slim waist, she reached for her binder and wrapped it snugly about her full breasts.

Again an unusual vibration blended with the wind, slightly out of kilter with the background noises. It almost sounded like a sigh. Listening intently, but hearing nothing more, Shannon thought her over active imagination was playing tricks on her.

Without delay, she grabbed her fringed, buckskin shirt and pulled it over her head and down over her slim body concealing the deadly knife on her hip—a weapon of which no one was aware. Then she searched in her bag until she located a small round jar. Unscrewing the top, she scooped out some thick, black liquid which she vigorously massaged through her hair, changing it from its glorious, golden red color back to a dull walnut brown.

Fingers of red pushed above the horizon, preceding the rising sun as she washed the last of the dye off her hands in the river. She had to hurry. Time was running out.

Snap!

Shannon jumped like a frightened rabbit at the sudden, sharp sound. Her heart leaped into her throat. Someone or thing was in the forest near her! An image of the grizzly rose before her eyes, and then reason asserted itself. She smelled nothing. At least if it was a bear, it wasn't upwind of her. Pulling her knife, she dodged into some brush upwind of where she had bathed . . . and waited. Silence.

After a few moments, she cautiously started back in the direction of the village.

Snap! It was a softer, more muffled sound this time. Whatever it was, it appeared to be moving away from her?

Studying the area about her, she observed nothing out of the normal. Lots of trees that could conceal a person . . . bears didn't consciously hide. Birds were singing as usual, and a squirrel dodged between two giant maples. A raccoon sauntered from behind a tree, and ran towards the river. A tiny twig snapped beneath a paw.

Relieved, and feeling a trifle ridiculous, she slipped the knife back into its sheath, and started jogging back towards the village.

Approaching the stockade, she slipped back into the role of Ian, but her step was lighter and firmer, and her eyes were not cast so low.

People were up and about in the village, with a few brave souls ambling down the path to the river for their morning ablutions. Smoke spiraled upward from the long houses as the central fires were stoked up.

Upon entering the building, smoke assailed her eyes and nose, making her cough and her eyes water. The first thing she observed upon her eyes clearing was that Little Feather's sleeping platform was empty!

"Little Feather?" she asked of Red Fox who was helping himself to a bowl of stew.

"He went out a while back. Must be feeling pretty good. Help yourself to some food, and let's get out of here. Understand?"

Shannon looked blank for a moment before replying, "Out . . . Little Feather out." That dog! She knew with a certainty that he had followed her! That noise she had heard was no raccoon! It had been Little Feather! the snoop!

"There's a bowl there," Red Fox said, pointing to the ledge above where she and Little Feather slept. "Help yourself and let's get out of here!" the youth repeated. "There won't be so much smoke once the fires are burning hotter."

Quickly, she filled her bowl from the big kettle bubbling over the fire and followed Red Fox outside, getting angrier by the minute thinking about Little Feather's duplicity. How dare he spy on her!

"Little Wolf and I are going to gather some of our friends and have a game of stick-and-ball. C'mon and join us, Ian. We'll teach you how to play. Since Little Feather is feeling well enough to go out, he probably won't need you. Grandmother can see to him this morning, and Wolf Running's grandmother is already tending him. You're not needed this morning. Understand?"

Shannon was looking somewhat blank at this long speech when Little Wolf, a youth a little taller and heavier than Red Fox and whose family shared the central fire with Little Feather and Iron Fist, joined them outside. Two long sticks with loops on the ends to which were attached nets where carried in one hand while he munched on a piece of cornbread held in his other hand.

Finally, she nodded her head and answered, "Ah . . . yes."

The three of them were strolling through the village when Shannon saw Little Feather ambling towards them. Anger rose in her like a forest fire crowning—and as dangerous—as she watched him. His roach was wet, and his skin was glistening. Obviously, he was returning from a swim in the river. And he was grinning from ear to ear! The sneak! The louse! The spy! She wanted to knock that smirk from his handsome face and beat on him. How dare he! And she couldn't act on a single thought without revealing her deception. Frustratioon and anger ate at her like a canker. Some day she'd even the score with the smirking warrior!

Shannon, watching as Little Feather approached, observed that the stitches were exposed to the air, but they appeared to be healing well. Hopefully, they wouldn't get infected from his morning excursion in the water. She was angry with him, but she didn't want him to die!

She reached out to examine his arm. The water had removed the dry poultice of leaves, but the splint was still intact. "Stupid!" she admonished, staring up into his dark eyes.

"Very stupid!" he repeated, his dark eyes glittering strangely into her lighter ones. He pulled his arm away from her hand.

The last thing he needed now was for her to touch him. Last night his little flaming-haired warrior woman had visited his dreams again . . . and not chasing a grizzly! And then to see her bursting forth from the river—like some water sprite—with glistening droplets of moisture spraying all about her and her hair flaming in the rising sun! The last lingering doubts about Ian and his warrior woman being one and the same had washed away on the current along with the ugly dye! He hadn't intended to go swimming or to spy on her when he followed her to the river. His only goal had been to protect her, but the glimpse he got of her glorious body and hair as the last of the dye rinsed away held him spell bound. From that point on, the necessity for an icy cold swim grew and grew!

"We'll find you later after Ian has checked the stitches and redone my arm. We'll be along in a short time."

Little Feather and Shannon went back to the long house while the boys went on towards the playing ground.

The long house was mostly empty with no one close to Little Feather's fireside.

"How dare you follow me?" Shannon attacked, at the same time, closely examining his stitches. "And you shouldn't have gotten these wet. It's only been three days since I stitched you up."

"How dare you go off by yourself!" Little Feather responded harshly. "And I checked the stitches on my side, and they looked pretty good. Besides I needed a cold swim . . . a very cold swim!" He glared at her.

"Well, I'm sure I don't know why you needed a cold swim! And I hope these don't get infected! And what do you mean 'how dare I go off by myself'?" Shannon tried ineffectively to rage in a hushed tone.

She knew he had watched her naked in the water, Little Feather mused, and didn't understand why he needed a cold swim? In what kind of culture could a person grow to adulthood and not know what happens between men and women? Well, he was certainly going to have his work cut out for him!

"It's dangerous!" he yelled at her. "People don't usually go to the river by themselves, especially not in the dark!"

"I did and nothing happened! And don't yell at me!"

"Nothing happened," he said quietly but forcefully, "because I was there! And I don't yell!" he added loudly and arrogantly.

"You can go to the river with the women and girls or with the youths, or even with the men, but don't go alone!" His voice had increased by several decibels.

"Right! You know I can't do that," Shannon replied sulkily.

"I know!" and now the rat was grinning from ear to ear!

"What's the matter, Ian? Don't you know that men like looking at women, and women usually like looking at men?"

"Yeah, well, your friends are going to look at you really strangely if they see you gawking at me the way you're talking about!" Shannon grumbled, examining his stitches.

Another problem to be resolved. She couldn't do without bathing! And she would die before she'd admit, especially to him, that she did enjoy watching him!

"These stitches look good, but they still need to be washed every day. Got any whisky, or can you get some?"

"Probably. But for how much longer?"

"Three or four days and they should be ready to be cut out."

Shannon was retying the splint minus the poultice when his grandmother returned to the long house.

Shortly thereafter, the two of them went in search of the boys and whoever else was willing to join in Ian's first 'lesson' in the stick-and-ball game.

Chapter 9

"It's hopeless, Little Feather," Tall Tree grumbled disgustedly, resting his racket on the ground and wiping sweat from his brow. "That boy has two left feet and two right hands! I have no idea how Ian could be so skilled stitching you up and so clumsy now. If I hadn't seen what he did for you with my own eyes, I would never have believed a retelling of it!"

The two men watched Shannon struggle to her feet and limp over the hard-packed ground after the ball. Red Fox had a confused look on his face and had obviously missed that move.

"Got spunk, though . . . gotta give him that!" Tall Tree was forced to admit with reluctant admiration and a shake of his head.

"He has, hasn't he?" Little Feather grinned, his eyes sparkling with humor and wondering when Ian was going to start 'learning' the game, although she had shown some progress the day before. She better catch on quick, or her teachers were going to scatter to the four winds in self-preservation!

Three mornings ago, after she had set his arm they had gone in search of the boys and he had put the netted stick into her hand for the first time and clumsy had become deadly.

That first morning while swinging the stick to get the balance of it, she had some how managed to get it caught between her legs, sending herself sprawling to the ground.

"Hey, Ian! You're suppose to hit the ball!"

Shannon glanced up at her tormentor. Running Weasel and his cronies, and another idea was born.

"What's the matter, Dummy? Can't stay on your feet? Go back with the Frenchmen! We don't want you here!" As the group strolled away, their raucous laughter drifted back.

"Your day is coming, my friend," Shannon warned, in Gaelic, to their disappearing backs, a grim smile on her shapely lips and a glint in her stormy grey eyes. "And if all goes well, in the not too distant future!"

Little Feather, who heard her words, suddenly realized that her mutterings always had a musical, pleasant sound to his ears . . . why, his little warrior woman was speaking in a foreign language! He smiled, impressed by her ruse and wondering what she had said to him on occasion. It was probably as well that he didn't know! The warrior did know that the expression on his woman's face meant trouble for Running Weasel.

"Don't let him bother you, Ian," Red Fox advised, helping her get untangled from her racket and back on her feet.

All went well in practice from Shannon's point of view, but not from her fellow players and teachers. Her first attempts at the stick-and-ball game were dreadful and dangerous. At one point the ball came winging its way at her, and she made a wild, clumsy swing at, missed and gave Tall Tree a glancing blow to the shoulder. She had pulled on the swing at the last moment, hoping it wouldn't be to hard.

"Sorry," she muttered.

Tall Tree thought nothing of it—the first time. It was a rough and tumble game with as much of the game learning to avoid other players' rackets as controlling the ball.

Little Feather dodged in front of her, coming so close that the aroma of sweat and his distinctive musky odor floated about Shannon, hitting her in the gut like the kick of a mule. Sensations tingling along her nerves, breathlessness, a wonderful flowering in her loins—totally foreign—assailed her, leaving her more confused than she was pretending to be! Her eyes, unbidden, followed Little Feather as a plant follows the sun. It only took a moment to collect her wits—and a whack of a racket to her shapely butt!

A few seconds later, grappling for the ball with Little Feather, she only succeeded in snaring her racket between his legs.

Down went the big man in a heap. Shannon was so close behind him that she couldn't prevent herself from tumbling down on top of him.

"Sorry," she muttered.

"I don't believe it for a minute!" he rumbled from under her, laughter filling his eyes.

"Well, maybe not!" she admitted, flashing him a grin that took away his breath.

While trying to disengage her arms, legs and racket from his, her hands slid across his broad, muscular chest. Shock and something else flared in her expressive grey eyes.

"Sorry," she mumbled again.

"Don't be!"

Little Feather, seeing the shock and passion that flashed through her eyes when her hands came in contact with his chest, and one never to waste an opportunity, managed to run his hands along her arms, breasts and waist while attempting to get her off him. And all in the matter of a second or two, and her response to him provided food for thought. So his little woman was attracted to him, although he didn't think she was aware of it yet.

"I'm not!" again, laughing at her.

She understood his reference and didn't know whether to kick him or kiss him! She realized that kicking him would be safer.

By the end of that practice session, frustration was high and tempers were short. Shannon stood leaning on her racket with a disgusting twinkle in her eyes that only Little Feather noticed . . . fortunately. Patience had been stretched to its limit with more injuries and bruises than was normal for the game. Red Fox had stumbled twice over Shannon's racket and been bowled over three times as Shannon stumbled and fell. Little Wolf had fared a little better. The deadly racket had found his feet only once. But she had fallen over him twice. After the second time Tall Tree tangled with her racket, he found a nimbleness of foot he never knew he had. He pitied his friend. Little Feather never found that quickness of foot to help him, which was strange—he had always been sure-footed for a man so large. He went down five times with Shannon tripping over him.

Not one of them had ever seen anyone trip over his own feet as often as Ian did. Maybe he really couldn't learn, and they were wasting their time. But Little Feather asked them not to give up, and he *was* their friend and relative—but he was going to owe all of them big for this favor!

The second day had actually been an improvement on the first day. Ian had seemed to develop the skill of getting the racket around the opponent without hitting anyone—very often. Tall Tree only got hit once, Little Wolf got tripped once, the racket missed Red Fox entirely, and Little Feather was bowled over only three times!

On the morning of the third day, Little Wolf decided he had been neglecting his target practice and left with some friends. Ian just wasn't improving enough for Little Wolf's liking, and he wasn't in the mood for anymore 'dodge the deadly racket in Ian's hand'.

"Coward!" Red Fox accused his brother, greatly tempted to escape with him. But he was positive that all Ian needed was encouragement and practice . . . a lot of practice. And he had seen improvement in Ian's performance the day before.

The only reason Tall Tree was still there was loyalty to his friend and a burning curiosity. Ian had been terrible the first day with noticeable improvement the second day. Almost as if he were learning something he already knew. As Tall Tree thought back on his previous encounters with Ian, the kid had always been slow moving . . . slow talking . . . said very little? His big floppy hat always covered his eyes, eyes that Tall Tree had seen sharp with intelligence when she was dead tired after working on his friend. Where had the idea come from that the kid was an idiot or different?

And then there had been Iron Fist's behavior. He had come out to watch Ian's progress several times. Every time Little Feather went down with the youth on top of him, a strange sparkle would come into the older man's eyes, and he never seemed disappointed with Ian's inept performance. And Little Feather? He was the biggest enigma of all. He had a sparkle in his eyes and a joy of living that Tall Tree had never seen in his friend. His friend had been all duty and somewhat aloof from everything else as far back as Tall Tree could remember. There was a mystery here and Tall Tree determined to solve it.

As Shannon awoke on the morning of the third day with Little Feather's arm over her and his long, strong body curled up behind her—as usual—she lay thinking in a half awake state. She was comfortable—really comfortable—and she realized with wonder that there was no place else where she wanted to sleep! Fortunately, for some reason she had been unable to fathom, he also wanted her sleeping with him. And she felt safe. Never in her life had she felt as safe as she did with him—whether in his bed, out and about in the village, or anywhere. But there was no time to ponder it now, as Wolf Running was screaming from the end of the long house.

After tending Wolf Running's wounds which were healing nicely, she cut the stitches from Little Feather's lacerations. As she had anticipated, the stitches had healed rapidly, leaving only fine red lines that would fade with time. Her step was a little more confident, and she held her head a little higher. She hoped the change in her attitude would be so slow that people wouldn't notice it happening but accept it as a normal consequence of her new environment.

So when they arrived at the playing ground, Shannon was in a wonderful mood. Today was going to be the day for massive improvement in her playing. The first few minutes were strenuous, she managed to stumble a few times and hitting Tall Tree really was an accident. As she dragged herself to her feet and started after the ball, a coarse, strident laugh shattered the friendly atmosphere.

Running Weasel! Something hard came into her eyes as she recognized the harsh voice. Glancing up, she observed the heavy-set youth and a little girl standing next to him, clinging to his hand. Surprise filled her eyes. The child was gazing up adoringly at him.

"Sunbeam, his Little sister," Red Fox informed her, noticing the direction of her gaze. "He's crazy about her. Understand?"

Shannon shook her head in the affirmative, replying, "Didn't know . . . liked anybody."

"You're not much good for anything, Ian, are you?" Running Weasel taunted. "I heard you were quite a healer, but I don't believe it! And it certainly isn't pleasing to the Great Spirit for you to be playing our sacred game!"

Shannon glanced questioningly at Little Feather. He had said nothing about the game being sacred, and she didn't want to offend anyone by profaning something that was sacred to them. As a matter of fact, no one had said anything, and a number of people had watched their practice each day.

"We play it to entertain the Great Spirit, and I'm sure He has been entertained during these past few days! But the skills are also important for our hunting and raiding. Understand, Ian?" Little Feather explained.

Shannon appeared to be contemplating his words, and after a few moments, replied slowly, "Yes." Then she turned and stared at Running Weasel. "You play. Ent . . . ent . . . enter . . ."

"Entertain!" Little Feather supplied, knowing—just knowing that his warrior woman was about to become very skilled at the stick-and-ball game. He actually felt sympathy for the brash youth.

"Yes, ent . . . er . . . tain Great Spirit!" Shannon presented a timid smile as though greatly pleased with her accomplishment and stared at Running Weasel for a few seconds. He was sap enough to fall into her trap, too arrogant to even see it.

"Friends," she pointed to some of his cronies who had gathered around him. "Let's . . . play!"

"You're kidding!" Running Weasel scoffed disparagingly, having watched some of their practice sessions. There was no way he was going to play against such a clutz. Little Feather and

Tall Tree were worthy opponents, but with Ian playing it wouldn't even be a challenge. It was simply beneath him to play against such an inferior being.

"You . . . think . . . Ian better slave," Shannon repeated his words tapping her chest and resting her stick on ground. "You win . . . Ian be slave . . . your slave . . . for seven days!"

"Hey, now, Ian! Wait a minute!" Little Feather was aghast. What was she doing? Had she lost her mind? She'd be killed!

"We get six players to your four since Little Feather and Tall Tree are the best players in the village," Running Weasel interrupted.

"I won't have any part of this nonsense, Ian," Little Father roared angrily at no one in particular. No one seemed to be listening to him. "Understand?!"

Shannon turned to Little Feather and slowly nodded her head, and shuffled the few steps to the big warrior. There was a twinkle of mischief in her eyes that hit him like one of their rackets.

"Another favor!" she asked so low that no one else heard her.

"You'll be killed!" he objected.

"I'm hard to kill, big man. Really hard to kill!"

Against his better judgment, Little Feather finally agreed. If she didn't get killed, he would be tempted to do it himself. It was a stupid stunt, and he wasn't quite certain on how she got him to agree.

Turning back to Running Weasel, she made the final challenge, "You win . . . me slave . . . Week . . . We win . . . you slave . . . week.

Arrogance was the hauty youths downfall. Running Weasel agreed.

The sun was high in the sky when the game started. Shannon swung at the ball and tripped. The ball flew to Little Feather's racket while her racket gave running Weasel's legs a stinging blow. The youth hadn't even seen it coming.

A few seconds later she dodged between two of Running Weasel's friends, claimed the ball and flung it at Red Fox. She tripped over an opponent and stumbled into Running Weasel, bowling him over.

As she scrambled to her feet, she saw Little Feather rushing towards her. Some imp from deep inside her pushed her hand out and brushed it against his hip as he flew by. She was shocked by her own audacity and turned away blushing. But his hip had felt firm under her hand, nice.

He nearly broke stride from the shock. Had it been deliberate? No . . . people were always running into each in this game. But . . . maybe . . . After sending the ball flying to Tall Tree, he glanced at Shannon, and her look was pure innocence. Too innocent! Was it possible that she felt this same extraordinary attraction that he felt? That was what he was working towards. He grinned at her innocent look. She turned away, and his grin grew larger.

As the game progressed, Running Weasel couldn't stay far enough from Shannon; she was all over him—her racket was all over him. The nimbleness that Tall Tree had developed escaped him and worst of all, the points kept adding up for Little Feather's team.

Gradually he began to realize that he had been suckered well and good. Anger made him careless. He swung his racket viciously at Shannon, who easily dodged it. Almost immediately he felt a racket shoved between his running feet and found himself flying through the air head over heels.

When the game ended, Shannon's team was victorious by a large score, and a much subdued Running Weasel limped off with his friends.

"Running Weasel!" Shannon yelled at his retreating back while she wiped the sweat from her forehead. No dye.

He paused, scowling back at her.

"In . . . morning!" she shouted to him.

Little Feather's eyes shone with appreciation as Shannon walked slowly towards him.

"Arm?" she asked.

"Fine," he answered, showing her the splint was intact and firmly held in place. She had rebuked him several times over the past three days about playing. But this time in her company had been worth the risk, especially today's game.

"Wait 'till I tell Little Wolf what he missed!" Red Fox shouted, jumping around from excitement.

"What are you going to have Running Weasel do for you?" Little Feather inquired.

After a moment's thought, she replied, "Be human!"

Red Fox stared at her as though she had grown horns.

Red Fox rushed off to find Little Wolf and relate to him what he had missed by being a coward. Tall Tree collected his wife, Evening Dove, from their small audience which dispersed leaving only Little Feather and Shannon.

He placed his arm companionably about his little warrior woman's slim shoulders, and they strolled back towards the long house, famished. "So what do you want to start 'learning' tomorrow?"

Chapter 10

Her heart thundered in her throat, and perspiration streamed down her forehead and into her eyes. Frantically, she swiped away the blinding drops, but it didn't improve her vision. The cave was dark, dank, with visibility nearly zero. In the far distance was a glimmer of light towards which she fled. But no matter how fast or hard she ran, the light kept receding in the distance. It appeared to be laughing at her futile, puny efforts!

Behind her echoed the soft slithering of the serpent's belly on the ground as it relentlessly pursued her. It's hot breath and poisonous saliva that dripped on the ground behind her pushed her to a final desperate burst of energy. Abruptly the light was blocked momentarily, and then it shone around the massive form of a gigantic bear. At that moment something rose from the path in front of her, and she felt herself flying through the air, screaming . . .

"Shhh . . . it's only a bad dream," a deep voice whispered in her ear, as strong arms pulled her close into a warm, safe place. "Shhh . . . go back to sleep. You're safe now. Shhhh . . ."

Feeling secure and protected as a bear cub with its mother nearby, Shannon fell back into a deep and dreamless sleep.

Little Feather lay with his arms wrapped snugly about his woman, wondering what horrible dreams could cause such distress. When it was in his power to slay her demons, he would do so. Slowly, he drifted off to sleep himself.

Grey sky shone through the smoke hole the next time Shannon awoke. Some movement or change in her body woke the man holding her, but he remained still and relaxed, pretending to sleep.

Shannon lay thinking for a while, too comfortable in Little Feather's arms to try moving—although she didn't think about that! That damn serpent! It had chased her in many dreams during the last year. She knew the serpent symbolized the traitor responsible for her father and brother's deaths and her present situation. But the bear? Twice now the bear had burst upon the scene and rescued her from the serpent. So the bear probably symbolized the help or knowledge she would get or need to bring the traitor to justice—a lot of help if the size of the bear was any indicator!

Carefully she removed Little Feather's arm and rolled over, facing him. Since he was sleeping so peacefully, she took this opportunity to study him, although it was mostly in her imagination. The long house was still too dark—with all the fires burned low—to see much of anything.

As she slid her eyes over his form under the bearskin, she admitted to herself that life *had* taken a turn for the better since he had taken her under his protection. She knew she hadn't saved his life . . . Wolf Running's . . . that she'd take credit for. She grinned in the dark . . . maybe Little Feather's, too.

Thinking about yesterday's game, she wondered what she was going to do with Running Weasel. And she reminisced about all the nonsense her new friends had taken from her! Of course, they hadn't suspected it was pretend—just that they were really good and patient teachers. None of her new friends would ever know how much she appreciated them! On impulse she leaned forward and kissed Little Feather on the mouth. The mouth had been a lucky shot as there was too little light to see his face clearly.

Little Feather shifted restlessly in his sleep, moving his hips away from her.

Not wanting to wake the sleeping man whom she knew needed his rest to heal, she rolled cautiously away from him and thought about the coming day—about bathing in particular! There was no way around it. She was going to have to take him as her protector—as if she needed a protector!

Abruptly, she pictured an area of rocks she had climbed around. Well, no problem! He could sit on those rocks with his back to her. He could protect her, which would keep him contented, and she could watch him, which would keep her happy! She dozed off again, with a smile on her face.

"Give it to me!"

"Yaaaa! Noooo! Go way! Yaaaa!"

Ungodly screeching and yelling pulled Shannon into startled wakefulness. Bright Eyes, that precocious imp, lay sprawled on the floor, clutching a corn husk doll to her naked chest and screaming in anger. Over her stood a stocky boy, maybe four or five years old, struggling to tear the doll from the little girl's grasp.

A grin spread across Shannon's face. Those two were always fighting over something. If Bright Eyes had it, it was guaranteed that her brother Boy-Who-Talks-A-Lot would want it. But the girl got her licks in, too. she'd kick, bite and scratch to get what she wanted. Occasionally, Laughing Woman, their great-grandmother and, also, the Clan Matron would shoo the two of them outside when they were making too much ruckus.

Little Feather whispered in her ear, "It's really time I made that little man his own bow and arrow. Then he could go and harass everyone else in the village, but he wouldn't wake us up so early in the morning!"

"It isn't early!" Shannon whispered back, and without thinking, butted him with her buttocks. Something hard pushed against her, and she pulled quickly away from him. "It looks like we're the only ones still lounging in bed," she burst out hastily.

Little Feather—still reeling from the midnight kiss—had been taken by surprise at her sudden shove against him and nearly burst out laughing as she leaped so quickly away. She was such an innocent! But not for long if he had any say in the matter.

He had been dreaming about his warrior woman again when he had been so rudely awakened by the children's quarreling.

They had been hunting together, but he couldn't remember for what they were hunting. He could only recall that it was a beautiful day with a warm breeze blowing on them, and the birds were unusually noisy. He was jogging along a path through some heavy old growth, and she was following behind him. But he knew they were hunting together. She still wore men's clothing and that silly hat, but her hair was a flaming red around it. The new dream had the same effect on him as the old one upon awakening! The first thing on his agenda was a swim in the very cold river.

"Up!" he ordered, shoving her legs over the edge of the bed to which she clung.

"Hey!" she yelped, grabbing for her cap and pulling it on down to her ears as she was pushed to a sitting position.

Running Feet, the children's mother, and an older woman, heavily marked by the deadly small pox, who were squatting by the next fire up the central corridor, glanced up at the sudden commotion.

Little Feather swung his long legs over the side of the sleeping platform. "Ian had nightmares last night, and we didn't sleep well."

"I'm sorry to hear that," the older woman, Smiles-A-Lot, murmured sympathetically.

"If the youth is troubled with dreams, maybe the dream interpreters could help him."

"There are those in the village," Little Feather explained to Shannon—bad dreams being the last thing on his mind at the moment—"who might be able to find the source of your nightmares and help the dreams to stop. Understand?"

After a few moments, Shannon nodded, although she already knew the source of her dreams.

"River?" the hunter asked. "Wash?" and he pantomimed washing.

Shannon looked blankly at him for a moment, and then a distinct twinkle appeared in her eye. "Wash . . . river. Good."

The big man was taken aback momentarily, wondering what his woman was planning. He was sure it would be interesting and probably not to his liking.

Outside of the long house, Running Weasel sat on a stump waiting for them. A sulky expression rested on his youthful face.

Shannon stood for a moment staring at the boy, wondering what she was going to do with him. A little inspiration would be nice, she thought, immediately followed by the words 'fire wood'. Well, ask and ye shall receive, she thought gleefully. The girls and women were always gathering firewood. A little help would not be amiss, and the experience might teach the youth a little humility and appreciation for the women in his family.

"Get . . . fire wood . . . for mother!" she ordered, pointing to Running Weasel.

"Collect wood for my mother?" Running Weasel repeated, aghast. "That's woman's work!"

Shannon nodded her head. "Slave work!"

A short time later as Shannon followed Little Feather to the river along the well-beaten path, the sun shone warmly through her buckskin shirt and made her head itch beneath her floppy hat. She envied the half-naked form moving gracefully in front of her.

They moved single file as they passed a couple of small groups of chattering women and two old men—sharing tales of their glory days—ambling back from the river. As soon as the path was clear, Shannon moved abreast of Little Feather.

"I didn't see many people around the village this morning. Where is everyone, or are we really that late in getting up?"

"You just didn't notice—too busy tending Wolf Running and myself—but most of the villagers are at the spawning grounds fishing. They'll be gone for several weeks."

"But the game players . . . ?"

Little Feaather laughed. "There are always people for a game! Men and boys taking a break from the fishing grounds, men returning from a hunt. There's always someone in the village ready for the action."

"Oh," was all Shannon could think to say, and then added, "Will we be going to the fishing grounds, too?"

"I hadn't thought to go. I, myself, returned recently to the village after a long absence."

"I know. Iron Fist spoke of you every time we came to the village. I never understood why, that is, not why he talked about you, but why he talked to me. I never let anyone think I was anything but . . . well, stupid . . . different."

"Oh, but he knew you weren't what you appeared to be! He figured that the deception might include the act of being 'slow'."

"Smart man."

"Would you like to go to the fishing grounds?"

"Would you be going there if I weren't here?"

"Maybe. But you are here, Ian." As he said it, extreme pleasure flowed through him. A sense of rightness, and he knew she belonged with him. He thought of her as his woman, his dream woman, his warrior woman. At least, he thought she had come to him in his dreams as the result of some unfulfilled desires of his. But as she walked beside him in the flesh, he also felt she belonged there. Could that be the meaning of the dream he had had that morning? Later, he would discuss it with his uncle and discover if the older man received any other impressions from the dream.

"Well, then, if that is where you would have gone, let's go there." Shannon responded, gazing up at him with a perky grin. His heart flipped in his chest, and he stumbled over his own feet, managing to catch himself.

By this time they were at the river's edge.

"Well?" Little Feather turned to her, blasting her with the full force of his smile.

"What now?"

Her heart flipped in her chest; she stumbled over an imaginary stone, and forgot her well-thought-out plan! "Ahhhm . . ." She scrambled to regain her thoughts.

"Uh . . . uh . . . upstream," she stuttered. Then she gained a modicum of self-control, and the words flowed out more smoothly, "I found a nice place yesterday . . . uh . . . upstream . . . uh . . . private. I don't want to be watched by *anyone*," she said pointedly, glaring at Little Feather from under the brim of her floppy hat, reminding him of a chipmunk standing on its hind legs scolding him. Although, he acknowledge that she was far more dangerous than she appeared at the moment.

"Lead the way," and he fell into line behind her, grinning at her backside. So, it would appear that his smile had the same effect on her that hers had had on him—scrambled her thoughts! Absolute momentary idiocy! He'd have to try it again and test his theory! He was feeling more comfortable with his dreams and the woman.

After a few minutes walk along the edge of the river, pushing their way through some undergrowth and around the boles of a couple of forest giants, they came to an area with a few large boulders strung along like pearls on a necklace and stretching halfway across the river.

She swung a shapely arm in the general direction of the large rocks, and informed him saucily, "You can sit on one of those with your back to the water while I take a swim."

"Now, you wait a minute! I can't protect you like that! I need to search the area for a ways back in the forest and make positive there are no prowlers around. I can't assure your safety sitting on that rock!" Little Feather protested, laughing at the same time. "And what about my swim?"

His little warrior woman's face developed a mutinous look, but after a moment, she conceded the wisdom of his plan.

"Alright," she agreed—reluctantly—to his plan. "I'll wait until you determine that it's safe to bathe here. Then you'll sit on a rock and keep watch while I get in the water. Once I'm in the water, you can go and take your swim on the other side of those boulders, prowl through the woods again, whatever you want to do—I don't care—but don't be gone long that time, because I'll stay in the water 'till you get back. If you're gone too long, I'll freeze to death!" She was babbling, and she knew she was babbling. Little Feather knew she was babbling, and he stood their grinning at her like she was an imbecile. God, how she hated this lack of control . . . this horrible indecisiveness! She would kill Shamus for exposing her to such embarassment. And Little Feather was no better—taking advantage of her at this dreadful time. She didn't quite know *how or why* he was taking advantage of her, but she knew deep in her gut that he was. It just frustrated her no end!

Little Feather couldn't help himself. He burst out laughing. "How thoughtful of you! And we wouldn't want you freezing to death, would we?" With that remark he disappeared into the forest.

Shannon ground her teeth in frustration.

Half an hour later, the warrior reappeared and, ignoring Shannon, started stripping.

"What are you doing?" she squawked

"I'm going to go for a swim," he remarked calmly. "Since we have no company, *I* decided I'd take my swim the same time you took yours! Save time so we can leave sooner for the fishing camp. If your uncomfortable with that, *you* can go swim on the other side of those rocks!" He pointed towards her string of rocks that protruded from the river, forming two swim areas. So saying he dashed, naked, into the icy river with her eyes glued to his powerful, muscular buttocks.

Damn! but he was easy on the eyes! Another of those almost irresistible urges flowed through her body. What would he think if she dashed out into the water and ran her hands over that magnificent body of his, especially those buttocks? Damn! the arrogant man would probably like it! She just knew he would, because she would like it! Damn! From where did such thoughts originate? What was wrong with her? She'd never had such crazy, irrational thoughts towards anyone before. An image of her father rose before her eyes. It was that same balmy summer day, and she heard his voice again, "Wild and wonderful, hinny!"

"Da," she muttered, "this can't be what you were talking about! It's too horrible for words!" Damn, but she hated taking orders, and she stomped past the row of rocks, cursing in Gaelic all the way, stripped off her clothes and rushed into the frigid water.

Racing through her morning wash, she was back on the shore and haphazardly dressed when Little Feather strolled around the barrier of rocks. She was frantically searching in her bag for the dye for her hair.

A strange glitter shone from his dark eyes as he stared at her flaming-red hair, and her musical imprecations from earlier still rang in his ears as she had intended. He knew he wouldn't have cared for what she had said.

"Why do you hide the glorious color of your hair?"

Rocking back on her heels, she stared up at Little Feather. "I've dug myself a pit, and now I need to get out of it with your help . . . remember, you promised?"

He nodded with a broad grin on his sensuous mouth, causing her to look quickly away.

"Most of the people in your village have seen me at one time or another as Ian, dark, drab hair, kind of slow moving, slow talking . . . you know the routine. What are they going to think if I suddenly show up with this . . ." She shoved her fingers through her bright auburn-gold hair, ruffling the curls about her face. "I really think that if I'm going to be around for any length of time, that the transition might be more acceptable if it's a little slower, and the reasons for the deception explained."

Little Feather could scarcely think, bird song faded, the breeze stopped blowing, time came to a stand still as Little Feather's mind crawled to a stop as he gazed upon the beauty before him. Her words almost flowed around and past him. If she were going to be around for any length of time? His face hardened, and his mind started spinning as her words penetrated the fog he was wallowing in. She was thinking of leaving?

"You would not honor your contract?" He understood about the six years left on the indenture contract.

She glanced up from her search, startled. "Of course I'm going to honor the contract or buy it from you. What made you ask?" She had recovered the dye and was rubbing it vigorously into her hair. The sunshine brightness was quickly concealed beneath the dark dye.

"Just a misunderstanding. Ready to go back to the village?"

"Yeah," she mumbled, fluffing her hair with one hand to hasten its drying. She picked up her bag from the ground and shoved the container of dye back into it and firmly shoved her floppy hat down on her head, concealing all but her lower face. The transformation was complete. The only thing left to do was wash the dye from her hands which she quickly did.

Together, in companionable silence, they started the trek back to the village, each lost in his or her own thoughts. Little Feather was lost in thoughts of his dreams and the woman by his side. He accepted his strong attraction to her which was good if his dreams were any indication of the future. Also, it would benefit him as well as her to help her in carrying out her plan to strip way that ugly disguise. If his friends thought he was attracted to a boy, he'd never live down the ridicule! The attraction he felt for his warrior woman was so strong, he knew he wouldn't be able to conceal it at all times under all circumstances—especially not if she gave him that gamine grin!

Shannon was also reflecting upon Little Feather and the unusual sensations he aroused in her—both frightening and thrilling! In truth, when she wasn't angry with him, she enjoyed the feelings and wanted more of them! which frightened her more than anything else. She felt she was losing control of her own body!

Ruthlessly suppressing her thoughts and feelings as she could do nothing about them at the moment, neither analyze and understand or control them, she turned her thoughts to Shamus and the promise to her dying father.

She was no closer to fulfilling the promise or of finding Shamus than of resolving her errant feelings towards Little Feather. A thought occurred to her. She couldn't discus with Little Feather the feelings he stimulated in her—that was unthinkable—but maybe she could unload some of her worries about Shamus and her vow to her father. She'd watch the warrior, get to know him, think about asking his help, and then decide. Could she possibly enlist his help to find Shamus without informing him of the whole truth? Yes, she had a lot to think about and observe in addition to carrying out her plan to get rid of her pseudopersonna.

Chapter 11

The fishing camp was a hubbub of activity when Little Feather and Shannon, accompanied by Running Weasel, arrived at the site. Lean-tos were scattered randomly throughout the trees and brush bordering the river the people were working. Intermingled with the lean-tos were scaffolds upon which fish, cleaned and scaled, were drying, and the air reeked with the smell of blood and dead fish. Water birds were screeching and squabbling over fish parts and entrails.

Shouting, laughter, and friendly bickering filled the air and children ran and played everywhere in the dappled light as the sun shone through the branches far above.

"Cousin! It's about time you got your ugly butt here!" shouted a young man, wading from the river and carrying a net filled with fish over his shoulders. Dropping the net, fish and all, among a group of young women, he strolled over to where Little Feather and his group stood watching the activity around them.

Shannon recognize the young man as Grey Turtle, one of the men who had fought the grizzly with Little Feather

When Grey Turtle reached them, he scrutinized Little Feather thoroughly. Little Feather still wore the splint on his arm. The lines from the stitches were red, but there was no sign of infection. Finally he nodded his head in satisfaction.

"Remind me," he said, turning to Shannon, "if I ever encounter a bear I can't handle, to call on you, kid!"

Little Feather cuffed his friend on the shoulder with his good hand, and Shannon muttered, "Ian!"

Grey Turtle looked startled, and Little Feather explained, "The kid's name is Ian. You didn't stick around in the village long enough to know, but Ian saved Wolf Running's life."

"Wolf Running's going to live? Wonderful!" The brave turned again to Shannon. "Ian, you must have magic in your hands! I saw what you did for Little Feather, but everyone had given up on Wolf Running. I commend you!"

"The False Faces . . . there first. The Spirits . . . helped . . . Wolf Running. I . . . helped the Spirits," Shannon mumbled slowly, eyes cast down.

Grey Turtle stared intently at Shannon. No one in the village had ever heard the kid string so many words together.

"Where's your brother?" Little Feather asked, gazing around the camp of several hundred people.

"White Feather? Oh, he's around some place," Grey Turtle said somewhat vaguely, searching the area for his twin. "The last time I saw him, he was regaling a group of young women with his lies! Trying to impress them with his prowess as a hunter and warrior."

"But not as a fisherman?!"

Both men laughed.

Grey Turtle glanced at Running Weasel and asked Little Feather, "How did you get him here?"

Everyone knew that Running Weasel was a bully, and avoided work whenever he could.

"Have you seen or talked to Tall Tree? He and Iron Fist assisted Ian and Basket Maker work on Wolf Running."

"Nah! He and Evening Dove are fishing a spot up river. Nobody sees much of them. I wonder how much fishing they'll actually get done!"

Little Feather grinned and, turning to Shannon, explained, "Tall Tree and Evening Dove got married a few weeks ago. Understand?"

Shannon thought for a moment, then nodded her head, saying, "Yes . . . married. Tall Tree . . . married," wondering what was so funny about the young people wanting to be alone. Then understanding hit her. Oh, *that*! But why anyone would want to do *that* was beyond her. Revelation hit her again! Oh, no! Those irrational feelings and urges couldn't be related to *that*, could they? She tipped her head, hoping no one would notice the blush that burned from her neck to the top of her brown-dyed head.

"Running Weasel lost a stick-and-ball game and forfeited a week of his freedom to Ian." Little Feather explained to his cousin.

"He lost a game of stick-and-ball? To whom?" Grey Turtle asked, clearly puzzled. Running Weasel was an excellent player when he wasn't cheating and bullying.

"Tall Tree, Red Fox, Ian and myself."

"He cheated!" Running Weasel grumbled. "He lied! He pretended he didn't know how to play when he really did! He tricked me into playing!"

"Ian didn't trick you, Running Weasel," Little Feather rebuked the boy. "Ian worked hard for three days to learn the stick-and-ball game." He turned to Grey Turtle with a grin, "Ask Tall Tree about the game. It was one to remember!"

"Three days?" Grey Turtle asked in disbelief.

"Ian's a fast learner! Apparently, no one had ever had the time or desire to try and teach him anything."

"A really fast learner," Grey Turtle repeated, staring at Shannon who had her head practically resting on her chest.

At that moment, to Shannon's immense relief, another voice was heard yelling, "Hey, Cuz, glad you could make it here!"

Another young man, identical to Grey Turtle strolled up to them.

"You're looking pretty good, better than the bear! Remind me not to go hunting with you again!" White Feather teased. He had several gashes healing on his right hip and leg.

"Has your 'fishing' been successful?

"Always, Cuz! Look at it this way. When I go into the water with my net, I'm going to have all the help I could possibly need. Probably get more fish than anyone else, too!" and with that remark, he sauntered away.

"And he probably will, too!" Grey Turtle said in a disgusted tone of voice.

During this exchange, Shannon had been watching all the activity going on around her. She observed a group of boys about Running Weasel's age along a stream that joined the river. Every few minutes, one of the boys would wade across the freezing water hauling a net with him. After a short time, he would haul the net back, and the fish scooped up would be taken to some women to clean and scale. The cleaned fish were placed on a scaffold to dry.

"Where . . . mother?" Shannon asked Running Weasel.

"I don't see her," he responded sulkily.

"Fish . . ." Shannon ordered, pointing to the boys she had been observing. "Take fish to mother!"

"You want me to go into that icy water!"

"Slave! no work . . . no eat . . . winter! No want honor bet?" Shannon asked the boy. Without honor, he might as well be dead, and he knew it.

The boy stomped off, muttering about idiots who didn't belong in the village.

"I've got to get back to the fish. Appears Mother and the girls are nearly finished with the fish I dropped there. Are you well enough for this, Cousin?" Grey Turtle inquired, concerned.

"No! Not in water!" Shannon hastily inserted.

"Yes!" Little Feather insisted, grinning at Shannon. "I was in the water yesterday and today. I'm fine." He gazed about the busy encampment. "My little healer here is overly concerned with his handiwork. I'll see you later. Going to show Ian around the camp."

"Later," Grey Turtle answered as he started back towards the river.

"C'mon, Ian . . . that's a boy's name, isn't it?" Little Feather asked, leading her through the camp.

"Yes, but it's safer at this time."

"You may have needed it among the whites but not here."

"Oh, I need it here! Especially here!" Shannon replied enigmatically.

"Little Feather!" a deep voice interrupted their conversation. An older man, wearing tunic, leggings, breechclout and moccasins, was waving his arm vigorously to get the younger man's attention.

"Grey Owl!" Little Feather stopped and waved his arm in acknowledgment.

"You're looking well so soon after your ordeal!" the older man remarked upon reaching Little Feather and Shannon.

"Good healer," Little Feather explained, gazing at Shannon, wishing she trusted him enough to share her true name with him. "Grey Owl is Grey Turtle and White Feather's father."

"Uncle? Your . . . uncle?"

"Not exactly," Little Feather wondered how to explain their relationship.

Grey Owl laughed. "It's hard for whites to understand our kinships." He turned to Shannon and explained slowly, enunciating each word clearly, "Older men are 'uncle' to all of the youngsters in the village, but specifically to our sisters' children and our brothers' children, but not to our wife's brothers' children."

"Understand?" Little Feather asked.

"No!" Shannon answered. Even as her full witty self, she would have to think about these kinships!

"No matter! Just call me 'uncle'," and both men laughed. After a moment, Grey Owl continued, "I heard Wolf Running was going to survive."

Not again! Shannon thought ruefully, awaiting the expected explanation which was delivered.

Grey Owl studied Shannon trying to form some picture or impression from former meetings with the youngster. Nothing came to mind except the Frenchmen's assistant, tending to the Frenchmen's business and then wandering off by himself. The children always collected about him. Somehow Grey Owl had gotten the image of someone who was slow—slow moving, slow talking, not very smart. From what he had heard from Tall Tree, that wasn't the fact at all! He wondered how he had acquired that impression.

"Your skills are a welcome addition to our village, young man. Good healers are always welcome." As Grey Owl was speaking, he was leading the couple to his lean-to where his wife, daughter and other female members of their clan were chatting while they cleaned the fish Grey Owl and Grey Turtle were bringing to them regularly.

"Ian," Shannon informed the older man. "Name Ian!"

"So," Grey Owl grinned at Shannon, unperturbed and replied, "my fine young healer, your name is Ian. But not for much longer I predict!"

"Come share our meal with us!" Makes-good-moccasins, Grey Owl's wife invited.

The smell of fish sizzling over their fire made Shannon's mouth water. They hadn't eaten in hours, not since a hasty meal upon first awakening.

A young girl, wearing a buckskin skirt and short tunic, shyly handed Little Feather a plate with a steaming fish on it. Her eyes kept shifting to the handsome warrior as he gingerly picked the hot flesh from the fish. Several other girls in their early teens would gaze at him and, glancing away, giggle among themselves.

Shannon couldn't help but notice their juvenile display of interest in the man sitting next to her and was irritated by it. Good heavens! Did all the unmarried women want to go into the forest with this warrior, regardless of their age, she mused somewhat hysterically. Damn! That sensation of something budding or flowering—just plain growing—deep in her abdomen was there again! Damn!

Little Feather glanced sharply at Shannon, noticing that she was only picking at her fish.

"You don't like fish?"

"I . . . love . . . fish!" Shannon snapped back.

Her sharp response took Little Feather by surprise, and he looked more closely at her. His woman was definitely upset about something. But what? What had he done? What had changed in their environment? The only thing he was doing was eating fish served by Frisky Chipmunk. He glanced up at the girl to discover her staring moon-eyed at him. Gazing about him, he realized immediately that all of the twins little sisters were gazing at him with adoration—hero worship! Could his woman have misunderstood the children's hero worship? Could his woman's—his little warrior woman's—irritation be plain old jealousy? Could he be so fortunate? With his luck, she wouldn't know it was jealousy!

"Saw you and thought I'd let you know our camp is over beyond those trees," said Iron Fist, pointing to a large clump of trees, as he and Deer Runner, Little Feather's adopted father, joined the group.

"Join us for a meal, Brother," Makes-good-moccasins extended the invitation to Deer Runner and his brother-in-law.

"Just a small bite, we just ate," he accepted a small piece of fish which he shared with Iron Fist. Turning his gaze critically onto his son, he remarked after a moment or two, "You're looking unusually well, for having encountered a grizzly so recently. You were most fortunate to have this young person so close at the time. Iron Fist informed me of the incident." Deer Runner, a big man in his late middle years with long black hair, turned his piercing gaze on Shannon.

He studied her for so long, she began to get antsy. Was it possible for him to see through her disguise? He examined her fringed buckskin breeches and shirt, a gift from Pierre and Jacques as they would wear better than the homespuns with which she had left the VanHooven's, and the silly hat that came down to her ears and shaded her eyes.

"I don't understand why I never noticed you before . . . Ian?" Deer Runner spoke slowly, thoughtfully. "I know you came to our village several times with the Frenchmen. But I really don't remember you, and it shames me. I want you to know, you have my deepest appreciation for what you did for my son and my good friend Wolf Running."

"The . . . Great Spirit . . . put me at . . . the . . . right place at the . . . right time. I'm pleased . . . I was . . . able to help," Shannon replied, stumbling over her words as though trying to locate the correct word in a foreign language.

Grey Owl looked on in amazement. "I can't ever remember you saying so much!"

"Not much say . . . hard words . . . not understand . . . not need talk."

Deer Runner glanced at his son. "Iron Fist informed me that you bought Ian's contract of service?"

Little Feather nodded his head. "I didn't want trouble with the Frenchmen—they're too valuable to me. They're going to try and get me some flintlocks."

Premonition knotted Little Feather's stomach as he anticipated his father's next words.

"In exchange for your life and Wolf Running's, would it not be appropriate to give Ian the contract to do with as he pleases?"

The words pierced his heart with greater force than he could possibly have imagined, and Little Feather's first thought was, let Wolf Running pay his own debt! Without the contract, how could he keep his woman by his side until she became comfortable with him and his people, until she learned to trust and love him, until she acknowledged her love for him? How could he keep her safe from other men when they discovered the truth about her? He almost burst into laughter! The thought of any other man with her instigated a driving rage within him! He was jealous!

"I was planning to destroy the contract, Father. I just hadn't gotten around to it." Little Feather replied lamely and turned to Shannon sheepishly. "I really did intend to destroy the contract. It just slipped my mind." It was the truth—sometime in future years when she decided to stay of her own volition—but they both knew that hadn't been his intention at the present time. He hoped it wouldn't do any irreparable harm. Knowing his prickly, little warrior woman, it probably would.

Free! She was free! Under no obligation to anyone! So what was she going to do in this strange land? Where would she start to find Shamus? What would she do without Little Feather?

That thought stopped her dead! *What would she do with out Little Feather?*

"You are welcome to stay in our long house as long as you desire," Iron Fist invited, knowing the problem her freedom might present to his plans for this young woman and his favorite nephew. "Laughing Woman would be delighted to have you as a guest and friend indefinitely."

For the time being, that seemed best. She still needed to discover who was responsible for the reward on herself and Shamus. There was so much she needed to learn to live and travel in this country, things that Little Feather could teach her. Would he still be willing to teach her if there was no contract between them?

"You promise . . . teach . . . things. Will . . . teach . . . still?"

Little Feather's relief was palpable. "A promise is to be honored," he answered solemnly And would he ever teach her! Everything she wanted to learn and everything he wanted her to know! Oh, yes! He would teach her! But not an inkling of his inner triumph showed on his chiseled face.

"Oh, Son," Deer Runner said as an afterthought. "I've heard a rumor going around. At the next Annual Council of the League, you're going to be recommended for Lone Pine status. Congratulations!"

Iron Fist and Grey Owl were both grinning with Deer Runner. Little Feather was speechless for all of a minute. "We'll have to wait and see what happens." As if there were any doubt but that he would become a guardian of the League!

The afternoon passed in a haze of activity. The knowledge of Ian's freedom spread throughout the camp like locust during harvest season. Red Fox and Little Wolf confiscated her and dragged her to the creek where they were fishing with their nets.

Never had birdsong sounded so sweet as it did that afternoon as Shannon hauled load after load of fish up the long winding path, through the brush and trees to the family's camp where Bright Flower and other women from their long house prepared the fish for drying. A good haul now meant full bellies next winter, maybe even some left over to trade with other tribes and maybe even the European traders. Free! Free! Free! The word chanted though her mind like a religious litany.

As she worked she munched on fish cooked for the purpose of keeping up everyone's strength. Free! Free! Free! And as she moved along the path with her load, listening to the birds, watching a squirrel who eyed her presence suspiciously from a tree branch, she felt something else that she could not remember ever feeling in her whole life before—safe! Oh, how bright the sun was shining, sparking through the tree branches—free! Free! Free!

She didn't say a lot or move very fast—that would have been out of character—but everyone suddenly took notice of the kid that few could remember from her visits to the village with the Frenchmen.

That night when it was too dark to fish, and everyone was satiated from eating, there was dancing and merry making. Some of the older men had groups of children and young people about them whom they enthralled with stories of great heroes and magical peoples. As the children fell asleep, they were carried off to their families lean-tos.

Finally, the fires died down, and the camp settled down for the night. An owl hooted in the distance warning the small forest denizens that it was starting its night's forage for food. The scurryings of small night creatures could be heard. And here and there throughout the camp fires popped and snapped as they burned low.

Little Feather and Shannon retired to the lean-to constructed earlier in the day. Everyone appeared to accept as the natural order of things that the guest of the Turtle clan would share a lean-to with Little Feather. And objecting never occurred to Shannon. Must have been the drugging effect of the balmy spring evening and that she was bone tired.

Chapter 12

Shannon couldn't keep her eyes off Little Feather. It didn't matter where she was or what *he* was doing. Dressed like all of the other men in breechclout and bare feet, he should have been fairly indistinguishable. He wasn't.

"Ian, pay attention!" Red Fox admonished. "You're letting fish around the net!"

Red Fox and Little Wolf had dragged her off to work the nets with them. Little Feather was fishing with the men and bigger nets.

"Sorry," she muttered. Dragging her attention back to her end of the net, she tightened it, trapping more fish.

"That's better," Little Wolf approved.

Together the three of them pulled the net ashore. Dumping its contents into a large basket, they helped Shannon hang it from her slim shoulders—it being her turn—to haul it to where Bright Flower, her sister, Snail Girl, and Snail Girl's daughter, Red Wing, were preparing previous catches for drying.

As she struggled under the load, not having done this much work in nearly a year except for the day before when her loads had been much lighter, Shannon's eyes drifted to where Little Feather stood chatting with Wild Rose whose family had shown up at the fishing camp earlier in the morning. Over his broad, muscular shoulders hung a basket full of fish about twice the size of Shannon's. His handsome face was alive and animated, chatting with the woman as they started walking towards his mother's encampment.

Irritation blossomed in Shannon's breast like a thistle bush. It was irritation! How did Little Feather have time to chat with that . . . hussy . . . when there was so much work for everyone to do. As a borage plant grows rapidly, so did Shannon's anger grow as Little Feather and . . . *that woman* . . . approached the camp site.

Little Feather, who had been observing Shannon as closely as she had watched him, knew the instant jealousy's monstrous head rose up in his woman's breast. As he observed her dump her load, his smile broadened; he couldn't help it. Her jealousy controlled her movements and her mutinous expression. She nearly ran over him as she stomped back towards the river. He nimbly jumped aside.

"Busy! Too busy . . . chat!" she muttered as she hurried past.

"Relax, Ian. There's always time to chat while we work!" he shouted to her fleeing back, adding fuel to the fire of her jealousy.

As she drew near the river, Grey Owl and White Feather approached her. Both men carried large baskets loaded with dried fish.

"We're heading back to the village. We thought you might like to come with us and check on Wolf Running," Grey Owl suggested.

She was seriously tempted, she really was. She wouldn't have to watch Little Feather paying so much attention to Wild Rose when he should be helping with the nets! But Red Fox and Little Wolf were devoting themselves to helping her learn more of their language and adjust to her place as a guest in their clan.

"Basket Maker tend Wolf Running . . . good hands. Thank . . . you for . . . thinking take . . . me," Shannon said, not looking directly at the older man. Pointing at Red Fox and Little Wolf, she added, "Brothers . . . help me . . . help speak, I help . . . fish." As an afterthought, she looked at White Feather and added, "Be safe! Watch out . . . bears!"

"We will!" White Feather promised, the two men chuckling as they strolled away under their heavy loads.

Shannon watched the two men disappear into the forest before continuing on to the river, a feeling of contentment and belonging flowing through her . . . in spite of her annoyance with Little Feather.

Glancing over her shapely shoulder, she saw the source of her irritation stretched out on the ground with his back and head supported on his elbows, chatting animatedly with *that woman* who was still standing idly about. His mother and other women of the clan were busy with the pile of fish which was nearly finished.

Now what caused that look of contentment on Ian's face as she watched the sachem and his son going into the forest, Little Feather wondered. And what could they have said to her? The look of irritation she cast in his direction—he had no doubt what caused that! How could he use her jealousy to his advantage, to awaken her to the feelings he suspected she harbored towards him? Maybe he had fed her jealousy enough for today. He really ought to be down at the river helping Iron Fist. Well, in a few minutes, he decided as he watched Ian return to the boys. He derived great pleasure from watching her, almost as much as holding her at night.

"Little Feather! You're not attending!" Wild Rose complained.

Turning his head politely towards the woman, he thought, oh, but I am attending!

As Shannon approached the river, she heard Red Fox shouting to her.

"C'mon, Ian!" he yelled. "We're losing fish!"

Dropping the basket, she hurried to where the boys struggled with the net.

"It's easier with the big nets to have more people," Little Wolf explained to Shannon.

"Sorry," Shannon mumbled. "Grey Owl . . . stop me. Want . . . know I . . . go with them . . . back village."

"Why didn't you go, Ian?" Red Fox asked as they untangled the net and set it to scoop up more fish.

"You help me . . . speak like . . . you," Shannon answered. "You . . . help . . . me learn fish, you help me learn . . . stick-and-ball . . . game," Shannon said slowly with great pride in her voice.

"By the way, I saw Running Weasel a ways upstream fishing with some of the other boys. Was that your idea?" Little Wolf asked.

"Yes, yesterday. But I . . . but I gave . . . mother . . . obligation today," Shannon replied slowly as though searching for the correct Kanien'kahaka words.

"You gave his mother his obligation of service?" Little Wolf asked, a grin slashed across his youthful face.

Shannon nodded.

"How wonderful!" Both boys laughed.

A few minutes of hard work later, they had another net full of fish to be taken to the camp for the women to clean. They dumped the fish into a large basket, and when Red Fox started to pick it up, Shannon protested.

"I take . . . it," she hastily offered.

"That's okay, it's my turn," Red Fox explained.

"I take. No hard work . . . . very long. Get strong," Shannon refused the lad's help.

Red Fox shrugged his shoulders. "Okay with us. But when you get tired let us know, and we'll take our turns. Okay?"

Little Feather, having observed the minor disagreement between Ian and Red fox, watched with amusement as his little warrior woman struggled from the river with a load much too heavy for her. What could she have on her mind to take Red Fox's turn? Whatever she planned, he was sure he'd appreciate it although probably not like it much.

The weight on her back, twice in a row, *was* too much for Shannon, although she would have died before admitting it. Inspiration! She knew exactly how to deal with Little Feather and . . . *that* . . . *that* . . . *woman*!

Shannon's sudden impish grin and the laughter in her eyes was the only warning Little Feather had. But in that instant he knew what she was going to do! And there was no time to get out of the way!

His warrior woman stumbled . . . right! . . . and the whole basket of smelly fish flew over him and Wild Rose! All he had time to do was raise his arms to deflect the fish from his face. Wild Rose was not so lucky.

"Ugh!" she screamed. "Oh! Oh! How could that incompetent idiot do this! Ugh!" she reiterated, shoving the flopping fish off her lap. Little Feather reached over and plucked the one off her head. Wild Rose jumped up and ran off screaming towards her family's camp site.

"Ian, are you alright?" Bright Flower, Little Feather's adopted mother asked solicitously, removing the basket from Shannon's shoulders and helping her up. "Those boys know better than to let you haul two loads in a row. It's too much if one is not use to it."

Helping to scoop up the fish, Shannon explained, "My idea . . . not work . . . hard . . . long time . . . want get strong!" She peeked up from under her floppy hat and gave Little Feather, who was now standing and trying unsuccessfully to wipe the slime from his breechclout and bare skin, a cheeky grin. "Now . . . get back work . . . help Iron Fist. Wild Rose help . . . family!"

"You're not going to get strong all in one day, Ian!" Bright Flower bustled about helping gather the fish. "You carry smaller loads, or you'll make yourself so sore you won't be able to carry anything!"

As Shannon started back to the river with her empty basket, Little Feather strolled along beside her.

"That was a slimy trick!"

"I tripped. You saw that," Shannon excused herself. "The load was just to heavy for me. I said I was sorry."

"Why don't I believe that?"

Suddenly Shannon burst out laughing. "You should have seen your face when that fish came at you! And Wild Rose!"

"But why?"

"Why what?"

"Why did you throw the fish at us?" Little Feather asked patiently.

"I don't know . . . Wild Rose annoys the daylights out of me. Has since I first met her, and she treated me like a worm!"

"Surely . . . not a worm!"

"Yeah, a worm," Shannon asserted.

"But you've been irritated with me, too. Why? What have I done?"

"I don't have a logical explanation for that either. Maybe I'm still angry with you for buying my contract. At least with Pierre and Jacques, I was moving about the country. There is someone I was looking for, and I don't know how I'll find him now. What you do is none of my business, and yet when I saw you with her, all I could think of was all the work we have to do, and you're wasting your time laughing and joking with her, and she should be helping her own family."

A sudden irrational wave of jealousy washed over Little Feather. A husband, maybe? A man she was planning to marry? He'd kill him if he had to!

"If I still had the right to tell you what to do, I'd tell you to come to the river and help me wash this mess off since you were responsible for it!"

"Little Feather! What happened to you? Pheeew!" Red Fox said, joining Little Feather and Shannon.

"Ian tripped, spilling the fish all over Wild Rose and myself."

"That must have been a sight to see!"

"It was," Little Feather said with a lopsided grin that flipped Shannon's heart.

"We're planning on catching another couple of nets full of fish and then quitting for the day and going hunting squirrels and rabbits. Thought you might like to go with us, Ian, start working with a bow."

Turning to Little Feather, she suggested, "You help . . . Little Feather, brother?"

As she said 'brother', revelation hit her again. Never in this life would this man ever be a brother to her! Shamus never aroused such irrational feelings as this man did. One moment she wanted to caress his whole wonderful body, and the next she wanted to break his good arm . . . or throw fish all over him! Her father's words returned to her again,

"Sometimes I didn't know if I was coming or going, whether I was up or down! That's the way it was between your mom and me!" Her father had been talking about love! Could she possibly be falling in love with this man? After only five days?—and months of hearing Iron Fist praise him? For the first time she admitted to herself that she *was* extremely attracted to the big warrior. She liked waking up in his arms, and damn! but he was easy on the eyes! And her reaction to Wild Rose, could it really be a healthy dose of jealousy?

Little Feather observed the look of wonder that passed over his woman's face—like the expression on a child's face when she sees her first butterfly—and wondered what she could possibly be thinking. It was as though she had just discovered something spectacular.

"You were just rebuking me for not doing my share of the work. Maybe I should stay and help Iron Fist!"

Caught by her own words! "Well . . . ah . . . your arm. Can't haul . . . too much yet! Can't . . . shoot bow . . . yet! Maybe come . . . show Ian? . . . You promised." Shannon was pleased with her quick thinking.

"Little Feather!"

They all turned at the shout. Tall Tree was emerging from the forest along the river and strolling towards them, a grin splitting his face from ear to ear.

As the man reached them, he explained, "Evening Dove is helping her family clean fish. Heard you were here, so decided to come down and see how you were doing."

After examining Little Feather critically, Tall Tree finally shook his head in disbelief and said, "Five days and you're nearly healed! If I hadn't seen it for myself I wouldn't have believed it!"

"You have magic in your hands, Ian," Tall Tree said, gazing at Shannon.

"It couldn't . . . . have been done . . . without you, Tall Tree." Shannon muttered from beneath her hat, getting tired of having to respond to this particular compliment. She hadn't saved Little Feather's life.

"You boys, finish the fishing you planned. I'm going to chat with Tall Tree. I've done enough fishing for the day with my bum arm." He gazed at Shannon who blushed delightfully for him. Fortunately, no one else noticed.

The cacophony of birds fighting over fish, the musty odor of the earth, and the salty tang of blood, filled the air as the boys and Shannon—dodging birds and bird droppings—went back to their net. Little Feather wandered off with Tall Tree to chat.

"I was going to come looking for you if you didn't surface soon." Little Feather informed his friend. "It appears that married life suits you well!"

"You ought to try it. But I don't think that is why you were going to look me up.

What's up. friend?"

"Another dream," Little Feather answered as the two men found a couple large rocks by the river and sat down, amazed as usual at his friends intuitive insight.

"Same woman?"

"Yea," Little Feather started, the picture of absolute misery as he sat with his head bent forward staring at the ground and with his hands folded between his legs. "We were hunting together. I was in the lead, and she was following, but she was armed the same as I was. But I don't remember what we were hunting. I felt good in the dream, happy as if everything was as it should be. She was suppose to be with me."

As he meditated upon his friend's words, Tall Tree picked up a flat stone and tossed it parallel to the water. It skipped five times across the broad stream sparkling in the spring sun.

"Your marriage partner?"

"Every time I dream about her—which is almost every night— I wake up aroused!"

Tall Tree laughed. "Well, I can't do anything about that! So you think you're suppose to marry this white woman?"

"With hair the color of the sunrise and eyes like a stormy lake," Little Feather added.

"Don't anticipate problems until you've met her! And you might want to talk to your uncle about this dream. I'm no interpreter."

"Maybe not, but I've noticed that you're usually correct." Little Feather was silent for a moment before adding, "And I have met her!"

For all of a second, Tall Tree was speechless. "There was a time when we shared everything with each other." Obviously, his friend had met this woman during the time Little Feather had been away.

"Wild Rose doesn't have a chance with you, does she?"

"This woman has had my heart since the first dream in which I saw her!"

"But there are problems, I assume."

"There are, but the worst thing is I don't even know what they are. So there is nothing I can do to solve them at this time. And I think she's attracted to me but doesn't know it!"

Now Little Feather picked up a couple of flat stones and skipped them on the water.

"Let me see if I understand this. You've met a woman, both in dreams and in the flesh, whom you plan to marry, but you're not sure that she's attracted to you, right? and you can't show her to anyone, yet, right?"

"That about sums it up. But you'll be the first to meet her when the time is right."

"This sounds like it's going to be fun. Mind if I watch and laugh?"

Little Feather slugged his friend on the shoulder and rose to his feet. "C'mon, the boys want to take Ian hunting small game. Ian wanted me to instruct him on the use of the bow. Want to come?"

"Sounds like a good way to pass the time. Looks like a couple more hours of daylight, and I imagine that Evening Dove will be tied up during that time." Tall Tree stood up and followed his friend along the river. "How is Ian doing with the clan?"

"He's picking up our language pretty fast. Seems he didn't talk much because he didn't have much to say, and didn't know our language. Let's go see if he can learn to use the bow as quickly as he learned to play the stick-and-ball game."

"Can I stand behind him?" Tall Tree asked seriously as they ambled along by the river back to camp.

The sun was warm on their backs, and a fish leaped in the river, falling back with a splash, as Little Feather slugged his friend on the shoulder again and replied, "You can't. I'm going to be standing there!"

Chapter 13

"Hey, Little Feather," Red Fox shouted when he saw his brother exiting the forest with Tall Tree. "The fish are running so well right now, we're going to bring in another net full. Then we'll take Ian on his first hunt!"

Waving his arm in acknowledgment, Little Feather and Tall Tree strolled over to the camp site. Little Feather, sitting on a convenient tree stump, pulled his pipe from his pouch and filled it with tobacco taken from another pouch. Taking a stick from the ground, he leaned it into the campfire and then held the lit end to the tobacco in his pipe. He inhaled deeply, enjoying the smoke.

Iron Fist sat nearby, drawing on his own pipe.

Tall Tree sat leaning against a tree watching his friend and his friend's uncle smoke. He'd never understood their penchant for the pipe. Even when he had to smoke the pipe at a council meeting or trading session, it burned his mouth and lungs, and it was all he could do to refrain from coughing.

Another young man sat by the fire, rubbing a bow handle.

"That is a beautiful piece of work, brother," Little Feather praised the handiwork of Standing Elk, the son of Snail Girl, Bright Flower's sister.

"Thank you, brother, for your kind words." The young man, still wearing the long hair of a youth as he had not yet gone on his first war party, blushed at the praise. Holding the bow handle up, he added, "It's nearly done. All I have to do now is string it."

Yelling and laughter from the direction of the river drew their attention.

Red Fox and Shannon were dragging the basket, which had been overfilled, and Little Wolf was pushing on it and picking up fish that keep flopping or falling from the top of the pile.

"Our children have no sense at all, sister! They will ruin that basket, and we'll have to make another one." Bright Flower said to Snail Girl.

"Something to do during the long winter," Snail Girl answered watching the struggle. "They have no idea the work that goes into making a basket like that!" Bright Flower responded, then added thoughtfully, "But they will next winter!"

As they watched, the three stopped tugging on the basket, and Shannon came shuffling rapidly back to the camp.

Little Feather, puffing enjoyably on his pipe, watched his woman's progress with great glee. It wouldn't be long before the whole village would knew the vivacious person he, himself, was coming to know—although, not understand! He drew another long, relaxing puff on his pipe.

As Shannon reached the camp, she wrinkled her nose and exhibited an horrific cough. Pointing to Little Feather's pipe, she wheezed out, "Awful . . . . dirty . . . smelly!" and started coughing again.

Then with an amazing recovery, she turned her back on Little Feather and asked the women, "Blanket? Use . . . blanket?"

Snail Girl gave her a bear-skin blanket which Shannon carried back to where the boys were waiting with the basket under the trees. The three young people pushed, pulled and tugged the basket onto the blanket.

"Appears that you're going to have to get another bear to replace that blanket!" Tall Tree suggested, grinning at Little Feather.

"My foot! They can get their own bear or shiver this coming cold season!" Little Feather objected, knowing full well that Ian, at least, was capable of doing just that, with a little help. He had never seen one bullet kill any grizzly!

Finally, with a great deal of tugging and sweating and Ian muttering in that foreign language again, the last basket of fish for the day arrived at the camp for the women to process.

"Now we can go hunting," Little Wolf puffed, wiping sweat out of his eyes. "At least for an hour or so." Then, muttered under his breath, "That should be long enough to get us all killed!"

Shannon, overhearing the remark, pretended not to have heard and struggled not to laugh. It was so close to what she had in mind.

"Are you coming, brother," Red Fox addressed Little Feather.

"With the greatest anticipation! I invited Tall Tree to go with us, if it's okay with the three of you?"

"Hey, that's great!" Red Fox answered. "I just thought of something, Little Wolf. What's Ian going to use for a bow?"

"A bow? . . . Don't look at me! I'm not giving him the means to do me in with!"

"A bow would be helpful if you want to teach Ian how to hunt." Little Feather suggested, grinning at his younger brothers, ignoring Little Wolf's remark.

"Don't be a jerk, brother!" Standing Elk rebuked the older man.

"You should learn a little respect for your elders!"

"He does have little respect for his elders," Tall Tree added helpfully.

Standing Elk ignored both men and handed Ian his old bow. "I finished a new one for myself a short time ago. I didn't know if I would have time to finish it today or not, so I brought my old one along with me. You're welcome to it, Ian. It should have about the right strength for you. You can borrow my quiver and a few arrows, too."

"Hey, that's great, brother! We really appreciate the gift," Little Wolf thanked his older brother. "Do you want to come with us?"

"Not today, I have other plans, and I don't want to miss the dancing tonight."

"He's going to go watch the girls!" Red Fox teased. "We plan on being back in time for the dancing."

During this exchange, Shannon had been studying the bow she had been given. It was a beautiful bow but smaller than a man's bow. "Thank you," she said to Standing Elk. "Much beautiful . . . much like . . . much appreciate."

"It's my pleasure, little brother. Good hunting," Standing Elk grinned at Shannon.

Red Fox and Little Wolf helped themselves to some cornbread from a plate by the fire, giving a piece to Shannon. Collecting their bows and arrows, they were ready for the hunt.

"Would you like to take the lead?" Red Fox asked Little Feather. "You're a better tracker than we are, and we don't have much time."

"Be my pleasure. Tall Tree can bring up the end." Little Feather agreed. "Ian can follow me with the two of you next."

As Shannon jogged behind Little Feather, observing his every graceful, coordinated move through the dappled light—first in the shade of forest giants, then in the fickle light that managed to reach the ground—she became aware of that knot that expanded of its own volition deep in her abdomen—again! Following on the heels of that unpleasant feeling, unwanted thoughts of the laughter they shared, his patience with her, his patience with Bright Eyes and the other children, his thoughtfulness towards his younger brothers burst into her mind. All in all, she realized with a start, a thoroughly admirable man. But, she didn't want *any* man now—not even an admirable one. Right now she had to concentrate on finding Shamus and then finding the traitor and bringing him to justice.

But, she rationalized, feasting her eyes on Little Feather's broad shoulders, his narrow hips and strong thighs—which she couldn't help studying since he was so close in front of her— while she had the opportunity wouldn't hurt. She would just have to bear with that knot in her abdomen that tended to grow and to rise to the level of her heart. Tingling sizzled along her nerves as she was overcome by a sudden urge to run her hands along his broad shoulders and down those slim hips . . . passion! What she felt for the man was passion!

The abrupt revelation so distracted Shannon that she tripped over her own feet and fell against Little Feather bowling him over from the unexpected blow.

They tumbled down upon the hard ground in a tangle of arms and legs and swirl of dust as Little Feather twisted in the fall trying to catch Shannon, and Shannon grabbing for his shoulders in an effort to catch herself. In the process her hands skimmed over his chest and shoulders, and his arms wound up around her. When they finally came to rest, she reclined on top of him with his arms about her. An altogether acceptable position from his point of view. Not bad from hers either. Even though it had been unplanned and not in her scheme of things, she got to satisfy the urge to touch . . . and touch . . . and touch!

Blushing a fiery red at the unbidden thought, she mumbled, "Sorry, I hope I didn't hurt you!"

Little Feather couldn't have been more delighted with this unexpected bounty from the Great Spirit. The caressing by her hands over his body hadn't been missed. He simply didn't know whether it had been deliberate or not. Her hardened nipples through her binder brought him to instant arousal, threatening to wash away his carefully constructed self-control.

When she attempted to scramble off him, she found herself held tightly for a moment or so longer than necessary. Glancing into his angular face, she was engulfed in his dark, glittering eyes and a look so raw and primal that it sent fear and excitement racing along her nerves. Then his eyes became shuttered.

"Not at all, Ian!" He laughed into her flushed face. "You don't weigh much more than a butterfly . . . a big butterfly!"

Hearing the rest of the party approaching, Little Feather quickly pushed her off, attempting to suppress his ardor. It was unthinkable that his family or friends think he was attracted to a boy!

"Your arm?" she questioned as she rose to her feet, brushing dirt and twigs from her buckskins.

"Fine. See." He held the arm out for her inspection. "The splint is as tight as when you replaced it this morning. I'm fine, don't worry."

Little Feather was rising to his feet when the boys and Tall Tree reached them.

"What happened?" Little Wolf asked, his voice full of concern.

"I . . . tripped," Shannon explained. "Knocked big brother down!"

"Must have been some stumble!" Tall Tree commented. Something didn't seem quite right. He glanced around but didn't see anything that could have tripped Ian.

"Ian was running too close, and I was caught unawares. That's all." Turning to Shannon, he asked, "You okay? Do you want to go on?"

"I'm fine. Okay to go on. I stay farther away!"

"Let me know if you need to rest. The rest of us are used to running for hours."

"No problem. Can keep up!" Shannon grabbed her hat from the ground where it had fallen and slapped it back onto her head

More time passed as they jogged through the forest looking for squirrels, rabbits or big birds, and Shannon was feeling the effects of the unusual exertion. She began to drop back. Soon Red Fox and then Little Wolf passed her. Each suggested that she let Little Feather know if she needed to rest. Pride was her downfall, and she kept struggling on, unwilling for Little Feather to see any weakness in her.

"You know, Ian, it's okay not to be able to keep up with Little Feather, but you have to let him know, or you're going to be lost in the woods," Tall Tree, the only one still behind her, stated mildly. "And that is very dangerous for someone who doesn't know the forests. You very possibly wouldn't be seen again. Do you understand what I'm saying?"

"Yes, I . . . understand. But I can . . . see him. He has . . . he has to stop . . . sometime. Start back . . . camp soon. Dark . . ." Shannon said, panting while pointing overhead where dusk was overtaking them.

The man behind her burst into laughter. "Not in your life time, Ian! He can keep this up all day and night if we didn't have to go back to camp!"

"Surely, not run nighttime. Can't see!"

"Well, I probably have to concede that one to you, although he does have the eyes of an owl. But there is no shame in not being able to keep up with an experienced hunter."

Shannon cursed profusely in Gaelic. She didn't want the party to have to stop on her account. There was a time when they wouldn't have had to rest because of her, but she had grown soft over the past year.

Tall Tree's heavy brows rose. He didn't understand the words, but the tone and expression were unmistakable. He grinned, wishing he knew what the boy was saying. He bet it wasn't complimentary to Little Feather. But why couldn't the lad just tell Little Feather he'd had enough?

As Shannon, now breathing heavily and muttering in that strange language under her breath, trotted beneath a low hanging branch, her hat was snagged by a twig and yanked off her head. She turned to regain it, and a wayward sunbeam that had struggled its way to the forest floor sparkled off the top of her head.

Tall Tree was startled to see several flickers like flame mixed in with the boy's dark hair, much brighter than would be expected for normal color variation. Little Feather's words came back in a flash, "her hair is like the rising sun." That would explain a lot but created even more questions. Why the disguise? His friend had a lot of explaining to do.

Little Feather was aware of the exact moment when his warrior woman started falling behind, and he had slowed his pace accordingly. But since they were almost at their destination, he decided to continue. Tall Tree would look after Ian.

Nearby there was a meadow occasionally visited by small herds of elk, and he thought the boys would be thrilled if they brought down one of the big animals.

As the trees began to thin, Little Feather motioned for his party to slow down and be quiet. Shannon and Tall Tree caught up after a few minutes. Before them lay a broad meadow with patches of green and a few early, hardy flowers scattered around. Many small trees grew at random across the field, and beneath the trees browsed a small herd of elk, unfortunately, it was a herd of bull elk, and they could turn mean! Little Feather wished his arm was healed enough to use his bow, but he knew it wasn't.

He motioned the kids to be quiet and move back from the field. When he thought it was safe to talk, he explained, "Bull elks, like the males of most species, are very unpredictable. I don't think there are enough of us to tackle them safely. What do you think, Tall Tree?"

His friend thought for a moment. "Boy, it's awfully tempting to try for them. We could shoot them from the maximum distance our arrows can fly."

"That distance is going to be a lot closer for the kids than for you, and I won't be of any help. Sure wish I had my flintlock with me!"

"Yeah, but you don't," Tall Tree responded.

"Hey, don't we get any say in this? After all this was our hunt!" Little Wolf protested.

"What would you suggest, little brother?" Little Feather asked patiently.

"Well, I noticed a natural funnel of trees on the east side of the meadow," Little Wolf blurted out, so excited he couldn't stand still. "If . . . if Tall Tree and Little Feather went over and hid by the end of the funnel, we could chase the elk towards you . . ."

"I can't pull the string on a bow, little brother. What would you have me do, throw rocks?"

Tall Tree grinned. He couldn't help himself. The image of Little Feather throwing rocks at a grown bull elk was too funny.

Little Feather frowned at his friend.

"Have . . . have . . . idea," Shannon added to the conversation.

Everyone looked at her in surprise, although Tall Tree noticed that Little Feather didn't seem as surprised as the others. Of course, knowing what he now new, Tall Tree, himself was more curious than surprised.

"Big brother, you stand . . ." she put her arms in the shape of a funnel . . . "wide end" . . . she wiggled her elbows . . . "and keep elk . . . moving towards Tall Tree. Only kill . . . . one elk. More . . . too much carry."

"I think Ian has an idea that might work, but you kids be real careful. Watch for any elk that turns on you. They can do it in the blink of an eye and trample or gore you to death."

A few minutes later, the two men were in place, and Red Fox, Little Wolf and Shannon had collected large forked branches to wave in the air.

Screaming, shouting and waving their branches high above their heads, the three young people raced towards the startled elk from three different directions, the hope being that the animals would escape in the only direction that was free to them—the east.

Several of the beasts escaped through the funnel before Shannon saw a large buck fall. She started jumping up and down shouting, forgetting that there were still a couple elk in the field rambling towards the funnel of trees.

Abruptly the biggest buck swerved from its easterly course and thundered towards her, totally unresponsive to her shouting and bow waving. Her heart thundered in time with the beast's hooves. She knew she would be trampled like so much dry grass or torn apart by its massive antlers.

Without thinking, she grabbed an arrow from the borrowed quiver, nocked it to the string and pulled with all of her strength. The arrow flew straight and lodged into the mighty beast's chest. The buck dropped at her feet. Reaction set in and she sank to the ground, trembling.

"Ian! Ian! Are you alright?" Red Fox was the first to reach her, followed within seconds by Little Wolf.

She could only nod her head as tears flowed down her cheeks. She was joyous . . . oh, so joyous just to be alive. The sharp tip of one of the antlers grazed her leg, leaving a trail of blood.

Shannon staggered to her feet with the boys' assistance, her emotions finally under control. Her heart rate had returned to normal, and she was no longer shaking like a leaf. "Where . . . where's . . . Little Feather and Tall Tree?" she asked, staring towards the funnel. "Shouldn't they be coming out of the trees by now?" burst from Shannon in her anxiety. Fear flew along her nerves. Anything could have happened to the men among the trees.

"It seems they should be," Red Fox answered with growing concern.

Filled with apprehension, Shannon discarded her image of 'slow' and flew across the field. With still no sign of the two men when she reached the trees, she screamed, "Little Feather! Tall Tree!" She raced past the fallen elk. Oh, don't let anything have happened to Little Feather! Don't let some elk have gotten out of control at this end as it had at her end!

"Over here!" Tall Tree's voice filtered through the trees.

Shannon burst through the trees following Tall Tree's voice. When she found them, Little Feather was leaning against a tree with his head thrown back and his eyes half closed. Blood was all over the left side of his chest.

"Little Feather!" she shrieked in panic. grabbing his shoulders and ignoring the blood. All pretense and question was gone. She knew that Little Feather was the most important man in the world to her. With tears streaming down her face, she shrieked, "Oh, my God! Don't you dare die! Not before I have a chance to tell you . . ."

Suddenly she noticed that the blood was flowing from high on his shoulder. A sneaky suspicion began to grow in her.

Carefully—in case she was wrong—she wiped blood from his chest. He groaned. No wound! Her suspicion grew. Blood still flowed from high on his shoulder. Grabbing his shoulders again, she pulled the limp warrior forward.

"Careful!" Tall Tree cautioned, but there was a strange sound to his voice.

Little Feather's head slumped forward onto her shoulder. Again no wound!

The panic she had first felt turned rapidly to anger. Roughly she shoved the big warrior's shoulders back against the tree. "What kind of . . ." Her words were cut short when his powerful arms pulled her tight against his chest. His dark eyes laughed into her stormy grey ones for a split second before his mouth came down on hers.

"Hurry up! The boys are coming!" Tall Tree warned.

For a split second, Shannon was pliant in his arms, enjoying the new sensations that flowed through her before her anger took control. Struggling out of Little Feather's arms, she raged, "You damn near scared me to death for this?"

"It seemed a pretty good idea at the time," Little Feather murmured, grinning from ear to ear, well satisfied with himself. He could work around her anger because she had responded wholeheartedly if only for a split second before she became furious. "We've seen white men and women 'kiss' and thought it might be enjoyable!"

"Obviously, you've blabbed to your friend that I'm not a boy! Or does he think you're a pervert? Maybe he's a pervert, too? No, I guess not, he's married!"

"He didn't tell me about you. Well, not exactly," Tall Tree tried to sooth the ruffled feather's of his friend's woman.

"And just what the hell is that suppose to mean? I damn well didn't run into you!" Shannon fumed, half in Kanienka'haka and half in Gaelic.

"You were going to tell me . . . ?" Little Feather asked, adding salt to the wound.

"Go to hell!" she said in Gaelic, shoving him back against the tree.

He couldn't keep the silly grin off his face, but he released her as they heard the boys coming through the woods.

Shannon stomped off towards the meadow. The last thing she caught was Tall Tree's voice. "I think she's attracted to you, but I wouldn't want to be in your place!" Now what was that all about? She hated being made to look the fool.

Shannon stood watching the busy bees flit about the wild rose bush. The sweet scent of the delicate pink flowers drifted on the breeze around her. Turning away from the bush, she gazed over a broad meadow filled with a myriad of flowers displaying all the colors of the rainbow. Gnarly, old trees grew at random across the field.

"Shannon!"

She looked in the direction from which the voice came. Little Feather strolled towards her waving his arm and calling her name. She waved back and started running towards him, her heart filled with joy. As she ran, the ground became soft and muddy, sucking at her feet. Great wild rose bushes sprang up in the meadow between Little Feather and herself, plucking at her hair and tearing her clothes.

A terrible bellow forced her head up from where she struggled with the thorn bushes.

Great drops of poisonous venom dripped from the gaping mouth of the red-headed serpent rising up behind Little Feather.

"Behind you!" she screamed. "Behind you, Little Feather!"

A ferocious wind had blown up and was howling over the meadow turned deadly thorn field, carrying her words away from Little Feather.

"No! No! No!" Shannon screamed, as the head slithered downward towards the warrior. At the last possible moment, he turned, beholding his terrifying enemy.

Tears flowing down her cheeks, blood flowing from multiple cuts and scratches all over her body, Shannon collapsed to the ground, trembling violently . . .

Shannon's thrashing about in Little Feather's arms woke him.

"Shhhh, Ian. Shhhh," Little Feather whispered into Shannon's ear. "Wake up, Ian, your safe! Shhhh, my little warrior woman, you're safe."

Still caught in the grip of the dream, Shannon lay trembling in his arms.

"Com'on, Ian, wake up. You're safe. I've got you," he murmured into her ear.

Her eyes snapped open but were still glazed, seeing something he couldn't.

"Oh, Little Feather," she wept mournfully. "It's going to attack you, and I can't help! You can't hear me!"

So, his little woman was dreaming about him! And apparently, something horrendous was happening to him, and it was tearing her apart. Rolling onto his back, he pulled her close to his side with his good arm. Gradually, Shannon's shaking stopped, and she fell into a more peaceful sleep without ever coming fully awake.

For a long time, Little Feather lay thinking about their future. From his dreams and his body's reaction to her, he knew that she was the woman for him. Her words tonight revealed the strong feelings she had for him. Whatever else her dreams were telling her, they could handle together. Rolling back on his side, he curled around his woman's slight form and drifted into a contented sleep.

The warm sun shining through the doorway of their lean-to onto Shannon's face brought her slowly awake. Warm and comfortable under the heavy bearskin blanket, she was reluctant to move. Warm and comfortable?

As her mind cleared, she felt Little Feather's arm holding her snugly against his powerful chest. The rise and fall of his chest against her back was deep and regular. How dare he after the trick he played on her yesterday?

His arm resting lightly across her breasts, now confined in the binder day and night, brought the tips into pebble hardness with dizzying effects on Shannon. Passion and anger warred within her.

Passion, being so new to Shannon, caused confusion, jealousy—she'd never experienced *that* before in her life—and insecurity emotionally. She had to admit to herself that she had never felt so secure physically as she did with Little Feather around. What if Little Feather didn't feel the same? And why should he have these crazy wild emotions for her? She simply didn't know what to do about these new up-and-down, unpredictable emotions.

Now anger was an old friend. A lot of time had been spent angry with Shamus, the perennial jokester with her, usually, the butt of his pranks.

Anger won. Little Feather had scared her silly over a stupid scratch! And his friend, Tall Tree had helped him! Obviously, Tall Tree was aware of her disguise, and if Little Feather hadn't told him, how did he find out? So, hell, did the whole village know?

It had been too late to skin the animals, so they had pulled the carcasses up into a couple of large trees to be dealt with in the morning.

On the return trip to the village, she had ignored the two men, devoting her attention to Red Fox and Little Wolf. Being the butt of a joke was not her idea of fun.

In spite of her anger, she had been unable to dispel that kiss. Like most young girls, she had imagined that first romantic kiss, and it *had* been more spectacular than she had ever dreamed. It had released something in her that made her want to jump, laugh and shout for joy. But for him, it had meant nothing but a laugh, and in front of his friend! Even now that kiss haunted her!

Grabbing his wrist, she shoved his arm off her and crawled out of the lean-to opening into the new day. The camp surrounding her was coming awake as people wandered off into the woods to relieve themselves after the long night. Women were stirring up the coals from yesterday's fires, and a variety of foods could be smelled cooking over the fires of the earliest risers with fish being predominant.

"Ian! It's about time you got up!" Red Fox shouted, returning from the trees. Obviously, he hadn't been up long either.

Shannon glanced with great deliberation at the sun that was hidden beyond the forest across the river.

"So I beat you by a short time!" Red Fox grinned as he help himself to a piece of stale cornbread.

"Where . . . where is Little Wolf?"

"Around somewhere," the boy answered nonchalantly. "The women are going to dress those elk we killed last night. Say, that was one fancy shot you made. I didn't know you could shoot. Thought we were going to teach you!"

"Lucky . . . shot. Desperate!" Shannon tried to lessen the boy's awe of her shot. "Kill or be killed!"

Lucky shot! My foot! Little Feather thought, listening to their conversation. He had awakened at his woman's first move. The instant she had grasped his wrist and moved his arm, he knew his path with her was *not* going to be straight and smooth. Apparently, she did not remember her dream or revealing her deep feelings for him . . . and she was still angry about yesterday! He sighed. What was life without a challenge?

A grin spread across his handsome face, the kiss was nice until the anger kicked in.

So, he and Tall Tree hadn't had time to think the plan through carefully. Tall Tree had come up with the idea initially. His friend had scarcely sufficient time to inform him of the conclusion he had drawn from Little Feather's description of his woman and Ian's red hair. The plan had really only been an impulse. At least, Little Feather would know if the woman was attracted to him, so said Tall Tree. Well! He knew! The grin was still plastered to his face! The problem was how to placate his prickly little warrior woman.

Rolling over onto his stomach, he crawled out of the lean-to and climbed to his feet. He took a cursory glance at the healing wounds on his side. The woman did beautiful stitches. Would his shirts and leggings be as neatly stitched one day? Somehow he didn't think so!

"Ian, would you mind redoing this splint. It's coming loose."

Shannon immediately turned to him to remove and replace the splint, all concern for the welfare of his injured arm. While she was tending him, she examined the healing wounds on his face and side. Everything looked good.

"I'm really sorry your feelings were hurt yesterday," he apologized for her ears only.

"You made me look a fool!"

"That was not my intention!"

"What was your intention? You pretended to be injured when you were not." Anger, never far from the surface, was starting to boil up again.

What could he say? That it was all to discover if she was attracted to him? To take advantage of her closeness to kiss her? Neither of these reasons sounded plausible, even to him. If this is what love did to a person, he might do without it. It didn't occur to him to simply say, "I wanted to kiss you." He didn't say anything.

She stared up into his dark, glittering eyes. "Would you have done it to any other woman you know?"

As he had never wanted to hold, kiss and be with another woman as much as he did Ian, he could answer in all honesty, "No!"

Shannon stomped away, angrier than she could ever remember being.

Now, what was wrong, Little Feather wondered, completely baffled for all of about three minutes when it occurred to him how she might interpret his careless word.

Hurrying after her, he suggested, "Morning necessaries? You shouldn't go off by yourself."

How she hated it when he was right! She followed him as he disappeared among the trees.

"I'll take this one," Shannon said, coming to a large clump of brush. "You keep going!"

Continuing farther among the trees, he berated himself. No matter what he said to his woman, she misunderstood him. He'd never had a problem communicating with others, and he had diligently tried to placate her feelings on the way back to camp, but she had simply ignored him. Could it be a language problem, Little Feather wondered naively. As he meditated upon the situation, anger began to grow in him. The misunderstanding wasn't *all* his fault. She was as stubborn as an old bull elk, not even willing to listen to him! Well, two could play her game! She wanted to ignore him. Well, he would ignore her, too . . . or try to, he admitted to himself. Finishing his business, he turned and started back for camp, ignoring Shannon as he passed her, and she fell in behind him.

Tall Tree and Evening Dove were entering the camp site from upstream as Little Feather and Shannon returned from their walk.

Shannon went in search of Red Fox and Little Wolf, too angry and embarrassed to desire the men's company.

"May the sun shine brightly upon your day!" Tall Tree greeted his friend. "Evening Dove is going to help dress the meat. I thought we might dry it here over the next couple of days 'till the fish stop running."

"May the sun shine brightly upon both of you this day. I had decided the same about the elk meat."

"I looked at the elk Ian brought down yesterday. Nice shot!" Tall Tree praised.

"Yeah, nice shot," Little Feather agreed grumpily.

Tall Tree's eyebrows shot up, and a knowing grin slid across his rugged face . . . "The sun isn't shining so brightly, huh, friend?"

"I'm going over and visit with Bright Flower. I'll let you know when we're ready to go after the elk," Evening Dove said, knowing that neither man heard her.

"Ah . . . yeah, okay," Tall Tree answered her absentmindedly.

"So she hasn't forgiven you yet?"

"No, not yet," Little Feather answered, then brightened a little. "She has terror dreams, had one last night, talked in her sleep, very enlightening. She cares deeply for me."

"Let me guess . . . she didn't remember the dream this morning!"

"Right." Little Feather strolled to the campfire and helped himself to some stale cornbread, his friend trailing behind him. They started off towards the river.

"Since she wants to ignore me, I'll ignore her in return."

"I don't know that that is such a good idea."

Little Feather scowled at his friend. "It was your idea that started this!"

"You didn't have to go along with it."

"Yeah, I know. If I'd had time to think it through, I probably wouldn't have done it."

"How was the kiss?"

Stopping, Little Feather thought for a moment, and then

grinned. "Good enough for another if I can discover how to get around her prickles!"

Both men started laughing.

"Little Feather!"

They turned to see Bright Flower waving her arm and pointing to the kettle over the fire. The men started back through the trees at the river's edge towards the group of people around the campfire. Everyone was standing or sitting around with a bowl in hand and eating. Iron Fist sat on his favorite stump, smoking his pipe. Shannon, Red Fox and Little Wolf were sitting, leaning against a big tree apart from the others, eating their fish stew and cornbread.

Helping himself to a bowl of hot stew, Little Feather wandered over to where the boys sat and slid down the tree next to Shannon. His bare hip above his leggings rubbed against her hip.

Shannon, sitting too close to Red Fox to move, had to sit and tolerate the big warrior next to her. Keeping her head down, she paid diligent attention to her stew and attempted to ignore Little Feather. Anger still burned in her breast like a bright flame needing to be quenched.

The heat from his hip filtered through her buckskins and warmed her thigh. She ignored it. The heat crawled its way up and down her leg. Unbidden, images of his arm around her each morning when she awoke came to mind. And the warmth. The heat continued to crawl up and into her abdomen. Shannon wished he'd get up and leave, go and keep Tall Tree and his wife company or something.

"That was a nice shot you made yesterday. That elk skin will make a nice warm shirt for next winter." Little Feather said companionably, deciding to follow Tall Tree's advice and not ignore Ian.

"Lucky . . . just lucky," Shannon muttered, mouth full of stew.

"Yeah, we thought it was a good shot, too," Little Wolf said.

"Well, if it was only a lucky shot, you'll need a lot more practice to become proficient," Little Feather suggested. "Maybe take in some target practice or even look for small game while the women are slaughtering the elk until they're ready for us to help carry the meat back to camp—probably until the sun is high overhead. What do you boys think of the idea?"

The boys, who had had enough of fishing for a awhile and even smelled of fish, thought it was a great idea. Shannon wasn't so sure. She wasn't sure she'd be able to hold onto her anger! Little Feather could be so considerate when he wanted to be!

"Little Feather!" a high feminine voice called.

Wild Rose! Little Feather groaned inwardly. He didn't know if the woman's presence would help or hurt his wooing of Ian away from her anger—probably hurt it—but either way, he could not rudely disregard the woman. Rising gracefully to his feet he strolled away, calling back over his shoulder, "As soon as you boys are ready, we'll leave. Tall Tree is going with us if none of you have any objections."

Shannon did, but couldn't very well voice them. Suddenly she felt cold and lonely with Little Feather removed from her side. The heat that had been radiating from the point of contact stopped cold dead. She wished she could make up her mind whether she wanted the warrior around or not! Damn! She was angry with him and at the same time lonely when he wasn't there! All in all, she was miserable! And to make matters worse, Wild Rose was back making those stupid doe-eyes at her man! Her man? Where had that idea come from? She didn't even know if he was attracted to her! But 'her man' did have a nice sound to it. Now if she could only make up her mind what she wanted!

As she ate her meal, thoughts flitted around in her head like bees, but one came back to haunt her. Joke or not, Little Feather had initiated that kiss. He must have wanted to kiss her. Oh, if only she knew for sure. If this is what Da meant about being in love, she wasn't positive, but she thought she might do without it!

Looking up from under her hat, Shannon observed Little Feather, Tall Tree and his wife, and Wild Rose laughing and chatting. Losing her appetite, she started shoving food around in her bowl.

"What's the matter, Ian?" Little Wolf asked solicitously.

"Nothing . . . just not . . . hungry. Must be sun hot on head.

"You don't have to wear that hat, you know. You'd be much more comfortable without it."

Shannon gave a noncommital grunt, but the hat stayed firmly in place.

"Well, I'm finished," Red Fox added, wiping up the last of his broth with his last bite of cornbread. "Let's go collect Little Feather and Tall Tree and see what we can run down today."

Later, as the boys and men were jogging through some underbrush, Little Feather called a short rest.

"Has anyone had any dreams of animals or hunting in the last few days?" Little Feather asked.

They looked around at one another, shaking their heads.

"Well, don't expect too much from this hunt then, since the elk gave themselves to us last night. That, in itself, is going to be a lot of meat to haul back to the village in addition to all the fish."

"How about some target practice for a while? The women should be finished with the elk by then and be ready for our help," Red Fox suggested.

"Okay with me. Any objections?" Little Feather turned to his friend.

"It's all the same to me."

While the boys and Tall Tree strung their bows, Little Feather assisted Shannon to string hers. With the bow strung, he stood behind her with his arms about her, showing her how to nock the arrow and sight along it to take aim on her target just in case yesterday's shot really had been luck due to desperation. Because of his fracture, he was unable to pull on the bowstring, so Shannon pulled it under his tutelage. When he was satisfied that she knew what she was doing, he moved away from her.

"What shall we use as a target?" Little Wolf asked.

"I'll break a branch on that maple, and we'll use that," Little Feather replied, pointing to a large tree about twenty yards away.

Shannon was still getting the feel of her bow and swung around.

"Hey, don't point that at anyone!" Tall Tree shouted, diving for the ground.

Red Fox and Little Wolf followed the warrior down as the bow swung in their direction.

"Sorry!" Shannon muttered.

Little Feather scrambled behind Shannon and helped her free the arrow from the string. She glanced in his direction with a distinct twinkle in her grey eyes as she repeated, "Sorry!"

The little minx! He hoped she wouldn't accidentally shoot someone, trying to convince them of her ineptitude.

"I'll be right back," Little Feather said, adding to Shannon, "Don't touch anything until I return!"

While Little Feather jogged to the tree he had previously indicated as their target, Shannon practiced stringing and unstringing her bow. Then she nocked an arrow and aimed towards the maple.

"Hey, don't do that!" Tall Tree shouted, leaping towards her to grab the bow and arrow from her hands. "Little Feather!"

Shannon jumped, startled by Tall Tree's shout, and the arrow was released.

Little Feather tumbled to the ground, praying diligently that her arrow would fall anywhere but where he lay. It did. It thudded into the tree next to where he had been standing breaking the branch. Had he been standing, she still would have missed him. What an archer! He smiled into the dirt before rising to his feet. Hopefully, that burned off the last of her anger at him.

"Kwa . . . eee! Kwa . . . eee! Kwa . . . eee! Kwa . . . eee." With the first cry sounding in the distance, the birds hushed their noisy chatter. The second and third cries came closer in a weirdly silent forest, and the fourth was heard receding to muted birdsong.

The smile died on Little Feather's face, and it took on a cold, hard, chiseled expression.

The boys, leaving their bows strung and in their hands, started back along the path they had recently come down.

The grim look on Tall Tree's and Little Feather's faces told Shannon that something was amiss.

"What's wrong, Little Feather?" she asked as he passed her.

"Stay close! Tall Tree will run behind you."

"But what's wrong? What's happened?" Shannon repeated.

"One of our chiefs has been killed!"

Chapter 14

Shannon heard the wailing before she saw the encampment. Oh, God! No! Not Grey Owl and White Feather! It couldn't be!

As they burst from the haven of the trees into the campsite, all was in turmoil. Makes-good-moccasins and her sister and daughters were wailing and screaming in great anguish, their pain uncontrollable. Their piercing cries tore at Shannon's heart, partly from their pain and partly from her father's and brother's deaths that she had never had a chance to properly mourn.

The deeper drone of the men's voices as they discussed the horrific event provided a counterpoint for the women's high piercing cries. The children in the camp moved about like silent ghosts. Even the dogs were abnormally quiet.

Shannon's heart sank It *was* the gentle Grey Owl and possibly White Feather. Death so soon among her new family and friends? Would the violence never end? The heart-breaking shrieks twisted her heart and wrenched visions of Paddy's twisted body with his head half blown away and then her father's with its gaping hole from just below the surface of her mind. She shook her head to rid herself of the grizzly scenes from the past. The evils of the present were sufficient without dredging up the evils of the past. This was here and now, and she needed to pull herself together as her services might be needed.

Grey Turtle was struggling to hold his hysterical mother who was flailing her arms and attempting to do herself and Grey Turtle physical harm. His own wrath, kept under tight control, raged and boiled as violently as the Great Thundering falls to the west.

Iron Fist was holding Little Robin, Makes-good-moccasins' sister, as she cried and grieved, pulling at her hair at her sister's terrible loss.

"No! No! It can't be true! He can't be dead!" In the next moment Makes-good-moccasins was screaming, "I want them dead! I'll tear out their hearts!"

The distraught woman was moaning, yanking at her hair and tearing at Grey Turtle. "Why! Why! No, he's not dead! I won't believe it!" she shrieked, shoving violently at her son. "Gray Owl will be back!" She sank into her son's arms, weeping her heart out. Then a hard, crafty look transformed her pleasant face into something Shannon would never have recognized nor would she ever forget it. "I want their killers caught! I'll tear them apart limb from limb!" She began struggling again, ranting, raving, scratching and digging at herself and Grey Turtle who fought to restrain her. Finally, she collapsed to the ground in exhaustion, but her sobs continued unbroken.

A stranger to Shannon stood in their midst eating a small piece of cornbread sweetened with maple sugar for energy to continue his long journey.

"Can you continue on, or do you need relief?" Little Feather inquired of the runner.

"No, I can make it to the next village, and a relief runner will take the message from there."

"Have you any information about what happened?"

"I don't. We're fishing the river south of here, and some of our people were returning to our village when they found Grey Owl's body—two arrows and a bullet—in the back!" The runner said grimly. "The body is about two and a half hours southwest of here. Those discovering it tied the body up on a tree branch to keep it away from predators.

"We knew you were up here, so I came here first before taking the message to the rest of the League."

"They only found Grey Owl? White Feather was with him."

"I don't know anything about White Feather, only Grey Owl was found. Sorry I don't have more information." The messenger shrugged his slim shoulders and shook his head, a solemn expression on his face."I've got to go. Everyone along the Trail needs to know about this as soon as possible."

The young man disappeared among the trees, and a few minutes later, the mournful cry of "Kwa . . . eee!" was heard in the distance.

"I am so sorry!" Shannon turned to Little Feather. "If there is anything I can do, tell me!" Shannon felt helpless and like an outsider with so much anguish surrounding her.

"Can you heal a broken heart? Can you restore a loved one?" Chiseled granite couldn't have been harder than the expression on Little Feather's face as he watched the agony that Grey Owl's wife was experiencing—an anguish Grey Owl's whole clan would share when they learned of his murder.

Little Feather hadn't meant to be so harsh with Shannon, but he shared the pain of those around him. Grey Owl had been another uncle and mentor to him all of his years in the village.

"If White Feather is still alive, I may be able to help him," Shannon offered.

"If he is alive, we will know that much more quickly who did this. No one touches a Kanien'kehaka without retribution!"

Shannon could only stare at the arrogant man before her. This was the man who had said he was sorry for hurting her feelings? If her arrow had missed the tree, her target, and hit him, would she now be on the receiving end of that retribution? That shot had been a juvenile act, she admitted, but she had still been angry. Good thing she seldom missed that for which she aimed!

Women and children were already scurrying hastily among the trees and campsites, collecting essential personal items, extinguishing cook fires, gathering together baskets of fish and elk meat packed that very morning. Much meat and fish was left hanging from tree branches. All was done efficiently with an eerie silence pervading the camp. The people communicated in hushed tones while Grey Owl's women cried and moaned, anger and sorrow equally blended.

Men from different campsites stood scattered about in small groups discussing the murder excitedly and what to do about it—the hotheaded young men wanting to take off immediately to exact their revenge and create havoc, the older men advising caution. Wait until Grey Owl's clan decided what they wanted done. Wait, don't act without thinking and planning.

"Little Feather, I need to find whoever may have some healing herbs with them. We're going to need them when we find White Feather." Assuming he's alive, Shannon thought, but kept those sentiments to herself.

"Okay, I need to talk to Grey Turtle. Let him know we're going seeking his brother, and that we'll return Grey Owl's body to the village."

While Shannon went among the older women in the camp looking for supplies, Little Feather sought out Grey Turtle.

"I just learned from the runner that White Feather may still be alive. Ian and I are going searching for him. If he is alive, he will undoubtedly need Ian's heeling skills." Little Feather informed his cousin, deep concern on his rugged face for Grey Turtle's grief.

The young man's handsome, bronze face had grown haggard and old, his eyes haunted.

"Do you really think I would let you go without me? My brother—my other half—is out there somewhere, Little Feather, preferably alive! But whether he's alive or dead, his attackers are dead men!" Grey Turtle did not question Shannon's accompanying them. He had seen her skill in treating Little Feather's wounds and knew that if his brother were alive, he would need her help.

"Ian, if you need to rest, let me know," Little Feather instructed. There was no way he was going to let her out of his sight until the danger had been removed. She was his to protect.

The noise of the camp being dismanteled were soon left behind. The only sounds to accompany them were the chirping of birds, the rustling of the wind through the tree branches, and the pounding of their own hearts as the trio set out to find White Feather and to retrieve Grey Owl's body.

The messenger had been wrong. After removing the body from the tree branch, they found three arrows and a bullet hole in Grey Owl's back, and he had been scalped. His basket, fish spilling out of it, lay on the ground where his body had first fallen. For some reason, he had not been carrying his basket at the time of the attack. Otherwise he might have survived. A second basket, with most of the fish still in it, was lying farther along the trail. There was no sign of White Feather.

"I could have been lying there with him," Shannon, horror splashed across her face, whispered to Little Feather who was examining his uncle for any scant sign of life. Grey Turtle, off in the bushes, could be heard vomiting.

"What do you mean, you could have been here with him?" Little Feather glanced at her questioningly.

"He asked me if I wanted to go back to the village with him." Shannon paused, watching Little Feather's examination. "Why are you looking for signs of life? He's been scalped!"

So that was what his uncle had been talking to her about. A chill trickled down his spine. He could have lost her before ever sharing his thoughts or feelings with her! But now wasn't the time.

He looked at her with a grim smile. "Scalping doesn't kill! Bullets and arrows do that." He pulled the arrows from the corpse.

"Will they help you identify who did this?"

"Yes, that's why they were left in by the ones who found him, but mainly I plan to return them!" Sunbeams, filtering down through the branches revealed the unrelenting resolve that marked his handsome face and hardened his voice.

"Oh!" A small grin slid over her face. If she'd thought about removing the bullets from her father or had had the time, she'd return them to the traitor—front or back, didn't matter.

Grey Turtle, having gained some control over his grief and shock, returned to his father's side. Covering him with the blanket he had brought, he gently lifted the body and, staggering under its weight, placed it back on the tree branch.

Shannon glanced at Little Feather, a silent question in her eyes.

"The villagers will be along soon, and he seeks to protect his family from more anguish."

Grey Turtle returned to the trail and, with Little Feather's and Shannon's help, collected the baskets and fish and placed them behind some brush.

"Now, let's see if we can find my brother." His skin had a pasty pallor beneath the bronze, but grim determination sculpted his comely face into harsh lines.

"You don't have to do this, cousin. Ian and I can find him."

"I have to. If he's alive, he'll be waiting for me. It's just the way it is."

Searching the brush on either side of the trail for fifty feet or so, they looked for blood or any sign that a person may have crawled that way. Slowly moving towards the village, they thoroughly examined every inch of the surrounding area. They tore through thick brush, rolled logs over, searched in hollowed-out trees—anyplace where a man might seek concealment.

They were still searching when they heard the villagers approaching. Remaining unseen, they waited until the people had passed and then continued their search.

"No point, at this time, in revealing that this is the place of the tragedy." Little Feather explained.

About half an hour later, Shannon found White Feather. He had managed to crawl into the rotted-out trunk of a large, old tree.

"Little Feather! Grey Turtle! Over here!"

Unable to see more than his feet, she didn't know if he was still alive or dead. One foot moved a little. Her imagination? It moved again!

"Oh, my God! Hurry!" she screamed. "He's alive!"

Both Little Feather and Grey Turtle, who were already hastening towards her, burst into a rapid run. Grey Turtle reached her first with Little Feather a second later.

The two men tore frantically at the rotted part of the tree around White Feather, pulling away large chunks of wood and enlarging the hole. Soon they were able to see enough to know that he had an arrow in his shoulder and a bullet low in his back.

How he had ever crawled into and stayed in that small space transcended Shannon's imagination.

Continuing to rapidly strip away rotted wood, they soon pulled White Feather from the hole and could observe the full extent of his injuries. He had been scalped also!

Forcing down the bile that rose in her throat, Shannon took some of the herbs from her pouch and started blending them with water she carried in a bladder. She mixed and listened.

White Feather opened his eyes, glazed from pain, and stared up into his brother's eyes. A ghost of a grin shaped his mouth. "What took you so long, brother?" His eyes drifted shut. "Oh . . . my head is killing me! This is the worst headache whiskey has ever given me! I swear I'll never drink again!"

"You've been scalped, you idiot!" Grey Turtle said in exasperation.

"Scalped?" White Feather's eyes drifted open, and a frown formed between them.

"Do you remember what happened to you and Grey Owl?" Little Feather asked gently, Shannon squatting beside him as she worked with the herbs.

"My father? . . ."

"You have an arrow through your shoulder, a bullet in your back, you've been scalped, and we just pulled you out of a tree!" Little Feather informed him grimly.

White Feather stared up at Little Feather, then his gaze went to his brother. Again a slight smile formed on his lips. "It must have been some celebration!" His eyes closed again

Shannon could only stare in disbelief at this exchange between the twins. She suspected that White Feather was more lucid than he sounded.

Grey Turtle stomped away.

"Your father is dead!" Little Feather told his cousin.

White Feather was silent so long that Little Feather thought he may have passed out or died.

"I know," he finally replied. Opening his eyes, he stared up at Little Feather. "I can't do anything to bring him back. Right now I don't know if *I'm* going to survive. The next best thing is to annoy Grey Turtle!"

"If you didn't already have an arrow through you, I'd put one there! This is no joking matter!"

"*You're* telling *me*?"

"Do you remember what happened?"

"Of course. I wish I didn't!"

"Well?"

"There were six Huron—five men and a woman—and a white man. They asked for sanctuary. We invited them to go to the village with us, but they declined. Said they had to go back to their camp which was somewhere nearby to collect their belongings. So we directed them to the village. Although the white man spoke French well, he wasn't a Frenchman. He spoke French with an unusual lilting sound." White Feather ceased talking for a few moments, resting and remembering. "Strange, but I thought I had heard it before. The man also had red hair . . . redder than anything I've ever seen!" He closed his eyes and was silent for so long that Little Feather thought he may have lost consciousness.

Shannon started with surprise. Could the man have been Shamus? Could her brother have changed so much during the past year that he was capable of such carnage against innocent people? God, how she hoped not. Then reason spoke in her head. "White Feather?" Little Feather questioned.

Grey Turtle returned and squatted down by his brother, listening.

"I'm still here, cousin . . . unfortunately." His eyes remained closed as he talked. "He asked if we might have seen a redheaded woman when we visited the Dutch trading post. Told him we had seen a few, but none such as he described—said she was absolutely gorgeous, with hair like the sunrise and eyes like a stormy grey sea! He appeared frustrated with our answer, but since there was nothing else we could tell them, they went on their way back to their camp." He stopped speaking to rest.

There was no doubt in her mind, if it wasn't Shamus then somebody else was looking for her. The traitor? Could it possibly be the traitor come searching for her? The one responsible for the reward? Could they be one and the same? But why would he want her or Shamus? Well, she had one piece of information now that she didn't have before. He was a redhead the same as she and Shamus. A relative?

"Father had rubbed his shoulder raw," White Feather continued, "from the basket strap and removed his basket to pad the sore. I took my basket off to rest my shoulders while helping him." He was silent for a while, staring up at the sky. "Pretty stupid, huh? Only moments passed when I heard a shot and my father fell to the ground by my side. Before I had time to do anything, I felt a bullet penetrate my back and an arrow my shoulder. I fell. A blinding pain shot through my head. I must have hit it on something because I lost consciousness." Another long pause. "They must have thought I was dead.

When I regained consciousness, my roach was gone, and my father was dead. I made it this far but haven't had the strength to go any farther yet. Was thinking about trying when I heard Ian. It was all I could do to wiggle my foot! I was afraid that he wouldn't see me.

"Enough talking, brother," Grey Turtle ordered gruffly. "We've got to get you patched up enough to get you back to the village."

Shannon applied the poultice, she had been preparing, to his scalp and tied it in place with strips of leather. "That should . . . pull out pus . . . and relieve some pain."

"Just think, bother," Grey Turtle teased, "let your hair grow in around your head, and you'll look just like the Black Robes!"

"Your hat will cover it, cousin," Little Feather intervened between the brothers. "Don't pay any attention to Grey Turtle."

"Little Feather," Shannon drew his attention, pointing to the arrow. "Easier to move him . . . with this broken."

"Cousin," Little Feather addressed himself to Grey Turtle. "We need some thick tree branches for a travois on which to haul White Feather."

"You think I can't handle what needs to be done?"

"I know you can tolerate what needs to be done. You could

do it if you had to, but you don't need to do it, and we do need the branches as soon as possible."

Reluctantly, Grey Turtle went in search of the needed wood.

Little Feather grasped the arrow shaft penetrating White Feather's back and snapped it a couple of inches from the skin. White Feather passed out.

"Have you ever dug a bullet out?" Little Feather questioned Shannon.

"Yes . . . I have."

"Did they usually live or die?"

Shannon stared at him for a moment, a slight grin forming on her shapely lips. "They usually lived."

"Will you do it here and now? While he's unconscious?"

"It might be safer for him to do it after we get him back to the village."

"There may be those who would object to your treating him. There's going to be a lot of stress in the village when we get back.

"You have that much faith in my skills?"

"I bear the results of your skills, and Wolf Runnling owes you his life." Little Feather grinned. "I would like to see White Feather in your debt."

"I need a fire immediately. I think between the three of us, there is enough water . . . I need some moss . . . I think I can manage with those things."

"And, Ian . . ."

Shannon glanced up at him.

"When things quiet down a bit, you and I need to talk about red-heads!"

Shannon looked down at White Feather again. She had hoped that piece of information had slipped by Little Feather in the emotional tension of the moment. No such luck!

Within a few minutes, Little Feather had a small but hot fire blazing.

Shannon withdrew from her pouch a slender sheath from which she pulled a long, thin knife and stuck the blade in the fire. Glancing at Little Feather, she saw his raised brows.

"My father had it especially made for me."

"Used much?"

"More than I care to remember. Help me roll White Feather over and keep him off that arrow."

The bullet had lodged in the hip bone about two inches from the spine. After a few minutes of digging, she had the bullet out. She quickly cleansed the wound and packed it with a poultice of knitbone, covering it with moss.

"I can't understand why they thought he was dead. Neither wound was fatal."

"All of the blood on his back, they probably didn't even realize how low the bullet had actually hit."

"Well, whatever the reason, I'm glad they didn't notice."

By the time Shannon was finishing the dressing, Grey Turtle had returned with the material for the travois. His appearance was more haggard and stressed than it had been a few minutes ago. He was at the end of his endurance.

"If you want to take White Feather on into the village, we'll go back and get Grey Owl's body," Little Feather suggested.

"Thank you, cousin, I'd appreciate that." Grey Turtle's relief was tangible. "I can manage here if you want to leave now."

A few minutes later, Little Feather and Shannon were on their way back to retrieve Grey Owl's remains.

It would appear that the time of reckoning was upon her, and nothing short of the truth was going to satisfy the warrior trotting ahead of her. Could she manage it without telling him about the reward?

Chapter 15

Fury raged within Little Feather as he trotted along the hard-packed earth. Someone was going to suffer for Grey Owl's murder!

But where did Ian fit into the picture? There was no doubt but that Grey Owl's killer was searching for her. Confusion and fury churned within him. Could she be in alliance with the killer? Could she have been party to the killing? Tearing pain ripped through his heart at the very idea.

Questions buzzed around in his head like angry bees as he ran along the beaten path back to Grey Owl's body. What explanations could she possibly give him about the man pursuing her? Could he *trust* any information she gave him, her having already lied to him once.

And his dreams . . . would they tell him to marry the cold-blooded killer of someone he loved? Revenge against the killer and his family raged in his heart even as a forest fire rages uncontrollably before it crowns. Had he interpreted his dreams incorrectly? But even his body responded positively to her! Was his body betraying him? His heart said no, she could not have been involved in the murder. His head questioned his heart.

The musty smell of moist earth rose about them, as swiftly and silently the warrior, with Shannon close behind, covered the tree and brush lined distance back to where Grey Owl's body had been concealed.

Anxiety flowed through Shannon like poison from a snake bite. She accepted that what she felt for Little Feather was love— at least it fit her father's description of love—but was it reciprocated? Was she about to die at his hands because she had no satisfactory explanation for why the killer of Grey Owl was searching for her? Maybe he cared enough to at least give her a chance to explain. A slight grin curved her shapely lips. He did enjoy holding her—every morning she awoke snuggled close to his chest, his arms embracing her tightly. But could she trust him with her deepest, darkest secret? The hundred muskets?

She had to decide what she could trust him with because soon he was going to question her concerning what she knew about Grey Owl's killer—at least she hoped he would give her the opportunity to explain. But what *could* she tell him? She didn't know who the killer was. She prayed fervently that it wasn't Shamus. He simply could not have changed that much in a year. Could he?

The journey back through the forest only took a short time before they were standing over Grey Owl's remains.

The expression of surprise on Little Feather's face was almost laughable. "I'm not going to be able to carry him! I forgot about my bum arm!"

"Let me have your hatchet, and I'll get some poles for a travois.," Shannon offered. At least he hadn't killed her yet. Maybe she would have her chance to explain yet.

Little Feather hesitated, indecision written all over his face. "Maybe we should have that talk first." He hated to think that she might try to harm him. He'd have to take her prisoner then or kill her if she wouldn't allow herself to be captured. Somehow, he anticipated that it would be the latter.

Shannon stomped over to a nearby log and flung herself down, hurt to the core that he could even contemplate that she would deliberately hurt him—and at a time like this, too, with Grey Owl's body just a few feet away. What kind of a person did he think she was that she could do something like that to someone she loved. Just because he didn't know she loved him was no excuse. She had sewed up his beautiful hide for him, hadn't she? She resigned herself ungraciously to the inevitable questions. She would answer honestly but offer no extra information. It never occurred to her that he might think she was in partnership with the killer.

"What do you know about what guides us?"

Shannon stared at him blankly for a moment. "What?" What did this have to do with the redhead who had murdered Grey Owl? Did he have some devious means of trying to trick her into revealing something she didn't know anyway? "I haven't the foggiest notion what you're talking about. I anticipated that you were going to ask if I had any idea who the redhead who killed Grey Owl might be." She decided that getting right to the point might be the best strategy.

A rustling in the brush drew her attention, and she watched a rabbit scurry away.

"All in good time. You visited our village a number of times with the Frenchmen. What did you observe while you were there?"

A ghost of a smile shadowed her lips. "That Iron Fist is a shrewd bargainer. Very few things can be hurried. A lot of ritual . . ."

"But nothing about our dreams?"

"That they're important to you. Why?"

Little Feather sat on the log beside her, contemplating how to explain his dreams and what they revealed to him. He realized he was taking a terrible chance. What if he had misinterpreted them? But telling her what he thought might induce her to trust him with the truth about herself, and if she had any idea who had killed Grey Owl, she might tell him that also.

"Within each of us is an inner self who is in touch with the future, the past, our desires and things we need or should avoid." He glanced at Shannon to determine if she understood him. Most Europeans were blocked from understanding dreaming by their prejudices.

She was listening avidly to his explanation. She nodded her head, indicating that he should continue.

"If we do not follow the guidance revealed by our inner selves through dreams, illnesses—mental and physical—occur to the individual and to the community. Do you understand what I'm saying?"

"I think so." Shannon had no idea why he was telling her about dreams, but if it kept him from the subject of redheads a little longer, that was okay with her—she had changed her mind about a direct confrontation. And what he was saying was fascinating.

"They tell us whether or not to go hunting and what will be willing to give its life to us. Our dreams tell us whether or not to go on raids. Often we have dreams that tell us who to marry . . ."

"Marry?" she interrupted in surprise.

He let her digest that information for a few moments before he continued. "Four nights in a row I saw you kill a bear. Your were dressed in buckskins, carried a flintlock and a knife on your hip. Your hair was flaming red without that ugly dye . . . I didn't know you would be saving our lives."

Shannon was shocked! "You saw me in dreams? Before we met?" A thrill trickled down her spine. As an after thought, she protested, "I didn't really save your life. Tall Tree and the twins, and Red Fox, too, would have taken down that bear!"

"Maybe, but I don't think so."

Shannon brought him back to the subject that interested her the most at the moment. "And your dreams?"

Little Feather glanced at her with a grin that was almost shy. "Since you burst into my life, you have been in every dream!"

"Good or bad?"

"Oh, definitely good!"

Now she understood why he was telling her about his dreams, and she knew what was coming. But he hadn't said anything about love! She wanted to cry. She wanted to stop his next words.

"I believe the dreams are telling me that you're meant to be my wife!"

Shannon stared at him, but suddenly turned inward as disrupted images passed before her mind. She was struggling to get to Little Feather. She was struggling, crying and her heart was breaking. All because she loved him so!

Her love shone from her eyes as she said slowly, "I . . . dreamed of you." Her thoughts turned inward, remembering. "But I couldn't . . . reach you . . ." Tears started trickling down her face as she relived her dream. "A gigantic serpent, with a red head and red and green stripped body, was rising over you, and it was going to eat you! I screamed and screamed, but you couldn't hear me, and I couldn't get to you! I was struggling through thick mud and terrible briars!"

Little Feather took her into his arms and comforted her even as he had during the night of the dream. "Ian . . ."

"My name is Shannon. But I'd prefer you to continue to call me Ian for now."

He liked the sound of her name. "Thank you. It's because of the serpent, isn't it? You do realize don't you that the serpent is probably linked to the redhead who killed Grey Owl and is looking for you. Have you dreamed of it before?"

"Many times since . . ." Distress and tragic memories filled her eyes with tears anew.

Abruptly changing his line of questioning, he asked."What do you know about the man who is seeking you?"

"That he's a redhead." The serpent in her dreams had *always* had a red head.

"How many red-headed men do you know?"

"Just about everybody in my immediate family was a redhead. Most of them are dead now. Of course, I have cousins, aunts . . ." her words became slower and faded as her thoughts ran down other paths . . . "and . . . uncles who are redheads." No, they wouldn't do that, she thought. They wouldn't have been responsible for betraying her father and causing his death. Her uncle had never shown any desire to be the O'MaGuire . . . but his three sons had, and they were all redheads!

"Your thoughts suddenly wandered away. What has been revealed to you?"

"What I should have seen long ago," she said on a sigh. "The serpent in my dreams always has a red head. It's always pursuing me with deadly intent, and I'm always fleeing for my life—until recently. In my most recent dream, it was after you.

But there were a couple of dreams in which a giant grizzly intervened on my behalf, before the serpent went after you!"

Shannon gazed up into the warrior's dark eyes. His arms still held her close, comforting her. "Oh, Little Feather, I wondered if the grizzly was you! Now the traitor is going to be after you!"

Her flow of words stopped as she remembered her dreams and her new knowledge. She enjoyed the pleasant, secure feeling of his arms about her. If only he loved her. Pushing that errant thought away, she wailed, "Oh, Little Feather, I think one of my cousins may have killed Grey Owl!"

"But why would they do that? Why are they searching for you?"

The hundred musket rewards! Now it made sense! Conal had put the reward on them to find them. She wasn't important to Conal except to get to Shamus. His younger brothers, Brian and or Kevin was in the colonies looking for them. Conal would never have risked his position as the O'MaGuire to come to the colonies!

"I don't know why they killed Grey Owl, except they're a bloody bunch of bastards who were also responsible for my father's and brother's deaths. The only reason I can think of for them to be looking for me is to get to my older brother, Shamus." As she spoke the words, Shannon knew with a certainty that her cousin's had caused the deaths of her beloved Da and her brother Paddy, and they were now hunting for Shamus to kill him.

"Why would they want him?"

"My brother, if he ever returns to Ireland, will be embraced into the heart of the clan as its leader. The O'MaGuire. He is loved by everyone!" she answered proudly. "My cousin Conal's position as head of the clan will never be secure as long as my brother lives!"

On impulse she blurted out, "Conal has put a reward on each of our heads for one hundred muskets!"

Little Feather was stunned. A hundred muskets! That was unheard of for anyone! His arms tightened around his woman. "So that is the reason for the disguise!" His heart swelled with pride and love. She had truly trusted him with her life!

"Yes!"

"This 'head of the clan' position must be much coveted!"

"It is."

Now it was more important than ever to maintain her disguise. Every warrior in his village would be willing to turn her in for a reward like that! Except him. But there must be a way to get those muskets without giving up his woman or her brother.

"C'mon, Ian. We've got a travois to make."

Standing, he pulled her to her feet, and before she realized his intention, he pulled her into his arms and gave her a passionate kiss. Then he handed her his tomahawk and sent her off to collect the necessary wood for the travois.

Chapter 16

An eerie stillness hung over the village as Little Feather and Shannon passed through the narrow stockade entrance A few young children played quietly about the long houses, and the ubiquitous village dogs had slunk away into the shadows.

Little Feather, with Shannon beside him, hauled the travois to the rear entrance of the house of the dead backing the stockade wall.

After depositing the body, Little Feather and Shannon went to Makes-good-moccasins long house to inform them that they had returned with Grey Owl's remains and to offer their condolences.

"Thank you, nephew, for bringing my husband back to the village." Makes-good-moccasins was slumped on the low platform at her fireside that she and Grey Owl had shared for years, tears streaming down her pale, gaunt face. Death and mourning, a heavy, suffocating cloak, hung over the long house, smothering all joy.

Grey Turtle accompanied Little Feather and Shannon out of the long house. Leaning against the stockade wall, he stared up at the roof of the building with unseeing eyes.

"He gave us our first bows. Uncle was planning to give them to us during our fifth summer, but Father gave them to us in the spring of that year."

"He always did think the sun rose and set in the two of you . . . never could figure out why!" Only a ghost of a grin touched Little Feather's lips.

"I never could understand why he liked you either. You caused him nearly as much trouble as we did!" Grey Turtle's eyes shifted from the roof to his cousin.

"If I remember correctly we were usually together in those pranks, along with Tall Tree." Little Feather was silent for a long moment, listening to the breeze rustling through the branches of the tree growing inside the stockade wall. "How is White Feather?"

Shannon studied Little Feather during the exchange. He appeared nearly as gaunt and stricken as Grey Turtle. His eyes were dark and hard with a haunted look she understood. The lines of his face were angular and hard. The softness that had been present by the river when he had laughed at her was gone. Her heart ached for this man who was hers, but at least he knew she was there for him if he needed her. Desperately, she wished she knew if he loved her, if he would be there for her. A dream telling him to marry her—no matter how wonderful the dream— wasn't the same as his heart telling him to marry her. Maybe it was normal for these people to marry without love, in the hopes or expectations that it would develop, but it wasn't for her. She just wished she knew. Her wandering thoughts were brought back by a heart-felt sigh from Grey Turtle.

"He lapsed into unconsciousness before we got back to the village. We asked the False Faces to come do a ceremony for him. They just left a little while ago." The young man—his face grey and haggard under the bronze—turned to Shannon. "Mother would like you to care for White Feather, if you would."

"Of course. May I see . . . him now, or would . . . that be inappropriate?" Shannon asked slowly, her words more fluid than five days earlier.

"If you can save his life, then anytime is appropriate!"

"And if I can't?"

Grey Turtle shrugged his broad shoulders. "His life is in the hands of the Great Spirit even now . . . but maybe you can lend . . . a little of your considerable skill!"

They followed Grey Turtle back into and through the long house to the fireside the twins shared. Crying, screaming and wailing going up and down the scale from very high pitched to very low could be heard emitting from all the firesides. Other villagers were quietly coming and going, bringing words of condolence accompanied by gifts of food, beads or metal items, bringing their valuable possessions in an effort to assuage the terrible grief that raged rampant throughout the long house. This was Grey Owl's wife's clan, and they grieved with her for her terrible loss.

Shannon knew that in some distant village, Grey Owl's mother, grandmother—if she still lived—aunts and all his sisters and their children were destined to experience the same horrible grief when they discovered the horrendous tragedy And elsewhere his brothers would join with other friends and relatives and grieve the loss of a much beloved sachem. The League of the Iroquois, itself, would mourn the murder of one of its sachems, and the consequences . . . she couldn't even fathom the consequences! This much she had learned on her visits to Iroquois villages with Jacques and Pierre—by listening.

Shannon had a stalwart heart, but she trembled now at the thought of anyone uncovering the reward that was on her head. Next to that thought, the thought of their linking her to the murderer sent adrenalin raging through her arteries. Could Little Feather protect her? *Would* Little Feather protect her?

White Feather was still unconscious, but now he burned with fever, and the arrow still needed to be removed. It was probably as much a source of the fever as the scalping, and she informed Little Feather and Grey Turtle of that fact.

Warriors with an arrow that penetrated their torsos often bled to death after it was removed, or died from fever.

"First, I need hot water, lots of moss . . . scraps of deer hide . . . some strips of deer hide or something to tie with," Shannon requested slowly, reviewing quickly what she would need. "Oh, and some more knitbone . . . Check with all healers in . . . village."

Grey Turtle left immediately to locate the supplies she needed.

"And some whiskey!" she yelled after his receding form.

"Do you think you can save him?" Little Feather asked, standing staring down at his cousin and friend.

"I'm going to do my best." She looked about the fireside, searching for a kettle to heat water and a dipper to fill the kettle from a bucket of water by the door. Soon water was over the fire heating. The kettle was too big in which to mix the herbs, so she continued hunting for a bowl. Finally, she found one—needing to be washed—under the sleeping platform.

"Men!" she muttered, taking some water from the kettle and cleaning out the wooden bowl.

"Did you need something else?" Little Feather asked distractedly as he continued to watch his cousin. He couldn't imagine life without the volatile, light-hearted White Feather. As he watched his cousin struggle for life, frustrated rage stormed within him. Whatever White Feather's clan decided they wanted, he would personally exact revenge from the people who did this!

"No, but shortly after Grey Turtle gets back, we'll be ready to remove that arrow."

Both men, having removed arrows before, knew what needed to be done.

"You know, cousin, you don't need to help," Little Feather suggested, offering to relieve Grey Turtle of the grisly task ahead of them.

Grey Turtle gave him a look that clearly said, try and stop me!

Little Feather shrugged his shoulders in acknowledgment of his cousin's decision.

When Shannon had the knitbone solution, the whiskey and the moss pads ready for use, she nodded her head for the men to proceed.

Together they rolled White Feather to a sitting position. The man groaned, and his head fell forward.

Grey Turtle muttered, "Sorry, brother!" With his hand holding a piece of hide against the arrow shaft protruding from his brother's back, he nodded to Little Feather.

Little Feather, grasping the shaft in front of the tip, pulled violently as Grey Turtle shoved.

"Aaaaiiiieeeee . . . ." White Feather's head jerked up as he screamed.

The arrow passed through his body leaving blood and puss spurting everywhere.

Shannon let the mixture flow for a few moments until the drainage was only blood. Then she slapped a pad of moss onto White Feather's back, ordering, "Hold that while you ease him back onto the bed! Keep your hand there pressing upward for now!"

Grey Turtle followed her directions explicitly, and if he noticed that her use of their language was instantaneous and efficient, he didn't show it.

After settling him to his back, Shannon worked quickly on the wound in the front of his shoulder. The initial spurt of blood lessened to a steady flow. Soaking up the blood with a pad of moss, she saw enough of the hole to pour whiskey into it. White Feather groaned. Soaking up more blood, she poured more whiskey into the hole. Repeating the process several more times, she finally poured the knitbone solution into the hole, praying the wound was clean enough that it wouldn't become poisoned, and the knitbone would stop the bleeding. She put several layers of hide over the wound and had the men turn him over with Little Feather holding the pad tightly to White Feather's shoulder.

The whole process was repeated on his back. The pads were tied tightly in place with strips of hide wrapped over and under his arm and around his chest.

Checking the bullet wound she had dressed earlier, she found it appeared clean, with no sign of poisoning.

"That's all I can do for him now, Grey Turtle, but here is some willow bark. I'm sure your mother or grandmother has some when this is gone. Put this much," she handed him a couple of pieces, "into a bowl of boiling water. Let it cool with the bark in it and give it to him to drink several times a day." She knew he wouldn't let anyone else take care of White Feather. "We'll be back later on to see how he's doing. See if you can get the False Faces in again."

"I will do that. Thank you, Ian, for all you have done for him." He gazed at her strangely, but said nothing about what he was thinking.

Shannon didn't realize that she had completely dropped her disguise as Ian from her speech and behavior.

Little Feather and Shannon left the smoky dimness of the long house and walked out into the chill, fresh air of evening. The sun was setting in the west, and the moon was becoming visible overhead in a cloudless sky.

"Brrrrr!" Shannon shivered and wrapped her arms about herself.

Dusk was settling over the land, and more people were moving about the village, carrying their gifts to the mourners

Shannon wondered how to broach the problem of needing to answer nature's call. The thought had no sooner passed through her mind when Little Feather spoke. He must have been reading her mind!

"Let's go collect a couple of blankets. I need to take a walk, and I imagine you do, too, after such a long time," Little Feather suggested, trying to allay any embarrassment his woman might feel with such a personal task. Whites had strange ideas about the most natural things they all shared.

"I was thinking along those same lines, and a blanket would feel good about my shoulders!"

In companionable silence they ambled through the village to their long house and collected a couple of blankets to use against the evening chill. Then they strolled through the entrance of the stockade. After attending their individual needs, Little Feather found a log and sat down, Shannon sitting beside him.

Little Feather sat, leaning forward with his forearms resting on his powerful legs and his hands clasped between his knees. The woman sitting next to him, whom he had considered to be his almost from the moment he had met her, he now thought of as his wife. Shannon . . . he liked the sound of it. Although the traditional exchange of gifts had not yet occurred, it would when she understood more about their customs and could give up her ridiculous disguise. But the exchange of dreams linked them irrevocably. Everything else would resolve itself in the proper time . . . with a little help!

"What happens now?" Shannon asked.

"About what?"

"Grey Owl's funeral. What can I expect? In the eyes of your clan and village, you appear to have made yourself responsible for me. I wouldn't want to cause you or myself any embarrassment."

He turned his dark eyes, glittering strangely, on her. "You *are* my responsibility!"

Shannon liked his protection but bristled at his possessiveness. She refrained from commenting.

"The funeral?" she brought his thoughts back to her question.

"A delegation of Younger Brothers will be here probably tomorrow, possibly the day after. They will make all funeral arrangements and bury Grey Owl. Long ago Grey Owl got permission to be buried in the Bear Clan burial ground, wanted to be near Makes-good-moccasins." He gazed at her with a slight grin. "They loved each other very much."

"My parents did, too." She was silent, reminiscing about the things her father had told her. She couldn't remember her mother. "What will happen tomorrow?"

"It will be similar to this afternoon. More gifts and words of condolences, efforts to help the family work through their grief. Villagers will eat together and talk about Grey Owl. He was much loved in our village by everyone—from the youngest to the oldest. Something scurried through the debris on the ground, attracting Shannon's attention, but it was too dark to see anything. In the distance, past the clearing that surrounded the town, the stockade wall formed dark, soft shadows. The waning moon, still nearly full, was glowing brightly over the village, casting its silvery light upon everything. Shannon pulled her blanket more tightly about her.

"It was on a night like this that Iron Fist found me," Little Feather spoke so softly that Shannon had to lean close to hear him.

"Near a village like this one." He stopped, remembering. His face filled with a heart-wrenching anguish. "It was ablaze with flames! I was standing on the edge of the clearing. I had just returned from killing my first deer. I'd be able to hunt with the men!" He rose from the log and walked to the edge of the clearing, the memories too painful to be tolerated at rest. "My mother, my little sister, my brother—mostly women and children perished that night. My father was away on a hunting trip with some other men. I don't know whatever happened to him."

"Oh, Little Feather!" Shannon, who had come up to his side, put her arm about his waist. "I'm so sorry! I can't remember my mother, but I was with my father when he died with a bullet hole in his chest."

His arm slipped around her waist as they stood looking towards the village.

"I was about to throw myself at the attackers, both Indians and colonists—there must have been hundreds of them circling the burning stockade—when Iron Fist grabbed me about the waist and pulled me back into the forest. I thought he was one of the attackers and fought like a wild animal!"

His teeth gleamed in the moonlight as he remember the fight. "Thank all of the powers that be that he was bigger and stronger than I—I was big for my age—and he finally subdued me. I was in my twelfth summer then. He brought me back to the village and Bright Flower adopted me into their clan."

Turning with her in his arm, he walked back to the log, regaining his seat.

"The first day I was here, after the gauntlet, the twins and Tall Tree came to introduce themselves to me, and from that moment on we were inseparable." He gazed in Shannon's direction, and she could see his teeth gleaming again. "We were the bane of Grey Owl's life! There was no other man in the village we harassed as much as Grey Owl! Oh, Iron Fist got his share of our rambunctiousness. But there was just something about Grey Owl . . . he was just fun! More often than not when we went hunting small game, he went with us.

He taught us more about hunting and woodcraft than anyone else."

Again he was silent remembering. "I'm going to miss him . . . we all are."

Shannon put her arms about him, placing her face against his shoulder. "I am so sorry!"

His arm slid about her, and he pulled her close. "You are so sweet," he murmured, resting his cheek on the top of her head. He lifted her chin to kiss her lightly on the lips to thank her for her comfort and for being there for him. The kiss that started out as a light kiss of appreciation quickly deepened into something more.

It subtly changed, growing deeper—more demanding. His tongue flicked lightly against her lips, tasting her sweetness. By the spirits, she was sweeter than maple syrup!

His passion, having been kept under tight rein since he had first seen her in his dreams, burst free, washing away his self-restraint and temporarily assuaging his grief.

Sweat beaded on his forehead! If he didn't gain some semblance of control, he would ravish her, and he knew she wouldn't appreciate that! He had to take this slow so as not to scare her to death—innocent that she was. But desire raged through him, wave upon wave crashing over each other.

Shannon was stunned! The touch of Little Feather's tongue against her lips had sent shockwaves of pleasure rippling through her body. Her nipples had hardened against her binder, and that little flame, burning deep in her abdomen flared into a conflagration, threatening to consume her. And all from a kiss!

"Little Feather," she whispered against his firm mouth, "I don't think this is such a good idea!"

He had felt her nipples harden against his chest and thought this was probably a very good idea. She was just confused from the passion she was feeling.

His mouth came down more firmly on hers again, his tongue gently demanding entrance. After a moment, her lips opened to him. Her teeth presented a slight resistance, but then opened willingly.

As his tongue plundered her mouth, her body trembled from the unfamiliar passion. Only the strength of his arms kept her from slipping off the log. Pushing her silly hat from her head, he ruffled her hair with his hand. It felt soft and silky to his touch. It smelled of walnut.

His hands slid down her back.

"Careful with your broken arm!"

She would think of something like that! Little Feather smiled. Her mind wasn't completely on what they were doing, but that was because she didn't know what was coming.

"I will be, my little wife," he murmured, speaking his thoughts aloud unintentionally. He could have kicked himself almost immediately.

Shannon stilled instantly. "Wife?" she asked.

"Shhhhh. Dreams must be obeyed!" he murmured against her lips, holding her close with the arm with the splint and freely roaming his other hand over her body. As he plundered her mouth, his free hand was busy under her shirt trying to remove the damn—her word, which seemed appropriate—binder. His kisses trailed distractingly from her mouth, along her chin, down her throat. His thumb ran over the hardened nipples through the binder.

She was distracted.

Finally, he found where the end of the binder was tucked in and released it. He almost sighed aloud in relief.

Suddenly, Shannonn felt her breasts free, and she could breath more easily . . . for all of a second! His hand gently cupped her breast and rubbed the nipple. She stopped breathing entirely.

His mouth was back on hers, his tongue playing with hers. She had never imagined the waves of pleasure that were rocking her world.

The next thing of which she was aware was that her shirt was moving up and over her head and cold air was caressing her hot skin. Almost instantly a blanket came up over them, and Little Feather was sliding to the ground with her in his arms, his blanket under them.

"Careful of your arm!" she shrieked.

"Hush, wife!" His mouth was back on hers, and the hand that had been caressing her breast was moving down her body to her breeches. That required a little help on her part, but it never occurred to her to object. Soon she was divested of all of her clothes, and his hand was roaming lovingly and gently over her body sending currents of pleasure along all of her nerves.

"Wife, you don't need to clutch me so tightly, and feel free to explore my body, too!"

And Shannon did with great pleasure. But when she came to the freshly healed lacerations, "Little Feather! We don't want to reopen any of these scars, it's only been a few days since I stitched you up!"

Little Feather groaned a little but responded only by placing his fingers on her most private of places and gently started to massage while he suckled at one breast.

Shannon forgot everything but what he was making her feel. "Oh, Little Feather! What's happening to me? I feel so strange." She was wreathing beneath his hand and pushing up against his mouth. "This is awful!" she moaned.

He stopped. "Awful?" Pulling his mouth away from her breast he stared into her passion-filled eyes and grinned.

"Don't stop!" she almost shrieked.

And he resumed his pleasurable activities.

"What's happening to me, Little Feather, my husband?" Her eyes were tightly closed.

He almost stopped again. "It's your woman's body coming alive to me. Open your eyes, wife," he commanded.

Her eyes blinked open.

"Do you enjoy what you see?"

"I can't see much! It's pretty dark!" She was breathing hard.

"Do you like what you see when it's light?" He asked patiently.

She thought of the times she had studied him—and they were numerous. She ran her fingers over the planes of his face, and shoulders and muscular body, bringing to life his image in her mind. "Oh, yes!" she breathed.

His heart skipped a beat. "Then let us enjoy one another, wife."

Her hand slipped up behind his neck and pulled his mouth down to hers. "I'm afraid, Little Feather. I'm afraid of the strength of my feelings. but I don't want to stop. I want you to touch me and love me. I want to touch you, husband." As she said the word, she knew it was true, he was her husband. "I want to go wherever this takes us."

"I'll be as gentle as possible. You'll never regret being mine." His mouth descended on hers, and they became lost in a world that belonged only to them.

His hands caressed her soft curves and elicited unimaginable sensations of pleasure. His mouth left trails of fire on her soft skin.

Neither were her hands idle. They sought out and explored every inch of his powerful frame bringing forth sensations he had never experienced with any other woman.

"Wife, I don't think I can wait much longer!" His cock was hard and throbbing against her thigh.

"Then don't!" she whispered into his ear.

Her body was throbbing beneath his hand, and he knew she was as ready as she would ever be. He rolled over her, balancing his weight on his forearms. He let his cock ride against her natural curve until the tip came into her entrance. Then at the same moment he sucked her tongue into his mouth, he drove home. He felt the resistance give way.

A sharp, burning pain tore through Shannon and forced a scream out before she could control it. Her eyes blinked open and stared into his shadowy face. Perspiration glistened on his forehead in the moonlight.

"If it hurts so much, why do people do it?" she asked through gritted teeth, but strangely enough the pain was already fading. She had been correct. There wasn't any reason do this!

"It only hurts like that the first time, you'll see. The next time will be pleasure only."

"Well, that may be. But I don't think there'll be a next time. Now that we're finished, can we get up and get dressed?"

She was desperately fighting disappointment and tears. She didn't know what she had been anticipating, but this wasn't it.

Little Feather couldn't help smiling. "Well, wife, we aren't exactly finished."

Returning his mouth to hers, he lovingly caressed her lips with his tongue. He didn't seek entrance at the moment, he was afraid she might bite him! He moved his hips until he was nearly out of the warm cocoon of her body. then he rode her curve back into her body.

Her eyes widened in surprise as the pleasure caused by his movements washed over her.

"It's only starting for us, wife."

And they rode together to a place where only lovers can go. Nor was Shannon disappointed.

"Little Feather! Little Feather!" a voice spoke frantically with a touch of humor into his ear as he floated back to earth. "Little Feather, I can hardly breath!" the voice gasped, two hands pushing against his massive chest. He came fully awake instantly and realized he must have collapsed upon her fragile body. He rolled off Shannon who took a deep breath.

"Oh, wife! Are you alright?" His voice was filled with chagrin. "I might . . . have killed you!"

"Oh, Little Feather!" she chuckled. "It wasn't that bad! It was just easier if you got yourself off me, but I would have managed, if you hadn't come to. I'm fine! Oh, husband! Will it always be like that between us?"

"I hope not! Not if I'm going to faint like a woman!" he said in disgust. "And collapse on you! You'd die!" he groaned, lying on his back with one arm thrown over his eyes, the thought of loosing her tearing his guts apart.

"Well, I hope it is like that every time. I'll just have to be on top. If I faint and collapse on you, at least you won't be in danger of suffocating to death!" Lifting his arm Shannon grinned into his eyes as she leaned on his shoulder, idly running her finger along the thin scars on his face.

Hugging her close, he murmured in her ear, "Don't ever tell anyone that I fainted like a woman and collapsed on you! I'd deny it! I'd never live it down!"

"I promise!"

He clutched her tightly to his chest. The thought of losing her brought with it thoughts of Grey Owl. For a few moments, in her arms, he had forgotten everything. He was thankful to her, his wife, for the gift of temporary forgetfulness.

Together they got up and dressed with Little Feather assisting Shannon to replace her binder. He plopped the hat on her head, and they started back to the village, each wondering what tomorrow would bring and when they would find another opportunity to slip away into the forest to enjoy one another.

Chapter 17

Through a cloud of choking dust, Shannon, sweat dripping into her headband, dodged towards the ball and caught it neatly with her net. Swinging her arm from the ground and fighting a powerful urge to sneeze, she gave the ball a mighty throw over her opponent to Little Feather who carried it away in his net towards the goal posts. Shannon sneezed. A player, a stranger to Shannnon, leaped over a fellow player and knocked the ball from Little Feather's net. Running Weasel slipped in between several players and snatched up the ball, tossing it to Tall Tree who quickly lobbed it through the goal posts. Loud cheers went up from the audience on the sides of the field.

Glancing towards the sidelines, Shannon smiled. Grey Turtle sat on a blanket upon which his brother lay, eyes closed, with his face turned in the direction of the game. Grey Turtle's mouth was moving animatedly, and she knew he was describing the game to White Feather. A short distance away Makes-good-moccasins and some other women and children were sitting, watching the lively game avidly. Suddenly, the woman leaped up, shouting and waving her arms. Shannon turned just in time to catch the ball . . . . in her stomach! The pain sent her spiraling into unconsciousness and . . .

Her eyes blinked open. What the . . . ? She was lying on her back with a heavy weight across her stomach and breasts, only her stomach hurt. Their bearskin blanket was pulled over their heads.

Beyond Little Feather, from his place on the platform, Shannon could hear Iron Fist's gentle snores.

Putting her hand on her stomach, she found Little Feather's knee, curled up in front of him and pressing heavily on her abdomen. There would have been no problem if she hadn't been there; unfortunately, she was! If she had been on her side, she could probably have tolerated the weight—thinking about it—she would have enjoyed it! But not on her stomach. That hurt!

The long house was in absolute darkness except for a slight glow from some of the fire pit coals. Shannon couldn't locate the smoke hole in the roof some twenty feet above her head. It was sometime in the late night or early morning hours.

She tried shoving Little Feather's heavy leg off her abdomen. It didn't budge. Great! How was she to wake him without waking Iron Fist or Little Wolf's family—the family who shared the fireside with them.

Several more times, she tried to push his leg off without success. Strange. His leg should have been a little more relaxed since he was sleeping. Sleeping? Taking a couple of deep breaths, she realized she was breathing easier than when she had first awakened. His leg no longer weighed as heavily on her stomach. He was awake! The jerk!

Elbowing him in the ribs, she heard him chuckle softly in her ear. She rolled on to her side and slid her buttocks into the curve of his hips, feeling his cock pressed firmly against her lower back. Her last thought as she slid into a comfortable sleep was that she would have to discuss her dream with him when she awoke in the morning.

Snap! Crackle! Pop!

Shannon came slowly awake. Little Feather lay snuggled up behind her with his arm about her. Could this be seen through the heavy blanket covering them? She fervently hoped not, for his sake as well as hers!

Peeking out from under the corner of the blanket, she watched Snail Girl, Little Wolf's mother, stirring up the coals from last night's fire and adding fresh wood to it. Her movements were quick and efficient and Shannon wondered idly how she had gotten her name.

A pair of legs passed behind Snail Girl and sat on her family's platform.

"Well, husband?" the woman asked softly.

"I gave the knife to Grey Turtle."

"The one in which you carved the wolf? The one you made for Little Wolf?"

"Little Wolf went with me to gift it to Grey Turtle."

"I am sure that helped to cheer him up. How is White Feather?"

"Still unconscious, Grey Turtle says he is not as feverish as before Ian treated him," he paused for a moment. "The knife did cheer him up. He said he would carve up the killers with it!"

The platform Shannon was lying on began to move. Since Little Feather was not stirring—although she didn't think he was sleeping—she knew that Iron Fist was getting up. Shannon realized now that Little Feather enjoyed having his arms around her too much to rouse himself before he absolutely had to.

The sleeping platform dipped slightly under Shannon, and she realized that Iron Fist was sitting at the end.

"May the sun shine brightly upon you, brother," Iron Fist said to White Elk, his brother-in-law.

"The sun would probably shine more brightly on you if you took another wife."

"You know, brother, this subject gets boring after awhile. I really think you're trying to put me out of my own home!"

White Elk burst into deep laughter. "I haven't said a thing about your taking another wife in a . . . oh, handful of days! And when is our good Little Feather going to take a wife? He's *years* past the age for marrying!"

"I guess you'll just have to ask him. I imagine when he finds someone who appeals to him, or a dream tells him to."

The platform rose under Shannon, and she knew that Iron Fist had risen. At the same time a jolt of pleasure zipped along her nerves as Little Feather's fingers moved over her binder, finding the sensitive tips of her breasts. She nearly jumped out of her skin at the unexpectedness of the caress. There was no movement visible through the blanket. His fingers continued exploring her breasts. He was taking the grossest advantage of her! Enough was enough! Scrambling towards the side of the bed, she managed to punch him in the stomach. With satisfaction, she heard his soft muffled, "Umph!"

Finally, extricating herself from the bearskin, Shannon managed to swing her legs over the side of the platform and pull on her floppy hat. Her buckskins were beginning to reek. How was she going to get some clothes to wear while she washed hers? Go swimming in her clothes and wash them? She shivered at the very thought of it!

"There will be some food to eat in a short while," Snail Girl said, busily stirring a kettle that was beginning to steam.

Little Feather slid to the edge of the platform and swung his long muscular legs over the side next to Shannon. He held his arm out for her to examine the splint which had come loose— probably from too much use the night before! She quickly realigned and restrapped it in place.

"We'll eat when we get back. We're going to look in on White Feather before we return." Little Feather explained, standing up and stretching his long, muscular frame.

Many people were now making their way through the cubicle on their way outside on their morning pilgrimage to the forest. Bright Eyes trailing behind her mother was coughing with an early morning dry throat.

Wolf Running entered their fireside from the interior of the long house. His lacerations a much brighter red than Little Feather's but without sign of poisoning. He was well on the road to recovery. In his arms was a heavy bearskin blanket, and he looked directly at Shannon.

"So you are the person I have to thank for saving my life. I don't remember much about that day." He shrugged his shoulders in apology.

"It's just as well that you don't."

"You look awfully young to be so skilled."

"I'm only one of many who worked on you."

His eyebrows rose at her skilled use of their language. He didn't remember much about the kid who had served the Frenchmen, but he recalled thinking how unfortunate that the kid was so slow. He wondered where he came up with that idea, not that it mattered.

"This is a gift for you, little brother, to help you sleep comfortably at night. Now you won't have to rely on that rapscallion sharing his blanket with you.

"It is . . . much . . . appreciated. Bring much . . . warmth . . . this coming cold season, Wolf Runneing . . . brother," Shannon mumbled, hugging the heavy, warm blanket close to herself. It seemed strange to Shannon to call everyone 'brother' or 'uncle', but that seemed to be the custom among these people. She just knew she would eventually call someone 'brother' or 'uncle' inappropriately. "I know . . . it will keep me . . . warm and comfortable . . . on many nights." Shannon glanced quickly and shyly at the warrior.

Wolf Running gave her another intense stare before shrugging his shoulders, turning and disappearing down the central corridor of the long house, again questioning himself on how he had ever concluded that the lad was slow.

Iron Fist was returning as Little Feather and Shannon were leaving. Little Feather gave him a big grin and a wink. Wonderful! thought Iron Fist and grinned back. Then, much to Iron Fist's delight, Ian gave him a cheeky grin and winked at him from under her floppy hat!

Early morning birdsong filled the air, and the night's dew still covered the ground. It wouldn't be long before the sun's warm rays burned away the dew. It was the time of day Shannon most loved, and today was sharper and brighter than most. She felt like shouting and jumping for joy. She didn't, but she felt like it! It must be love! She couldn't get rid of the silly grin concealed beneath her floppy hat.

Later, as Little Feather and Shannon were returning from answering nature's call, Shannon remembered her dream.

"Little Feather, I had a dream last night. It wasn't like the dreams of the serpent. This was like something that could or was happening.

"And?" he asked, glancing at her. He knew there had been no dreams of terror. She hadn't awakened him with the thrashing about that usually accompanied her nightmares. The only time she had awakened was when he had placed his leg on her stomach. It had only taken a few minutes for her to wake up from the unusual weight. A smile crossed his face at the pleasant memory. Life with her was going to be fun.

"We were playing a game of stick-and-ball. You and Tall Tree were playing. Even Running Weasel was playing a sportsman-like game!"

Little Feather stopped and stared at her intently. "Do you remember anything else?"

"Yes, there were lots of people participating, most of them I knew . . . a few I didn't recognize. Everybody was having a great time! Grey Turtle was sitting on a blanket, describing the game to White Feather who was lying on the blanket with his eyes closed. Oh, Little Feather! Makes-good-moccasins was there with some other women, and they seemed to be having a good time! What could it mean? It was so real!"

He turned her to face him and held her by the upper arms. He didn't dare take her into his arms which is what he wanted most desperately to do. They might be seen.

"Ahh . . . my sweet little wife!" He spoke so softly, she had to lean towards him to catch his words. "One day you will understand what dreaming is all about! I need to talk to Iron Fist after we check in on White Feather, but I think your dream is self-explanatory."

Their first stop back in the village was at the Bear Clan long house to tend White Feather.

They found Grey Turtle sitting on the sleeping platform, leaning against an end post, talking to White Feather who lay unconscious and covered with a heavy bearskin blanket. He was telling a lively version of the Creation Story with the beautiful Sky Woman's fall to Earth. A sheepish expression passed over his face when his cousin and Ian entered his fireside.

"Hello, cousin. I didn't realize how much I relied on the conversations my brother and I had—good, bad or indifferent. I just feel like I need to talk to him. I've been up all night talking about everything that came to mind." His face was haggard, with dark circles underscoring his eyes. He looked terrible!

Since no one had taken time to stir up the coals in his fire pit or to start a new day's fire, a chill permeated the fireside. Within a few minutes, Shannon had a cherry fire blazing merrily while the men conversed.

"That's woman's work!" Grey Turtle objected. Little Feather hadn't noticed her activities.

"Where I come from when one is cold they build a fire, doesn't matter whether it's a man or woman, and I'm going to need hot water to tend his wounds."

"Sorry, I'm just not thinking this morning." Grey Turtle apologized.

"Why . . . don't you rest . . . for while. I'll sit . . . with White Feather . . . after I finish tending his wounds," Shannon suggested. Then turning to Little Feather, she said, "Why not . . . go talk . . . Iron Fist? I'll be along . . . later."

By the time, she had finished speaking, Grey Turtle had already slid down on the bed and was sound asleep. "Better wait a minute!" She smiled at Little Feather. "I may need your help to move White Feather around!"

With Little Feather's help she cleansed and dressed all of White Feather's wounds. So far there did not appear to be any sign of poison forming. She had been puzzled by his prolonged unconsciousness until she found the bump on the side of his head. Then she remembered him telling Grey Turtle about hitting his head when he fell. Head injuries were unpredictable. It didn't seem to be a big bump, so hopefully White Feather would be regaining consciousness soon.

Little Feather left as soon as they were finished, and Shannon settled herself comfortably on the mat on the sleeping platform. Leaning back against a post, she began talking to White Feather.

Over the next couple of hours, she talked about her home in Ireland,and her family—mostly dead now. She talked about the mighty Cuchulain, legendary hero of Ireland. Stories of Cuchulain had been the bedtime stories her grandmother and later her father had told her. And she talked about her love for Little Feather— all in Gaelic.

As she talked, Shannon was unaware of the people who came to the corridor opening to the twins fireside to listen to Ian talking. Although they didn't understand what was being said, they enjoyed the sound. It was musical—pleasant to the ear and soothing. Everyone who heard Shannon speaking, came to realize it was nothing more than a foreign language, and wondered why he or she had once thought it the gibberish of a mentally-impaired person. They could only shake their heads in puzzlement.

The False Faces entered the fireside at White Feather's mother's request, so Shannon . . . wandered outside.

A group of strangers were entering village, maybe thirty men and women. They were carrying baskets and a variety of containers, and appeared to be dressed in their best finery. Their tunics, skirts, kilts, leggings—even their tobacco pouches were heavily decorated with the finest embroidery.

Little Feather came up behind her as she stood staring.

"Who are they?" Shannon asked, mouth hanging open, awestruck.

Smiling at her expression, he explained, "They're our Younger Brothers come from west of the Kanien'kahaka. They are here to make all funeral arrangements for Grey Owl and to bury him. That relieves his clan, his wife's clan and anyone grieving from the responsibility of tending to such a stressful responsibility. That is our way."

After watching for a few minutes they returned to Grey Turtle's long house, but a man stood outside to turn away anyone from entering. The False Faces were still within.

"That's okay. I need to go visit a bush," she said, smiling at Little Feather. "And I haven't eaten yet!"

"What!" Little Feather exclaimed, shocked. "Someone should have brought you food!"

"It's okay. They probably thought I had already eaten, and I spent the morning talking to White Feather."

They were on their way out of the stockade when her stomach started growling.

"We'll hurry!" Little Feather laughed.

Later, while Shannon was eating a bowl of delicious stew—at that point any stew would have been delicious—and a piece of cornbread, she asked, "What did Iron Fist say about my dream?"

"What I had already suspected. That we need to organize a healing game of stick-and-ball."

"A healing game?"

"To restore their hearts, their thoughts . . . their lives back to normal. To restore White Feather to health. Iron Fist has already gone to our village chief to discuss it, but you weren't the only one to have such a dream. Little Wolf had one, too!"

After Shannon finished with her meal, they started back to determine if the False Faces had left White Feather's yet.

"Oh . . . Ian . . . that bearskin Wolf Running gifted you with, we'll use it under us when we go a pleasuring!"

She blushed beautifully.

"Ian! Little Feather!"

They stopped and waited for Red Fox and Little Wolf to catch up with them.

"Have you heard?" Red Fox asked breathlessly. "A healing stick-and-ball game is being organized! Little Wolf dreamed about it! Grey Turtle was out a little while ago, and he dreamed of a game also, and I heard Uncle say that someone else described the same dream, too!" Red Fox bounced around in his excitement like a bird a-courting.

"Ian was the third person to have the dream," Little Feather informed his young brothers.

A couple of hours later, after the Younger Brothers had performed the Condolence Ceremony for Makes-Good-Moccasins and all the mourners in her long house, the stick-and-ball game commenced.

About half the Younger Brothers played while the rest prepared Grey Owl for burial. Many women came and went from the sidelines as they prepared food for everyone to share after the game.

Grey Turtle and his brother were on the blanket as Shannon had visualized, with Grey Turtle describing the game to the unconscious White Feather. Makes-Good-Moccasins and some other women were near the blanket, and the game went surprisingly as Shannon had dreamed it, except she kept her eyes on the ball and suffered no mishaps.

Somewhere towards the end of the game, shouting, screaming and crying drew the attention of the participants. White Feather's eyes were open!

The game broke up as the players went to share the clan's joy even as they would share in the deep sorrow that would follow the burial.

During the game other strangers had arrived and joined Makes-Good-Moccasins and her clan.

"Who are the newcomers?" Shannon asked Little Feather as they strolled back to their long house.

"That's Grey Owl's clan—brothers, sisters, his mother and her sister—most of his clan."

Shannon nodded her head in understanding."I need to go back and check on White Feather—make sure he's okay. Will it be inappropriate for me to be there?"

"No, you'll be welcome," Little Feather responded without hesitation.

"I'll be along in a while. I have gifts for the twins. You might want to give something to Makes-good-moccasins."

"I have nothing to give anyone. I have only the clothes on my back, and even they are in dire need of a good scrubbing!" Shannon wrinkled her nose in distaste.

"Yeah, we do need to do something about your clothes, but in the meantime you have the elk skin that is rolled up in the storage area at the end of our sleeping platform."

"That would make an appropriate gift?"

"Very appropriate. It is customary to say words of condolence when giving the gift. Something like, 'I give you this gift that it may wash away your tears that you may once again see clearly."

"How beautiful!"

When they arrived back at their fireside, Shannon immediately retrieved the rolled-up skin and left again. Little Feather shoved things around on the ledge above the sleeping platform until he found what he was searching for—two long hickory sticks that had been aging for the past two winters. Taking the two sticks, he left the long house and found his favorite stump, upon which to sit, near the door.

Shannon, after feeling utter frustration and helplessness at not being able to do anything to help relieve Makes-Good-Moccasins grief, was thrilled that she finally had something she could offer to the woman, something that was her own.

"Ian!"

Shannon stopped and gazed about. Tall Tree was waving his arm and striding towards her, carrying a large bearskin over his shoulder.

"Hello, Tall Tree. I have a gift to give Makes-good-moccasins. Little Feather told me what words to say when I give it to her!"

Tall Tree smiled at the obvious joy that Little Feather's woman was experiencing at being able to give something to the grieving woman. She would fit in well with their people.

"I want to express my regret for the ah . . ." he hated the word 'trick'—that wasn't what they had intended, " . . . incident when we were hunting. Little Feather didn't reveal your secret to me. He did tell me that his dreams indicated he would marry a flame-haired woman, and he admitted he had already met her, but he wouldn't tell me anymore than that."

Shannon stopped walking and watched Little Feather working on the hickory sticks as she absorbed Tall Tree's every word. He had told Tall Tree he was going to marry? Contentment filled her. "Okay. How did you decide his dream woman and I were one and the same?"

"Remember when you were running in front of me, and your hat got snagged?"

After thinking for a moment, she nodded her head, knowing where he was going with his explanation, and regretting thinking the worst of Little Feather . . . her husband, although he hadn't been at that time . . . well, maybe he had been.

As she studied Little Feather and listened to Tall Tree's explanation, Wild Rose approached Little Feather with something in her hands. Shannon couldn't tell what it was, but jealousy rose in her like sap in a tree!

"You moved through some sunlight, and I saw strands of hair that flamed in the light. It wasn't too difficult to put his description and your red hair together and know you were the woman he was talking about."

"What is that hussy doing with my . . . ah . . . Little Feather?"

Tall Tree grinned at her slip, wondering what she had been about to say, and gazed towards his friend. Wild Rose! She wouldn't be so bold as to approach Little Feather at a time when the village was mourning the loss of a beloved chief, would she? And so bold as to bring him a betrothal gift without first having her mother verify with Little Feather's mother that it was acceptable to him? Not even Wild Rose could be that brazen!

They watched as Wild Rose placed the basket at Little Feather's feet and turned to walk away.

"She just asked him to be her husband."

"What?" Shannon shrieked.

"Shhhh . . . you don't want to attract attention to your feelings for him, do you? It would be rather awkward, don't you think?" He was grinning at her. He couldn't help himself. He was enjoying his friend's dilemma so much! "But usually the mothers of the prospective couple verify that the union is agreeable to both parties. It appears that Wild Rose has initiated this action on her own. I know of no conversation between their mothers."

"Well, he damn well better say no!" she muttered vehemently.

As they continued to watch, Little Feather, picking up the basket, stood up and called to Wild Rose. He spoke to her, and then they started walking towards Tall Tree and Shannon.

As they waited for the two to catch up with them, Tall Tree

assured Shannon, "Your secret is as safe with me as it is with Little Feather. He's my best friend, closer than a brother, and I would never betray him nor she who is dearest to him."

As Little Feather and Wild Rose reached them, Little Feather explained, "Wild Rose, mindful of my feelings for Grey Owl, thought to cheer me up. I suggested she take her gift to Makes-Good-Moccasin's long house as there are many people there who need the cheering up more than I do." He stared pointedly at Shannon who tipped her head to hide the blush that rose into her face.

Wild Rose, obviously unhappy with the change in her plans, sulked, but accompanied Tall Tree and Shannon to present her gift to the grieving family.

So, Shannon thought, the giving of a gift by a woman was a proposal of marriage. She glanced into the basket Wild Rose carried . . . cornbread! Shannon had no idea how to make cornbread! She wondered if it had to be edible.

Shannon's gift and words of condolence were received with gratitude and pleasure along with a trickle of other gifts that were being presented in a steady flow. After giving the rolled up elk skin to White Feather's mother, Shannon went to check on her patient.

White Feather was propped up on furs talking with Tall Tree who had just presented him with the bearskin when Shannon arrived.

"I was just leaving. I need to talk to Little Feather. We are going to need to find their trail before it gets any older."

"Ian, will you stay with my brother while I'm gone," Grey Turtle requested of Shannon. "Don't let him do anything foolish—like chasing all the girls in the village!"

"When he's capable of chasing the girls, I won't be able to stop him!"

"Come and get me when you and Little Feather are leaving," Grey Turtle addressed Tall Tree.

"We won't be leaving 'till after the burial, probably not until morning."

Little Feather was going to be leaving in the morning? A tremendous disappointment washed over Shannon. She had realized that he was going to track Grey Owl's killers, but she had been expecting to go with him. Now that would be impossible, having to stay here with White Feather.

Makes-Good-Moccasins, on the arms on two strangers and with several women, staggered through the fireside, softly sobbing.

"The dressings can wait," she said, and stepped out of the way, as White Feather swung his long legs off the sleeping platform.

Grey Turtle assisted his brother to a standing position. White Feather swayed and Shannon caught him on the other side. Together, she and Grey Turtle supported White Feather, and they followed the other mourners out of the long house and joined others going to the Bear Clan burial grounds.

Little Feather met them on the way and took her place supporting White Feather.

Some of Grey Owl's bones had been broken to place him in the traditional sitting position. By him in the hole were placed his favorite moccasins and tobacco pouch, a woman from his clan placed a bowl of oil by him, and several other gifts were placed in the hole with him. Sobbing—loud and soft-screams and wails rose about Shannon on all sides, and she could hear the deeper angry voices of men as they promised Grey Owl they would exact revenge for his murder.

Later that night, lying close in Little Feather's arms—they had placed her new bearskin blanket over both of them—she reminisced over the day just past and thought of the day to come . . . and worried about Little Feather. He was going after the killers and could be killed himself. And she worried about Shamus. Was he already dead in this wild land at the hands of his own relatives? No, she answered herself. If he were dead at their hands, they wouldn't be hunting her. So thinking, she sank into a restless sleep.

Chapter 18

The path up the mountain was twisted and torturous, bordered by steep cliffs. It slithered around monstrous boulders and under rocky ledges.

Shannon stood at the bottom of the mountain, straining to catch sight of Little Feather as he struggled his way up the steep inclines and winding trails. In and out between her legs and over her feet, strutted, rubbed and purred a big black cat. "Go away, kitty. Go away, kitty!" she repeated several times, shoving the pesky animal away.

She gazed up the mountain trail again to see how far Little Feather had progressed He was only a tiny figure in the distance, but the glint of sunlight reflected off his gun. A rock or pebble or something rolled under his foot causing him to slide towards the rocky cliff.

Slapping her hand over her mouth, she gasped. Her heart stopped from fear momentarily and then raced as adrenaline pumped through her veins, but there was no way she could help him. This was his struggle.

The damn cat rubbed up against her legs again, purring contentedly. Again she pushed it away.

As she stared at Little Feather, the mountain began to tremble!

"Little Feather! Little Feather!" she screamed, but he was too far distant to hear her words of warning.

As the mountain continued to shake, Little Feather grabbed onto a stunted tree! Above him, the serpent, head weaving back and forth, giant mouth gaping and emitting a horrible roar, rose up from the peak! She screamed and screamed!

Little by little, the mountain with its rocky, winding trail vanished as lumbering, grey cloud masses rolled in. As she strained to see through the cloud cover, she thought she saw Little Feather change into a giant grizzly! But she couldn't be sure. The last glimpse she caught, from where she had last seen Little Feather, was a blinding flash as a stray sunbeam ricochet off his gun.

Tears streamed down her face, as she sank to her knees. The cat purred into her ear . . . and purred . . . and purred . . .

"Shhhh . . . shhhhh . . ."rumbled softly into her ear. "You're okay, Ian. Shhhh . . . . wake up, Ian. Everything's okay. Shhhhh."

Shannon's eyes snapped open. Orientation took a few seconds longer. Stale smoke permeated the fireside. Somewhere down the long house she heard Bright Eyes crying fretfully, and another child whimpering. Little Feather's arms were wrapped tightly around her.

"I'm awake," she whispered over her shoulder to Little Feather. "It was awful!"

She snuggled back against him. "It was awful!" she repeated.

Her heart raced against his hand over her breasts.

"C'mon," he whispered into her ear. "Let's go out. I need to know what you just dreamed, before we go tracking Grey Owl's killers."

Silently, they collected their bearskin blankets against the night chill and left the long house, stepping out into the pale silvery light of the moon and dark shadows that were the village at night. An owl hooted in the distance on its nightly forage for food. Stars twinkled against the velvety backdrop of the infinite sky while large clouds moved slowly at random.

Grey was crawling up the eastern sky as they wrapped their blankets tightly about themselves against the early morning chill and strolled across the silent village. Wandering through the clearing that surrounded the stockade, they found a couple of stumps upon which to sit and talk.

"Pretty bad, huh?"

"Ah . . . very bad. But they're always bad when I dream about the serpent," and she proceeded to recount her dream.

Little Feather sat in silence so long, pondering her words, that Shannon wondered if he had gone to sleep. Finally, he asked, "You didn't see me die?"

She gazed up into his much loved face. "I never see you die. I've never seen the serpent win, but I've never seen it loose either. Do you have to go Little Feather? Can't other's go? I know the men who did this terrible deed have to be caught . . . stopped. But you're the only one I ever see in danger!"

"Maybe that's because you have feelings for me . . . Shannon . . . my wife." The words rolled smoothly and sweetly off his tongue. He put his arm about her shoulder, pulling his own blanket over hers. "And you're in danger, too, wife, as long as your cousin is looking for you and has that reward on your pretty head."

"I know, Little Feather, my husband," the last words were whispered as she leaned her head on his shoulder. "I just don't want you to go. What about your arm? You still can't use your bow."

"I can use my gun . . . I can use my tomahawk . . . I could beat them to death with a tree branch if I had to!" He hugged her more closely to himself. "Don't worry, I'll be fine! Besides, Tall Tree and Grey Turtle are going with me. If we think we can't defeat them, we'll come back and get help."

"I just don't want you to go . . . Oh, I know you have to, but I don't have to like it," she sobbed quietly.

He turned her face up to his and kissed her gently on the lips. The passion that burned so close to the surface between them roared out of control.

Little Feather was the first to break the kiss.

"Whew!" was all Shannon could manage to say.

Little Feather grinned, feeling much the same. "I need to discuss your dream with Iron Fist before we leave, but he won't be up for a little while." He paused, then whispered in her ear. "I can think of nothing nicer than a little pleasuring to spend the time. What say you, Shannon—my wife?"

"Why not? It could be the last time!" she couldn't help grumbling, even as she anticipated the pleasure they would share.

He chuckled. "I assure you, my prickly little wife, it won't be the last time!"

Going farther into the cover of the trees, Little Feather turned Shannon into his arms, keeping his blanket about her, and brought his mouth down upon hers. His tongue caressed her lips with an urgency that she shared. Her lips opened willingly to him.

While Little Feather had her attention focused on his mouth, his hands were trailing over her back under her shirt, after the elusive binder end! It wasn't in the same spot as before!

She giggled! She actually giggled at him who couldn't tolerate giggling!

"Would you like a little help?" she asked into his mouth.

"No! I'll find it myself! I won't be defeated by a piece of cloth!" And true to his word, he found the end and quickly had her breasts free for his exploration.

They lost her blanket in the process.

Her arms slithered up and around his neck, and she murmured into his mouth, lovingly, "We're going to freeze!"

"Problems! Nothing but problems!" he muttered, letting go of her long enough to spread one blanket, pull her down, and cover them both. "Is that better?"

"Much!" she chuckled.

He resumed kissing and exploring her body, skillfully managing to remove her shirt and breeches while she dealt efficiently with his breechclout. Little Feather played her body like a master violinist, bringing her body alive with his touch.

Slowly, her hands roamed over his back, acquainting themselves with the satiny smooth skin, taut over powerful muscles. The feel of his powerful hips sent shock waves of breathtaking pleasure through her. Last on her tour of his body, she shyly brought her hand between them and grasped that part of him that had been created for joining, sliding her fingers along the hard, velvety length of him.

A tremor ran through his body as he groaned and unsteadily removed her hand.

"Did I hurt you?" she asked in confusion. She had only intended to give him pleasure the same as he did her.

"Oh, no!" he forced out in a deep, trembling voice, laughing at her from passion darkened eyes. "It's just more pleasure than I can handle at the moment!"

"Oh! In that case, it's okay!" and she resumed her loving administration.

"No, it's not okay!" and he removed her hand again. "Our time is running short, breath of my body and beat of my heart!"

Shannon stilled for a moment, staring at the man next to her. What a beautiful sentiment!

"In that case, my husband," and she helped him roll on top of her.

Together they rode the lover's path to that place of ultimate pleasure.

"Little Feather! Little Feather!" a soft voice tickled his ear.

Oh, no! not again! He opened his eyes and found himself half on her and half at her side. He could see the white gleam of her teeth in the moonlight as she grinned into his dark eyes. He flopped over onto his back and bent his good arm over his eyes.

Shannon moved his arm and grinned into his face. "Pretty good, huh?"

"One day, when you're on good terms with everyone in the village as yourself and my wife, don't you dare tell anyone that every time we go a pleasuring, I faint like a woman! I will deny it!"

He hugged her close to him, and she only grinned into his handsome face . . . no promise this time!

Little Feather pulled her to her feet.

"Now I'm freezing!" she protested.

"I'll help you dress . . . with pleasure," he grinned at her minor discomfort. "And day will be upon us soon, he added. "I have a couple of extra tunics that should cover a breechclout and leggings to your satisfaction, so you can wash your clothes," he suggested while he helped her dress.

"I was wondering what I was going to do. They're getting pretty ripe!"

"I've noticed!"

"I imagine *everybody* has noticed! I'll figure out a way to take care of it later today."

As they were returning to the village, the sky started to cloud over. Within minutes a spring storm was upon them forcing Shannon, who in the stress of the moment earlier had forgotten her hat, to pull a square of leather from her pouch and to cover her head in an effort to try and protect the dye in her hair. All she had to do was enter the long house with flaming-red hair and black streaks running down her face. Now *that* should elicit a raised eyebrow or two and some questions. The storm broke in all its fury, and the deluge saturated them almost immediately and made the paths about the village slick with mud.

Slipping and sliding, and with lots of laughter, they returned to the long house without incident.

Shannon stood in the doorway watching the rain, and eating a delicious bowl of deer meat and vegetable stew and cornbread, and hoping the storm would blow over before she had to check on White Feather. She loved the rain. It reminded her of home where it rained more often than not. The depression that she usually felt at memories of Ireland and her family was not as strong as in the past. Sadness was still there, but it was far overshadowed by the joy of her relationship with Little Feather. She marveled that she had had to come half way around the world to this wild place in order to find the wildest thing in life— love.

Strolling back through the vestibule into the smoky interior of the long house, she heard Little Feather and Iron Fist discussing her dream and wondered what their interpretation would be. From deeper within the building, she could hear a very cranky Bright Eyes fussing and crying. Even more distantly within, she could hear other children fussing. Apparently, it wasn't a good day for the children. Idly, she wondered what Boy-who-talks-a-lot had done to his little sister this time.

"I think the dream is advising you to go and challenge and defeat the demon. I think you already suspect who that is," Iron Fist suggested shrewdly.

Little Feather nodded and glanced up as Shannon entered the fireside. He rose to his feet and started rummaging through his possessions on the storage ledge above the sleeping platform. After a few minutes, he pulled some items off the shelf.

"Here are those clothes I promised you," he said, holding up the tunic before her. It reached to her knees.

Looking down the garment, she flashed Little Feather a gamine grin. His breath lodged somewhere in his chest, and his heart did a flip. She was so beautiful, and she was his!

"Yes, this should do!" she responded humorously.

Glancing at Iron Fist, the only other occupant of the fireside, she explained, "I need something to wear while I wash my clothes. They're beginning to reek to high heaven."

"So I'd noticed," Iron Fist replied with a touch of a smile.

Knowing, from the Black Robes who visited the village occasionally, what a propensity whites had for their 'privacy', Little Feather suggested that if Ian changed quickly, he and Iron Fist could momentarily waylay anyone wanting to pass through.

"You'll be surprised how fast I can be!" Shannon responded, shoving Little Feather towards one open doorway to the central corridor while Iron Fist took his place at the entrance to the vestibule.

"I was planning on going to the river later. Now I won't have to . . . all done!" she said in jubilation.

Iron Fist refrained from laughing. Little Feather didn't. Shannon reciprocated his laughter with a smile. A foot of legging had to be rolled up, and the tunic did hang to her knees—and very baggy! She had tied a long strip of rawhide about her waist. All in all, she was going to wash her clothes as soon as she looked in on White Feather.

"Mother will wash those for you. And don't go to the river by yourself!" he ordered. "It's too dangerous!"

Shannon's eyes began to sparkle. She hated being given orders!

Iron Fist smoothly intervened. "I will go with Ian to the river, and I will teach him our customs and traditions, but it *is* too dangerous to go alone," the last he addressed to Shannon.

"I appreciate your willingness to go with me, Iron Fist . . ." he raised his eyebrows questioningly at her . . . "Uncle, and I'll be honored to learn anything you wish to share with me." Turning to Little Feather, she added, "Your mother has enough to do without doing my clothes, and I've been doing my own wash as long as I can remember. When are you leaving?"

"I'm on my way over to Tall Tree's now. Then we'll go by and collect Grey Turtle."

"How long do you think you'll be gone?"

"There's no way of determining that. First, we'll try and locate their trail. If that's unsuccessful, we'll visit other villages, probably go to Fort Orange and see what we can discover there. A redhead traveling with natives should be fairly noticeable."

Little Feather gathered some extra moccasins, ball and powder for his flintlock, and his bow and arrows which he slung over his back. His knife and tomahawk already hung from the cord that held his breechclout in place. Rolling up his bearskin, he tied a deerskin cord about it and hung it across his shoulders. He put a few chunks of pemmican and maple sugar into a pouch and added the pack to the others hanging on his back. Then he headed outside with Shannon close on his heels.

The rain had stopped, although water still dripped from the eaves. They dodged through the miniature waterfalls.

People were hustling about through the village, mud and all, going about their business. There was no place for a private goodbye

"Be careful, Little Feather!" she murmured, devouring him with her eyes, wanting to grab hold of him and never let go.

"We'll be okay, Ian. This is a part of our lives, something that must be done. Would you think more of me if I avoided my duty?"

"No. I know you have to go. Hurry back." She mouthed the word, "husband!"

He flashed her a smile that stopped her breath in her chest, and then he turned and strolled towards the long house in which Tall Tree lived.

Shannon admired his graceful movements, long, firm stride, easy swing of his shoulders and arms—a man with a purpose. Her man.

After tending White Feather's wounds which were healing well, Shannon was standing outside of the long house with Iron Fist when they watched the three men leave the village.

"He'll be back safely," Iron Fist assured Shannon. "I think your dream, although it was frightening, revealed that Little Feather would defeat your enemy and therefore his enemy."

They stood in companionable silence for a few minutes.

"Why don't you go and get those clothes that are in such desperate need of water and we'll go down to the river? I know some stories—about Little Feather—that might entertain you."

Shannon didn't hesitate a moment but dodged inside and retrieved her garments, and they strolled down to the river with Iron Fist chatting as they went.

Chapter 19

Shannon lay in the dark, snuggled in her heavy bearskin blanket, listening to the rain on the roof and thinking of Little Feather. He'd only been gone a day, but already she missed him more than she could possibly have anticipated—his teasing smile and easy laughter, often at her expense, his lovemaking. She smiled into the dark, thankful for the night as her neck and face grew warm at the thought of their passionate pleasuring. How presumptuous she had been to think there was no reason to do *that!* Well, Little Feather had taught her differently!

Curling herself into a ball, and listening to the pitter patter of the rain on the bark shingles and to several children fretting from further within the long house, Shannon, a wistful smile on her face, drifted into sleep, being carried away to a land of sunshine and flowers where only she and Little Feather, *her husband*, existed. The last conscious thought to float through her mind was she would learn how to make cornbread and present it to him after her problems were resolved. The rain continued its gentle tempo on the roof, and the children continued to fret.

*   *   *

"If you weren't so stubborn and didn't insist on being up and about so much, your shoulder probably wouldn't be bleeding again!" Shannon, her floppy hat firmly in place on her head, sat on the platform next to White Feather, scolding as she put a new dressing on the wound. "At least it doesn't appear that poison is developing!"

"I had to relieve myself!" White Feather defended his actions with a mischievous grin.

"And it took four girls to help you?" Shannon scoffed as she removed the dressing from his scalp. That, too, looked good, and the scar was going to be fairly small. "You're healing really well. Do you people all heal so rapidly?" she asked, thinking of Little Feather and Wolf Running.

"Probably because those four girls gave such a boost to my spirits!" He gave her a conspiratorial smile. Suddenly, his eyebrows rose. "Ian! You've never gone a pleasuring with a girl, have you?"

"I've gone a pleasuring," she answered cautiously but honestly, keeping her face averted, "but this isn't about me! Your brother and Little Feather made me promise to make you rest so you can get well . . . I can't imagine why!"

Ignoring her comment, he continued talking as though she weren't there, "Now who could we get to go a pleasuring with you, a white boy? No offense, Ian," he assured Shannon, glancing quickly at her. "After what you've done for Little Feather, Wolf Running and now me, you're as close as any brother could be . . . well, except maybe Grey Turtle." He paused and laughed before continuing with the matter at hand. "It's just some of the girls aren't attracted to . . . well, light skin."

He shrugged his shoulders and winced at the pain the movement caused.

"White Feather, forget it! I promised I'd take care of you while they're gone, and I'm going to do just that!"

The frown left his handsome face and was replaced by a big smile. "I've got the perfect girl for you!"

"White Feather, you're ignoring me!"

"Of course, I'm ignoring you! You don't make sense! What youth your age doesn't want to try out his prowess with the girls? Wild Rose would be perfect for you!"

"Wild Rose?" Shannon choked and suppressed an almost irresistible urge to laugh. She had an acute sense of humor, and this definitely struck her as funny. "The one who's always falling all over Little Feather?"

"And half the other men and youths in the village!" White Feather snorted in derision. "But she's experienced when it comes to a pleasuring!"

Shannon blurted out the first thing that came to mind to stop this crazy conversation, "Where's your little sister? She's usually here watching while I change your dressings?"

"Frisky Chipmunk? I haven't seen her this morning. I think she only stops here to watch Little Feather. She plans on marrying him when she grows up!"

Shannon shook her head in amazement. It appeared that everyone had a crush on her man . . . but then, so did she! She grinned beneath her floppy hat.

"I'm going to check in on your mother and sister and see how they're adjusting so soon as the funeral. I might be able to assist in working through their grief or cheer them up in some way."

"Ian, just don't do any woman's work!"

She found Makes-good-baskets spooning up some liquid from an herb mixture that cooled by the fire into a bowl for Frisky Chipmunk who was still lying in bed.

The girl, about eight years old, stared at Shannon from glazed eyes. "I can't get up! I feel awful!" she moaned. "So weak . . . ohhhhh!" she groaned as her stomach heaved and emptied its content of liquid into a bowl that was by her head.

"How long has she been like this, Aunt?" Shannon inquired, placing her hand on the child's forehead. The girl's skin was burning.

"She was listless last sunset. She was out in the rain yesterday and got chilled. This should bring down her fever"—she held up a bowl filled with an herb water solution—"and settle her stomach."

"Is there anything I can do? Get anything? Run any errands?" Shannon offered.

"I don't think so, Ian, but thanks for the offer. My sister, Little Robin, has gone to ask the False Faces to come."

"If later you decide there is anything I can do to help, just send one of Little Robin's girls for me, okay?"

The woman nodded as she gently lifted the child's head and shoulders and encouraged her to drink a little of the herb tea.

The sky was cloudy and overcast, and the air carried the chill of an early spring storm as Shannon left the long house.

She was deeply disturbed. Bright Eyes and Boy-who-talks-a-lot had both been listless and feverish this morning. She couldn't remember if they had been caught out in the rain yesterday or not. Still, extreme worry lurked in her mind.

Pulling her hat down tightly over her head, Shannon tied her leather scarf over the hat for double protection and went trailing through the sucking mud that filled the village in search of Iron Fist to discuss her suspicions.

After going from long house to long house inquiring for him and finding illness starting in several of them, she finally located Iron Fist down at the river with Red Fox, Little Wolf and several other youths from the village.

"Iron Fist, I need to talk to you. Alone, if it's okay?"

"Of course," he responded with concern in his voice, looking at her intently while they walked a short distance away from the young men.

"Bright Eyes and Boy-who-talks-a lot are sick . . ."

"Probably out in the cold and rain yesterday."

"I thought that could be it but Frisky Chipmunk, Makes-good-baskets' daughter is sick also—fever, too weak to get up, vomiting. And there are people in other long houses who are becoming ill."

A somber expression passed over his face. "I wasn't aware of that. I'll need to talk to the village chief immediately."

"Have there been any other European visitors to the village in the past few weeks?"

Iron Fist's smooth brow wrinkled into a frown as he thought back over the time in question for a few moments. "Some Black Robes traveled through from Fort Orange going west to French territory. We provided them with hospitality for a couple of days. That was almost half a moon ago." Iron Fist sighed with regret. "You'd think we'd learn, wouldn't you. This isn't the first time they've brought illness to us."

Shannon's heart sank as he was speaking. Neither of them wanted to give the dreaded name to what they suspected was starting to breakout in the village.

"I think we should treat this with caution until we know what we are facing," Shannon suggested. "Anyone who is not already ill with fever or has not been in touch with anyone who is ill should leave the village immediately, set up a temporary camp—no contact between the camps and the village, nor should the boys return to the village."

"Red Fox and Little Wolf have been exposed to Bright Eyes and Boy-who-talks-a-lot. They shouldn't be with those who have had no contact, and the people from those other long houses where illness is beginning should probably camp here with our boys and the people from our long house who aren't ill yet," Iron Fist added his thoughts on the matter.

"Two camps then? One for people who have been exposed but aren't showing signs of illness and one for people who haven't been exposed to the sickness?" Shannon shrugged her shoulders. "Sounds like a good idea. Probably should have someone to direct people to the different areas."

Rain started falling—not a good omen.

When the situation was explained to them, the boys, immediately started collecting branches to construct lean-tos for themselves and other members of their family who would be joining them shortly. Blankets and food would be brought out to them. They, in return, would provide water and fresh meat to the village entrance.

Iron Fist and Shannon started running. Before they reached the village, they passed several families hurriedly seeking refuge in the nearby forest.

One man stopped long enough to explain, "There's illness in several long houses. One child has already developed pox on his face and palms of his hands. It's smallpox! Stay away!" Then he hurried after his family.

"Wait!" Iron Fist called after the fleeing figure.

The man stopped but didn't return. Iron Fist walked towards him, stopping a short distance away. "We are establishing two areas for camps. If you have not been exposed to anyone who is taking ill, set up your camp north of the string of rocks on the river. If you have been exposed, we are setting up a camp over there." Iron Fist pointed in the direction where the boys were working. "Also if possible, it would be very helpful if you would consider staying here—away from the trail—and directing people to the two areas."

The man listened and nodded. "I need to tell my family to go above the rocks on the river, but I'll return and do as you ask."

'Iron Fist nodded his appreciation and turned towards Shannon. "You'd better stay out of the village, Ian," he suggested. Little Feather would have his hide if anything happened to her that could have been prevented.

"It's okay. I've cared for smallpox victims before and never gotten the disease. I think I remember my grandmother saying something about my having a very mild case when I was very young."

More families, carrying and dragging needed possessions, came scurrying past them out of the village to be directed to one of the two camps. The disease, more dreaded than the freezing rain, drove them out into the torrential deluge.

Pandemonium reigned in the village. Whole families packed their most necessary belongings helter-skelter into baskets and on travois and ran from the village amidst lightning, thunder, heavy freezing rains, and wind released upon the land by an unfeeling heaven. Babies cried and whimpered in confusion as their parents' panic touched them. Some very young children were in everyone's way as they sought reassurance—that didn't exist that day—that everything was okay.

Other children laughed and joked, thinking it was a grand lark, never having seen an epidemic that swept away most of their loved ones and a third or more of a village.

Half an hour ago, Shannon had been worrying about Little Feather's safety and feeling sorry for herself because she was so lonely with him gone. How trivial her problems had suddenly become! And Little Feather? The sickness, although it's presence had not been known, was already in the village when he left. Would he or any of his companions fall prey to the most feared of the white man's diseases with no one to care for them? Her heart sank lower. There was nothing she could do for them but hope and pray. Worrying would not help them, nor would it help her. Anyway, Shannon had a horrible feeling that she was going to be too busy to worry about Little Feather and his party for a long time to come.

"I'll meet you at the long house after your meeting with the chief and council." She started to walk away but stopped and called after him, "I've been thinking," she said as she walked back towards him, "Back home there were a couple of outbreaks of smallpox over the years. Those people who hadn't had the disease and parents with small children would seek out those victims who had the mildest cases and expose themselves or their children to it." She paused, thinking. "I think that's how I got it. You get smallpox once, you don't get it again. The people would try to get a mild case and then never have to worry about it again." Rain continued to pour down around them. Swiping water from her eyelashes to clear her sight, she waited for some comment from her friend.

Iron Fist studied her thoughtfully. Everyone knew that if one survived the deadly disease that they never got it again. But to deliberately expose one's self? That was a novel idea. He watched as people scrambled to get away from the village.

"How many people died?" he asked thoughtfully

"A few," Shannon admitted honestly, "but far fewer than those exposed accidently, and remember, exposure was only to those with the mildest cases."

"I will think on this and discuss it with the council, but the people will do what they want." He shrugged his broad shoulders philosophically. "Right now fear and panic are controlling them with good cause."

Iron Fist sloshed on through the mud and rain to the long house of the village chief, while Shannon ran, slipping and sliding, towards their long house.

Dodging through the waterfall flowing from the overhanging roof that formed a porch outside the building's vestibule, she darted into the storage room and shook out her scarf and loose, floppy hat. Satisfied that no dye was running from her hair, she hurried into the main corridor of the long house.

The building was smokier than usual—if that were possible—as several older women fed the fires. A straggly dog nipped at her leggings. Bright Flower, face gaunt and strained, hair unkempt and hanging in a tangle down her back, paced the long corridor, crooning to Boy-who-talks-a lot who slept fretfully in her arms.

Running Feet sat in a pile of furs on her bunk with Bright Eyes curled up in her lap, crying hoarsely. The young mother, tired and tears streaming down her cheeks, was trying with little success to encourage the child to drink herb tea from a wooden bowl. "Why? Why do they bring their evil upon us?" she sobbed.

Grey Wolf, Iron Fist's father, brought in a large waterskin and set it on the ground, leaning it against a support pole. Smiling Woman gave him a weary but grateful smile. Thin lines around her eyes, normally not seen, were now clearly visible.

"Was Iron Fist with you when you returned to the village?" the older man, who, in spite of his age, was a handsome, strong man—an older version of Iron Fist—asked.

"As soon as we returned to the village, he went on to the chief's long house."

"Good! I'm on my way there now." Turning to his wife, he continued, "I'll be back as soon as possible."

Smiling Woman acknowledged his words with a thin, tired smile as she poured some water into a large kettle over one of the fires.

Shannon threw her hat onto her bunk—no one would take notice of so trivial a thing as her hair under the extreme stress and seriousness of the situation—and directed her attention to Boy-who-talks-a lot whom she lifted from Bright Flower's arms.

"You look like you could use a break, Mother. Let me tend to the boy for a while." Bright Flower breathed a sigh of relief and lay her weary body on her platform for a much needed rest, not even surprised that this strange white boy was assuming so much quiet control of the situation.

"It's smallpox, isn't it, Ian," the woman asked wearily, her voice filled with fear.

Shannon nodded her head. "A child several long houses over has developed the pox. Have you had the disease?" she asked Little Feather's mother, who showed no signs of any pox marks.

"No!"

"Oh, Mother! You should leave now!"

"And you, Ian?" the woman smiled gently at her.

"I have cared for smallpox victims before and never got the disease. I think I had a mild case when I was very young. I'll be fine. But you won't if you stay."

"I won't be in the rain either!"

"Don't be difficult, Mother! Red Fox and Little Wolf are making a lean-to. It should be finished by now. You can stay there. Iron Fist will show you where they are when he returns."

While Bright Flower reluctantly—succumbing to the sensible suggestion—gathered items she would need, Shannon, with Boy-who-talks-a-lot in her arms, turned her attention to Running Feet.

Fear was stamped on the young woman's face as she gazed at Shannon and shook her head in the negative. "I haven't had it either!" she muttered in a hushed, trembling voice.

Going from person to person still in the long house, Shannon soon learned that no one had had smallpox except Smiles-a-lot. So much exposure, so few who had had the disease. Shannon's head started to ache. But this was no time to quit or to anticipate the worst She continued to assess the situation, and strangely enough, no one questioned her authority.

After determining who had not had the disease, Shannon checked everyone for signs of the illness and found only three people who were sick: Bright Eyes, Boy-who-talks-a-lot and Standing Elk, Snail Girl's oldest son and the young man who had given Shannon his bow and arrows.

Shannon fervently prayed that this would be the extent of

the illness in their long house, but due to the extensive exposure feared there would be more victims.

Later, after Iron Fist and Grey Wolf returned, everyone—except for the ill, Shannon and Smiles-a-lot—packed up a few meager belongings and joined the exodus from the village, going in search of Red Fox and Little Wolf. The plan being that whoever developed fever would be brought back immediately to be cared for by Shannon and Smiles-a-lot.

Shannon watched with a heavy heart as the last of Little Feather's family disappeared through the stockade opening. Turning, she found Smiles-a-lot behind her.

"I'm going to visit the other long houses where there are sick people and suggest they and others who have survived previous epidemics come here. If we pool our resources, we might come through this better than trying to fight it individually."

"It can't hurt to ask,"

"While I'm gone, Grandmother, would you check and see what healing herbs we've got. Especially check for garlic. My grandmother used it for just about everything. I used to think it was just to annoy English soldiers she encountered. But who knows, she was right about everything else she taught me." As she talked she returned to Little Feather's fireside to retrieve her hat and scarf.

That night when Shannon finally fell into bed and snuggled into her bearskin robe, she was tired, cold and lonely, but there was also a sense of accomplishment. Fourteen people with pox had been brought to their long house along with four more people who had already survived previous epidemics. Seventeen sick so far and six to care for them.

The care givers had decided on relief shifts with two people sleeping at a time, And, it had been decided unanimously that Shannon be one of the first two to get some sleep while the others kept the fires going and the herb teas brewing. The smell of garlic filled the long house, and the storm had decreased to a light drizzle on the roof as Shannon drifted into an exhausted sleep. Her last conscious thought was where was Little Feather and was he all right.

Chapter 20

The shower that had begun before Little Feather and his friends left the village grew more violent as they backtracked to where Grey Owl and White Feather had been attacked.

Searching the area as thoroughly as possible in the pouring rain revealed nothing that would help them to determine the direction in which their query fled.

"Let's continue on to the east. Fort Orange is in that direction, and they may try for it. Any other suggestions?" Little Feather inquired, glancing at his friends.

"East is as good as any direction, although you might consider the fishing camps to the north if we don't discover anything along this trail," Tall Tree suggested.

Little Feather's mind was divided between the search and Shannon. At some point he was going to have to confide in his friends and enlist their aid in pilfering the muskets.

As the rain fell throughout the morning, the ground became softer and muddier, harder to traverse.

"I don't know about you, Little Feather, but any sign there might be, I think we would probably miss in this weather. I think we ought to hole up at least until the rain stops." Tall Tree offered, pulling his foot out of the sucking mud.

"I agree," Grey Turtle said. "They've got a three day head start on us. I don't think a few hours will make much difference. If it's raining on them like it is on us, chances are they're holed up somewhere to." He swiped water from his eyes.

212

"I was thinking the same thing," Little Feather agreed, wiping raindrops from his own face.

"There's a dense thicket in an oak grove not far from here. It should provide us with some protection until the storm blows itself out."

A short search revealed the thicket, and a short time later, the three men were fairly comfortable waiting for the weather to clear.

Little Feather pulled out his pipe, filled it with tobacco, tamping it down. and lit it from the small coal he carried in a clay pot in his pouch. He drew a long satisfying drag on the pipe. This was as good a time as any to enlist his friends' help in acquiring the muskets.

"We need to talk about Ian," Little Feather started, taking another long drag from his pipe. He blew it out and continued, "Tall Tree knows part of the story, but there is more."

"You mean that our good healer Ian is a woman?" Grey Turtle suggested with a smile.

Little Feather choked on the smoke in his lungs, and his eyes watered.

"She'd better be," Grey Turtle continued, "from the way you've been ogling her, or there are things you've never told us!"

"Is her disguise that easy to penetrate?"

"Her disguise is fine. You were the give away!" Now Grey Turtle was laughing at his friend's expression.

Little Feather had been concerned with how long he would be able to conceal his feelings for the woman. Obviously, it hadn't been long! Little Feather gazed at the rain dripping from the opening of their shelter and slapped his forehead. "I can't believe I was so obvious!"

Then he explained to Grey Turtle, "I saw the woman in dreams before I met her. I discussed the dreams with Tall Tree and Iron Fist. Then she burst into my life much as I had seen her in the dreams." He took another long puff on his pipe, exhaling it slowly. "And my life hasn't been the same since!"

"Your future wife?"

Little Feather nodded his head. "In the dreams, she's a warrior with flaming red hair."

"Well, that doesn't sound like our Ian," Grey Turtle remarked, then grinned, "Her hair is dyed, isn't it?"

"It is," Tall Tree added to the conversation.

"And the warrior bit?" Grey Turtle asked, intrigued.

"The day we brought down the grizzly . . . ?"

Grey Turtle nodded his head.

"Well, while I hovered between unconsciousness and consciousness, she took my musket and riffled through my pouches until she found the ball and powder. Hers was the ball that finally brought down the bear!"

"There was only one shot! The Frenchman's!"

"There were two! I watched her shoot!"

Grey Turtle was silent pondering this information. Gradually a frown formed between his eyes. "The man who killed my father and tried to kill my brother was a redhead . . . and he was looking for a flaming-haired woman . . . Ian?"

"That's what we needed to talk about. He's her cousin. He and some of his brothers were responsible for the death of her father and another of her brothers."

"So, Ian has another or more brothers," Grey Turtle questioned shrewdly, "that this cousin would like to see dead . . . and Ian, too . . . maybe?"

Tall Tree had been listening intently to all of the information with which he was unfamiliar. "Why would he want to kill Ian and her brother?"

"The why isn't important. It's a family position or something that they want. What is important and the reason for Ian's disguise is that the cousins have put a reward of one hundred muskets on each Ian and her brother."

"Dead or alive?" Grey Turtle asked instantly.

"Don't even think it!" Little Feather warned him.

"I was only teasing you, cousin. I've seen you look at Ian! I assume you have some plan on how to obtain the muskets?"

"Not yet. But I think if the three of us start considering the problem now, by the time we catch the man, we'll have some plan of action for getting them."

"Does this mean we can't kill him right off?" Grey Turtle questioned.

Little Feather cast him a look of utter disgust. "You're more like White Feather than you care to admit!"

Grey Turtle rolled his eyes in mock dismay. "Oh, no! Never like White Feather! Never!"

"You wouldn't kill him right off anyway!"

Grey Turtle and Tall Tree laughed—not a light-hearted laugh but a sinister laugh that boded ill for their prey.

After a couple of hours, the bulk of the shower blew over leaving only a light rain falling with the sun attempting to break through the clouds.

Travel was hard, and progress slow through the soft, muddy ground as they traveled in a northeasterly direction in search of fishing camps.

As they slogged persistently through the muck, it started to rain—again! a slow steady drizzle. The mud oozed beneath their moccasins, and the light rain remained with them throughout the rest of the day.

This was the hardest and most necessary journey Little Feather had ever undertaken, each step taking him farther and farther from the woman he loved, but at the same time, each step bringing them closer to the resolution of her problem . . . closer to the time when he could shout to all and sundry, "This is my woman!"

He had waited a long time to meet this woman, and great was his reluctance to leave her behind. But she *was* the most capable person to provide care for White Feather.

Would she be able to keep her identity hidden? How many people had already deduced her secret from his behavior? Would she have time to touch up her hair as necessary? Would any Europeans come into the village who might have seen the posters and recognize her through her disguise? Worry plagued him. He should have brought her!

Monotony was the keynote of the journey as the miles slid beneath their moccasined feet.

The minutes passed. An hour passed. Squirrels and chipmunks scurried away from the constant thud of feet. A snake slithered across the trail in front of Little Feather and disappeared into a pile of leaves. They moved steadily and persistently in single file. It was wet, and cold and muddy!

Finally, in the early evening, the rain ceased and the sun appeared—again—from behind a cloud, burning off the remaining haze.

The sound of children laughing and screaming, dogs yapping, the deep voices of men shouting to one another and the buzz of women's voices reached them long before they arrived at the fishing camp.

"Ho, brother!" a big man, from the Turtle Clan in another village, waved his arm vigorously and shouted to Little Feather as he plowed from the water, hauling a net full of fish with him.

"Ho, Bear Man!" Little Feather shouted back with deep pleasure, rushing forward to rub the huge man's broad chest. "It's been too long a time since I feasted my eyes on my friend and brother! What are you doing here? I heard you had married and moved far to the north!"

"Come, my friend. I want to introduce you to my wife. We're visiting my family for a while."

Bear Man introduced his wife, Flower-in-Spring and her uncle and the uncle's young wife to Little Feather's trio. While making the introductions, he held his small, pregnant wife in the crook of his big, muscular arm.

"So, you're the one who tamed this wild man!" Little Feather smiled at Bear Man's wife, feeling envious of the big man. He wished Shannon was here under his arm being introduced as his wife. Soon, he thought. Soon all would be as it should be.

Later while they shared a repast of hot, steaming fish that melted in the mouth, Little Feather broached the subject of their purpose for being there.

"Grey Owl was murdered a short time ago, and we're on the trail of his killers."

"I can't believe Grey Owl is gone! We hadn't heard anything. I am so sorry," Bear Man said to Grey Turtle. "Is there anything we can do?"

"My mother would appreciate a visit from you and your wife."

"It's done! Do you know anything about the ones who perpetrated this atrocity?"

"One is a white man with red hair, traveling with five Huron men and a woman. Have you encountered a group like that?"

"A few weeks—maybe a moon—a man such as you described passed through our village," Flower-in-spring, answered in her soft voice.

Bear Man gazed at his wife and then back at Little Feather. "That's right, I'd forgotten. He was hunting for a man and a woman . . . red-haired like himself. Said they were very dangerous people. Said he would pay a hundred muskets apiece for them! Sure would like those hundred muskets! But haven't seen anyone who fits that description."

"He would have killed Grey Owl after he left us. We have no idea where he might be now," Flower-in-spring spoke again. "But you might ask around in camp. It's so late, why don't you stay with us for the night?"

"Thank you for the invitation. We were going to ask for hospitality for the night as we can't go far in the dark," Little Feather smiled at Flower-in-spring.

After spending the evening wandering about the camp asking people if they had seen or heard of the red-haired man, the trio constructed a lean-to for the night. The night turned into three days as the rain continued intermittently.

On the third day, the sun finally came out and started drying up the land. Also on the third day, a family, from a fishing camp to the west, came to visit friends. When they heard of Little Feather's and his friends' quest, they sought out the trio.

"We saw the redhead and the Huron you are seeking about three days ago in our fishing camp. They were searching for a redheaded man and woman. Said he would pay a hundred muskets for each of them! We told him we couldn't help him, and they left. They left our camp traveling west," the young man informed Little Feather. "We've been moving up and down the river. We hadn't heard about the sachem's death. Sorry we can't be of more help."

"You've been a tremendous help," Grey Turtle replied. "Without your information, we would have traveled east to Fort Orange and wasted precious time."

When Little Feather, Tall Tree and Grey Turtle departed from the camp, three young warriors accompanied them on their search.

Chapter 21

"Ian! Ian!" A desperate voice sobbed by her ear, and a hand shook her roughly. Shannon opened one bloodshot eye and stared at the heavy-set boy standing by her bed. In his arms, Running Weasel held the limp form of his little sister, Sunbeam. "Please, Ian, help her!" the youth pleaded with tears running down his cheeks. "I don't know what I'll do if anything happens to her."

Shannon swung her legs over the side of the bed and rubbed her burning eyes. There was more smoke and steam in the long house than usual with all the fires burning constantly. Fisher Woman, a survivor of a previous epidemic, hovered nearby. "I tried to stop him from coming into the long house, but he wouldn't let me take the child. Said he would only give her into your care." She shrugged her narrow shoulders.

"It's okay, Fisher Woman. I'll take care of it," Shannon said in a soothing voice, trying to settle the other woman's frazzled nerves. Taking the child from Running Weasel, she warned,"We'll give her the same care we give to everyone. We make no promises. She's very sick, Running Weasel."

"Please, Ian, let me stay and take care of her! I'll do whatever you say!"

"No! Absolutely not! Now get out of here! You've already exposed yourself to more than is tolerable!"

"Please! I' . . ."

Shannon shouted,"No!" and physically shoved him from the long house. The sun was shining! The sun was shining for the first time in three days! And her eyes hurt abominably. As a matter of fact her head hurt abominably!

"Let me stay and help, Ian. I won't be in the way. Surely, there is something I can do?"

Shannon couldn't think. God, she wished she wasn't so tired, but they were all tired. She knew that Running Weasel wasn't about to leave the village. So, what could he do that would really help? Her mind was beginning to clear as she came more fully awake. What were they all tired of doing? What would be a big help to everyone? Move some of the tea brewing and food preparation outside! The long house had become a steam bath, and Shannon knew that had a lot to do with short tempers and lack of sleep.

"Yes, Running Weasel. There is something you can do that would be a great help to all of us. But under no circumstances are you to come into the long house again. Understand?"

The youth nodded meekly.

"Good," said Shannon and explained what she needed him to do and the herbs they needed from other people in the camps. If people didn't have the herbs, then he needed to organize search parties to go looking for what they needed in the forests and fields.

As Running Weasel, with firm resolve, trotted across the muddy ground towards the stockade entrance in search of supplies he would need, Shannon turned into the hot, smoky long house with Sunbeam in her arms. The first thing to do was to try and get some garlic brew into the child and to bathe her in cool water to try and reduce her temperature.

Big-as-a-bear, once a large man but now shriveled and wizened from age, was feeding pieces of wood to the fires.

"Grandfather," Shannon spoke to the old man respectfully, "we can let two of the fires burn low from now on at night. Running Weasel is going to keep a fire burning outside to make some of the teas."

"That is very good," grinned the old man from his pock-marked face. "A sweat lodg is a good place for a specific purpose.

I don't feel the need for visions right now. Right now I need the energy to get the job done. Let's leave the visions to the shamans!"

"Definitely!" Smiles-a-lot agreed emphatically, wiping sweat from her brow and pushing some strands of moist hair from her face. "Let me take the child, Ian, and you go back and lie down. You had only been asleep a short time when the boy burst into the long house."

"I wondered why I felt so bad! But I'm awake now and don't think I could go back to sleep, I'll see if I can get Sunbeam to take any garlic water. She's awfully listless. I can only hope. You go on with what you were doing, Grandmother," Shannon suggested to the older woman who had a bowl of steaming broth in one hand and a wooden spoon in the other.

"I was just going to try to get some broth into Boy-who-talks-a-lot. He's not doing very well."

"It's early days yet," Shannon murmured as she picked up a bowl and dipped it into the garlic brew. Now, she wondered, how do I get Sunbeam to take this. The child was more like a rag doll than a human being. She watched the child for a moment and realized that Sunbeam was sucking in her state of semiconsciousness. After a few moments search, Shannon found a clean rag and dipping it into the broth watched the child suck the liquid from the rag and swallow it. Half an hour later, the bowl was empty.

Shannon used the technique to successfully get the broth into two more young children, one of them being the boy who first broke out with the pox three days earlier. Smiles-a-lot fed four children using the rag technique while Fisher Woman gave bowls of broth to the rest—the total number of the sick now reaching twenty-one. Runs-like-the-wind, a young Huron who had sought refuge from their village and Thorn-in-the-foot were sleeping.

Shannon had just finished bathing Sunbeam and gotten the child into a fitful sleep when a loud shout came from the long house doorway

God, what now, Shannon thought, but only said, "Big-like-a-bear, would you please see who that is and don't let anyone—absolutely anyone—in who is not sick and has not had small pox in the past! I need to bathe Boy-who-talks-a-lot."

The old man moved away from the kettle he was stirring and moved with a surprisingly light step for one so old towards the vestibule. A few moments later he returned grumbling, "No one listens to the old people anymore. No respect for age and wisdom . . ." Behind him trooped the False Faces—strong religious tradition in conflict with common sense.

Shannon felt like pulling her hair out or spitting wooden nails. Each day they had come, and each day she had forbidden entrance to all who had not had the disease which was most of them.

"Honored, Sirs . . ." she began when one of the False Faces attempted to push her aside.

"The sick need our help and intervention with the Spirits," a deep voice came smoothly from behind the grotesque mask.

Shannon was tired, distraught and her nerves were frayed to the edge. She had no other excuse. "OUT!" she screamed and grabbed the False Face by the arm and spun him around and shoved him into the line of False Faces following him. "Out! Get the hell out of here! How is your getting sick going to help these people, your families or the village?"

By this time the False Faces were milling around outside of the long house.

Shannon had calmed down a little. "I don't mean any disrespect, but your Spirits don't seem to have done a really good job on protecting your people from white men's diseases. To be perfectly honest, the white men's God hasn't done a very good job either!" She shuffled her feet hoping she had not irreparably damaged her budding position with these people. They might sacrifice her to those Spirits before Little Feather returned.

"The best protection against this disease is to get it and survive. We only have six people in there who have survived small pox. That's not very many to take care of the sick who number twenty-five or so. All we're asking is that anyone who has not had the disease not expose themselves at this time."

One of the False Faces spoke up. "I heard that white men expose themselves to the disease in order to get the disease with the hope of surviving."

"Not exactly. Some people will expose themselves and their children to someone with a mild case—that is *mild* case of small pox. Most of the people in there are far too ill to risk that kind of exposure. Have any of you had small pox? Even a mild case?"

Two men stepped forward.

"You are welcome to go in and minister to the sick," Shannon invited, waving her arm towards the door. "The rest of you, I fervently plead with you not to go in. Your deaths would not serve your families or the village. But you and your families could help by finding us more garlic, birch bark—whatever other herbs your healers use in fighting fever—water, fresh meat, fuel and help in keeping the fire Running Weasel has going outside. Those things are desperately needed as I'm sure more people will be taken sick."

Two men went inside, and the other six filed silently and thoughtfully towards the stockade entrance. From that day forward, the sick house did not lack for any of the items needed in caring for the ill. Each morning there was fresh meat and fuel with herbs and water by the gate.

Each day when Shannon collapsed on her bed for her period of rest, she was thankful for the two False Faces who ministered to the sick each day. There was an air of tranquility in the long house that had been missing before. She was also thankful for the others; she knew they were instrumental in their receiving fresh supplies each day. But her heartfelt gratitude to her fellow workers was beyond words. They worked unstintingly and without complaint. Her last thought each day before sleep overtook her was of Little Feather. Where was he now? How was he? Was he missing her as much as she missed him?

As Shannon stood outside of the long house on the morning of the fourth day enjoying the warm sun and getting some much needed first air, she saw a small group of people coming through the gate.

Two men were assisting a woman who was obviously too weak to walk on her own. With them was a young woman Shannon recognized as Tall Tree's wife, Evening Dove.

"My mother is ill. We were told to bring her to you, Ian. Can you help her?" Evening Dove sobbed, The young woman had visibly aged at least ten years in the past four days.

"We'll do the best we can, Evening Dove. We don't promise anything. Wait here with her while I get help to take her inside."

"We'll take her in," one of the men offered.

"No!" Shannon almost screamed. Lowering her voice, she explained, "Only the sick and those who have survived other epidemics go in. It's safer that way. I'll only be a minute." So saying she entered the long house and returned in less than a minute with Runs-like-the-wind.

The men were reluctant to entrust the two youths with the woman.

"We're stronger than we look, and we need to get her inside and lying down as soon as possible," Shannon explained apologetically as she slid her arm under the woman's arm and took her weight while Runs-like-the-wind did the same on the other side.

"Her name's Black Bird," Evening Dove said, trying to hug her mother, but Shannon pushed her away.

"You've been exposed enough. Please leave the village, but come to the gate each day, and I'll let you know how she is doing.," Shannon offered, touched by the girl's concern.

The men and girl started to leave, but the girl turned back to the long house.

"I can't leave! I just can't leave my mother! Surely there is something I can do, Ian?"

Shannon, just inside the vestibule door, turned back to the girl. "I'll be back out as soon as I get your mother settled. Whatever you do, stay out!"

Shannon and Runs-like-the-wind put Black Bird in a fireside by herself as they did not yet know how sick she would get. Those people most ill were in adjacent firesides while people who seemed less ill were in firesides several firesides away.

"See if you can get some garlic tea into her, Brother." those who took the garlic tea earliest seemed to do the best. The young man nodded at her before going to get the tea. Shannon returned outside to the waiting Evening Dove.

"I just can't leave!" the distraught young woman insisted.

At that moment, Running Weasel came through the gate with an armload of wood for his fires. He was losing weight and looked haggard. There were few people willing to relieve him of the task of keeping the fires burning and herb teas brewing. He got less sleep than she did.

Shannon grinned. "You're a godsend!" she told the girl—who looked totally confused—with heartfelt appreciation. "Running Weasel could certainly use your help. He wouldn't leave either after he brought his little sister in. Now his help is indispensable!"

Running Weasel blushed from the unexpected praise.

"Will you help him keep the fires going, Evening Dove. He brews up our herb teas and cooks up meat and vegetable broths for the ill. I don't know how we would get along without him, but he needs relief, too. Will you do this for us?"

"Of course!"Evening Dove agreed immediately. Turning to Running Weasel, she said, "Just tell me what you want me to do, and I'll do it."

Shannon returned to the long house with Running Weasel's voice floating in the background.

The days fell into a regular routine for the care givers, giving garlic and birch brews to everyone, encouraging people to drink meat and vegetable broth, bathing people, cleaning up vomit from people who couldn't keep the broth down, helping those strong enough to go outside to relieve themselves, cleaning up after those too weak to get up, and treasuring their times of rest whether lying down or walking outside for a breath of fresh air.

Every day or so, one or two new patients were being brought in to the sick house.

One day—Shannon had lost track of the time—when she went outside after her sleep period, Evening Dove was bursting with news.

"Oh, Ian, someone from one of the fishing camps came into camp—the camp where there was no exposure—last night. He said that Tall Tree, Little Feather and Grey Turtle spent several days there. That was when it was storming so much. Anyway, they received news about Grey Owl's killers and are now tracking them to the west. Your big brother said to tell you that all is well, and things will be different when he gets back." Evening Dove stopped her rush of words, then added, puzzled, "Does that make any sense to you? But that was exactly what Little Feather said."

"Yeah, it makes sense." Shannon responded slowly, her heart soaring. Little Feather was okay. At least he had been when the storm ended some days ago. How many days ago was it now? Shannon couldn't remember. Death and illness all around her, fatigue weighing her down like a too-heavy basket of fish being carried constantly day after day, days all blurring together like an unfinished painting, but her dreams that night were ever so sweet!

Chapter 22

Hearsay! Always hearsay! The redhead was here four days ago. Left in that direction. The redhead was here three days ago. Looking for a redheaded man and woman, said they were dangerous people, is offering one hundred muskets to anyone who delivers them to the redhead. Little Feather's heart sank to his toes when he heard that piece of news. He had been hoping that piece of news would be withheld for a little while longer . . . like until they had caught the redhead and relieved him of the muskets.

Little Feather and his companions followed the elusive trail with unrelenting determination. The buds grew bigger on the trees, and the birdsong at sunrise was louder and more boisterous each day. Squirrels, chipmunks, and foxes skittered away into the forest before the constant, monotonous thudding of their feet upon the ground.

"Little Feather, take a break!" Tall Tree grumbled to his friend. His stomach growled loudly at that moment, adding its protest. Their pemmican had run out two days earlier. "A few hours break isn't going to make much difference in our pursuit, and we need meat."

The others nodded heartily. Little Feather was a hard person to keep up with.

Little Feather flopped down on the ground under an old oak tree and leaned back. Looking at Black Bear, Red Hawk, and Grey Elk, he suggested, "Why don't you three see if you can chase us down some rabbits . . . yeah, rabbit does sound good."

He paused for a moment, gazing around the area they had stopped in. "Sometimes when I'm running, I tend to forget where I am. I don't lose awareness of what's happening around me . . . Just where I am—if that makes any sense. Sorry, I forgot about eating!"

Some chuckling ensued from his companions before the three youths who had joined them earlier disappeared into the forest to forage up some food—hopefully some rabbits.

Grey Turtle and Tall Tree joined Little Feather on the ground under the tree.

"Any thoughts at all on what the redhead is up to or where he's going?" Grey Turtle asked.

'It appears he's trying to cover as much territory as possible at random to spread the news of the people he's hunting and the reward he's offering."

A noise from the branches above them drew their attention, only to have an acorn—probably the last one still hanging from the tree-drop on Little Feather's nose. A very angry squirrel chattered noisily from far above them.

The men burst out laughing, relieving some of the extreme tension and frustration of the hunt.

"Have you come up with any ideas yet on how to get those muskets?" Tall Tree inquired after he stopped laughing.

"No, I guess I'm relying on inspiration at the last moment!"

"Well, don't rely to heavily on inspiration, and stop thinking so much about Ian. She'll be there when you get home," Grey Turtle grinned at his friend.

"I don't think I let thoughts of Ian interfere with my days too much," he responded grumpily.

"I wasn't referring to your days! But you talk half the night through!"

Little Feather scowled at Tall Tree.

His best friend laughed and shrugged his shoulders. "Must be stress!" he grinned.

Little Feather snorted at his friends and, getting up, strolled off amongst the trees to relieve himself.

Later that evening as the men sat around the fire enjoying

their repast of roast rabbit, a branch was heard snapping in the forest.

"Ho, brothers! I am a runner seeking hospitality for the night," a voice bellowed close on the snap.

"Come and set yourself at our fire and share our rabbit," Little Feather invited.

A big man dressed only in breechclout and moccasins emerged from the trees. Across his broad shoulders was slung a bow and quiver full of arrows. He carried a musket in the crook of one arm, and the ubiquitous pouch carried by all men bounced against his chest.

"I'm Turtle Man," he introduced himself. "I carry a message across Iroquois land."

"I'm Little Feather of the Turtle Clan." Little Feather returned the courtesy. "You're a runner?"—runners were usually slim and fleet of foot—"What is the message you carry?"

Turtle Man grinned at Little Feather. "I'll race you at any time you choose," he challenged as he helped himself to some rabbit.

There were some chuckles from Little Feather's friends. That was a race they would like to see.

"Perhaps another time," Little Feather responded amiably. The man was a runner, and running was his business. "What is the message you spoke of?" he promted their visitor.

Turtle Man finished his rabbit, and his face took on an extremely somber expression. Little Feather and his friends knew that the news coming was not going to be good . . . and it wasn't.

"Small pox has broken out in Standing Bear's village . . ."

Varying gasps and exclamations of dismay brought Turtle Man's words to a halt.

"How long?" "How bad?" "How do you know?" The questions rushed at the messanger.

"Your village?" he asked sympathetically. "I was in that vicinity three days ago. I was stopped by guards well outside the village. It all seemed so well organized," he paused, a puzzled expression on his face. "I caught a glimpse of some funny-looking white kid—

dressed in clothes obviously not his and a weird floppy hat. Seems he was in charge of caring for the sick . . . couldn't have been more than about twelve summers. Not nearly as many sick as I've seen before, but enough. That's all I can tell you. It's all I know."

"Well, do we go back?" Tall Tree asked of his companions in general. Each man was thinking of what he had to lose.

"There wouldn't be much you could do if you did go back." and the runner explained about the camp arrangement. "Even the False Faces aren't allowed to do rituals for the sick unless they, themselves, have survived the disease."

Grey Turtle snorted, "And who's going to stop them?"

Turtle Man grinned at that. "I heard that the white kid—I think his name is Ian—physically threw them out early on in the sickness. I would sure like to have seen that!"

"I can imagine that," Little Feather murmured softly, his heart swelling with pride at what his warrior woman was doing for his people, and at what risk to herself?

All thought of returning to the village without the muskets died. He would give Shannon his share of the muskets as a marriage gift.

Dark had fallen by this time, so the men set camp for the night. Little Feather and Grey Turtle took the first guard duty. As Little Feather moved silently about the camp of sleeping men, his mind was half on guard duty and half on Shannon. Would she get sick? He wished fervently that he had brought her with him. He had so recently found her, he couldn't contemplate her being sweep away by the white man's disease. With great difficulty, he pulled his thoughts away from his woman—he could do nothing for her at the moment except catch her cousin and bring his head and the muskets to lay at her feet.

The sudden flap of wings, whoosh of air and a high pitched squeal alerted Little Feather that a predator was on the prowl for food, and that it had been successful . . . even as he, himself, would be successful.

For the next seven days the small band tracked the elusive redhead and his band of Hurons. At one village after another they heard the same disappointing news. "The redhead was here five days ago . . . looking for a redheaded man and woman . . . a hundred muskets . . ." "He was here three days ago . . . a hundred muskets . . . heading north . . ." "Four days ago . . . collecting furs . . ." "Here two days ago, left traveling east" Little Feather and his companions followed every lead over rivers and streams, through forest and field from village to village, only taking time to hunt when it was absolutely necessary. Finally, they arrived at a fishing camp to discover that their prey had been there a day earlier and traveled north when he left.

"It's about time!" Little Feather said with relief and great feeling as they pursued the trail north. Fourteen risings of the sun had passed since he had left his feisty, little warrior woman, and his body was burning for her.

"Brother, you've never been so impatient before on a hunt!" Tall Tree teased. "I'm the one who should be anxious to get home . . . with a beautiful wife waiting for me!"

"Oh, shut up!" Little Feather responded ungraciously but knowing that his friend spoke truly. He had never had such a hard time focusing on the task at hand.

"You're not doubting yourself, are you, Friend?" Tall Tree questioned more seriously.

"Don't, cousin. We'll get those guns and my father's killers!" Grey Turtle assured Little Feather. "It's not your fault that the redhead's trail has more twists than a snake's back."

A storm blew fiercely across the land that day, the huge hailstones forcing the hunters to seek temporary shelter under the largest trees. But it was the kind of storm that, though violent while upon you, passed quickly.

Three more days passed uneventfully without a sign of the redhead and his Hurons. The trees were leafing out, squirrels were more obvious in their activities, and the birds were more exuberant in the early morning. Little Feather and Tall Tree were itching to get back to their women. Grey Turtle was totally obsessed with revenge, and the three young warriors who had joined them at their first stop were still anxious to achieve glory in this particular hunt.

Then, traveling along a trail with thick brush and tall trees surrounding them on all sides, limiting their visibility and heightening their senses, they rounded a curve in the path and, in the shade of forest giants, surrounded by saplings and shrubs just leafing out and turning green in response to spring, and with birds singing their joy of life, the hunters encountered their first positive, but grizzly, signs of their query—a small party of men, women and children massacred on the trail. The men, three of them, all had bullet holes and arrows in their backs. Their bows and arrows were still on their shoulders. The two woman had struggled with their assailants but to no avail. Their garments had been ripped from their bodies and both had been violently ravaged. One woman's brains were spilled out upon the ground from a skull split open with a tomahawk, and the other had multiple slash wounds. Both had strands of red and black hair clutched tightly in their hands. Two young children and an infant had been slain with their parents. All had been scalped. Blood was everywhere, and the air was rank with its salty smell.

"Why?" Tall Tree muttered, gazing in horror at the carnage.

"Hates the Haudenausaunee?" Little Feather replied grimly. "He's traveling with Huron, and there's no love lost between them and us. Probably some renegades who weren't brought to heel last winter."

"Well, we'd better catch them pretty quick here before there are more atrocities to be avenged!" from Grey Turtle. "If anyone else finds them first, there may not be enough left for us to exact revenge! At least there won't be if we find them first!"

"Just don't forget in the heat of the moment that we need to find out where those musket are before anything else is done," Little Feather warned his friends.

Little Feather addressed himself to Black Bear, one of the young warriors who had joined them on the fourth day of their search. "You know what needs to be done."

"I'll pass the word. I think they're from the village west of mine. Someone will return to retrieve their bodies. Send a message to me when you bring them in. I want to be there."

After covering the bodies with large branches and brush to provide some protection against predators, the hunters, with all senses alert to danger, proceeded silently but swiftly along the path leading east.

Dusk was falling over the land and full dark caught them before they found another village or encampment.

"Best to sleep far from the trail and no campfire," Little Feather suggested. There was no argument from his comrades.

Their meal consisted of a few pieces of rabbit saved from an earlier meal and water from a nearby stream. Tomorrow they would have to take time to hunt for food.

"I'll take first watch with Grey Elk while the rest of you sleep," Tall Tree offered.

Shoving some branches together for his head, Little Feather curled up in his blanket and fell asleep almost immediately.

He was sitting on the bank of a stream, the grass beneath him soft, green and fragant. Overhead in an azure sky floated a few puffy, white clouds. All around him birds sang lusty songs.

But it was the sight before him that held him spellbound.

Shannon, naked, played in the water before him, joyous as a water sprite, her auburn-gold hair swirling about her like glittering sunbeams. Her eyes—a soft grey—glowed mischievously as she splashed him and dared him to come and catch her.

Her eyes widened with delight at the speed with which he leaped to his feet and divested himself of his kilt and dashed towards the water, his cock fully aroused. But in that moment before she splashed him again he saw her eyes glow appreciatively as they roamed over his naked form. He grabbed her through the flying water before she had a chance to flee and pulled her, laughing and struggling, up against his hard body and placed a ravishing kiss on her laughing mouth. Her arms wrapped themselves around his neck, pulling him closer.

A groan was wrenched from somewhere deep within his chest as she rubbed herself seductively against him, her passion-filled eyes gleaming into his own.

Covering her mouth again with his own, he slid his hands down her slick body.

"Shannon," he murmured, "you're a fire raging in my blood! I don't think I'll ever get enough of you!"

Suddenly his whole body started to shake. Shannon slipped from his arms and panic gripped him. What was happening? He was being pulled away from her.

"Little Feather, wake up!" a familiar voice whispered softly by his ear.

Little Feather's eyes snapped open and stared up into the shadowy face of Tall Tree. He could see the shine of his friend's teeth in the moonlight.

"I think that a pleasuring is a personal matter, and you were talking in your sleep . . . again and quite loudly at that!" his friend chuckled softly

"Thank you, I think!" Little Feather muttered. He had dreamed of Shannon every night that they had been on the trail, tonight being the most vivid.

The next day fortune smiled on them. They arrived at a village about half a day after the redhead had departed, and he was traveling to Fort Orange with many furs to trade for supplies! The villagers willingly provided Little Feather and his warriors with food for their journey when they heard of the massacres committed by the redhead and his Hurons.

Two hours after leaving the village, they discovered two more victims of the marauders. They were getting careless as the man, bullet holes and arrows in his back, still clung to life.

"Red Hawk!" the man choked out, grasping the hand of one of Little Feather's companions. "Took our furs . . . Fort Orange . . . attacked . . . red . . ." the man choked out before dying.

Tears filled Red Hawk's eyes as he squatted and placed a blanket over the young woman who had been stripped and raped. "Ah . . . little sister, I shall grieve for you after I have avenged you," he murmured softly to the dead woman, taking one of her hands in his own.

Red Hawk, a youth probably in his late teens, stared at Little Feather from eyes cold, hard, and suddenly very old. "They're close by! I will carry the message back along the trail and to my village, but I will return! When you catch them, you wait until I get back before you start anything serious! My sister and her husband will be avenged!"

"You're going to have to wait your turn or join us at our village! That's where they're going. My father's clan will want them. They slaughtered my father first, but I promise to save you a piece!"

"It would appear that Ian's father and brother were first," Little Feather put in mildly. "And they are threatening . . . him! You're all going to have to wait your turn!"

Red Hawk was soon swallowed up by the trees along their back trail, while Little Feather and his friends continued to trot along the winding path to the east.

Chapter 23

"I don't believe a word of it!" scoffed Standing Elk, even though he came each morning to the fireside where Shannon was telling the tales of her homeland. "Nobody could do those things!"

"And going to war over a brown cow!" added Red Fox who had been brought in with fever on the fifth day of the epidemic. He had been sicker than Standing Elk with higher fever and more pox, but he had been able to take the garlic brew and meat broth from the beginning and was now recovering well. The thought never occurred to the young men that their own warriors had had many skirmishes for less reason than that.

"I tell you truly, Standing Elk and Red Fox, Chuculain and Maeve did just that!" Shannon laughed from where she perched on a bunk holding Boy-who-talks-a-lot's listless body. The child's face, little arms and legs were covered with pox, and the last few times she had tried to force broth on him, it had trickled from the corners of his dry mouth. She feared the child wasn't going to survive this epidemic. All she could do now was hold him while she told her fantastic stories.

"Chuculain was a mighty warrior and shaman. Great was his magic and many were his deeds. My grandmother told me many tales of him"

Standing Elk and Red Fox again snorted their derision, but the younger children were spellbound even though they had heard the stories before when the white boy had come to their village with the French traders. Adults who were well enough often joined the story sessions. Everyone liked a good story about heroes and great deeds whether they were Shannon's stories about the great heroes of her people, or the stories of Sky Woman, The Brothers or the Trickster told by Big-as-a-bear.

She burst into a cheery song that rolled like the waves of the ocean, light, lilting highs, and long rumbling lows. It was a song about the mischievous Fair Folks that her grandmother had sung to her. After singing the songs, she would recite the stories in their language.

The long house was smokey and filled with the scent of garlic and broth, sickness and death. Shannon's eyes burned as usual, but she was determined to finish her stories as they gave such a boost to the children's morale and helped to keep her mind off Little Feather for a short time each day. She had heard snippets of news about him occasionally from people passing by via Evening Dove and Running Weasel, but it had been over a week since she had heard anything. Following story time, she always went out and visited with Running Weasel and Evening Dove, getting all the news from the camps and waiting anxiously for any word from Little Feather.

Other children lay on the platform behind her and more reclined on the bed on the other side of the fire totally enchanted by the wondrous tales of heroes and the Fair Folk. Later each day while Shannon was taking her break, Big-as-a-bear would regale the younsters with their own tales of heroes and monsters.

"Let me take the child," Black Bird, her own pox already starting to dry up, offered as Shannon sang to the other children. The woman's illness. fortunately. had been mild, and she was already recovering. All curiosity at the strange white boy's behavior had long since disappeared, and the strange reddish-gold sparkles in his hair drew no comments.

"Is that a song to your God?" Smiles-a-lot asked, at the same time putting up two fingers indicating that two more people had succumbed to the disease. Shannon's heart sank—although, it was not reflected in her singing—and she nodded her head slightly to acknowledge the message. When she was finished, she and Runs-like-the-wind would quietly remove the corpses through the back door of the long house and take them to the House-of-the-Dead. So far nine people had died, and the number of sick was at forty.

"No, this is about the little people who inhabit the hills and vales back home—very mischievous and curious people. Whenever something disappeared when I was very young, my grandmother would say the Fair Folk had taken it, and if I looked very closely, I would find what they had left in its place," Shannon laughed quietly. "These are very special little people—no bigger than this tall"—she measured an inch or so between her fingers—"with tiny wings."

"You're teasing us!" Standing Elk objected from his chosen place across the fireside. He was less ill than most and maneuvered on his own to this spot each day to listen to Shannon's songs and wild stories about her homeland.

"No, I'm not!" Shannon protested earnestly. "Sometimes in the forest on a night when the moon is full, you can hear the fairies dance and sing, but if you get too close, they'll disappear, or worse, take you with them and you'll never be seen again!"

"The Spirits of the Forest!" Thorn-in-foot, a woman badly scarred from her experience with smallpox in the past, said with sudden enlightenment. "Everything has a spirit. What you call Fairies, we call the Spirits of the Forest! It's the spirit in trees and rocks and animals. Even the water, we believe has a spirit living in it."

"Something like that, except these are little people in their own right who share that spirit your talking about. And these little people are very mischievous!" She tweaked the nose of the child lying next to her, and he giggled.

The children loved her stories, and the tales helped distract her little patients from their illnesses.

"Haven't heard anything about Tall Tree and Little Feather," Evening Dove, a frown on her gaunt face, informed Shannon later in the day. The young woman had lost much weight during the past couple of weeks but never complained of the hard work she was doing.

Movement from the gate drew their attention. Running Weasel was coming towards them with an arm load of wood. He had lost a lot of weight and had developed the masculine form of an adult.

"I would never have believed a person could change so much!" Shannon murmured.

"Love for his little sister. He talks and thinks and dreams of nothing else.' Evening Dove said, turning her eyes towards Shannon.

Shannon's eyes were covered with her floppy hat. "Strange about Sunbeam. Seems she should be dead by now or showing strong signs of recovery. But she did drink some broth this morning, and that's a good sign."

Running Weasel had reached them by this time and was listening avidly to Shannon's report about his little sister.

"And she chuckled slightly at one of my stories this morning, Running Weasel!"

"And my mother?" Evening Dove put some wood on the fire, keeping her eyes averted.

Shannon smiled slightly. No matter what she told the young woman, Evening Dove would not believe her mother was getting better until she could see for herself. "I tell you every day that she is getting better. Her sickness was very mild, and she is already helping with the others. A few more days . . . a week and she should be ready to leave"

Shannon left the village and made her way into the woods in the opposite direction of the camps. Her trips were always brief and filled with anxiety that someone might catch her squatting to pee. She worried about her hair and wore her hat all of the time— when she remembered—now. She worried about Little Feather, wondering if they had caught up with her cousin yet. She worried about Shamus. Was he alive or dead? Had her cousins caught and killed him? Had disease gotten him? She hurried back to the village, no more refreshed than when she had left.

It became an endless round of forcing herbal tea on people to weak to help themselves, poultices or herbal solutions poured on open wounds, endless cooking and care, but gradually some people were getting better and helping with the other sick people. And some people died . . . among them Boy-who-talks-a-lot. That day Shannon couldn't bring herself to tell her stories. She was too choked up with tears.

But after that one day of mourning for the chubby little boy who died nothing but skin and bones, Shannon forced herself to find time each day to tell her wondrous stories to the children and adults interested in listening.

On the fourteenth day of the epidemic while Shannon was getting the daily news of the camps from Running Weasel and Evening Dove, a woman was carried into the village between two men—Iron Fist and Deer Hunter. The woman was Little Feather's sister, Running Feet. A sharp pain shot through Shannon's heart. What if she could not save Little Feather's beloved sister . . . as she had been unable to save his favorite nephew.

Before the men reached her, she yelled for Big-as-a-bear to come and assist her in carrying the woman into the long house.

"When did the fever develop?" Shannon asked the men.

"Just this morning," Iron Fist answered.

Shannon felt some relief that the woman had come in as soon as the fever started.

"I'll be back for some garlic broth as soon as we get her lying down," she called to Running Weasel who was feeding the fire about twenty feet from the front of the long house. "You, two," she addressed herself to the men, "get out of the village now. We will do our best for her." And she did. Shannon spent the long afternoon forcing garlic broth on Running Feet. The fever slowly rose and dropped only to rise again in several cycles. Between the times of forcing broth on the young woman, she bathed her with cool water. Fortunately, there were enough care givers and recovering people to take care of the needs of everyone else.

That night she ached all over as she fell exhausted onto her sleeping platform. Pulling the bearskin blanket over her head, she shut out the world and fell asleep to dream about Little Feather.

Always they made tender love, passionate love, or funny love. Each morning she always awoke with tears in her eyes, wondering where he was and if he was okay. Then she pushed the heavy blanket down, shoved thoughts of Little Feather from her mind and resumed her caregiving activities.

Five days—and a lot of care—later, Shannon knew that Running Feet had passed the crisis and was going to survive. Bright Eyes'—who illness was milder—poxes were nearly dried up. Although Red Fox's illness was more severe, he developed few poxes. Standing Elk was already recovering with most of his poxes dried up.

After Running Feet came down ill, no one else developed the fever. By the twenty-first day, twenty-seven people, of the seventy-two who had gotten sick, had died.

That night when Shannon collapsed on her bed she knew the epidemic was over. She pulled the heavy blanket over her head and cried silently. She was exhausted, she was jubilant, she was lonely.

Chapter 24

Long rays of pink and gold stretched up into the western sky, and the eastern sky was already growing a dusky grey when Little Feather's band first detected the pungent odor of smoke in the air.

"A campfire? Couldn't be the redhead? He couldn't be that stupid, could he?" Grey Turtle asked with disgust in his voice.

"Maybe they're that sure that no one would be trailing them?" Tall Tree responded. "Maybe they decided they couldn't be linked to the killings. They've been going pretty freely among the villages and camps, or maybe it's just another group of travelers or hunters like us," Little Feather added to the conversation. "But we won't find out standing here speculating. Let's just stroll into the camp, and if it is the redhead, we'll see what their story is." Little Feather shrugged his broad shoulders while speaking. "Seems as good a plan as any."

Grey Turtle chuckled. "Good idea! I wondered what you'd come up with."

"And what will our story be?" Grey Elk, their fourth member questioned.

"We're hunting . . . what else?" Little Feather grinned. "Started out this afternoon and haven't caught sight of anything. Saw the smoke from their fire and thought to request hospitality for the night."

"All friendly like? Just cozy up to them?" Tall Tree asked.

"Why not? We aren't suppose to know who they are or what they've done. But keep your eyes sharp and your wits about you.

At no time forget that these snakes strike from behind! We'll get what information we can before we take them prisoners. It's possible, although not likely, that no amount of torture would elicit the information we want, and there are many people along their trail who want a piece of them."

"What information?" Grey Elk asked, the newcomer not having been informed of the hunters full mission.

"Well, my friend," Little Feather explained, "every place they've been they've ask about a redheaded man and woman . . ."

"I know that. No one has seen these people."

"But it's not the people we're interested in," Little Feather said patiently. "It's the muskets! We want to know where they are, how well they're protected, even if there is some code used to access them."

"You're after the guns!" Grey Elk's eyes widened in surprise. The thought of going after the guns had not even occurred to him. He looked at Little Feather with new respect, even awe in his dark eyes. He was familiar with the tales of the legendary Little Feather of the Turtle Clan which was largely why he was here now. The opportunity to go with Little Feather on any journey was every boy's dream. He grinned. "Wonderful! And so simple!"

Tall Tree raised his eyebrows and shrugged his shoulders. "Very simple. Took lots of thought, that idea," exclaimed Tall Tree irreverently, not holding his friend in such awe as the youth did.

"After that, Grey Turtle and Red Hawk get their time with them. Then they'll get turned over to Grey Owl's clan," Little Feather continued, ignoring his friend's comment.

"What about Ian?" Grey Turtle asked.

"I don't think . . . he'll care much what happens to them. One other thing, try to place yourselves close to the Huron. I will lean my musket against my legs while I eat. When I pick it up and explain that I'm going into the forest to relieve myself, that will be the signal to attack. We want them alive if possible but not at the expense of your lives, except for the redhead. Him, we need alive!"

They followed the scent of smoke through the trees and around brush and shrubs.

After a short time, voices—raucous laughter and grunting—accompanied the acrid smell of smoke and the sweet aroma of roast rabbit.

Little Feather and his three companions scoped out the campsite and its occupants and found they were the marauders they had been pursuing for days. The elation they felt did not show on their faces—neither did their disgust—as they strolled into the light cast by the campfire.

The redhead lay near the fire, with his pants down, grunting over the woman who was spread-eagle with her hands and feet tied to stakes driven in the ground. The six Huron were staggering around the camp making lewd comments about their companion's performance. Each held a bottle of whisky that he was alternately waving around and drinking. No one noticed in the midst of their merry-making they had company standing on the edge of the light produced by the campfire.

With one final heave of his buttocks, the white man threw his head back and roared out his release. The woman winced. One of the half-drunk Huron staggered over to them, held the woman's struggling head as he poured whiskey down her throat and over her mouth, waiting his turn.

As the white man struggled to his feet and was attempting to pull his pants up, he discovered the four strangers standing near the trees, studying his campsite He knew he was at a slight disadvantage even as his visitors knew it. Three of the strangers were carrying flintlocks resting easily in the crooks of their elbows. Loaded? Probably not. People didn't usually carry loaded muskets, and Indians weren't smart enough to think ahead. But no point in taking chances at the moment, and they might provide a little fun before he killed them. His thoughts flowed in rapid succession over his face. Best to bluff at the moment. He never doubted for a moment but that he could best these ignorant savages.

"Hey, come and join us, friends!" he invited jovially, but his shrewd blue eyes revealed that he was not as inebriated as his companions.

The four men stood looking at one another with puzzled expressions

"So my dirty, rotten Mohawk visitors, you don't speak French!" The smile never left his face. He yelled to one of the men drinking heavily from his bottle, "Hey, Shorty, you speak the Mohawk lingo, don't ya?"

Shorty almost dropped his bottle when he saw the four Kanien'kehaka warriors lounging by the trees.

"Ask them what they want?" the redhead ordered.

Shorty relayed the message to Little Feather who appeared to be the leader of the group.

"We've been out hunting, no luck yet. Saw the smoke from your fire and came to ask your hospitality for the night. We didn't realize you were strangers passing through our territory until we entered your campsite."

The Huron recognized the subtle threat and sobered a little before he relayed the message to the redhead.

"So they want a little hospitality, huh?" He stared down at the woman staked out on the ground as the Huron took his place. "They can have all the hospitality they want. She's got enough for everybody! And there's whisky all around! Tell them they're welcome to share everything we've got," and he laughed heartily, glancing slyly at the flintlock Little Feather carried. "And no more drinking! Pretend to drink a lot, but no more!"

The big warrior didn't miss the interest shown by the redhead in his gun.

The four Kanien'kehaka warriors refused the services of the woman and the whisky but gratefully accepted the warmth of the fire and some roast rabbit.

"From which direction did you come?" Little Feather inquired, glancing around the small camp. Six back carriers were scattered about leaning against trees, each fully packed with pelts . . . stolen. From one of the carriers hung many scalps, more than had been taken since Little Feather had started tracking them.

"We have a village in Seneca territory. They accepted us after the breakup of our nation." Shorty answered. "The hunting has been good for us this past cold season, and we're just passing through your territory on our way to Fort Orange."

"Why not trade with the French? They would have been much closer than Fort Orange."

"Just wanted to learn what the Dutch are like as traders, and what they have to offer."

The warrior using the woman howled out his release, and another man took his place.

"Sure you don't want to have your turn with her?" the white man questioned through Shorty.

"No, we need to keep our minds and spirits on the hunt," Grey Turtle responded, barely resisting the urge to grab the white man and skin him like a squirrel.

Rabbit meat sizzled merrily over the fire that crackled and popped in the fire pit. Night was full over the forest, and the fire with the weird shadows it cast upon the camp and its occupants was their only source of light.

"Have you seen any game today?" Little Feather asked innocently. In a soft tone, for Tall Tree's ears only, he explained the white man's orders to his men about drinking.

"So they plan to try and kill us after we go to sleep!"

"Had you ever doubted it? Too bad we're not going to sleep!"

Tall Tree, while apparently eating, passed the message along to the other two members of their party.

"We haven't spotted any game within hours of here," Shorty replied.

"Ask the slime if they have any knowledge of a redheaded man or woman in the area. Tell him they both have grey eyes— not blue like mine—and that the man is big and brawny, mean as sin! The woman is gorgeous, lively, fights like a hellcat! She might be in disguise. We'll give one hundred muskets—flintlocks at that—to anyone who can help us locate either of them—two hundred for the two of them!"

Little Feather silently breathed a sigh of relief but waited patiently for Shorty to relay the message. He had begun to wonder if this was the group they had been trailing. Casting the white an expression of feigned amazement, he gasped, "Nobody has that many flintlocks!"

After the message was interpreted to the redhead, he smirked in return, saying, "We do!"

Little Feather appeared to ponder the question about the man and woman for a moment after Shorty had translated it for them. Gazing at his companions scattered about the camp, he received a variety of responses.

"If I recollect correctly, it seems like a man fitting that description sought hospitality from our village a number of moons ago. He was loaded with pelts and on his way to Fort Orange. But I imagine he is long gone from these parts by now. You might get information there. Why are you hunting for them?"

"It's none of their business what we want with them, they can't help us anyway." he responded after Little Feather's answer was relayed to him. "But after tonight what they know won't matter anyway. I sure do like killing these Iroquois, and then taking the whore . . . ummm, um!"

His companions laughed at the joke they were pulling on the ignorant Kanien'kehaka.

"They're brother and sister. Shannon and Shamus Maguire. Oh, by the way, my name is Kevin Maguire. Shamus is a monster! He rapes women and eats little children!"

Little Feather couldn't resist glancing towards the woman who was being raped by the fire while everyone sat around chatting as though nothing were happening.

"He brought shame to our family!" Kevin mourned, tipping the bottle of whisky and making a big show of drinking. Most of it ran down his chin.

"What of the woman?" Little Feather questioned, studying Kevin but addressing his words to Shorty.

"Oh, she's a sly and deceitful one! Helps her brother in his evil doing! But we believe she knows where he is. Oh, the shame of it all!" and he took another slug of whisky, dribbling it down the front of himself. His shirt was becoming quite wet.

Little Feather resisted both the urge to laugh—the man was nearly as good an actor as Shannon—and the urge to punch the man in the mouth for slandering Shannon, Little Feather's woman.

"I think we will hunt these people for you. Two hundred muskets is a prize not to be ignored," Little Feather decided, with the appearance of great contemplation.

"Well, I appreciate that, friend," Kevin said jovially. "You, you piece of slime, couldn't find a door if it was right in front of you." His friends laughed, although Shorty modified the message.

"How do we find you to collect the guns?" Little Feather asked.

"We've been hunting those two for a year without discovering a trace of them until now. You think you can find them more easily?"

"I always run my query to the ground!" Little Feather said arrogantly. "Where do we find you to collect the reward?"

Kevin considered the question shrewdly. He didn't like the arrogant Indian. The man made Kevin feel insignificant. But these hunters would be dead by morning, so where was the harm in answering the question. A smile slithered across his face . . . they would die knowing where the guns were and that *they* would never get their hands on them!

"I like your kind of confidence, my friend," the arrogant redhead said boisterously, pretending to take another drink. "We have a small trading post near Ft. Fontenac out of which we work. My brother Brian operates the post while I deal with outlying trading and information. But the post is heavily guarded. My brother is a most suspicious person!" Kevin burst out laughing. He sobered slightly and said, "I don't think I got your name, friend?"

"I am Little Feather of the Turtle Clan of the Kanien'kehaka. These are my friends: Tall Tree, Grey Turtle and Grey Elk"

So much for simple plans. All six Huron stopped, motionless—even the one raping the woman—on hearing Little

Feather's name. This man had terrorized their trapping and trading lines for two years! The hatred was palpable! Mayhem broke out! The Huron scrambled for their weapons, but alcohol made them slow and clumsy—knocking their muskets and tomahawks about, and the Kanien'kehaka were close by their sides—and not clumsy—as originally planned. Within moments the six Huron had been rendered unconscious and bound like animals.

Little Feather's gun had come up the instant the Hurons had dived for their weapons. There had been no time for Shorty to explain to the redhead who Little Feather was.

"Welcome to *my* territory, friend," Little Feather spoke in his best French and friendliest tone of voice.

"That gun isn't loaded!" the redhead sputtered.

"Oh, but it is! Would you like to challenge me? Incidentally, I loaded it before entering your camp. Thoughtful of me wasn't it? For an ignorant savage?"

"You never did encounter Shannon or Shamus, did you? You only wanted the guns!"

"Good planning for an ignorant savage, huh? For future reference—although I don't think you have much future—alcohol dulls the senses. That's why this ignorant savage never drinks!"

Little Feather glanced about him to see who wasn't doing anything at the moment. Tall Tree was the first to have his captives tied.

"Tall Tree, tie this *slime* ball up, would you?"

Little Feather stood for a moment, looking about. "Did any of you men think to bring any slave collars with you?"

"Don't look at me! I was at the fishing camp! This was a spontaneous decision on my part!" Grey Elk protested.

"Oh, shut up!" Grey Turtle admonished the young man. "No one is blaming you for our forgetfulness!" He turned to Little Feather, grinning. "How did we forget the slave collars? Weren't we planning on catching them?"

"I guess we all had other things on our minds," he responded, a little sheepishly, thinking of Shannon, White Feather and Evening Dove.

Red Hawk strolled from the forest, carrying the forgotten items. "I didn't know if you had brought any slave collars, so I brought some just in case they might be needed."

"Put them on!" Little Feather grinned, waving his hand in the direction of their prisoners. "Tonight we sleep well!"

"Grey Elk and I will take first watch. Grey Turtle and Red Hawk take the next, and you and I will take the last one," Tall Tree informed Little Feather.

Little Feather, carrying his gun, made his last trip to the woods for the night. Returning to camp, he found a spot away from the fire and curled up in his blanket and fell asleep instantly.

Chapter 25

The serpent had two heads, one of them appeared to hang limply while the other swayed and roared in violent rage and dripped poisonous venom that boiled and steamed when it hit the ground. Shannon leaped and dodge its deadly maw while swinging and slashing with her sword, hacking away large chunks of flesh. Little Feather carved away at the serpent with his tomahawk, great pieces of flesh falling away.

"Look out, Little Feather!" Fear drove Shannon to an even greater effort to distract the beast as its gigantic serpentine head swung over Little Feather like a hammer of destruction.

At the last possible instant, he leaped out of harm's way and swung a mighty blow at the monstrous head. The head reared back and then struck again.

Shannon screamed, waving her arms violently but to no avail. Little Feather couldn't hear her.

Suddenly something was constraining her. Struggling to free herself only caused the spider-like web to constrict more tightly about her. A piece of the web brushed irritatingly against her cheek, but she was so tangled up, she couldn't reach her face to remove the irritant. Her heart was throbbing in her chest, sweat rolled off her forehead and tears streamed down her face. She could no longer see Little Feather!

The irritant continued across her face . . .

Her eyes snapped open. The bearskin blanket was tangled about her, and Bright Eyes—emaciated to the point of painfulness—was tickling her cheek with a feather. After a few minutes struggle with the blanket, she won. Extricating herself, she grabbed the child into her arms and dragged her under the cover.

"Hide! Hide!" Bright Eyes chortled gleefully.

"Hide from your mommy?"

"Yes!" and the child giggled and squirmed under the blanket.

Running Feet entered the fireside, appearing tired and haggard and with new pox marks marring her lovely face. A long time would pass before she and the rest of the long house would get use to Boy-who-talks-a-lot being gone. Everyone, including Shannon, found themselves looking and listening for the boy's bright smile and incessant chatter

"I have lost my little Bright Eyes. Where could she have gone?"

Giggling and squirming under the blanket!

"If I can't find her, I shall cry and cry and cry! I shall miss her so much!"

The child threw the blanket back and screamed happily, "I's here, Mommy! I's here! Don' cry!"

Bright Flower, among others, had returned to the long house that morning. The lesions on the people who had survived were well along the way to being dried up, and they had returned temporarily to their long houses.

"Come and join us for a meal, Ian," Running Feet invited in her soft, sad voice.

Shannon, in Little Feather's clothes—they kept her in touch with him—swung her legs over the edge of the platform. "I'll be along shortly."

Shannon strolled out of the long house and breathed deeply of the fresh air. Gazing about, she was delighted to see new leaves burgeoning on the trees and flower buds swelling.

Walking past the stockade entrance, she found some tiny violets bursting from the ground, and the hardy dandelions were pushing up everywhere. Smoke tingled her nostrils. The long houses in the new village were in varying degrees of completion and would soon be livable.

Where was Little Feather? Three weeks had passed since his departure, and there had been no word in weeks. She could only pray that he and Tall Tree and Grey Turtle were well and safe.

Finishing her morning necessaries, she wandered back to the village. The day was too nice to spend it inside, and she resolved to spend as much of it as possible outdoors. Maybe she would go and help with the new village. Most people would be there.

Iron Fist and Standing Elk were leaving the long house as she was returning.

"Are you men on your way to the new village site?"

"It's going to take everyone working together to get the new village ready for habitation as soon possible." Iron Fist answered.

"Don't over exert yourself, Standing Elk, or you'll wind up flat on your back again."

"Will you tell me some more stories about the fairies and Cuchulain?" he asked with a grin.

"Just don't overdue it!"

Then she asked Iron Fist the question she asked every day that she saw him, "Have you heard anything from Little Feather?"

He smiled at her sympathetically. "Be patient, my young friend. Little Feather is fine. Sometimes these hunts can take a while. But the rewards for which you wait at the end are worth it."

Shannon walked on into the long house, not much heartened by Iron Fist's words. They didn't relieve the ache of loneliness, nor make the waiting any easier.

Several women collected personal items to be moved to lean-tos, their temporary lodgings, until the new long houses were finished or at least the sides and roofs were up.

Bright Flower and Smiles-alot were dishing up bowls of stew, one of which was handed to Shannon. "Let's go outside, my young friend. You've been cooped up too long and need some fresh, clean air. Smiles-a-lot is praising your work to everyone. The long, hard days you put in caring for our people."

Gratefully accepting the food, Shannon followed Little Feather's adopted mother outside with Smiles-a lot trailing behind.

The two older women found stumps to sit on while they ate, and Shannon sat on the ground, leaning against a tree.

Gazing up at Bright Flower, Shannon protested, "I didn't work any harder or do any more than anyone else! Smiles-a-lot was often up and working when I collapsed at night! And Evening Dove and Running Weasel kept the herb teas brewing day and night outside the long house. Without everyone working together, it would have been a whole lot worse. Even the people bringing food and water to the village gate were indispensable."

"But, Ian, there were times when we were all ready to quit— fortunately, not all at the same time! But you kept going and driving us. Thank you," Smiles-a-lot said, reaching out and ruffling Shannon's hair.

Oh, God! She'd forgotten her hat. Shannon's gasp was audible as her heart sank. With her mind full of Little Feather and the danger he was in, she had forgotten to put her cap on upon rising! And she hadn't had time to touch up her hair in weeks! Jumping up, she dodged into the long house to retrieve her cap.

"After we finish eating, I think we should do something about making your hair all one color," Smiles-a-lot murmured as though Shannon hadn't collected her hat. "Don't you think so, Bright Flower?"

Shannon's head jerked up until her startled grey eyes first met Bright Flower's and then Smiles-a-lot's surprised but twinkling ones. During the preceding three weeks Shannon and the sister of Little Feather's grandmother had developed a deep and abiding respect and affection for one another.

"That obvious, huh?" Shannon couldn't help grinning, resigned to at least part of her secret having been discovered.

Both Bright Flower and Smiles-a-lot nodded.

"I was going to tend to that this morning but over slept."

"We want you to know that if ever you need our assistance, it's yours," Smiles-a-lot said. "Whatever in your past, you are hiding from, among us you have earned the right to be yourself."

Bright Flower nodded her agreement, but Shannon wasn't secure enough to confide yet . . . maybe soon.

As good as their word, the women accompanied Shannon to the river where they assisted her to conceal the glorious, flaming color of her hair.

While walking back to the village, Shannon asked Bright Flower the question that had been stressing her since she knew the whole village would be moving. "How will Little Feather and others, away from the village now, find the new village?"

"Signs will be left by the clearing around the old village indicating the direction of the new one and how far it is," Bright Flower laughed.

"That simple?"

"That simple."

Later that day, while people who had recovered from the illness were hauling personal possessions from their long houses to the lean-tos, Evening Dove, came searching for Shannon.

"Ian!" Evening Dove called when she caught sight of Shannon.

Shannon waited until the pretty, young woman caught up with her. "I have a gift for you!" She handed a heavily beaded tunic, leggings and moccasins to Shannon. "You saved my mother. I made this tunic for Tall Tree, but I want you to have it. My mother's sister made the leggings and moccasins just for you. Now you won't have to wear Little Feather's clothes," she said ingeniously.

"Thank you!" Shannon murmured, deeply touched. "But won't the tunic be too long, if you made it for Tall Tree?"

"I cut it down for you, Ian!" Evening Dove giggled.

"Bright Flower! . . . Mother . . . Smiles-a-lot!" Shannon could scarcely contain her pleasure. "Look what Evening Dove and her family have given me!"

The two women studied the gifts, praising the exquisite workmanship and fine materials.

While the four women were discussing the gifts, a False Face strolled up to them. He stopped in front of Shannon and started shaking a turtle shell rattle he carried in one hand. Moving the rattle about her head and up and down her body, he chanted softly.

Shannon recognized the False Face as one who had visited the long house many times during the epidemic but was totally puzzled by his present behavior.

The man was obviously perplexed also when he spoke to her. "We thank the Great Spirit for sending you to us in our time of greatest need. You have earned the name I now hang about your neck . . . Boy-who-cares . . . several times you visited my visions. I saw this epidemic, and all the long, hard work you did, the lives you saved, the inspiration you provided when fatigue and depression weighed the people down. But the person in the vision was a woman with hair like the setting sun. I've never had a vision that was so right and so wrong!"

Gasps, quickly stifled, rose about them. The False Face appeared not to hear as he departed, but Shannon heard them.

Shannon gazed fearfully into Bright Flower's shocked face . . . which abruptly broke into a brilliant smile. Then turning her attention to Smiles-a-lot, she found the same broad grin.

"Ian, if you ever want to talk, I'm all ears!" Evening Dove gushed with a smile that wouldn't be contained.

Shannon returned her smile but felt only relief that the women showed no signs of anger at her deception, nor did any of them press her for an explanation. They never mentioned it.

Her new name spread quickly among the villagers, and everywhere she went people greeted her as Boy-who-cares.

"Boy-who-cares!"

Shannon, hauling Little Feather's possessions on a back carrier, glanced about to determine who was calling her. Running Weasel approached her with an armload of things he was transporting to his family's campsite.

"Grandmother would appreciate it very much if you would share a meal with us. You can imagine how much it means to us that you saved my little sister's life." She very probably had preserved this branch of the Wolf Clan.

"Thank you, Running Weasel for the invitation. I'd be glad to join your family when I have time. I'm just glad I was able to help."

Late that afternoon, a runner passed through the village. Men, women and children bustled about him to hear his news.

"More people have been slaughtered along our trail. When the message got to me a few hours ago, I was told that Little Feather from this village was close on their trail, and probably has caught them by now."

A thrill of excitement and pleasure flowed through Shannon. *Her* man was okay! And *her* man was doing what he had to do to protect her and his people. Her heart and head swelled with pride.

Someone handed the runner a drink of water.

"Can you rest a while?" someone else asked.

"Another runner will take over in the next village. One other message—someone passed through my village a short time ago hunting for a redheaded man and woman. He is offering two hundred muskets to anyone who can turn this couple over to him."

"He must want them desperately," a man commented. "What did they do?"

"He gave some crazy story," the runner replied. "The muskets would be nice though!"

A woman handed him some pemmican which he was chewing as he vanished among the trees.

Shannon cast her gaze towards Bright Flower and knew instantly that the woman understood the reason for the disguise, but nothing was said at that time or later.

That night Shannon shared a lean-to with Iron Fist, Red Fox and Little Wolf.

The boys discussed the merits of different girls in the village.

Shannon pulled her bearskin over her head in an unsuccessful attempt to block out their conversation. At this young age, they were already doing *that?* And thoughts of *that* immediately brought images of Little Feather to mind!

"Ian . . . I mean Boy-who-cares, with whom would you like to go into the woods?"

Damn! Was everyone going to try and match her up with someone? The blanket behind her shook. Iron Fist was laughing!

"I'm going to sleep! There is a lot of work we need to do tomorrow," she mumbled from under her blanket. And she went to sleep with no further problems.

She was swimming, and the water was crystal clear and warm. Water splashed over her from behind. Spinning about, she got another spray of water in the face. Wiping the droplets away, she saw Little Feather laughing at her. She leaped at him through the water, splashing him at the same time. He caught her in his powerful arms and brought his sensuous mouth down on hers. Her arms wound up about his muscular neck and pulled him closer. She couldn't get enough of him! His cock was hard against her belly, and she rubbed herself against him. He groaned with the pleasure of it. He pulled her up against his body and spread her legs about his waist . . .

Her eyes snapped open. Someone was gently massaging her breasts through her binder! Grabbing the hand she stilled the motion. "Go back to sleep, my prickly little wife!" was whispered so softly in her ear that no one else could possibly have heard it. Little Feather was home! and safe! She grasped his hand in her own and did as he said, went back to sleep.

Chapter 26

"You can't go! and that's it!"

"I am going! and *that's* it!"

"Oh, my prickly little wife. It's my duty—and privilege—to protect you, and this is too dangerous. You're *not* going!" His voice rose suspiciously, sounding a great deal like anger which he prided himself on not displaying.

Little Feather and Shannon were lying naked between their bearskin blankets in a secluded glade. They had completed wild, fantastic, ecstatic lovemaking moments before. Her head rested on his shoulder, and his arm held her close.

A stream gurgled nearby, and birds were flittering amongst the branches far above and singing lustily all about the intruders. A squirrel scampered up an oak looking for left-over acorns from the preceding year. New leaves were peeping out of their winter sheaths, giving a green haze to everything. All in all, the day was a beautiful spring day.

"I'm not prickly! and I *am* going!"

"Oh, Shannon . . . *Boy*-who-cares . . ." he grinned at her. She punched him in the shoulder.

"Iron Fist, a couple of other sachems, and some members of Makes-good-basket's clan will be accompanying us as far as the Central Fire. At Grey Owl's home village, members of his clan will be joining us. They will be going for the traditional Condolence Ceremony and the confirmation of a new Clan Sachem. You *will* stay with Iron Fist when our trails separate, and we continue on to Fort Fontenac. And *that is that!*"

Shannon, deciding she was getting no where with the bullheaded man next to her, made a strategic withdrawal. She had until they reached the Onondaga territory to convince him to change his mind, and if the worst case scenario came to pass, and she couldn't get him to change his mind, she'd simply follow after him. The thought never occurred to her to obey him is this decision. God, how she hated taking orders!

Leaning forward,she kissed his chin and started to caress his chest. He rolled towards her, eyeing her suspiciously at the sudden change in her behavior. He suspected he knew her well enough to know that some devious planning against him was taking place. But he wasn't going to reject the gift she was offering. Seize the moment, he thought, and he did. Taking her into his arms, he brought his mouth down on hers in a long, passionate, satisfying kiss.

"Three weeks was longer than forever! I missed you so," Little Feather murmured into her mouth.,

One day and a lot of pleasure making later, Little Feather and Shannon accompanied by a large host of villagers—whole families— departed for the Central Fire of the Extended Long house. The seven prisoners, led by White Feather and Grey Turtle, were tied slave collar to slave collar and limped along at the end of the column.

Some beatings had occurred at the time of capture, and the prisoners' Achiles tendons had been cut to prevent escape, but no serious harm had been done to them, the decision being made to turn them over to Grey Owl's clan, and anyone who wanted to could attend the disposition of the murderers. Little Feather had informed Shannon that Grey Owl's murderer had, in fact, been her cousin Kevin, but Shannon had been too busy with Little Feather to bother confronting the man. That would come in time.

Little Feather, Shannon, Tall Tree and Evening Dove strolled together as a group.

"I am going!" Shannon insisted. "Boys my age often go on raids!"

"How many summers do you have?" Little Feather asked, hoping to distract the stubborn woman from the raid. It didn't work.

"Enough summers to go an the damn raid!"

Evening Dove giggled from behind them.

Little Feather, glancing back over his shoulder, discovered Tall Tree grinning broadly, too. The big man stopped. "Is there some joke going on here that I don't know about?"

Evening Dove giggled again.

Little Feather cast Tall Tree a questioning glance.

His friend raised an innocent eyebrow, saying, "I don't mind gigglers."

"That's not what I meant!"

Evening Dove who had to struggle to keep a secret, burst out, "I know you're not a pervert which I had begun to wonder— along with others!"

A moment passed before Little Feather grasped the meaning of Evening Dove's words. When he did, his gaze went immediately to Shannon. "How?"

"It's a long story, but your mother and Smiles-alot know, too."

"Then I can tell you," he bent and put his nose to her nose, "that you can't go because it is inappropriate for a *woman* to go on a raid . . . and dangerous," and he was dangerously close to yelling.

"But, Little Feather, I can use a gun proficiently. I'm good with a bow—they both remembered her just missing him with the arrow. You've never seen me use a knife, but I'm as good with a knife, too! It's so recent since you injured you arm that you might hurt it again using your bow too soon."

Bringing his hand up to his forehead in a sign of irritation and frustration, he grumbled, "I'm not going to hurt my arm, you're probably great with a knife. But you're not going, and that's that!" But he had a horrible intuition *that* wouldn't be *that*.

Sulking, Shannon dropped back with Evening Dove and Tall Tree.

"He really is correct. Raids are too dangerous for women. He's only trying to protect you because he cares," Tall Tree observed seriously.

"Not you, too! Why don't you go up and plan your stupid raid with him?"

"Oh, we have days for that yet!" He shot back over his shoulder, his dark eyes twinkled with humor as he left the women behind and caught up with his friend.

That evening as the sun set amidst a bright red and purple sky, the group stopped and set up camp for the night. While Little Feather and Shannon were constructing their night's shelter, Red Fox and Little Wolf joined them.

"Boy-who-cares, how about coming and sharing our lean-to tonight. Talk about girls!"

"Do you know that tomorrow is apt to be a nice day?" Shannon asked, tipping her head enough to see the boys from beneath the brim of her hat while her eyes remained in shadow.

"Huh?" both boys muttered in unison, totally confused.

Little Feather snickered from behind her as he worked on their lean-to. Serve him right if she went, but then she would only be punishing herself, too.

"What I mean is that there are other things to talk about besides girls,"—the boys looked totally confused now—"forget it! Thanks for the offer, but I don't think so. I haven't caught up on my rest from the sleepless nights of the past three weeks. I'm pretty tired, want to sleep. Thanks anyway."

Little Feather chuckled again. "Sleep?" he murmured.

She blushed beneath her floppy hat, nor did she get much sleep that night, although she felt surprisingly refreshed in the morning with a healthy glow to her cheeks.

So the days fell into a routine. Each day Shannon pleaded, begged and threatened Little Feather to coerce him into taking her on the raid to obtain the guns. He adamantly refused. She sulked and spent a lot of time with Evening Dove. Their friendship, started during the epidemic, developed deep and close on the trail.

"What?" Shannon shouted one day as she and Evening Dove trailed behind Little Feather and Tall Tree. She and Little Feather had had another one of their disagreements over her going on the raid. "What do you mean if the Turtle Clan adopted me, Little Feather and I couldn't be married?" Shannon asked more quietly as Little Feather glanced back over his shoulder at her.

Evening Dove tried to explain the intricacies of who one could marry and who one couldn't marry.

"Well, I just won't let them adopt me!" Shannon insisted stubbornly.

"Oh, being adopted into any clan is more important than marriage," Evening Dove said seriously. "Marriages break up. You hope they'll last, but sometimes people grow apart. It happens. But when you're adopted into a clan, you belong to that clan forever. Your children and grandchildren belong to that clan forever. You always have family, someone to help when needed. Someone to share in you joys and sorrows. Understand?"

"Oh," was all Shannon could think to say. A long time had passed since she had had that kind of family. She also came from a clan—an extended family, but her clan was full of jealousy, anger, hate . . . more than she had realized until recently.

Shannon scuffed her feet in the dust of the trail as she thought about this important event. They were hiking along a river with broad open fields along each side In the distance she could see a village stockade. They would probably build their shelters in the open field about the village that night, and there would be much eating, and gaming. They might even get a stick-and-ball game going.

That evening Shannon went with Red Fox, Little Wolf and Running Weasel about the camp and village finding willing opponents with whom to game. During her time with the French traders, she had learned that gaming was a national past time with the Iroquois. The boys lost about as many games as they won, and all of the games with other youths was filled with bravado talk of girls and hunting. Finally, when Shannon got thoroughly bored with the boys, she split and went in search of Little Feather who was gaming with Tall Tree, the twins, and some men from the village. They appeared to all be good friends and were completely absorbed in the game.

Men! Shannon thought disgustedly and wandered off by herself. Settling herself on the bank of the river, she thought about the changes that had come about in her life over the past year. No doubt about it, Little Feather was the highlight of her year and Shamus was the low point. The worry she felt for her brother hung like a black cloud over all her thoughts and activities. Even the love she shared with Little Feather was experienced through the black cloud that was forever present. Was Shamus alive or dead? Had he been captured by the British? Was he even now lying in some unnamed, unmarked grave? There under the starlit sky and a full moon, Shannon was overwhelmed by thoughts of her brother, and tears flowed down her cheeks. Maybe the problem was that things were going so well for her, and she didn't know how they were for him. The river murmured softly to her as it flowed gently past. It seemed to say, "Tell Little Feather, tell Little Feather." Listening to the river, Shannon resolved to tell Little Feather about Shamus and ask him to help her find her brother when the muskets had been retrieved.

Slowly she made her way back to their shelter, and fell into a troubled sleep long before Little Feather finished gaming.

"Little Feather, I'm going to see Kevin," she informed him the next day, ignoring the fact that he stood in front of her in a breechclout, having lost his beautiful tunic to some man in the village. If he thought that she would be making his tunics, she might give it a try—she wasn't even sure about that! But it certainly wouldn't be of the quality of the one he had lost. But he did look good in his breechclout! Shannon couldn't help grinning at him as she eyed him from head to toe.

With nothing more than a disgusted grunt, Little Feather lead her back to where the prisoners were under guard.

Shannon studied Kevin dispassionately for a long while as he stared defiantly back, being use to having the savages gather and gawk at his red hair, and take pokes at all of the prisoners with their spears and arrows. The women and children pulled the prisoners hair and beat them with sticks. All the prisoners had multiple bruises and cuts.

Finally, she asked, "Why?" in Gaelic.

His eyes widened in surprise and recognition. "Well, if it isn't the bitch herself!" Gazing at Little Feather, something akin to admiration shone in his blue eyes. "So the dirty savage knew where you were all the time!"

"Why, Kevin? Was Clan leadership that important?"

"Oh, the leadership is important. Conal lives for it. He asked your father for your hand in marriage. That alliance would have sealed his position when your father and brothers died fighting the English." He sneered at her.

"I never knew that Conal wanted to marry me, and if I had known I would have refused." Now it was her time for enlightenment. How could they have been sure that her father and brothers would die in battle. One of them had shot her father and Paddy!

"My God! You were in the battle that day! You shot Da and Paddy! That's the only way you could be sure they would die!"

His lips twisted into a satisfied leer.

"You know you're a dead man, don't you?" Shannon said mildly to her cousin. "My husband's people will see to that . . . in a most gruesome way."

Shock and disgust flowed over his face. "You wouldn't marry my brother? But you would marry this savage?"

She gave an elegant shrug to her slim shoulders. "Such is life, my dear . . . and dead cousin!"

"We'll see," he muttered under his breath, so low that she almost missed it as she turned and departed for their campsite.

But she had heard, and as she strolled back among the trees, the words stayed with her. Why was he so sure he wasn't going to die?

"He actually admitted shooting my brother and father, Little Feather!" her voice shook with rage, tears and frustration as they dismantled their shelter in preparation of moving on. "I want him dead, Little Feather, now!" She saw again the blood flowing from her father's wound—put there by her cousin's hand. She felt the blood on her hands and saw it on her shirt in that musty damp cave.

As they walked, Little Feather directed her away from the camp to a secluded spot. Flinging herself into his arms, she wept from a broken heart. Holding her in his strong arms, he comforted her until the hard crying became broken sobs.

"Why is he still alive?"

"Taking him was so easy that he wasn't killed in battle. There really wasn't any battle. The Huron will be turned over to Grey Owl's clan to be disposed off. I was planning on taking your cousin with us. He may come in useful in obtaining the guns."

"I think you ought to kill him now. He's dangerous—worse than a snake—and needs to be watched every second."

"He *is* being guarded every second. Grey Turtle and White Feather will keep him from escaping. After we collect the muskets, he'll be turned over to Grey Owl's clan and the twins and their mother will be there for his disposal. Don't worry, my little wife, he'll get what he deserves." With that he guided her back towards their campsite.

Three days later they camped in the clearing surrounding Grey Owl's home village. Two columns of the villagers formed, and the prisoners were forced to run between the groups who beat the running men with branches, sticks and clubs with much laughter, jeering and cheering when the men stumbled or fell. The Huron were then taken into the village, and Kevin, battered and beaten and barely conscious, was returned to the custody of White Feather and Grey Turtle.

Early the following morning the whole band of several hundred people departed for the Central Council Fire. A festive atmosphere hung over the group, lots of laughing and visiting among people who hadn't seen each other in a long time, and gaming . . . every time people stopped for any reason games would be started. Children ran and played everywhere.

"I'm going, Little Feather! And that's that!" Shannon insisted a little desperately as they approached the point where the two groups would be separating.

"You're going with Iron Fist to the confirmation of Black Hawk as chief of the Bear Clan, and *that* is *that*! and I don't want to hear any more about it!"

Boy, could Little Feather be stubborn as an ass when he wanted to be! Just like Shamus! After this raid she would have to persuade the stubborn man to help her hunt down Shamus. She fell back in her sulk and walked with Evening Dove. Tall Tree joined his friend.

That night after a very satisfying love session, Shannon approached the subject again. "Little Feather, take me with you. You could leave me where you think I would be safe, and I would stay there."

He contemplated the matter for all of two seconds, "No!" He knew her well enough to realize she wouldn't stay any place unless it was what she wanted. He only hoped Iron Fist could keep her by his side.

Early the next morning, Shannon, standing beside Iron Fist and Evening Dove, observed the band of twenty warriors under Little Feather's leadership jog off to the west. She was already planning on following the stubborn man.

"He'll have my hide if you do!" Iron Fist reminded her mildly, reading her stubborn resolve on her face.

"No, he won't. Are you going to tie me up to keep me here?"

"I could."

She cast him her gamin grin. "You could, but I don't think you will. I think Little Feather hopes I'll stay here, but I don't think he expects it. And there is something else that bothers me . . . when I told my cousin he was going to die a horrible death all he said was 'we'll see'. My cousins aren't cowards but nobody wants to be captured by the Iroquois, or so I've heard, but he wasn't even concerned."

Gazing thoughtfully down the path Little Feather had taken, she pondered the problem. Why was Kevin so sure he wouldn't die at the hands of the Iroquois? He probably suspected that Little Feather would keep him alive until they got the guns, but then . . . Kevin didn't think he'd die at the hands of the Kanien'kehaka . . . why? Maybe he thought he'd be rescued? But how would he have gotten a message out after he was captured? Not after, Shannon realized, before! Prearranged signals! If he wasn't at a certain place at a certain time, a message would be sent to Brian at Fort Fontenac. Why hadn't she thought of that before? Her father had used this method of maintaining track of his men. Damn! She realized that Little Feather and his band were likely traveling into an ambush somewhere between here and Ft. Fontenac, depending on how long it took to relay the message to Brian that Kevin was missing.

"Iron Fist, I have to go after Little Feather and his band," she insisted to the man standing by her.

"Why, Boy-who-cares? He knows what he's doing. He'll be back soon, and then the two of you can take up your lives without deception. If you're there, he's going to be worried about you, and that will split his attention. That will get him killed quicker than anything else! Wait for him to come back!"

"Waiting is one of the things a woman learns, Boy-who-cares," Evening Dove said, gently. "Every time Tall Tree leaves, I worry about him, but he's about men's business, and I wait and pray for his safe return. It's one of the things about being a woman we have to get used to."

"I suspect they're going to be ambushed. Kevin is too positive that he's not going to die at the hands of the Kanien'kehaka. My father had a prearranged method of signals that let him know when someone wasn't where they were suppose to be at any given time. If someone disappeared, he would know almost immediately and could start searching for them. I suspect that when Kevin didn't make an appearance in Fort Orange, such a message was sent off to his brother Brian. It's only a suspicion, Iron Fist, but I have to act upon it," she pleaded with her friend.

The older man meditated upon her words. They made sense. "You're going to follow him, aren't you?"

"Yes, I've got to."

"Will you at least take someone with you . . . Standing Elk, maybe?"

"He's not tried in battle."

"And you are?" Iron Fist smiled gently at her. Her response amazed him, although he realized that it shouldn't have.

"I am! Do you know anyone who would lend me a musket and ball and powder. I'm going to need more arrows than I've got, and is there any possibility that anyone in this group might have a sword that they took as a souvenir from some European?"

"A sword?" Iron Fist sounded stupid even to himself. "I'll see what I can do. Check with Red Fox and Little Wolf about the arrows. They may have some extras. And the musket . . . you can take mine."

Shannon looked at the older man in amzement. "I didn't know you had a musket. Little Feather said you didn't like them."

Iron Fist shrugged and grinned, "C'mon," was all he said.

Through some stroke of magic, Iron Fist actually located a sword with belt and sheath, and Evening Dove collected some pemmican and water for her friend to take with her.

Iron Fist and Evening Dove watched as the transformation occurred. Shannon strapped the belt with sword about her slim waist, and it hung over her hip as though it belonged there. On her other hip was a long deadly knife that Iron Fist had never before noticed. He didn't realize that it had been concealed beneath her tunic. Her quiver was full, and she had the hardest, coldest eyes he had ever encountered. The Ian-Boy-who—cares—he had come to know was gone, and before him stood the warrior woman of Little Feather's dreams. Iron Fist could only hope that Little Feather wouldn't skin him alive when he found out that he had let the woman follow the men. But Iron Fist also acknowledged that there was no way he could have stopped her.

Then Iron Fist and Evening Dove watched as Shannon trotted down the same path the men had taken half an hour early.

Chapter 27

After following the trail for about three hours through broad meadows along the river, Shannon entered into a shadowy, heavily wooded area, the musty smell of rotting vegetation rising about her—a perfect place for an ambush. Continuing on the trail more cautiously, she remained alert to any sign of danger, relying heavily on the birds as a first indicator. But they continued flitting about among the trees and chattering as always.

About half an hour after entering the forest, she heard the abrupt volley of gun shots, followed immediately by blood-curdling screams, shouts, grunts, and groans from somewhere in the distance. The cacophony indicated a full scale battle was in progress.

Her heart stopped a moment and then resumed a hard, rapid pounding. Her eyesight became keener, noticing things she hadn't noticed a moment earlier, and sounds that slipped by her before now sounded like drums as the adrenaline pumped through her veins.

Bursting into a frantic run, she fled through the brush, ignorant of the grasping, clutching branches and briars that reached out to waylay her. The sound of yelling and screaming drew her ever forward. When the gunshots, curses and screams reverberated all about her, she veered off into the trees to the side of the trail to reconnoiter. She liked to know what she was getting into— better chances of survival.

Finally, she was able to see the battle scene clearly between the trees and young saplings. There were more French, Indians and Whites than she had seen in one place in a long time. Little Feather's party appeared to be outnumbered about three to one. A white was even now cutting Kevin loose.

An arrow through the heart of the white ended that scenario, but the bonds had been cut sufficiently that her cousin freed himself and crawled away into the darkness between the trees without anyone—except Shannon—seeing the escape. At the same time Little Feather was struggling with two warriors and a third was sneaking up on him from behind. Another arrow removed the attacker, but went by Little Feather's head so close he felt the breeze. Anger rose up in him like a tidal wave. If he survived this ambush, he was going to kill that woman of his! His sudden rage and fear for his warrior woman drove him into a killing frenzy. Swinging his musket like a club—there was no time to reload in hand to hand combat—he brought it up into the throat of one of his opponents, felling him like a tree. A second later, the makeshift club came crashing down on his other attacker. Club in hand, he quickly scanned the area about him and saw that Tall Tree was in the greatest danger battling with two warriors and two colonists. He joined the fracas swinging his club with deadly accuracy and intent on keeping the ambushers so busy that they wouldn't notice that a lot of the arrows taking out their people were coming from outside of the battle area. He was going to kill her personally!

Even his mindless rage faded into insignificance when an abrupt blood-curdling, animalistic scream of pure fury sliced through the forest. Birds scrambled for the sky in a mad rush. For a moment in time, all action on the battle field froze.

A chill of premonition trickled down Little Feather's spine. What could make such a terrible sound? the Windigo? Could the monster, itself, be here? No one had ever seen the Windigo, but he had heard about it during his sojourn in the north country. He had paid no attention to the stories, but he couldn't help thinking about it now. The sound had made his heart skip a beat . . . but only one beat. The battle resumed between Little Feather's band and the ambushers.

The scream tore through the forest again, sending the birds into a mad flurry for the sky a second time. A split second later it was followed by shouts, shrieks and more gun shots added to the fracas.

Movement was so rapid, Little Feather could scarcely follow it. It was as though demons had risen form the bowels of the earth to join the battle . . . but on whose side?

The Kanien'kehaka were used to speed and brutality, but what they witnessed left them with a strong sense of admiration and a deep burning hatred as they recognized their traditional enemy from the far south. Just what Little Feather and his band needed at the moment! It had been years since the Cherokee had raided this far north.

The attack was made against the Europeans with no effort to take prisoners. The new invaders of the Extended Long house Territory were natives but not like any Shannon had ever seen. Sachems didn't fight on the offense. That was left to warriors, but these demons all had long, black hair flowing over copper skin. It seemed they weren't worried about the enemy taking their scalps.

Breechclouts and leggings clothed their muscled bodies, and they fought with war clubs, tomahawks and knives. Four of the strangers were standing guard over the wounded natives from both sides of the battle.

The eerie howl of rage reverberated through the forest again as a tall, brawny, bronze-colored warrior, garbed as his companions were, tore around a curve in the trail. He was brandishing a broadsword clutched in both hands and dispatched two of the European raiders in seconds.

Little Feather's breath stuck in his throat from shock. The young warrior had flaming red hair and eyes as cold and grey as a stormy, winter sky. With a sinking heart, Little Feather saw Shannon's face except the lines were carved in granite. He wondered what his warrior woman was thinking at the moment, watching her brother behave like a wild man.

In moments the one-sided battle was over with the bloody corpses of the defeated Europeans and their native henchman scattered over the trail and throughout the forest.

Little Feather motioned for his fighters to desist for the moment. Redhair wasn't killing natives for whatever reason, and Little Feather didn't really want to kill his woman's brother if he could help it. Actually, he wasn't sure he could!

Redhair's men were rounding up all the natives into one group. Didn't they know the difference between Huron and Kanien'kehaka? And when was his woman going to make an appearance? Surely she recognized her brother, even he, Little Feather saw the resemblance.

Redhair motioned for a wounded Kanien'kehaka to remove his leggings.

He's a pervert! Little Feather thought with aversion, forgetting for the moment that some of his own acquaintances thought he had the same problem.

His woman's brother or not, Little Feather leaped at Redhair, who, taken by surprise was carried to the ground. In a flash Little Feather was yanked of Redhair, thrown to the ground with a knife at his throat with two, burly warriors crushing the breath out of him. But surprisingly they made no attempt to harm him.

Shannon, who had recognized her brother's warcry when it first left his lips, vowed she would kill him! He had been living with natives while she had been living in disguise pretending to be an idiot . . . his idea! She had been worried about him during this whole past year, while he had been living a life of ease and comfort with these people. She'd kill him!

But when she saw Little Feather—her husband, only the formalities needed to be seen to—thrown to the ground with a knife at his throat, she went absolutely berserk!

Grabbing her sword from its sheath, emitting a blood-curdling scream every bit as chilling as her brother's, she burst from the trees. With a flying leap, such as Little Feather had never seen before, she drove her feet into her brother's powerful chest, bowling him over. Within seconds she dispatched the men holding Little Feather down, the one with the knife—a kick to the chest—and a blade swinging such that he couldn't follow it with his eyes sent the rest of them scrambling for safety.

"Hey, Ian . . . Boy-who-cares . . . Shannon, I'm okay! Relax before you get yourself and all of us killed." He didn't really believe that for a moment, she seemed to have things well under control. His warrior woman!

Redhair came up fighting mad with a ludicrous expression on his handsome face that rapidly changed when he realized who had tackled him.

"Shannon? . . . Is it really you, little sister? I had heard their was an idiot traveling with some French traders in Iroquoia. Wondered if it could be you. Certainly hoped so."

"You leave this man and his friends alone!" She yelled before his words registered with her. "You're here looking for me?" she added.

"Shannon, I'm fine, really I am!" Little Feather reiterated as Shannon stood over him with her sword at the ready between her hands. The only problem he could see was a strong urge to laugh, and at the moment he wasn't sure either the brother or sister would handle that well.

"I told you they were crazy!" Kevin, who had been recaptured by the Cherokee, muttered.

"Shut up!" Shannon and Shamus both shouted simultaneously in Gaelic. Kevin subsided.

"The man is safe, little sister. Have him pick out his people from this group and they'll all be safe, and you can tend the wounded."

Shannon, sheathing her sword, relayed the message to Little Feather who, getting to his feet, called his men to gather about him which they did. The rest of the warriors were held captive by Redhair's men.

"Well, little sister, who is this man, and what is he to you that you protect him like a old she-cat?" Shamus asked, wrapping a muscular arm about her slender shoulders and leading her to a log on which to sit.

"Well, big brother, where the hell have you been this past year?"

Tipping her chin up, Shamus grinned shamelessly into her angry face. "I asked you first!"

Little Feather, not understanding a word that was being spoken, resolved to learn their language immediately. He didn't appreciate being talked around.

Shannon, pointing to Little Feather, answered, "He's my husband or will be as soon as we can legalize it by their traditions!"

"What?" Shamus roared, coming up off the log and heading for Little Feather.

Little Feather, understanding the body language if not the words, was ready to land the first blow if necessary.

Shannon grabbed one brawny arm and tugged to get Shamus's attention. "What's your problem, Shamus? Leave him alone!"

"If he's your husband, he's suppose to protect you!"

"Well," she admitted reluctantly, "I'm not suppose to be here. He left me with an uncle, but I figured out that Kevin had an ambush planned for him. I couldn't just let him die, could I?"

"So still disregarding what you're told for your own good!" Shamus repeated stubbornly, completely ignoring her indispensable assistance.

Shannon didn't like the sound of that at all!

Shamus' arm tightened around her, and when she attempted to pull away, he clamped her arms to her side! Damn! He hadn't tied her up in years! She had been so worried about his welfare, she had forgotten about his rotten side!

"You let me go, you brute!" she screamed.

Little Feather had had enough! Nobody was going to abuse his woman! Glancing around, he realized that all of his men were ready to attack, even though they didn't understand what was happening.

With four guns pointing at Little Feather, he kept advancing.

"Little Eagle, tell him I'm not going to hurt my sister, just package her up and give her to him as a gift! I'm going to teach him how to deal with her in future when she is disobedient!"

"You wouldn't! You rotten dog!" Shannon growled at her brother through gritted teeth.

Little Eagle relayed the message to Little Feather who stopped where he was, and a big grin spread across his face.

His men, confused, were muttering among themselves at the revelation that Ian-Boy-who-cares—was really a woman. Then smiles broke out among them as they realized that Little Feather's interest was not in a boy, as many had feared, but in a woman!

"Hey, Black Bear!" Shamus called to another of his men."I need a rope!"

"I'll never speak to you again! I'll kill you for this, Shamus!"

He ignored her and tied her hands and feet, dumping her unceremoniously at Little Feather's feet. "When you want her to stay some place this is the way to do it!"

Little Eagle translated Shamus's words, and many of the men chuckled.

Shannon blushed, furious with her brother.

"I thank you for your kind advice," Little Feather said through the interpreter as he pulled Shannon to her feet and untied her. "And for this most precious gift you have given me. But it is also a fact that if she had not disregarded my wishes in this matter, that I and probably many of my men would be lying here dead even now," he replied, completely disregarding his former anger. The responsibility to discipline her and protect her were his and no one else's. "And my prickly little wife will not disregard my wishes in the future, will she?" and he squeezed her shoulders sufficiently to cause her discomfort.

A gasp went up from among his men at Little Feather's acknowledgment of her as his wife.

Shannon gazed up into his eyes and murmured, "I won't disregard your wishes in the future, Little Feather." Then for his ears only, "Unless I think it's necessary!"

"And, my prickly little wife, do you think it's necessary to go on this raid with us?" Shannon stared up into his beloved face and knew that it *was* his duty to protect her. All he wanted was her safety . . . and she felt he would be safer for the rest of this raid. Shamus, knowing their cousins as well as he did, would be there also.

"I think I would like to spend some time with Iron Fist and get to know Evening Dove better."

Little Feather's eyebrows shot up in amazement. He had been expecting an argument.

"Tall Tree," Little Feather called his friend. "Would you accompany Ian back to the Central Council Fire?"

"With pleasure," Tall Tree answered, with thoughts of Evening Dove on his mind.

Five of Little Feather's warriors escorted Tall Tree and Shannon and led the prisoners from the failed ambush by slave collars back with them.

Chapter 28

Shannon stood on the footpath that disappeared into the broad plain that bordered the river, staring into the distance. Her floppy hat covered her eyes, but a troubled expression marred her beautiful face.

"Come, my friend," Evening Dove's soft voice murmured from behind Shannon.

"Standing here each day will not shorten the time until he returns."

"I know when I left him, Evening Dove, that I thought he'd be safe, but I can't help worrying now. My cousins were responsible for my father's and brother's deaths They're totally unpredictable, more crooked than snakes and cruel as hell."

"I don't think you have to worry about Little Feather," a deeper voice said as Tall Tree stepped up with Evening Dove. "And from the looks of your brother, I'd say he can take care of himself. As far as the Cherokees go, I never thought to see the day when they would follow a white and not attempt to kill us every chance they got. Note, I said attempt. They aren't usually successful!" He grinned slightly in his attempt to cheer up his best friend's woman.

"Come on, Boy-who-cares-a-lot—I'll never get use to calling you that knowing who you are," Evening Dove giggled.

"Well, you'd better until Little Feather returns with those muskets! If anything happens to Boy-who-cares-a-lot before he gets back, he'll have my head—best friend or not. He's waited too long to find her, and where would you be then Heart-of-my-heart?"

Evening Dove giggled before repeating, "Come, friend. The Condolence Ceremony is going to be starting soon. It will help to pass the time more quickly and might even take your mind off Little Feather for a short time."

The ceremony didn't distract Shannon from her anxiety over Little Feather. That night she slept badly in the shelter she shared with Iron Fist. The sun rising the next morning found her out staring along the trail disappearing to the west among the spring blossoms sparkling in the early morning sun and trees scattered about the plain. A gentle breeze tugged at her hat.

"Really, Boy-who-cares, couldn't you at least wait until the dew is off the grass?" Evening Dove complained mildly, shaking the drops of moisture from her moccasins. "And it isn't really safe to be out here by yourself now that we know there are Cherokee in the area."

"With the village so close, I thought I'd be safe."

"You know, it was the Cherokee who stole away Iron Fist's wife and son many seasons ago. I was very young when it happened, but I remember people talking about it. I can only imagine how Little Feather would react if something like that happened to you."

"I am sorry for the worry I cause you, Evening Dove. I don't mean to, but God, I am so lonely for him, and my loneliness drives me here each day, hoping to catch sight of him returning. I know my fear for him is irrational—well, partly irrational anyway—but I can't help it!" Shannon stood with her arms wrapped tightly about herself and her voice shook slightly, tearing at her friend's heart.

"I know, I feel that way each time Tall Tree goes on a raid. Even a hunt can be dangerous—look what happened to Wolf Running—but you can't let it control you. That's why we have clan support, and when the worst does happen, we have our condolence rituals and ceremonies to help us get through the bad times—and there's always revenge!" the young woman said seriously. "Come. Today a new chief, chosen by the women of the Bear Clan, is being confirmed. Come and enjoy the festivities."

Evening Dove tugged gently on her friend's arm. "At least try to enjoy them. If you can't do that at least pretend," the young women giggled. "Iron Fist is trying so hard to distract you from your worries. He knows your worrying isn't going to change anything. Try to relax and enjoy yourself. Little Feather will be back soon, and I'm sure he will take care of all your loneliness!"

Shannon gave her friend a sheepish grin and blushed at the thought of how Little Feather would wipe away all of her loneliness. And her friend was correct. Standing here day after day was not going to bring Little Feather . . . and Shamus . . . back any sooner. It was really time she tried to keep herself occupied.

Following Evening Dove back to the village for the confirmation ceremony, she diligently tried to shove thoughts and concerns for Little Feather to the back of her mind. She really did try. It just didn't work.

Finally, all the festivities were over. All the games imaginable had been played, and even a stick-and-ball game had been organized in which Shannon had been coerced by her friends to play. Nothing had removed the emptiness in her heart or her anxiety for Little Feather, but she hadn't gone out to the trail again either, not wanting to worry her friends. The time had come to go home.

"Boy-who-cares, will you help me take down the shelter and haul the wood to that pile over there?" Makes-good-baskets asked Shannon's help in dismantling her shelter. The wood from the shelters was being stacked as firewood for the villagers.

Shannon had just taken the last of the wood to the pile, when she heard a desperate shout, "Get those children away from the river!"

Three young children were playing dangerously close to the river bank. Shannon, being the closest, fled towards the children, her heart pounding in fear that she might be too late. In horror, she watched as one youngster toppled off the bank and into the water. After shooing the remaining two children back towards their anxious families, she clamber down the bank and into the icy water to retrieve the third child. Fortunately, the water was clear, and the current had carried the child only a short distance downstream. Shannon, being a strong swimmer, caught the child easily. By the time she drugged the child to shore, other people had already gathered to help her. Someone lifted the child from her arms, and other hands pulled her ashore While she was spitting out water and catching her breath, she heard the child start to cry and knew he was okay.

With assistance, she crawled up on the bank and lay there gasping. Someone dropped her hat onto her head. Laying there she realized that she hadn't thought about Little Feather at all. She decided that she would rather worry about Little Feather than go through another experience like this one.

"Thank you ever so much, Boy-who-cares, for saving our only child!" said the young mother, clutching the boy to her breast. The other mothers thanked her profusely for preventing their children from harm and promptly scolded their errant offspring.

By the time the camp was disbanded and the children collected ready to start the long journey home, Shannon was exhausted. She dragged her feet every step of the way as each step took her farther and farther away from Little Feather. Gradually she fell to the end of the column.

"This really isn't going to get Little Feather back to you any quicker," Iron Fist said, walking beside Shannon. His patience seemed to be infinite. "Any slower and you'll lose sight of everyone. And if we're back here by ourselves—obviously, I can't leave you here alone—we could just disappear and never be seen again." That was an exaggeration. He'd likely be killed, and she would never be seen again. "Now how do you think Little Feather would feel if he came back with all those muskets and you were gone?"

Shannon hated reasonable people, but she increased her pace and was soon up in the middle of the column with White Dove and Tall Tree. Iron Fist was delighted and relieved at her reluctant cooperation.

Grey Owl's clan dropped away from the group as they approached their village, but before leaving, the family of the child she had rescued gifted her with blankets, new moccasins, tunic and a new bow with a quiver full of arrows. After many expressions of gratitude, thanks and many farewells, Iron Fist and his people continued on.

Two days later, a runner coming from the west joined the travelers for a meal. Yes, he had encountered Little Feather's band a few miles south of Fort Fontenac. No, they weren't on their way back at that time. They were still moving towards the fort. Sorry, but that was all of the information he had. How many days? Oh, maybe five or six.

That news gave a boost to Shannoon's spirits, until the insidious thought penetrated her mind that anything could happen in those five or six days.

"But anything could have happened in those days!" Shannon confided her anxiety to Evening Dove.

"We still have a couple of days before we get home, and we're almost out of meat. Tall Tree and some of the men and youths are going hunting. Why don't you join them. You're getting downright morbid, my friend. Little Feather will get back in fine shape and you'll be a basket case!"

Shannon perked up a little. She liked hunting, and it would provide a temporary diversion from her own overactive imagination.

Three uneventful days later they arrived back at the new village which was bustling with activity. The men's hunt several days earlier had produced three deer and some rabbits and squirrels. There would be feasting tonight!

"Ian . . . Boy-who-cares!" a voice shouted from behind her.

Turning, Shannon saw Running Weasel and Sunbeam approaching her. She greeted the two with a big smile.

The little girl wrapped her arms tightly about Shannon's neck. "My brother says I'm here because of you!"

"Oh, no," Shannon denied. "Your brother worked day and night to help everyone, and many other people helped too. We're all glad you're still with us. What would we do on a cloudy day if you weren't here with us?"

Shannon stood up and, glancing at Running Weasel, found him giving her a strange look.

"I never could have done the job that needed to be done without everyone, including you, who helped." Her voice was serious as she tried to impress upon the youth his invaluable assistance.

The young man's eyes became shuttered as he said, "We're collecting saplings for the long houses. Will you come and help us?"

Shannon was confused by her new friend's attitude but only shrugged her shoulders. "Sure, just give me time to take this meat and my equipment to our long house," she stopped talking and looked about with a puzzled expression on her face. "By the way, Running Weasel, where is my long house!"

The expression on Shannon's face was so comical that Running Weasel burst out laughing. When he calmed down, he chuckled, "It's in the same location in this village as it was in the last one."

"Oh, do you know if there has been any word of Little Feather?"

"Not that I know of."

Shannon nodded her head in acknowledgment of his comment. "I'll meet you at the gate in a few minutes."

As Shannon struggled under the weight on her back, she passed several people who greeted her in a friendly manner, but gave her the same strange look that Running Weasel had displayed.

Later, while Shannon was helping Running Weasel and other young people collect the saplings for their long house, she noted that everyone was friendly and helpful. She felt like she was one of the tribe—a very good feeling—but several times, she caught men staring at her with . . . unusual expressions to say the least. Some appeared to be looking at her speculatively—heads cocked to the side, although they looked away immediately. Others were eyeing her with open curiosity, that she could understand having experienced it frequently during the past year. The final expression she encountered seemed to be disgust. Now why would anyone feel disgust towards her. It was more than she could fathom. She resolved to discuss it with Bright Flower later.

"Why is everybody looking at me so strangely? Have I grown horns or something?" Shannon complained. "Oh, my God! I haven't dyed my hair in the past couple of weeks. Someone must have noticed even though I try to keep my hat on."

"No, no. It's nothing like that," Bright Flower tried to sooth Little Feather's woman's frazzled emotions. "The False Face has been spreading the story of his vision of the epidemic and the red-haired woman who struggled so valiantly on our behalf . . ."

Shannon groaned.

"The people are just curious," Bright Flower continued, ignoring the interruption,

"and trying to determine if you really are the red-haired woman. Some people are just disgusted by the deception if you are in fact deceiving them. Some are just relieved after observing Little Feather's behavior towards you."

"Oh," Shannon replied, not knowing whether to be relieved or not.

A few mornings later when Shannon was returning from the river with two water skins, Evening Dove waylaid her. "Come and see what we have for you!" she said, bouncing around, barely able to contain her excitement.

"Is Little Feather back?" Little Feather was usually the first thought in her mind.

"Noooo . . . you'll know when he gets back. No, this is a different surprise." Evening Dove took one of the water skins. "Anyone who may have wondered about you before, won't if you continue doing woman's work!"

Shannon snorted. "Where I come from, when water is needed any and everyone gets it!"

"I hate to be the one to remind you, but you are no longer where you come from," Evening Dove said a bit briskly. Then immediately apologized, "I'm sorry. I know there are many bad memories from your past, but today we try to create a new good memory." So saying Evening Dove giggled and tugged on her friend's arm.

After the young women had taken the water to Bright Flower, Shannon followed Evening Dove to her long house. Evening Dove's mother, Black Bird and some other family members were there. Evening Dove could scarcely contain her excitement.

"Here this is for you!" she said, handing Shannon a most beautiful dress—soft doeskin, beautifully embroidered with fringe around the bottom and the sleeves!

"It's gorgeous, Evening Dove," Shannon said cautiously, clearly puzzled. "But why . . . how . . . ?" She looked inquiringly at the young woman.

"Don't be angry with me, Ian." Evening Dove was vibrating with excitement, although slightly subdued by her friend's reaction to the gift. "Most people already suspect the truth—that False Face really has a big mouth—and there was something I wanted my mother to consider, but I had to tell her the truth."

"And everyone else?" Shannon questioned caustically. Little Feather was not going to be pleased that Evening Dove may have placed her in danger. "And does Tall Tree know what you have done?"

To Shannon's surprise, Evening Dove smiled broadly at her question and answered honestly, "He approved whole-heartedly, although he has no say in this matter."

Now Shannon was totally mystified. Bending her head slightly and leaning forward, she waved her hand slightly, "Well, what's going on? Don't keep me in the dark!"

This time Black Bird started talking."I apologize if we have offended you in any way," here she frowned at Evening Dove, "but I thought you knew what my daughter planned. She wants us to adopt you, and we all think it's a wonderful idea!" This time the older woman looked at Shannon with a slight smile. "We had already been thinking about it before we knew the truth. Now it's even better.

"I went to see Bright Flower today, and she had no objections—said something about wanting to see Little Feather happy," Black Bird said with a definite twinkle in her eyes, "and we would be honored if you would allow us to adopt you into our clan, the Wolf Clan," Black Bird said diffidently, regretting not having discussed it with the girl before.

Shannon burst into tears and fell into Evening Dove's arms. The girl had really planned the most wonderful present of all for her. Now she would be able to marry Little Feather according to their traditions.

"Is this a yes or a no?" Black Bird asked with a slight smile.

"Oh, it's a definite yes!" Shannon burst out through her tears.

"I also took the liberty to talk to Bright Flower about Little Feather . . . if he might be receptive to my new daughter as his wife." She stared sternly at Evening Dove. "I hope I was not premature in presenting your petition based on what my daughter told me about your feelings."

Shannon shook her head 'no', followed rapidly by a 'yes'. "Oh, my God!" and burst out crying again.

"That was an okay . . . you approve? Or an 'I'm going to kill your daughter?'"

"Oh, things are going too fast! . . . to have a family all at one time . . . and to be engaged to be married . . . it's all too much to comprehend!"

"Well, I must caution you, Bright Flower wasn't sure, as he isn't home for her to discuss it with him, but she thought he might be receptive to the idea."

Shannon burst into tears again, embarrassing herself no end!

Over the next several days, the two young women were inseparable. Although, Shannon still wore her boy's clothes, she discarded the floppy hat to let people become used to her hair that was already going auburn again.

"So what do we call you now, my fine young friend," asked a middle aged man who had survived the epidemic. He didn't care whether the white person who had been instrumental in the recovery of so many of their tribe was purple with white polka dots, boy, girl, neither or both! But he did find the situation humorous.

Shannon grinned at him and replied, "Shannon."

"Nice name. Nice hair. I'm glad your one of us. See you at the ceremony tonight," and he went on his way.

"Does everyone knew about the adoption ceremony tonight?"

"Of course, silly! It's a big thing! And we want everyone to know that you are becooming an official member of our family. There will be much gift-giving, eating, dancing and lots of fun!" Evening Dove put her arm around her best friend—soon to be sister.

That evening turned out to be everything Evening Dove promised. The only dark spot to the festivities was that Little Feather wasn't there. After the evening ended and people went to their own long houses, Shannon collected her meager belongings, adding them to the wonderful gifts of clothes, jewelry and tools used by women she had received, and leaving Little Feather's clothes at his long house, moved into the long house where Tall Tree and Evening Dove had a fireside.

Early the next morning, news came that a strange cavalcade was moving towards the village.

Shannon, in a tunic and skirt given her by her new sister, rushed to the entrance of the stockade with Evening Dove and Tall Tree, Bright Flower and others.

The cavalcade appeared strange indeed. There were two wagons pulled by horses, one driven by a red-haired giant and the second driven by Little Feather. Accompanying their own warriors were other warriors who wore their black hair long who were immediatly recognized by warriors at the village entrance, sending them scrambling for their weapons! There were women and children scattered amongst the group.

Shannon started to run up to Little Feather, but Evening Dove grabbed her arm and pulled her back. "It won't hurt for him to wait. Well, it won't hurt much!" Evening Dove giggled.

Little Feather looked about for the floppy hat. How he had missed his little warrior woman! But the hat was missing! In its place he got a glimpse of flaming red hair, but it disappeared almost as soon as he saw it. Then he was surrounded by friends and family—basically the whole village—throwing questions at them. Where had they gone? What happened? Why the wagons? Where did the horses come from? Why were they with Cherokee warriors? Who were the women and children? Obviously, they had been successful at their chosen mission, and who were the strangers, and . . . and . . .

"Whoa! Hold on, and we'll tell you everything!" Little Feather laughed, still looking for the floppy hat.

"Very successful raid, nephew!" Iron Fist congratulated Little Feather. "But I didn't know you could drive horses!"

"Anything can be learned, uncle!" Little Feather answered with amusement and suppressed excitement, still looking around for Shannon.

The red-haired giant strutted over to where Little Feather and Iron Fist stood conversing.

"Shamus, this is my uncle, Iron Fist," Little Feather said. Shamus had learned Kanien'kehaka almost as fast as Shannon.

"Iron Fist. This is the Iron Fist?" Shamus asked, making no sense to Iron Fist.

When Little Feather nodded, the big red-haired man shouted something back to the group of people who had accompanied them. A middle-aged woman and teen-age boy separated themselves from the crowd and walked slowly forward.

Iron Fist stared and turned an ashen color. "Shining Star!" he whispered in disbelief. "By all the powers that be . . . my wife!" He started running towards the beautiful woman, than slowed down, unsure of his reception. She started running towards him with open arms. Iron Fist lifted her high into the air, laughing and crying. Then, still holding his arm about his wife, turned his attention to the young man standing by her, not knowing how to greet this stranger with the long hair.

The woman turned to his son, saying, "This is your father, Iron Fist of the Turtle Clan of whom I've told you so much."

The young warrior scrutinized Iron Fist from head to toe, finally nodding his head in approval. He reached out and rubbed Iron Fist chest in the typical Iroquois greeting. His mother had taught him well, and Iron Fist was pleased and returned the greeting. The three turned back towards Little Feather.

"Now that was a sight worth coming all the way from the Smokey Mountains to see! How long have them been separated?"

"Thirteen years! He found me looking for them."

"Glad to be of service. Now where is my prickly sister . . . I like that expression of yours for her. And I know, I've got some ruffled feathers to sooth. I was suppose to rescue her over a year ago."

"I don't know," Little Feather answered, puzzled. "She wasn't angry with me when she came back. After all I didn't tie her up to send her back the way you suggested."

"Yeah, that wasn't one of my better ideas, but she had me riled good!"

The village held a big celebration that night, guns were passed around and many put aside to be delivered to other villages. Little Feather kept twenty to give Shannon as a wedding gift if he could figure out how to marry her traditionally. He had never seen clan relationships as being a problem before. He'd have to talk to Iron Fist and see what solution they could come up with.

In the meantime, there was dancing and feasting, but at no time did Little Feather spot Shannon, nor—even more confusing—would anyone tell him where Boy-who-cares was. Some people actually laughed at him when he asked, but no one would answer him, including his mother and Iron Fist.

"Just wait." "Be patient," were the answers he got. Even his sister was uncooperative. He couldn't stoop low enough to ask Bright Eyes who would look at him and giggle!

By the next morning, he was irritable as a bear and in no mood to talk to anyone.

He sat on a stump outside of the long house, the sun bright and warm about him, the birds disgustingly cheerful, his mood black as a thundercloud, trying to determine what had gone so terribly wrong. Abruptly all of the normal hubbub of noise about him stopped, and he heard whispers, and giggles. Looking up his heart stopped . . . and then resumed a rapid thudding.

People were standing by their long houses and along the street, silently watching as a flamed-haired woman walked with slow, unsure steps up the street towards his long house. The soft doeskin skirt swayed gently about her shapely legs.

A silly grin grew on his face. He couldn't have removed it if his life depended upon it. He felt so light he thought he might float away with the joy that was bursting inside of him.

Shannon, eyes sparkling and a shy smile on her face, placed the basket of cornbread she had worked on all night with Evening Dove's help at his feet. She waited silently, anxiously for his reaction. He picked the basket up and carried it into the long house. He should have realized that something was up. Everyone from the long house was there, all with big grins on their faces, including Shamus and Iron Fist with his wife and son who no longer lived there but were now visitors. A few moments later, he reappeared at the door. "C'mon in, Shannon, and eat with us," he invited.

She shyly entered the long house behind Little Feather. The cornbread was broken into pieces and passed around to be eaten with the stew that everyone had in their bowls.

Taking a bite of her cornbread, she immediately spit it into her stew. "God! That's awful!" she stuttered, noticing that no one else was eating theirs. They must have already tasted it!

"It's okay, honey," Little Feather said soothingly, putting his arm about her shoulders. Then he took the bear claw necklace he wore and placed it about her neck. "You kill the bears, and I'll cook them!"

Shannon burst into tears and rushed from the long house, mortified but clutching the necklace.

Little Feather shrugged his broad shoulders and followed his prickly little wife out of the long house.

The sun shone warm on his bare back. The children's laughter rising up about him seemed more cheerful, and the lusty birdsong beat down upon his ears as he watched his beautiful wife flee out of the village. He broke into a run as he followed her. Making up was going to be such fun!

the end